PRAISE FO

SHORTLISTED

'Inspiring and infur
is an utterly captiva
politics into the
impossible

'Fantastic. Conveys all the in social situation
in a way that's vivid, hard-hi ally compelling.
It feels like we're living it, her than just learning about it'

Frances Hardinge

'This is a lovely and engrossing novel about three girls caught up in the Suffragette movement and WW1. It's Sarah Waters for teens, pitch-perfect, historically accurate, very romantic and a jolly good read'

Robin Stevens

'Historical fiction at its best'

Hilary McKay

'Just wonderful – warm and witty and genuinely wise'

Stephanie Burgis

'A very realistic portrayal of the struggles faced by women during the early 1900s'

UK Vote 100

'Nicholls has brought alive the young women of the past to empower the next generation'

'Children's Book of the Week', ***The Times***

'Each voice is distinct, resonant and authentic . . . uniquely special'

Guardian

'[A] chocolate box of a novel . . . books such as this are all the more to be prized'

Telegraph

'Timely, informative and hugely enjoyable . . . the book excels at what fiction is best at: inviting empathy and understanding for others'

Irish Times

'*Things a Bright Girl Can Do* is relevant for every generation'

Evening Standard

'A fascinating and emotive read for any budding feminist'

Scotsman

'A captivating YA novel . . . *Things a Bright Girl Can Do* explores sexual identity, the grim realities of poverty and war and the fraught nature of first love. Its appeal will reach readers of any age'

Red Magazine

'Nicholls explores difficult questions about poverty, empowerment, sexuality, pacifism and war with wise sensitivity. An excellent read'

INIS

'Offering a historical snapshot of a society in turmoil, this comprehensive coming-of-age novel is a thought-provoking and highly engaging story of love, life and hope'

BookTrust

'The politics of the time are skilfully woven into the personal stories of Evelyn, May and Nell, touching feminist, LGBT and social issues . . . This inspirational novel is very welcome'

Bookseller

'This novel is the perfect tribute to the incredible women who blazed a trail during the early twentieth century, and its inspirational scope and storytelling excellence cannot be praised enough'

Lovereading

'A sheer delight . . . Nicholls ensures that every voice is authentic and credible, every experience real and immediate'

Teach Secondary

'An inspiring novel'

WRD

THINGS A BRIGHT GIRL CAN DO

THINGS A BRIGHT GIRL CAN DO

SALLY NICHOLLS

ANDERSEN PRESS
LONDON

This edition published in 2018 by
Andersen Press Limited
20 Vauxhall Bridge Road
London SW1V 2SA
www.andersenpress.co.uk

6 8 10 9 7

First published in hardback in 2017 by Andersen Press

British Library Cataloguing in Publication Data available.

ISBN 978 1 78344 673 5

Printed and bound in Great Britain by Clays Ltd, Elcograf S.p.A.

To all my babysitters, without whom this book would have been even later than it actually was.

February
1914

*Reforms can always wait a little longer,
but freedom, directly you discover you haven't
got it, will not wait another minute.*

Unfinished Adventure, Evelyn Sharp

Strange Happenings Outside a Playhouse

'You tell me that women are weak-willed! You tell me that women are weak-spirited, and foolish, and ignorant, and only fit to stay at home and raise the children.' The woman on the orange crate paused, then added, 'Hardly seems fair on the children, does it?'

There was laughter from the crowd. Evelyn, always fascinated by the Suffragettes, said, 'Hold up a minute, can't you?' to Teddy, who stopped at once.

A man in the crowd called, 'A woman's sphere is the home! Do you contest it?'

'Her *sphere*, yes. Not her *prison*. You may as well say a man's sphere is the office, and take his vote as well.'

More laughter. This time, Evelyn joined in.

'Oh, come!' It was an older, rather apoplectic-looking gentleman. 'A woman doesn't need a vote! Her husband votes for her, and if she's not happy with his choice, she has a hundred ways to make him change his mind. *That's* a woman's proper influence, not the ballot box.'

'Indeed?' The Suffragette was enjoying this. You could

tell. 'It's rather hard on the unmarried woman or the widow though, isn't it? And the husband.' More laughter. 'I'm not sure your idea of proper influence is very complimentary to either sex.'

A young woman in a fur coat was pushing her way past Evelyn.

'Ooh!' she said, to the man beside her. 'I do think these women are perfectly horrid. As if any *lady* would want to stand on a nasty box and shout things at delivery boys.'

Evelyn bristled. She opened her mouth, but Teddy put his hand on her arm.

'Cool it,' he said. Then, before Evelyn could argue, he nodded at the Suffragette on the orange crate. 'She's doing rather well, isn't she?'

'I think she's splendid,' said Evelyn.

'Isn't she, though?' It was another Suffragette, one of the ones who were standing at the edge of the crowd, passing out handbills. This one looked about twelve, although Evelyn supposed she must be older. She had long, loose fair hair under her tam o'shanter, and a wide, toothy smile.

'Would you like a handbill? We've a meeting at the Albert Hall next week; you must come along if you're interested. There's more about it in *Votes for Women*, only that's a penny.'

'All right,' said Evelyn, fumbling for her purse. The woman on the orange crate was lecturing her audience on the iniquity of British divorce laws. Evelyn took her copy of *Votes for Women* and scowled at the front page.

'Look here,' she said suddenly to the girl. 'You Suffragettes think girls should be able to do all the things men can, don't you? Live in flats on their own, and get degrees, and – oh, everything. Don't you?'

'Lord!' said Teddy, audibly.

'Oh yes,' the girl said. 'But the vote is the first step. Those things will follow once we get the vote, and heaps of other things too – state orphanages, and old-age pensions – why!' Her little white face flushed. 'Once women have the vote, we'll never go to war, you know. What sort of woman would send her sons off to be slaughtered?'

'You,' said Teddy, 'have obviously never met my Aunt Gwladys. Evelyn, Mother and Father will be wondering where—'

Behind them, there was an outraged roar from the crowd. Evelyn turned. The Suffragette on the orange crate was clutching her cheek, her mouth open in shock. As Evelyn watched, another missile was flung at her; she ducked and it missed. A boot-black and a man selling hot chestnuts at the edge of the crowd whooped appreciatively.

The apoplectic gentleman called, 'I say, steady on! Mind the lady, can't you?!'

The chestnut-seller pulled an awful face. 'Go on!' He yelled at the woman on the orange crate. 'If you was *my* wife, I'd take a stick to you!'

'Evelyn,' said Teddy. 'I'm frightfully sorry, but we're going to have to look slippy if we want to catch Mother and Father. We'll miss the first act at this rate.'

'I know,' said Evelyn. But she didn't move.

'Why don't you stay at home where you belong?' the chestnut-seller roared. He picked up a handful of chestnuts, cooling on the side of his brazier, and flung them at the Suffragette's eyes. She ducked again, but did not step down from the crate.

'Evelyn—' said Teddy.

'Cheese it, can't you, Jimmy Boon!' It was another woman, standing in the doorway of the shop behind them. 'Some of us are trying to listen to the lady!'

'You can cheese it and all, you daft cow!' the chestnut-seller yelled. He pulled back his arm and flung a final chestnut in her direction.

It hit Evelyn square on the jaw.

She liked to say, later, that was the moment when she made up her mind.

Evelyn

Evelyn Collis was seventeen years old. And despite what certain poets might have to say about it, she was finding this more of an impediment than an ornament.

She was the second of four children. Her brother Christopher – known as Kit – was nineteen and away at Oxford. Evelyn, though she loved her brother in a dutiful sort of way, could not help resenting the fact that he'd been given everything she had ever wanted, without asking for it or even seeming to care very much when he received it. Christopher had been allowed to do everything at an earlier age than she had. He'd been sent off to boarding school – something Evelyn had always secretly longed for – and now her parents were paying for a university course he didn't seem to even particularly enjoy. This was especially galling since Evelyn had discovered a desire to go to university herself, and her family had been decidedly unsympathetic.

Evelyn went to a small day school in Belsize Park, where playing the piano and speaking good French were considered the most important parts of a girl's education. But, unusually, the girls also learnt Latin and Ancient Greek.

These were taught by a Miss Dempsey. Evelyn loved Miss Dempsey, and she loved Classics; loved that sense of lifting the lid on a world that was thousands of years old. At the end of last term, Miss Dempsey had said casually to Evelyn, 'Have you thought about taking the Oxford entrance exam?'

Evelyn was so surprised she could only stare. Girls at her school rarely went to Oxford. It was nothing she'd ever considered in relation to herself. She'd never thought much about her future at all, except to suppose in the vaguest sense that she would get married and have a family.

'No?' Miss Dempsey had said mildly. 'Perhaps you should.'

And that was all that was said on the matter. But the seed, once planted, had begun to grow in Evelyn's mind.

Young women at Oxford couldn't earn a degree. But they could go to the lectures, sit the examinations, and learn just as much as the young men did. Evelyn was becoming dimly aware that Classics, as taught to girls at her school, only touched at the edges of a world of knowledge that stretched seemingly infinitely into the distance. And that world was something she was beginning desperately to want a part of.

She had tried to explain this to Teddy, who'd been sympathetic, but baffled.

'I do see it's jolly unfair and all that,' he'd said. 'But does it really matter that much? There's no earthly use girls learning things, unless they're planning on forswearing men entirely and going to teach rotten little girls how to spell. And I would hope you aren't going to do *that*.'

But Evelyn couldn't explain why she wanted to go. Did one have to have a reason for wanting and wanting something?

She raised the subject of Oxford with her mother at Christmas. The two of them were coming home from a bridge game at the house of one of Evelyn's mother's friends. They'd done well, which had put her mother in a good mood, and Evelyn thought it unlikely a better opportunity would arise.

'I spoke to Miss Dempsey about next year,' she said diffidently.

Her mother wasn't paying attention.

'I should have known Mrs Weston had that ace,' she said. 'She'd hardly have bid otherwise.'

'Hmm,' said Evelyn. 'Miss Dempsey thinks I could go to Oxford if I wanted. She tutors girls for the exams, you know. In her spare time, I mean, not at school.'

'Really?' said Evelyn's mother. 'That *is* a pretty compliment, darling. You must tell your father when we get home.'

'Yes,' said Evelyn. 'Only – I think I'd like to.'

'Like to what, dear?' her mother said. 'Oh look, there's the vicar. No, darling, don't wave, he wants a stall at the bazaar, and I really *can't*, not after last time.'

'Go to Oxford,' said Evelyn fervently. 'I want to go to Oxford next year and study at one of the women's colleges. And Miss Dempsey thinks I could.'

Evelyn's mother looked at her in astonishment. If Evelyn had demanded a motor car, she couldn't have been more surprised. There were so few professions open to women, and those that were hardly demanded a degree. A university education, from Evelyn's mother's perspective, was simply an expensive way of unfitting one's daughter for matrimony.

'But, darling!' she said. 'Whatever for?'

'I don't know what for, exactly,' said Evelyn. 'Do I need a reason? I'd just like to, that's all.'

She could see that this was exactly the wrong thing to say, and she hurried on before the moment should pass.

'Just to learn things, you know – Latin and Greek and ancient history and all that. It'd be jolly useful having someone in the family who knew about classical civilisation, don't you think? And anyway, what use is university going to be to Kit? He's going to work for Teddy's father, isn't he? It's all decided.'

'But, darling,' said Evelyn's mother, again. She was a little dazed. Evelyn had been thinking of very little except Oxford for nearly a month, but this was an entirely new idea for her mother. 'Christopher will meet all sorts of people who'll be useful for him in business. He has to earn his own living, darling – but there's no thought you'd ever have to do that. These university women lead very sad lives. I'd hoped for better things for you – a husband, and a family, and a home of your own. Don't you want that?'

'I don't know what I want,' said Evelyn. 'I could go into business like Kit, or—' She struggled to think what careers were open to respectable women. 'Or give lectures, perhaps. Does it matter? And anyway,' she finished desperately, 'I don't see that I'm giving up a family and all that. I could still have all those things *and* a degree. Teddy wouldn't care.'

Evelyn's mother noted Teddy's name with relief. She was

very fond of Teddy, but she had never been sure exactly how Evelyn felt about him.

'I'm sure he wouldn't, dear,' she said comfortingly. 'Teddy's a very nice boy. But you can see it from our perspective, can't you? Going to Oxford costs a lot of money. Why don't you see how you feel next year when you leave school? I expect by then you'll be much more interested in golf, or something. But if you still want to crib up on stuffy old languages, perhaps your father and I could find you a Latin master to come and give you lessons. Far cheaper, and you could stay at home, which would be ever so much nicer, wouldn't it?'

Evelyn didn't answer. She was rigid with fury, and shame that she couldn't explain to her mother this desire that she couldn't quite explain to herself. Her mother fussed with the umbrella and pretended not to see.

'There!' she said. 'It's about to rain. And just when we were nearly home too.'

Evelyn was struggling with herself. At last she burst out, 'But it isn't fair! Really it isn't, Mother! Why should Christopher have everything and I have nothing?'

There was quite a lot Evelyn's mother could have said to that. But she contented herself with the standby of mothers and nurses the world over. 'Well, dear. Life isn't fair, you know.'

'No,' Evelyn agreed. 'But it ought to be.'

By which her mother assumed that the argument was over.

But as far as Evelyn was concerned, it had barely begun.

The Lioness

'It's not fair! It's the most beastly rotten thing that's *ever* happened to me! I hate her! I hate him! I hate the whole ghastly lot of them!'

Evelyn had worked herself up into a fine rage, pacing up and down the schoolroom, twisting her gloves in her fury. The occasion of her rage was another conversation with her parents about Oxford – this time armed with a very politic letter from Miss Dempsey. It had not gone well. Unlike Teddy's father, who owned several factories, Evelyn's father worked in a government office, doing something dull-sounding with figures. There was no money lying around to educate girls who would only go and get married once they finished university anyway.

Teddy was sitting on one of the ancient nursery armchairs, his sketchbook on his lap. Evelyn's younger sisters, Hetty and Kezia, loved Teddy's sketchbook, mainly because of all the pictures of naked girls from art school that they weren't supposed to know about. Most of the pictures in Teddy's book were of girls. Life-class nudes. Girls in tearooms. Art-school girls, all modern and hatless and sophisticated. Kezia, late for school, running to catch the omnibus. Hetty curled up in the nursery armchair, reading *Little Women* for the hundredth time, a dash coming out of her mouth saying – *Do you think Jo ought to have married Laurie, Evelyn? I do. Do you think, if you won't marry him, Teddy might marry me?* And dozens and dozens and dozens of pictures of Evelyn. Angry Evelyn. Thoughtful Evelyn. Evelyn in her school skirts. Evelyn dressed for dinner. Evelyn thumping resentfully at the piano. Evelyn reading. Evelyn frowning. Evelyn, her whole face alive with a smile that most of the world never saw.

He was sketching a rapid pencil-portrait of her now, her cheeks with their high colour, the furious, busy motions of her feet. Most of his thoughts were on the picture, almost all of the rest were on how much he would like to jump up and kiss her – right now, on the mouth – just to see what she would do. He had only the vaguest idea what she was saying, which was less dismissive than it sounds, since she'd been saying the same sort of thing over and over all afternoon.

Teddy's and Evelyn's fathers had been at school together. Teddy was very much the youngest of three sons, the unexpected pet of parents who had long assumed their childbearing days were over. His mother suffered from nervous headaches, with the result that Teddy spent much of his early childhood being hurried out of the house with his nurse. On cold or rainy days, they would be sent to the Collises'. To Teddy, the Collis house had been a place where he could slide down the bannisters, charge around the nursery, and shout as loudly as he wanted. Although he had never quite articulated this to himself, 'home', to Teddy, meant the Collises' shabby nursery, their long wilderness of a garden, and Evelyn.

Teddy and Evelyn had been engaged since he was in knickerbockers and she in pinafores. He'd proposed to her again, more or less seriously, last year, but Evelyn had laughed. She'd no intention of marrying anyone for a good while yet.

Now she was – technically, at least – a young woman, and Teddy a young man, another mother would have made some effort to keep their relationship respectable. But Evelyn's mother couldn't bear to admit that her daughter was nearly an adult. Evelyn would be 'coming out' at some point in the summer and would be expected to let down her skirts, put up her hair, attend grown-up parties and dances and generally advertise her availability for matrimony. Her mother had no idea how one was supposed to mother a young woman, and was rather dreading it.

'Oh, rather,' Teddy said absently now, sensing a pause in the stream of words and taking a guess at what he was expected to reply. 'Dashed unfair.' Flick, flick, flick went his pencil, catching the falling strands of her hair.

'And it isn't just Oxford!' said Evelyn. 'It's everything. Why, you and Christopher could be *anything*! Explorers! Soldiers! Inventors! What can girls be? Governesses, or teachers, or lady companions, or *mothers*.'

The last was spat. Teddy said, 'It's not so bad as all that. Modern girls can be heaps of things. You could be a lady doctor like Mrs Garrett Anderson. Or a writer – or an artist. Plenty of girls go to art school.'

'You can't just *be* an artist or a writer,' said Evelyn

furiously. 'You've got to have a *metier*, or talent at least. And I don't, not a jot. And I don't see how I could be a doctor when all the science they do in my school is 'nature walks' on the Heath. And it's *Dr* Garrett Anderson, not Mrs.'

'You could always marry me,' Teddy said mildly. 'I'd let you go to Oxford.'

'Ass,' said Evelyn. She wanted to stamp her foot in frustration. 'It isn't just about *me*,' she said. 'It's about us all! *All* women! How can women *live* like this? How can women like Mother just go on – not *caring*?' Her eyes were shining with rage. She looked, thought Teddy, magnificent. Like St Theresa, or Joan of Arc, or a goddess; Athena, or Diana, one of those ones who were always dashing about on a chariot full of righteous indignation. The urge to kiss her grew stronger, until his whole body was tingling with it. It was rather unsettling.

'Oh, quite,' he said hurriedly. 'Rotten show all round.' He began to sketch a lioness, of the sort Britannica was always dragging around with her, following his pencil-Evelyn. 'Only – begging your pardon – if your mother and father say you can't, what are you going to do about it?'

'Hang Mother and Father! I'm not talking about Mother and Father!' She stopped pacing and faced him.

'Oh dear,' he said. 'You mean the Suffragettes, don't you?'

'And what if I do?'

'Oh,' he said, again. 'Oh dear.' He laid down his pencil and rubbed his eyes, wondering where to begin.

Of May and Her Mother

A week after she had sold Evelyn a copy of *Votes for Women* and promised them a future free of war, May Thornton was eating breakfast with her mother.

'So then Miss Aitchson said Boudicca was an aberration of nature, and a nice girl like myself wouldn't want to take a barbarian like her as a model, would I? But I said I would. I think it'd be ripping to be Boudicca, and have my own chariot, and fight the Romans, except I told Miss Aitchson if I was Boudicca, I wouldn't go to war, because I'm a Quaker and we're pacifists. I said if *I* were Boudicca, I'd use diplomacy and political wiles instead. Miss Aitchson said it wasn't ladylike for women to involve themselves in politics. But *I* think if your country's been invaded by the Romans, you've got to do something about it, haven't you? Even if they *did* bring central heating and straight roads and all that? But then Miss Aitchson got out of it by saying that we weren't studying the Romans now, we were doing Henry VIII. I *do* think Henry VIII was a wart, don't you, Mama? I don't think it's very royal to chop off your wives' heads, even if they *are* witches. Do you?'

'Don't drip egg on your school skirt, darling,' said May's mother, who was reading a letter and frowning. 'Though I always did think Henry VIII a frightful man. I'm sure Mr Freud would have simply dreadful things to say about the inside of his subconscious. And really, I must go and complain to that school of yours. They're positively Victorian. I told Miss Cooper I'd be very willing to come and give you girls a lecture on the true history of the matriarchal society, but she never did reply.'

May and her mother lived in a narrow terraced house in one of the more respectable streets in Bow, in the East End of London. May's father, who had died when May was a year old, had been the headmaster of a free school for the education of the poor. When he'd died, May's mother's friends had expected her to move back to one of the nicer areas of London. But she'd stayed.

The house was a cosy, chaotic republic, full of books, and music, and incendiary ideas. May's mother was a vegetarian, a suffragist, a pacifist, a Quaker, a Fabian, a Bolshevik sympathiser and a believer in Rational Dress for women. They were looked after by their housekeeper, Mrs Barber, who had 'done for' Mrs Thornton since she was a new bride, and listened to all her ideas with a slightly pained resignation. May's mother had handed her numerous pamphlets and articles explaining the digestive benefits of lentils and black-eyed beans, but she had remained unconvinced.

You know best, my dear, she seemed to say. *But couldn't we just have a nice chop once in a while?*

As a little thing of five or six, May had sat in the offices of the International Woman Suffrage Alliance, solemnly sticking postage stamps to envelopes to aid the suffrage cause. There was a photograph of her aged seven standing outside Buckingham Palace wearing a white muslin frock and holding a banner reading FOR HEARTH AND HOME. Aged ten, she had met H. G. Wells, and had shaken his hand and asked him earnestly whether he really believed there were men on Mars.

Right now, May's mother was still frowning at her letter.

'Are you frightfully keen on going to the Albert Hall this evening, darling?' she said. 'Because I did wonder about going to see what Sylvia Pankhurst is doing instead. What do you think? Would you mind?'

May looked up from her egg in surprise. She and her mother were suffrag*ists* rather than Suffrag*ettes*; they wanted the vote, but they didn't use violence to get it. Suffragettes threw stones through windows, slashed paintings in the National Gallery and detonated petrol bombs in deserted houses. May's mother thought behaving like this set back the campaign – who would want to be associated with crazy, violent women like that? She preferred to work through peaceful means, like petitions, and marches, and articles in the press. The Suffragettes were rather scornful of women like May's mother, pointing out that these methods had been used with little success for forty years before Emmeline Pankhurst had entered the fray.

Sylvia Pankhurst was Emmeline Pankhurst's socialist daughter. She lived not far from May and her mother, and ran a local suffrage movement for East End women.

'Miss Thumpston gave me a very interesting article that

Miss Pankhurst had written for that paper of theirs,' May's mother was saying. 'She says – and I think rightly – that our movement is too concerned with recruiting the middle classes, and ignoring the struggles of working women. Naturally, I disapprove of her methods, but she's really doing astonishing things for the women here. I thought I'd like to go and take a closer look, if it's something that would interest you?'

'If you like,' said May, who always enjoyed doing things with Mama. Her mother smiled at her.

'Now, run and get your things, or you'll be late for school. Give me a kiss before you go.'

May slid out from her chair. Her mind was already on the day ahead – gymnastics this afternoon, and the results of last week's geography test, and whether Barbara and Winifred would be speaking to each other this morning or not.

She had no idea that this evening's excursion was about to change her life for ever.

Button Badges

'Listen!' said Kezia Collis, sitting up in bed.

'Is it them?' said Hetty. Her pyjama jacket was half over her head, and her voice was therefore somewhat muffled. She wriggled her shoulders and tugged the jacket down, then ran to the door. She could hear voices in the hall, and Teddy's laugh, rising high and delighted up the stairwell. Hetty felt that even if she lived to be a hundred, she would still recognise Teddy's laugh.

It was the evening of the mass suffrage meeting in the Albert Hall. Evelyn had told her mother she was going to a lecture at her high school.

'It's about the Pre-Raphaelites,' she said airily. 'So I told Teddy he could come too – you don't mind, do you?'

Hetty charged across the landing and leant over the bannisters.

'Evelyn! Teddy!' she called. 'Do come and tell us about it! We aren't a bit asleep!'

Evelyn paused in the middle of unwinding her scarf and looked up with a small frown. It would be just like Hetty to spoil things by telling their mother where she and Teddy had been. But before either girl could say any more, their mother appeared in the hallway.

'Hetty! Aren't you two in bed yet? How it could take you half an hour to put on pyjamas, I really don't know. What in heaven's name has Miss Perring been doing?'

Miss Perring was the younger girls' governess. All three girls went to school, but for everything else, from taking Hetty to school to supervising prep and darning their stockings, Kezia and Hetty were Miss Perring's responsibility.

Miss Perring was a small, grey, wispy woman, who gave the impression of life having passed her by. The children vaguely despised her.

'Oh, it wouldn't have done a bit of good if they'd been in bed,' said Teddy. He tipped his head up and turned the full force of his smile on Hetty, who was leaning as far over the bannisters as she could, her long hair dangling around her face. 'How,' he said, 'could I come to visit and not say hello to young Henrietta?' And he bounded up the stairs two steps at a time, while she stood on the landing beaming foolishly.

Kezia was twelve; small, wiry, fierce and terribly superior to plump, mousy, ten-year-old Hetty, the family baby.

Both had been consumed with curiosity over the trip to the Albert Hall, but were rather uncertain how they felt about Suffragettes: Kezia thought it rather grand to swank about not letting any man tell you what to do, but she did wish they didn't look so frumpy and earnest while they did it. Hetty thought that of course women should have a vote – and if

Teddy and Evelyn were going to be involved it *must* be all right – but could it really be ladylike to throw things through windows?

Teddy, meanwhile, had attended the meeting under duress. He'd already had several heated conversations with Evelyn about the Suffragettes, and had come along this evening out of an uneasy sense that one really oughtn't to let a schoolgirl go to a political meeting on her own. Probably, he suspected, he ought to be forbidding her to have anything to do with these women. But something in him revolted against the idea. He and Evelyn were going to be married one day, if he had anything to say about it, and he didn't *want* the sort of awful Victorian marriage where one ordered one's wife around. He *wanted* equality, or as close to it as he could get.

But this, of course, was the problem. He and Evelyn were not equal. In so many ways she was still a child, and an appallingly sheltered child at that. She wasn't allowed to read newspapers. She wasn't allowed to meet boys – beside Teddy himself, of course – and he was pretty sure no one had ever told her the facts of life. Teddy knew perfectly well that Evelyn's mother trusted him to look after her, and that allowing her to join women who set off bombs and smashed windows was not at all how she expected him to behave.

If it came down to it, he didn't much like the idea of it either.

The four of them held a solemn powwow in the night nursery. Now they were growing up, the night nursery was officially the younger girls' room, and the day nursery the schoolroom.

But it had been the nursery for so long that even Evelyn forgot to call it by its official name. There were heaps of nursery things still there; an old rocking horse that no one had played with for years, a battered collection of old games piled up in the nursery cupboard, *Just So Stories* and *Mother Goose* still leaning companionably on the nursery bookcase beside *Robinson Crusoe* and *The Hound of the Baskervilles* and *301 Things a Bright Girl Can Do*.

Teddy sat at the end of Hetty's bed, and pulled the eiderdown over his legs in a friendly manner. There was no fire and the room was cold.

'Tell us everything!' Kezia commanded.

'Did you blow up pillar boxes and sock policemen in the jaw?' said Hetty.

'Did you get arrested?'

'Hush!' said Evelyn. 'Mother will hear, and then we'll be for it. And no, of course we didn't. It was just people talking. Look, though! We brought you badges.' She threw the badges to Kezia and Hetty. Little round enamel badges in the colours of Mrs Emmeline Pankhurst's Women's Social and Political Union: green, white and violet. VOTES FOR WOMEN, the badges said. 'But for heaven's sake, don't let Mother and Father see you wearing them.'

'Who was there?' said Kezia. She took her badge and turned it over and over in her fingers. The mark of rebellion! 'Was Mrs Pankhurst there?'

'She *might* have been,' said Teddy. 'There were simply hundreds of people.'

'All women?'

'No, men too. All the speakers were women though. There was a lady – well, I suppose she wasn't a lady really – who worked in a mill, talking about how hard it was, and how all the mill-girls wanted the vote. That was jolly interesting. And there was a lady from Wyoming – in America, you know – where they have suffrage already, talking about what they'd done with it.'

'What *is* suffrage?' said Hetty.

'The vote, juggins,' said Kezia. 'Did you put your name down to get put in gaol?'

'It wasn't like that,' said Evelyn, rather thoughtfully. 'They didn't have a gaol list pinned up anywhere. We signed the petition, though. And I took out a subscription to *Votes for Women* – only, I'm having it delivered to Teddy's house, because I don't want a row.'

'You wouldn't go to gaol though,' Hetty said anxiously. 'Would you?'

Evelyn looked at her with scorn.

'I would,' she said. 'I wouldn't want to, but I would. It's not as though I have any freedom to give up now, anyway.'

'I say!' Teddy said. 'It isn't as bad as all that, is it?'

'Yes,' Evelyn said. 'It is. It absolutely is.'

And Hetty, peering at her solemnly over her button badge, was suddenly afraid.

Speaking Out of Turn

Miss Sylvia Pankhurst was speaking in the Bow Baths Hall. This was quite an occasion. Miss Pankhurst had been released from prison a week earlier, to recover from the effects of hunger strike. Her licence for release having now expired, she was liable to be arrested at any opportunity, which lent a certain air of daring to the whole enterprise.

The Bow Baths Hall was full of people. There was a list of Suffragette speakers, and the rumour of Miss Pankhurst rippling out through the crowds. Would she come? There were mounted police outside the hall, watching the women as they went in. If she *did* come, she would surely be rearrested.

The audience was mostly women, mostly working-class East End women. Another girl might have felt self-conscious, but May never felt self-conscious. The air was thick with the scent of sweat and human bodies. All around May and her mother, people were whispering:

'Is she coming?'

'She won't come. She was only released last week.'

'She'll come all right. She always does.'

'Is she here? Do you know?'

'We'll be ready if she is.'

They were. The woman who had spoken thumped her walking-stick meaningfully on the floor, and May realised with astonishment that it was, in fact, not a walking-stick at all, but a stout wooden truncheon. A woman behind her had another stick just the same. May felt a ripple of something that might have been fear, but was closer to excitement. She nudged her mother and pointed to the sticks.

'Do you think they're going to fight the policemen?' she said. Her mother frowned.

'If they do, keep well back,' she said. She looked around the hall. Police violence against the Suffragettes had been growing. 'Perhaps we shouldn't have come . . .' she said uneasily.

May looked around. There was a boy beside her watching them with open curiosity.

'*Will* it be dangerous?' May asked him. He looked startled, and shook his head, rather furtively, as though ashamed of being caught looking.

'Nah. You'll be all right. Just stay inside till it's over.'

He was about her own age, or a little younger. And – May realised with a jump of surprise – he wasn't a boy. He was a girl. A stocky girl, with short brown hair, in breeches and jacket and a flat cap like a boy. A girl holding a stick like the women preparing to go up against the police. May felt a shiver of something like excitement go through her. She'd heard the Suffragettes described as 'mannish' or 'unsexed' before – these were common cat-calls, she'd even heard them used against her own mother. But they were intended as insults. This girl was 'mannish', but she was in no way 'unsexed'.

Quite the opposite, in fact.

Erotic was not a word many of May's friends would have used; sex was not something most middle-class girls were expected to know anything about. But May had had it all explained to her at the age of twelve, with the help of the *Family Medical Encyclopaedia*. Eroticism was a relatively new concept however, and she found it thrilling. At fifteen, all sorts of unexpected things were erotic for May. Thousands of women, marching down the Strand, waving banners and singing suffrage songs, that was erotic. Poetry was erotic, good poetry anyway, the power, and the rhythm, and beauty of it. The back of the girls' heads in school, their long shiny hair with the school ribbons, all in a row. And a girl with a cockney accent in a flat cap sent a shiver down her back. Like knowledge. Like a recognition. I *know* you, May thought, illogically. I *know* you.

The girl turned back to the women she was standing with. May – suddenly desperate not to lose her – said, 'You aren't going to hit a policeman, are you? Are you going to get arrested?'

'Na,' said the girl. 'The stick's just to defend meself. They're wicked cruel to women, policemen. But we's ready.' She kicked the stick casually with her foot, and added, 'We does self-defence classes in Victoria Park on a Saturday.'

Even that was erotic, the violence, even to a pacifist like May. You didn't have to approve of a thing to find it erotic.

'Do you think Miss Pankhurst's here?' May asked. The girl nodded.

'I 'spect so. Probably in disguise,' she added, knowingly.

Just then, the gaslights dimmed. The people hushed. May waited, expecting to hear the old, familiar arguments. But what she heard was a voice from behind the stage curtains. 'Friends and comrades,' it said, and there was an instant murmur from the crowd.

The girl said, 'It's her! That's her!' Her face was rapt.

May said, 'Mama, it's Miss Pankhurst!' and a woman behind her said, 'Shh!'

'They would like to stop me speaking to you –' the voice was saying. May leant forward, thrilled, and became aware of a commotion behind her.

Fists were hammering at the door, voices calling, 'Open up in the name of the law!'

'It's the police!' the girl said delightedly. 'But they won't let them in – look at them!'

She was right. The crush of people in the hall was pushing against the door, blocking the policemen by the sheer force of their bodies. The crowd was cheering:

'That's right!'

'Keep them back!'

'Let her speak!'

'But I am here today to tell you –' Miss Pankhurst had to raise her voice to be heard above the clamour. Then, suddenly, there was more movement at the front of the hall. May drew in her breath. It was hard to see in the dim light, but figures were scrambling up onto the stage – two or three men, it looked like – and heading towards the curtain. Voices shouted from the audience:

'Miss Pankhurst!' and, 'Miss Pankhurst! The police!'

'Plainclothesmen!' said the girl in the flat cap, in an ecstasy of indignation and excitement. 'The stinking rats! Who do they think they are?'

Miss Pankhurst appeared from behind the curtain. She was younger than May had expected, with a long, plain, rather melancholy face. She'd been hunger striking only the week before, May remembered. The plainclothesmen made a rush for her. More voices were shouting from the floor:

'Jump!'

'Jump!'

'Miss Pankhurst, jump!'

Miss Pankhurst jumped. Off the stage and into the audience, which caught her. The women roared. The policemen leapt after her and into the crowd. They began pushing against the massed women, but the women pushed back. Miss Pankhurst was being carried over their heads – or – was that her? No, it was another woman wearing her hat. Where had she gone? May was bewildered and exhilarated. The policemen fought their way through the Suffragettes, who fought back joyously, with fists and sticks and knotted lengths of rope; 'Saturday nights', they were called, May knew.

Her mother grabbed hold of her arm.

'Are you all right?' she said, breathlessly. May nodded.

'It's wonderful!' she said, but her mother didn't seem to think so.

'We should leave!' she said, but May couldn't see how.

They were being crushed on either side, and the crush was fiercest around the door, where the policemen were still fighting for entrance. May was being shoved on both sides by elbows and shoulders and pressing feet. A woman barrelled against her, pressing her into the girl in the flat cap. At the front of the room she saw – to her horror – a policeman lift a chair and smash it against the head of a woman who was obstructing his way through the melee. They had their truncheons out, she saw. Another policeman lifted a woman by her collar and threw her aside. The Suffragettes cried out in rage and flung themselves against him.

'You said we wouldn't be hurt!' May's mother yelled furiously at the girl in the flat cap. The girl ignored her. She was looking at a woman who was standing on a chair and peering through the hall's windows.

'They're all around the hall!' the woman called down. 'They've got reinforcements – on horseback!'

Another woman was forcing her way through the crowds, yelling. She was clambering up onto the backs of the other women. She was clawing at the window. She was carrying a fire extinguisher, and – heavens! – she turned it on and aimed it at the men outside. They could hear shrieks and yells and the screams of the horses as the water reached them. Outside, May could hear the men cursing as they pulled back from the hall. The Suffragettes cheered and rushed at the door, pushing out of it and into the melee.

May's mother called, 'May!' in terror, but May was swept along in the crush, pushed up against the girl in the flat cap. Despite her panic, a small part of her brain thrilled to this.

'Why are they trying to get out?' she yelled, over the pandemonium. 'Aren't they afraid?'

'Course they ain't!' said the girl, scornfully. 'Miss Pankhurst's got to get out somehow, ain't she?' She gripped her stick, and for one brief, unpacifist moment, May wished she too had brought a weapon to use against the policemen and help free Miss Pankhurst.

The crowds were fighting at the door. May was banged against the wall. Her chest was crushed, her skin red and sticky with heat. She felt breathless and a little dizzy. She kept hold of the sleeve of the girl in the flat cap, and to her relief, the girl didn't try to break free.

The press of bodies pushed them through the narrow doors and out into the welcome cold of the March evening. The noise the women were making was immense. The mounted police were still struggling to control their horses. May didn't know much about horses, but these were obviously unhappy; their ears were back, and their eyes were wide, and although they were no longer rearing, they were moving in little distressed dances, as the policemen tried to soothe them. The policemen were pushing back against the press of women. Evidently they still hoped to trap Miss Pankhurst inside, and they were pushing back against the Suffragettes, trying to get to the open door, but with little success. They had heavy oak truncheons, and horses, and they were, for the most part, bigger and stronger than the women. But the women had sticks and cudgels and Saturday nights. The women were furiously determined. And there were many, many more of them.

The girl with the flat cap was forcing herself forward. May just wanted to escape. She could hear her mother's voice in her ears; 'One day, one of those women will get herself killed.' A Suffragette had died last year, at the Epsom Derby, although they said that was a suicide. One of these women could easily be killed, tonight.

But if she ran away, she would probably never see the girl again.

The girl was yelling terrible things at the policemen, the sort of things May's mother would definitely think gave the suffrage movement a bad name. She still clutched a stick, which she was struggling to bring upright.

May cried, 'Oh, for heaven's sake, let's get to the edge.' She was finding it hard to breathe. The girl began to force her way sideways in the crush. May was relieved, then a horrible thought struck her. Perhaps the girl didn't want to escape. Perhaps she just wanted to get closer to the policemen.

She fought to keep up with her, but it was almost impossible. Elbows and knees and hips and suffrage placards banged against her body.

'Oh, please,' she gasped. 'Please, let me through.'

And then suddenly, the pressure relaxed. The policemen were pulling back, admitting failure. May surged forward with the rest, struggling to keep her footing. She saw an old woman pushed to her knees, and shouted a warning. But the crowd ploughed forwards regardless, those at the front crying out indignantly at those pushing behind them, even as they themselves were forced to trample the woman down. For the first time, May was really afraid.

And then they were free.

The noise of the crowd was still deafening. The air smelt of sweat and fear and horses and coal-smoke from the nearby houses. May grabbed the girl by the arm and dragged her, stumbling, out of the press of bodies and into an alleyway. The girl was gasping for breath. All May's ribs were bruised and sore. She stumbled, and they fell together against a wall, sucking in air like long-distance runners.

'Are you all right?' said May, urgently. The girl took in a long, shuddering breath, and raised her head. Her face was red, and her hair stringy with sweat.

'What d'you do that for?' she demanded. 'We was winning!'

'We could have been killed!' said May. She felt dizzy and rather dazed. Her whole body was tingling.

'So?' the girl demanded. She thrust her face up against May's. All May could think was how much she wanted to kiss her. She leant forwards, almost unconsciously, and the girl jumped back, unnerved.

'Bloody hell!' she said. May stopped. 'Who *are* you?' she said.

'I'm May,' said May. 'May Thornton. Who are you?'

'Nell. Ellen. Nell. Nell Swancott.'

Pleased to meet you, May almost said. She wanted to giggle.

'What the *hell*—' the girl began, but what she was about to say, May never discovered.

There was a shadow at the end of the alleyway, and a voice said, 'May! I've been looking for you everywhere!'

It was her mother, looking dishevelled, her face flushed and her hair a marvellous bird's nest. There was a sharp, anxious note to her voice, which was most unusual for May's mother.

'Whatever were you doing hiding down here? Didn't you know I was looking for you?'

'I was just . . .' May turned back to the girl, to explain.

But she was gone.

Coney Lane

Nell made her way down the alleys towards home in a daze. She felt bruised and sore and bewildered. But more than that, she was filled with an excitement so strong it was dizzying.

Did that just happen? Did that girl really just try to kiss her?

Part of her – a very large part – wanted to turn back and find her. To say, *How did you know you could do that? Do people do that where you come from?* Perhaps posh girls like May kissed each other all the time. Perhaps everyone did.

But she couldn't ask. And she couldn't persuade herself to go back. In Nell's world, girls like May flashed past at a distance. Sometimes people you knew got jobs working in their houses, sweeping their floors and minding their children. Sometimes you came across them at closer quarters – working in the infirmary perhaps, or marching with the Suffragettes. But you couldn't just go up to them and demand to know why they had tried to kiss you.

And you certainly couldn't ask them to kiss you again.

• ● •

It was late when she got back home, gone nine. She let herself into the house – nobody in Poplar locked their front doors – and climbed the stairs to the two rooms the family rented. The kitchen was, for once, quiet. Her parents were sitting by the fire; Mum darning a tear in Dot's petticoat, Dad mending the sole of one of Bernie's boots. The younger children were asleep next door; the baby in an orange crate by the bed. Later, Bernie would be turfed out of the bed and onto the sofa he shared with Nell's older brother, Bill. Bill, who was sixteen, was out somewhere, as usual.

Mum looked up as Nell came in.

'All right, lovey?' Then, seeing her face, 'Weren't trouble, were there?'

'Bit.' She felt the teapot on the table – still warm. Good. She poured herself a cup. 'Should've seen them Suffragettes, though! They was bloody brilliant.'

Her mother frowned.

'You just be careful, my girl,' she said. 'Marching's one thing, but I don't want you setting fire to no postboxes, you hear me? We ain't standing bail if you ends up in't clink.'

Nell glanced at her father, who grinned at her.

'Always liked a girl who were handy with a match,' he said.

Nell's mother whacked him. 'And you can keep your mouth shut, and all,' she said.

The East End of London was the heart of the docklands, and one of the poorest parts of the city. Fourteen people lived in

Nell's four-room house – her family of eight in the two rooms upstairs, and Mrs O'Farrell and her five children in the two rooms below. The other houses on their street were equally full. Most of the people Nell knew lived noisy, outdoor lives; in and out of each other's houses, in and out of each other's business.

All kinds of people came to the East End from the docks: Jews from Eastern Europe, Lascars on the boats from India, Irish migrants, even a few men from the West Indies and Africa. There was a strong tradition of activism – Nell's father could remember the Dockers' Strike of 1889, and had once gone to hear the Labour MP Keir Hardie speak at a rally in Victoria Park. And now there were the Suffragettes.

Nell had found the Suffragettes last year, when she was fourteen.

She'd known about them vaguely, of course. She knew where the Women's Hall was, and one quite often saw them in the street, standing on top of orange crates, shouting about women's rights, and giving out handbills. It was good sport to watch them arguing with the men who tried to heckle them. And sometimes people threw things at them, and that was even better.

Mrs O'Farrell, their landlady living downstairs, said the Suffragettes were disgraceful women who ought to be at home looking after their husbands. But Nell's father liked them.

'Nice to see a lady looking out for herself,' he'd say. And, 'They're all right, they are. They know what's what.'

'Would you like to be a Suffragette, Mum?' Nell asked her

mother, but she just sighed, and said, 'With six kids and a house to keep! I ain't got time to go marching on Parliament. Not but what I wouldn't like a vote, mind. But whoever listens to what women want?'

Nell's mother was a piece-worker. For most of Nell's childhood, she had made shirts for a factory in Poplar, for which she was paid four pence per shirt. Each shirt took an afternoon to finish. It was hard, demanding work, but Mrs Swancott took it because it could be done at home, and she could nurse the baby and keep an eye on Johnnie, who was three. Nell's dad was a stevedore on the docks.

Nell had always been a tomboy, as far back as she could remember. She had always resented the bitter gender segregation of Coney Lane, where the girls sat on the steps and minded the family baby, and the boys played cricket, and soldiers, and other noisy, rowdy games.

'Mind the baby!' was a command she'd grown up with since early childhood. It never occurred to any of the Coney Lane mothers to yell it at the boys; looking after the baby was women's work, as was helping with the never-ending washing, and mending, and black-leading, and baking. Both Nell and her sister Dot had been taken out of school every Monday to help with the weekly wash, along with most of the other girls in their Board School. Even as a little girl, Nell had complained.

'Why's it always me what has to do it? Why can't the boys help?'

But her mother always had an answer.

'Because you'll have to run a house one day, and it's never too soon to learn how.'

Nell had huffed at this.

'No fear!' she'd said, right from when she was Dot's age. 'I'm not going to marry, ever, *or* have children. I'm going to live absolutely alone in a house with just me in it, and live off bread and dripping and pork pies.'

But no one had believed her.

Nell had always been restless. As a child, she'd followed her brother Bill into the cricket games, demanding her right to 'play too'. Nell was good at cricket, better than Bill was, so no one had argued much.

The boys' clothes went way back too. It was hard to run or climb or fight in skirts and petticoats, and Nell had always hated the way she looked in them. With her square face and jaw, she felt like a toy soldier dressed as a ballerina doll. (None of the Swancott children had toy soldiers or ballerina dolls, or indeed any toys at all, but Nell had seen them in the toyshop on the high street, and been fascinated.)

How did girls *cope*, squeezed into petticoats and pinafores and bodices and corsets and combinations and stockings and suspenders and spencers and all the rest of it, all day, every day? It was awful. You were too hot in summer and you were *squeezed* all the time, and you didn't have *pockets* – how did girls cope without *pockets*? On Sundays, when Nell was forced, protesting, into a Sunday frock, she felt like she was being slowly smothered to death.

'I look more like a boy anyway,' she'd said. 'So why shouldn't I dress like one?'

Her mother hadn't objected. There had been a rough few years after Nell's father had left the army when he'd struggled to find work, and if Nell wanted to wear her brother's cast-offs, her mother didn't have the money or the energy to complain. The other children had mostly accepted her as a sort of honorary boy, and if anyone said anything cutting, Nell's fists soon taught them otherwise.

It got harder once she'd left school at fourteen, though. Nell had wanted to get a job as a delivery boy, like Bill. (Her Auntie Betty had married a grocer. Bill had gone to work for him the previous year, and all the Swancott children had learnt to ride on his bicycle). But she'd gone round every shop in Poplar and no one had wanted to hire a girl, even a girl in breeches, so she'd settled for a job in a jam factory instead.

She worked as a packer, which was not difficult, but it was dull. You had to fill up empty packing crates with jars of jam. That was it. When you'd filled one crate, you went and fetched an empty crate and did the same thing over again. The other packers were all girls, Nell's age or mostly older. She didn't dislike them, exactly, but they baffled her. Leaving school had changed everything, for everyone. The other girls her age were suddenly interested in clothes, and hairstyles, and boys, none of which Nell cared about at all. And the boys had begun to care about cigarettes, and pomade, and making fools of themselves in order to catch the girls' attention. Nell, cut off from both groups, was lonely and resentful, and full of a baffling, miserable rage, which her mother put down to 'growing'. It was a strange, lonely, rather miserable time, until the day she saw the advertisement in the newspaper.

It was an old copy of *The Suffragette*, wrapped around a

bag of chips bought by one of the girls in the jam factory, and the advertisement read:

DO YOU WORK IN A SWEATSHOP?
WE CAN HELP!
FAIR WAGES FOR FAIR WORK.

And underneath was the address of the Women's Hall, the centre of the women's campaign for the vote in the East End.

Nell had torn out the advertisement and taken it home with her.

The family were – at that time – going through one of their periodic rough patches. Nell's little brother Bernie had diphtheria, and since there was no money to send him to the infirmary, he had had to be nursed at home. This meant that the work her mother could do was limited, since much of her day was taken up with nursing him, and the additional cost of the doctor's bills were putting their usual strain on the family budget. This meant less food for everybody. It meant they got 'behind' on the rent, which since Mrs O'Farrell lived below them, made life rather difficult. Mrs O'Farrell rented the whole house from another, grander landlord, and sublet the two upstairs rooms to the Swancotts; if they couldn't pay their rent, she couldn't pay hers either. Nell's mother borrowed money from Uncle Jack, and from neighbours, but doctors were expensive, and Bernie showed no signs of getting better.

Nell hated her mum's work. She hated how much Mum toiled over every shirt and she hated the pittance she was paid. In the jam factory, a woman's wage was less than a man's, whether you were paid by the hour or by the number of boxes you filled. It was the same everywhere. Women teachers were paid less than men. So were women in mills, and factories, and country houses, and shops, and tearooms, and palaces – Nell was hazy on how the monarchy worked, but she was pretty sure that King George got paid more than Queen Victoria ever had. The argument was that a man had to earn enough to support a family. What widows were supposed to do was never explained.

The next day, Nell had gone to the Suffragettes' shop on the Roman Road, with the newspaper advertisement in her hand, and told the women about her mother. There were two ladies in the shop; one was 'gentry', but the other was an East End woman like Nell's mother. They'd taken the particulars, and told Nell they'd use her evidence as part of their campaign against sweated labour.

'But you can't *ban* sweatshops,' Nell had said. 'Can you?'

'You certainly can,' said the Suffragette woman fiercely. 'You'll see.'

And she'd given Nell a handbill, with details of the local meetings, and the Young Suffragettes club.

A week later, a woman had come round to their house with an offer of dressmaking work for Nell's mother from a socialist organisation. Nell's mother had wept, and Nell's father had shaken her hand and told her he'd always thought women would do a better job of running the country than Mr Asquith did. Nell's father didn't have a vote either; to do so he would have had to own land worth at least £10, or pay £10 rent a year. Nell's father was a great admirer of Miss Pankhurst.

'Ruddy marvellous work you ladies are doing!' he said, and

insisted on opening a tin of condensed milk and making the woman a cup of tea.

The next week, Nell had presented herself at the Young Suffragettes club, and spent a bewildering evening listening to suffrage arguments and making banners out of old bedsheets. The week after that, she'd helped give out handbills while a lady in a Suffragette rosette had stood in the street on a soap box and argued with passers-by about equal pay for women. Nell thought the whole thing was marvellous.

She'd been a Suffragette ever since.

Sandwiches

Evelyn's local Suffragette group held meetings every Thursday evening. Evelyn had been along to one of these and found it rather dispiriting; like the dullest sort of committee meeting, much more interested in minutes and organising and dividing up the mundane work of newspaper-selling and shop-staffing and handbill-distributing than in slashing paintings in the National Gallery and setting off petrol bombs. Evelyn had hoped for a revolutionary cadre, and – to Teddy's great relief – had found something much more like a Mother's Union organising committee.

She had, however, agreed to take a slot selling *The Suffragette* on street corners.

'I thought Saturday morning would be best,' she said to Teddy. 'On the high street, or maybe outside the church. Somewhere where lots of Mother's friends will see me.'

Evelyn had not told her parents about the Suffragettes. She was hoping they'd find out in the most public and dramatic way possible.

'Perhaps I could sing,' she said thoughtfully. 'Or shout revolutionary slogans. Do you think one shouts?'

'What exactly do you think is going to happen when your parents find out about this?' said Teddy, amused despite himself. 'It's hardly going to help you get to Oxford, is it?

Evelyn flushed.

'I don't know,' she said. 'And I don't care. They subjugated me, *and* they've ruined my life, and they damn well ought to know it.'

But selling copies of *The Suffragette* on street corners proved a rather dispiriting task. Most people hurried past without buying anything. Some were openly scornful and combative, including a middle-aged lady who told her very plainly that a woman's concern should be her husband and children, not politics. One or two pointed and jeered. A young man in horn-rimmed spectacles told her giving women the vote would be a disaster, because one week out of every four, women were biologically incapable of rational thought. This was rather a shocking thing for a strange man to say, and for a moment Evelyn was blindsided. Then she told him furiously that that meant three weeks out of every four they *were* capable, which was more than could be said for men.

Several tried to interest her in their own pet campaigns. Evelyn had to listen for nearly twenty minutes to an elderly gentleman from a temperance society, who clearly saw her as a tame subject for conversion. After he'd finally left, he'd been replaced by a woman who had explained that Suffragettes were all very well, though she didn't have time for that sort of thing herself, but what was *really* important was the poor little heathen children in Africa, and would Evelyn like a pamphlet, since she was here? You see, the thing was . . .

Evelyn also had to deal with two men wanting directions, a young lady wanting to know the time, and an elderly lady who told her at great length about her granddaughter, who was just Evelyn's age, and was having *such* difficulties.

She hadn't even seen anyone she knew, except a couple of girls from school, who had stared. What was the point of being publicly humiliated, if you couldn't annoy your parents while you did so?

Desperate measures were obviously necessary. So, a month later, she signed up to walk around Hampstead wearing a sandwich board advertising the next Suffragette rally in Hyde Park. If that didn't attract her parents' attention, she felt, nothing would.

The ladies of the West Hampstead Franchise Society assembled on Saturday morning in the suffrage shop, feeling somewhat daunted. Evelyn was wearing a white muslin 'party' dress, with a VOTES FOR WOMEN rosette affixed to her shoulder. Miss Wilkinson, the local organiser, was in green, while Miss Colyer was in a violet costume, which had looked rather well at home, but now seemed decidedly . . . *visible*. All of the ladies were wearing sandwich boards of the type worn to advertise CLOSING DOWN SALES and FINAL REDUCTIONS, and were carrying leaflets advertising a rally protesting the fact that the Free Irish were still allowed to campaign in Hyde Park while the Suffragettes had been banned.

There were eleven ladies present, including Evelyn, Miss

Wilkinson, and Miss Colyer, a young English teacher who had never done anything more daring than try to sell copies of *The Suffragette* in the street and retire in confusion when a sign-painter asked why she thought she should have a vote when he didn't. Miss Colyer was studying herself with some alarm in the little mirror on the lid of her powder compact. Evelyn rather sympathised. Fortunately for Miss Colyer, the mirror was too small to show the true horror of her predicament.

'I feel like a belted knight,' said Miss Wilkinson, in a tone of some amusement. 'If anyone knocks me over, I'm going to have to lie flat on my back until someone picks me up.'

'I feel like a character in a pantomime,' said Miss Colyer. She peered at herself anxiously in the glass. 'I do wish we hadn't got to do this in Hampstead. It's so much easier to be plucky when you don't have to worry about bumping into the neighbours.'

'I shouldn't worry,' said Miss Wilkinson drily. 'I doubt any of the neighbours would recognise us in this get-up.'

Miss Colyer brightened momentarily, then paled as she remembered that worse fates awaited a Suffragette than being recognised by the neighbours.

'They won't . . . throw things, will they?' she said.

'They might,' said one of the other women. 'But you needn't worry about stones – they never throw them hard enough to matter. And you soon get used to mud. It's the rubbish *I* mind. Rotten vegetables, and apple cores, and banana skins, and all that sort of thing.

'Oh,' said Miss Colyer. She and Evelyn exchanged a worried glance.

• • •

The ladies of the West Hampstead Franchise Society marched down the street with an air of controlled terror. To Evelyn's disappointment and mild amusement, their one aim seemed to be to finish their route as quickly as possible, preferably before anyone they knew recognised them. All were armed with handbills, and a few even managed to thrust one in the face of the more obvious gawkers. Miss Wilkinson, in fact, actually approached several passers-by, with a smile and a cheery 'Votes for women?'

But in this she was alone.

The sight of eleven ladies dressed in sandwich boards and suffrage colours was enough to cause comment at best and outright ridicule – and rotten vegetables – at worst. A young man selling newspapers on the corner yelled, 'You oughta be ashamed of yourselves!'

Miss Wilkinson stopped and turned majestically to face him, nearly causing Miss Preddle, who was behind her, to walk into her wooden front.

'Oh, *lord*!' said Miss Preddle.

'I don't see,' she said to the newspaper-seller, 'what I have to be ashamed of.'

The newspaper-seller was clearly rather taken aback by this direct attack.

'No,' he said, 'but see here. Why should women have the vote? They don't pay taxes.'

'Certainly they do,' said Miss Wilkinson. 'I myself am a schoolmistress – I pay taxes. Perhaps you think I shouldn't? In which case, I'd be delighted if you'd pass on that opinion to the government. I'm sure they'd be interested to hear your thoughts.'

There was some laughter and a few ironical cheers from a butcher's boy on a bicycle, who had slowed to listen. The newspaper-seller scratched his chin and made the best of a bad situation.

'Naw, but,' he said. 'Men go to war, don't they? They die for their country. Women don't.'

'Some men go to war,' said Miss Wilkinson. 'And some do not.' Her expression made it very clear which sort of man she thought the newspaper-seller was. 'And under our current system, those who do, do not vote. And women, who risk their lives every time they bring a child into the world, also do not. As far as I can tell, risking your life for your country rather loses you your right to vote than otherwise.'

Evelyn was rather impressed with this piece of logic. A man could only vote in an election if he'd been resident in the country for the previous year, which naturally ruled out most of the armed forces.

A small crowd was gathering. Miss Wilkinson looked around to acknowledge the few scattered cheers that greeted this last sally and gestured to the other Suffragettes to start giving out handbills.

Miss Colyer said, in the tones of one about to face a firing squad, 'I do *believe* that woman there has a little boy in my Sunday School.'

'She'll hardly recognise you guyed up like this,' said Miss Preddle encouragingly. Miss Colyer sighed and turned to a very grubby little girl in a white smock lugging a baby.

'Would you like a handbill?' she said hopefully.

'Coo!' said the little girl.

'Oi!' said the butcher's boy, who was evidently growing bored. 'Suffragette!' Miss Colyer turned, and the boy lobbed half a fish-paste sandwich at her. It hit her left cheek, and the boy hooted, while his friends cheered. The woman with a little boy in Miss Colyer's Sunday School looked scandalised, and hurried away.

Miss Colyer pulled out her handkerchief, wiped her face, and sighed.

'Goodness,' she said. 'It's all very well, sacrificing yourself for your cause, but I do think men have it easier. At least people cheer when you go off to fight in the wars. I *think* I'd rather be blown up than have people throw things at me in the street.'

Evelyn thought she rather agreed. This was not the glamorous outlaw life she'd hoped for.

'I think we should set fire to things,' she said darkly. 'At least if you're setting fire to deserted manor houses, you don't have to deal with frightful missionary women, and butcher's boys throwing sandwiches.'

'Just wives in attics, and hunchback recluses,' Miss Colyer agreed. 'And spiders.'

'Hunchback recluses,' said Evelyn, 'would be no problem *at all*.'

May Morning

When May wanted something, she usually got it. She wanted to see the girl in the flat cap again very much indeed. So a few weeks later, she said to her mother, 'I don't think we got much look at what those East End Suffragettes were doing, do you? I mean, mostly we saw what the policemen were doing. Can't we go and look at something a bit more hopeful?'

May's mother said, 'Goodness, darling! Wasn't last time enough for you? You could have been killed!'

May didn't think she had come *very* close to being killed, but she knew better than to argue.

'Not *everything* they do can be as dangerous as that,' she said, instead. 'They do pageants for May Morning in the park, don't they, and things like that? There must be *something* safer we could go to.'

Most local suffrage societies were members of two larger organisations: the more peaceable National Union of Women's Suffrage Societies, led by Mrs Millicent Fawcett, and the more militant Women's Social and Political Union, led by Mrs Emmeline Pankhurst. The East London Federation of Suffragettes, however, were members of neither.

Two months after the meeting in the Bow Baths Hall, and the ELFS were holding an anti-sweating demonstration at the Kensington Olympia. There would be stalls advertising Miss Sylvia Pankhurst's work against sweatshops, and other, similar organisations; stalls selling products produced by women paid a living wage; and, the star attraction, a group of actual sweated labourers, doing their daily work in public.

It was exactly the sort of project that sparked May's mother's interest, despite a vague concern that the women were being treated as 'exhibits in a zoological gardens'. This turned out not to be the case, however. All the women were eager to explain their life to the crowds. Some had their children with them – and these naturally attracted a great deal of interest.

'How does one manage to look after children and work at the same time?' May's mother asked one woman, who had a baby and a little boy.

The woman said, 'Well, you can't, ma'am. Not without as he goes and gets hisself into mischief. I just keeps him strapped in his high chair, and he ain't no trouble.'

May's mother said, horrified, 'You mean he sits in his chair *all day*?'

May glanced at her mother and edged quietly away. She wasn't interested in sweatshop workers anyway.

She was looking for Nell.

The hall was a huge, cavernous space, with a high glass ceiling and stalls and people everywhere. But May wasn't looking for an attendee; if Nell was here, she would be working, which was easier. Even so, there were a lot of stalls, a lot of women handing out leaflets, a lot of people who might have been Suffragettes or might just have been stewards; it was hard to be sure.

May had gone nearly all the way around the Exhibition Hall before she found Nell. She had a handful of bills about women's suffrage, which she was evidently supposed to be giving out, but right now she was taking a break. She was leaning against one of the pillars by the entranceway, smoking a pipe, and looking out of the door.

May, watching her from the shelter of a stall about a woman's co-operative in Bow, thought she had never seen anything so attractive in all her life. The flat cap worn low over her eyebrows. The slow, sensual drawing in on the pipe, then the release of smoke. The boy's shirt tucked into the breeches, with the short, dark hair curling over the collar. After the first moment of uncertainty, there was really nothing masculine about Nell. That was what was so exciting about it. A boy who looked like a boy would have meant nothing to May. A girl who looked like a boy, however . . .

Another girl would have been nervous. May simply went up to her and said, 'Hello.'

Nell started. For a moment, she looked almost panicked. At last she said, in obvious confusion, 'You're that girl.'

'Yes,' said May. 'Would you rather I went away? I can if you like.'

Nell's eyes bulged. She choked on her pipe-smoke, and began to cough. As May watched, she bent over, still coughing. May waited. At last, wheezing, Nell said, 'It's all right. You can stay.'

'Huzzah!' May beamed at her. 'I say, I am sorry about the other day. I didn't mean to frighten you. You needn't worry, I won't kiss you again if you wouldn't like it.' Nell flinched, and looked around in obvious alarm. May was rather amused. 'Don't fuss,' she said. 'No one's listening.'

Nell grabbed her arm. She dragged her through the doorway to the hall, past the clerks at their desks and out onto the street.

'Who *are* you?' she said.

'I told you,' said May. 'My name's May. Mama and I came to hear Miss Pankhurst speak, because we think she's interesting. And then I came here today because I wanted to see you. Because I think *you're* interesting. You *do* want to see me again, don't you? Because I can go away if you don't.'

She waited. At last, almost reluctantly, Nell said, 'I don't want you to go away.'

'I thought you didn't,' May said cheerfully. She sat down on a bench, and the girl, still reluctant, sat down beside her. She looked at May rather sullenly, her fingers playing with a loose thread on her cuff. May, who was rarely daunted, said, 'You're a Sapphist, aren't you? Like me?'

'You what?'

'A Sapphist. Like Sappho. She was a poet. It means a lady who loves other ladies. Like me.'

The blank expression had gone. Now Nell's dark face looked almost hungry.

'You mean there's other folk what does it?'

'Of course there are!' May leant forward eagerly. 'Heaps of the suffragist ladies are in love with each other.'

'Not really, though?'

'Oh yes. Miss Payne and Miss Jones have a flat together. That's what the newspapers mean when they talk about 'mannish' women, only they don't like to come out and say so, because it isn't a bit respectable. And there's the Ladies of Llangollen – they weren't Suffragettes, but they had a house together, and were friends with Shelley, and the Duke of Wellington and – oh, heaps of people. Mama told me about them.'

Nell still looked dazed.

'Are you off your chump?' she demanded.

'I don't think so,' said May. 'How would you know, though? If you were? Do you ever wonder about that? I do. A girl in my form told me once that ghosts are people who don't know they're dead, and I used to worry for simply ages after that I was a ghost and didn't know it. But—'

'Stop,' begged Nell. 'Please. You do make me head ache. I'm supposed to be giving out handbills, not listening to you talk cobblers.'

May subsided.

'Sorry,' she said. She watched Nell. The bent head. The boys' flat cap. The fingers still playing with the threads on her jacket sleeve. The urge to kiss her was almost overwhelming. She could feel tingles of excitement running up the inside of her arms. Nell looked up and caught her hungry look.

'That's enough,' she said. 'Not here.'

'All right,' said May. She smiled at Nell. 'Don't worry,' she said. 'I'll find somewhere.'

Knickerbocker Glories and Blood

It was Hetty's birthday in May. She was eleven. Teddy took her and all her sisters for knickerbocker glories at the ice-cream parlour on the high street in honour of the occasion.

'Why haven't you been arrested yet?' said Kezia, to Evelyn. This, to Kezia, was the whole point of being a Suffragette. What better way to annoy Father and Mother than being thrown into a prison cell? Ideally one with rats and straw and chains. Kezia had a decidedly medieval view of the justice system.

'They don't seem to be very arrest-y sort of Suffragettes in Hampstead,' said Evelyn. She scooped her ice cream out of the bottom of the glass, and frowned at it. She wasn't *entirely* sure what she thought about being arrested. The Suffragettes had a policy of refusing to eat in prison, to protest the government's refusal to treat them as political prisoners. The government had decided to force them to eat anyway. Evelyn had read an account of a hunger strike and force-feeding in *Votes for Women*, and it had sounded deeply unpleasant. The woman had been strapped to a chair, kicking and fighting, while the feeding-tube was rammed down her throat. Later, alone in the cell, she had forced herself to vomit up the food again. Somewhere in this process, her eyes had turned completely bloodshot – a surprisingly disturbing detail. Force-feeding wasn't supposed to happen any more, but it still did sometimes, Evelyn knew. Either way, getting arrested seemed rather extreme.

'I already told you,' said Teddy cheerfully. 'If you want to annoy your father, we could just elope. Much less hassle, and rather more fun, don't you think? A small castle of our own in Gretna Green – a herd of highland cows in patriotic ribbons – bagpipes at the reception would be rather jolly, wouldn't they?'

'Ass,' said Evelyn. She wasn't entirely sure what she thought about Teddy, either. Of course, she couldn't imagine marrying anyone *else*. But wasn't love supposed to feel like a hurricane?

Teddy didn't feel like a hurricane. Teddy felt like home.

She didn't say any of this, of course. Instead, she said, 'Father would never let you get away with it. He'd come and fight a duel for my honour atween the clumps o' purple heather. And then you'd shoot him – the young swain always does – and leave me pale and sorrowing on his bloodstained breast. Which might make family occasions rather awkward.'

'Steady on,' said Teddy. 'You might get lucky. He might shoot me!'

Evelyn licked the last drop of ice cream from the pointed tip of her spoon.

'Or,' she said, 'we could do this instead.'

She opened her copy of *Votes for Women* and showed him

the page. It was an advertisement for an action a few weeks away. The king would be in procession down Pall Mall, and the assembled Suffragettes would try and pass a message to him. Hetty and Kezia scrambled to see.

'It's a march!' said Hetty. 'A proper march! Do you think there'll be girls with flowers – and trumpets – and singing . . .?'

'No,' said Teddy gravely. He took the newspaper from Evelyn and frowned at it. 'I think there'll be violence, and arrests. Your women have a rotten time on these things, Evelyn. I'm dashed sure I wouldn't want to go.' He was looking at her intently. She scowled. Being told what to do always made Evelyn pig-headed. 'You aren't really going to do this, are you? It's bound to be frightfully dangerous.'

Evelyn took the paper back from him.

'I jolly well am,' she said. She saw his expression, and something in it made her falter. She pushed on regardless. 'And if you don't like it, you can just come with me, that's all.'

He didn't reply, but she could see how troubled he was. He said no more, however, until the ice creams were finished and the four of them were up on the Heath. Hetty had new birthday roller-skates to play with, and even Kezia was not too old to resist the lure of a clear path and a newly oiled set of skates. Teddy and Evelyn wandered behind them. He took her arm and tucked it into his and said, 'Don't you think you ought to chuck this in now?'

She didn't answer. Teddy said gently, 'Evelyn . . . how much does it matter, the vote? You *can't* think it's worth the things these women do. Setting off bombs, arson attacks . . . Marches are one thing – I don't say I'm against marches – but rallies like this one . . . they're dangerous, Evelyn. I've been reading those papers too; people get hurt at those things. They get arrested, and then it's all hunger strikes and force-feeding and whatever else that dreadful man Asquith dreams up. Is a vote worth dying for? Is it worth *killing* for?'

'Now you are being absurd,' Evelyn said. 'Suffragettes don't kill people. You know they don't. Damage to property only.'

'Oh, don't they, though?' said Teddy. 'What about that business in Ireland, then?' And, seeing her uncomprehending face, 'You *must* have heard about that, Evelyn.'

Evelyn glared. The world, as far as she could tell, was full of things she *must* have heard of. None of the Collis girls read newspapers, as Teddy knew perfectly well. There was only one newspaper in their house – it arrived in the morning, was read by Evelyn's father over breakfast, put into his pocket, and taken off on the omnibus, from whence it was never seen again. The only news Evelyn knew about was the sort everyone talked about, like the sinking of the *Titanic.*

Teddy explained. In 1912, four Suffragettes had tried to set fire to a packed Theatre Royal in Dublin, where the prime minister, Mr Asquith, was due to speak on Home Rule. One of the women had tried to set the reels of film in the cinematograph box alight. The fire had quickly been extinguished, but had it not been, the consequences could have been disastrous.

'And there's that woman at the Derby last year,' Teddy went on. 'The one who was queer in the head.' Evelyn did know about her. Emily Wilding Davison. She'd thrown herself in front of the king's horse and killed herself.

'She wasn't queer in the head,' she said. 'She was a martyr

for freedom. A *soldier*. If a soldier did something like that, you'd say he was a hero.'

Teddy sighed.

'I know you want to go to Oxford,' he said. 'I can't for the life of me see why, but I can see it must be perfectly beastly to have everyone tell you you can't. But how is it going to change anything, joining these women?'

Evelyn scowled. She didn't know the answer to his question, exactly. Only that she was fed up of taking things without a fight.

She said this to Teddy, who laughed.

'When did you ever take anything without a fight?'

'I mean it!' Evelyn said furiously.

'So do I,' said Teddy. He watched her fondly. 'See here,' he said, 'you *don't* believe all that bosh the Suffragettes talk, do you? You *can't* think Parliament's going to start handing out old-age pensions, and free orphanages, and equal pay and whatever else, do you, just because women have a vote? I mean, it all sounds jolly nice. But you know it's a pipe dream.' He paused. 'Don't you?'

'No,' she said. 'No, I don't. And even if it is a pipe dream . . . Teddy, I don't care. I can't know that something is possible, and sit back and not do anything to make it real.'

Secrets and Confidences

May's school was a small, rather shabby but very respectable establishment called Brightview School for Girls, two 'bus rides away from Bow. May liked Brightview well enough, particularly the plays and the gymnastics. There were twelve girls in the Fourth Form, including May's particular friends, Barbara and Winifred. Winifred thought Emmeline Pankhurst was a harpy, but of course girls ought to have the vote if they wanted it. Barbara thought it would be rather splendid to go to prison, although she couldn't imagine *her* mother marching in the street, and didn't May think it queer to have a mother who did? But mostly they weren't that interested. Winifred's father was a vicar, and Winifred had to spend Sundays helping her mother run the Sunday School. Barbara's mother put on musical evenings, at which Barbara was forced to hammer out beastly sonatas on the piano. Parents were awfully peculiar creatures, everyone knew that.

It wasn't unusual for girls at May's school to develop feelings for older girls. May herself had had several very *interesting* encounters with Fifth Former Margaret Howard in the stationery cupboard. But so-called romantic friendships were not quite the same thing as Sapphism. It was understood that they were just something that happened when you were at school and didn't know any boys, and when you grew up and met your future husband, those feelings would be replaced by something 'real'. May knew perfectly well that what she felt for the girl in the flat cap was 'real', but she also knew without being told that this view of things would not be accepted at Brightview. She had never even tried to talk about Sapphism with Barbara and Winifred.

She kept her confidences for a party the next week, held by one of her mother's Bolshevik friends. For a Bolshevik, the friend lived in rather a grand sort of house in Bloomsbury; inside, however, in keeping with Bolshevik principles, it was furnished in an incredibly chaotic fashion. The room the party was held in was larger than the entire ground floor of May's house, and full of an odd assortment of dining-room chairs and battered occasional tables. Several of the chairs were missing their backs, and in one corner of the room a whole strip of wallpaper was peeling off the wall.

May and her mother paid their respects to the Bolshevik, then May looked eagerly around the room. She soon found the person she was searching for: a girl of eighteen or nineteen, perched on a window-seat, drinking red wine out of a teacup and swinging her legs. Her dark hair was bobbed and her lips were painted bright crimson. Between them rested a black cigarette-holder, with a lit cigarette glowing in its end.

This was Sadie Van Hyning, a daughter of an acquaintance of May's mother. All the year she was thirteen, May had nursed a deep and fervent passion for Sadie which, naturally enough, had been met with a detached but affectionate amusement. Sadie herself was in love with a terrifying young woman called Priscilla, who – rather daringly – lived entirely by herself in a bed-sitting room in Bloomsbury, worked as a sort of social secretary for an old woman in Mayfair, and was rumoured to be an anarchist.

Sadie was the sort of young woman Winifred or Barbara's mothers would have entirely disapproved of. May's mother thought she was rather sweet. May adored her.

'Sadie!' she called. 'Sadie!'

Sadie glanced up, and raised one black-gloved hand in acknowledgement. May pushed her way through an earnest-looking cluster of socialists and sat herself on the window-seat beside her.

'Hullo, my darling.' Sadie put the black-gloved hand (still holding the cigarette) around May's neck. 'Come and tell Sadie all about it. I can see you're simply bursting with it, whatever it is.'

May wriggled with pleasure.

'I'm in love,' she announced. Sadie raised her eyebrow in an elegant fashion. May, rather disloyally, wondered if she'd practised in the mirror.

'Darling!' she cried. 'Not really! And who *is* this divine object who's stolen your heart? Tell me *everything*.'

May did, with great willingness. She could talk about Nell for ever, she thought – or, she could to the right person at least. Sadie listened with an uncharacteristic patience.

'Don't you think she sounds tremendous?' May finished rapturously. 'I bet you simply long to meet her, don't you?'

'My dear, she sounds perfectly ravishing,' Sadie said. She blew a smoke ring over May's head. 'You will be careful though, won't you?'

'Careful?'

'Mhmm. A girl like that . . . well . . . her mother might not be as understanding about her abnormalities as yours is. You won't go blabbing your little love affair all around the houses, will you?'

'Of course I wouldn't!' May was indignant. 'And it isn't an *abnormality*. Mama's got a frightfully interesting book all about it, that says we're just as normal as anyone else is.'

Sadie laughed.

'Of course we are, darling,' she said. 'All the same, though. I don't know that they'd quite see it that way in Poplar.'

A Drawing-room Meeting

Teddy's mother looked at the invitation card in her hand and sighed.

'A talk by Mrs Proffitt on theosophy,' she said. 'I suppose I ought to attend – she'll be most offended if I don't. But really! Can't people think of more interesting things to hold meetings about?'

It was Saturday afternoon. Teddy's mother, who was very fond of Evelyn and vaguely aware that there were difficulties at home, had invited her round for 'tea'. Evelyn had gone willingly enough – she liked Teddy's parents. One got the distinct impression that they felt they'd 'done' parenting with Teddy's two older brothers, Herbert and Stephen. When Teddy himself had arrived, they'd more or less let him bring himself up, which he had done, it must be owned, with a fair degree of success.

Mrs Moran was heavily involved in the local church and the Women's Institute, which meant an awful lot of fêtes, and galas, and lectures, and recitals and, as in this case, 'drawing-room meetings'; where a speaker was invited to lecture to a collection of the hostess's friends. Evelyn had sat through enough of these evenings herself to sympathise. They were usually a frightful bore.

'It could be worse,' she said. 'Last week, some awful female from Mother's church made us sit through *two hours* of magic-lantern slides from the Holy Land. *Two hours*! You wouldn't have thought there *were* two hours' worth of slides from the Holy Land. I say, though!' She sat up. 'You should hold a lecture on the Suffragettes! They're jolly interesting. They do drawing-room meetings. You could get someone to talk about being in prison, and hunger strikes, and how to throw stones through windows. Only, they'd prob'ly try and recruit everyone to the cause, but I don't suppose your friends would mind that. They can always say no, can't they?'

'Well, of course they could,' said Teddy's mother, brightening. She was a nice, rather tired-looking woman some fifteen years older than Evelyn's mother, very kind but with a permanent sense that the world was a little too much effort to negotiate. 'I must say, I do think they're awfully plucky young women. Do you think Mrs Pankhurst would come and talk to us? That *would* be a coup.'

'Um,' said Evelyn. 'Well. Probably not. I think she's quite busy running the WSPU, you know.'

'Oh yes, I suppose so,' said Teddy's mother. 'Well, how about someone who's been in prison, then? I'm sure that would sound very dramatic on the invitation cards. I've never met anyone who's been in prison – well, except for Edith's young man, who did three weeks for stealing a set of fruit knives. I had to speak very firmly to Edith about him – *not* at all the sort of character one wants visiting one's kitchen. And then all the silver cake forks disappeared, and I was *sure* it was him, and really, I was in quite a quandary, because one can hardly accuse someone of something like that without proof, can one? But then it turned out Peggy had put them away in the drawer with the table-napkins, so it was all a fuss about nothing. But a prisoner of conscience is a different thing altogether, isn't it?'

'I don't exactly think any of the Hampstead Suffragettes have been to prison,' said Evelyn carefully. 'But I expect Miss Wilkinson will know someone who has. I'll see what I can do.'

A Supper Guest

'May I have a friend round for supper?' said May. It was evening. She was doing her French prep at the dining table; her mother was writing letters on the other side.

'Of course, darling,' her mother said. 'Is it someone I know?'

'No,' said May. 'She's a new friend. But I swear you'll like her.'

She wrote Nell a letter, at the address Nell had given her, formally inviting her. The reply came by return of post, accepting, but explaining that Nell did not finish work until six o'clock, so would be a little later than invited. May went to explain to her mother, who raised her eyebrows.

'*Who* is this friend of yours, darling?' she said, and May said airily, 'Oh, just someone I met.'

When Nell rang the bell, however, May answered the door herself, not trusting Mrs Barber to understand that Nell was the person invited to supper. She found Nell waiting uncertainly on the doorstep. She knew the gentry 'dressed for dinner', but the only decent outfit she owned was her Sunday frock, which she abhorred. She was damned if she was going to wear it to visit this new . . . new . . . whatever May was. Nell was very suspicious of people who 'played up' to the upper-classes. She told herself fiercely that if the Labour MP Keir Hardie could wear a cloth cap in Parliament, surrounded by all those toffs in toppers, she could wear factory clothes to May's.

But here on the doorstep, she did wonder if that might have been a mistake.

May had, in fact, changed out of her school gymslip and into her green velvet in honour of Nell's visit. But in general she and her mother did not dress for dinner, except when guests were expected. Twentieth-century Quakers might not dress in Quaker grey any more, but needless extravagance was frowned upon. She beamed when she saw Nell, and said, 'Hello! Come in! Come and meet Mama!' and the tightness inside Nell relaxed a little. For the first time, she allowed herself to look forward to what might be coming next.

Nell seemed unsure of herself, May thought. Nervous. She nodded at May's mother, and said, 'Nice to meet you, ma'am.'

May's mother said, 'It's so lovely to meet you, Nell. What a sensible outfit that is! And please don't call me ma'am. We're an egalitarian household here.'

She stayed quiet all through supper, answering May's mother's questions with her eyes down. May listened with interest to her answers. She learnt that Nell had five brothers and sisters, that her father was a stevedore, and that she herself worked in a jam factory. Her table manners were exaggeratedly polite, which amused May, who had rather expected her to tip up the glass like Pip in *Great Expectations*. She didn't know that Nell was desperately watching the two of them to see how it was supposed to be done. And her eyes went round when introduced to Mrs Barber.

After supper, May's mother said, 'Why don't you take a slice of seed-cake up to your room, girls?' and Nell's eyes went even rounder.

'Coo!' she said, as they went out. 'Cake, whenever you wants it! You is lucky.'

'Not *whenever*,' said May. 'Only when Mrs Barber's been baking. The stairs are through here, past the parlour.'

Nell peeped round the parlour door, which was the one formal room in the house, and the only public room which was kept free of the endless clutter of suffrage handbills, and newspapers, and banners, and rosettes, which spilled all over the back room, Mama's bedroom, and the hall. It was a dark, rather old-fashioned room, with a stuffed weasel in a glass case, a stiff Victorian ottoman in faded brocade which nobody ever sat on and Mama's piano against the wall. Nell said, 'Coo! What a room!'

'Isn't it ghastly?' May said. 'Mama uses it for piano lessons mostly. I'm supposed to practise in here too, but I'm trying to persuade her to let me drop it. It's not like I'll ever be any earthly good at piano, and you can't think what a bore it is, bashing out all those beastly scales every day.'

Nell didn't answer. May glanced at her; she looked a little

bewildered. She wondered suddenly if that 'Coo!' had been admiring.

'Come on,' she said. 'I'll show you upstairs.'

May's bedroom was rather plain. There was a bed, with a rose-coloured counterpane, and a print of Sir Isumbras at the Ford over the mantelpiece, and a dressing-table with a mirror which had been moved to May's room because it had begun to spot, and a china shepherdess, which May kept out because it had been a present from her grandmother. There was a little bookcase with three untidy shelves of books, and a chest of drawers which fitted nowhere else, and an enormous mahogany wardrobe inherited from an uncle. Around the dressing-table mirror, May had stuck up picture-postcards, mostly on suffrage themes, although there was one advertising A LOVELY DAY IN MARGATE, and a couple showing Figures from High Life. These were both of aristocratic ladies in ball gowns, and looked rather incongruous in the utilitarian room. May saw Nell looking and said, pointing to a dark-haired woman in a long silk dress, 'She's my favourite.'

She gave Nell a conspiratorial smile, but Nell did not smile back. She was wary, May could see. There was a tightness to her, a tenseness, like a boxer, readying for a fight. May had never actually seen a boxer readying for a fight, but there was something in the muscles along Nell's back that reminded her of a picture in a storybook she'd had as a little girl. You could see the shape of Nell's muscles through the tight cloth of her jacket. The clothes she wore were evidently second-hand. They'd been cut to fit someone tall and thin and on Nell, who was short and broad and squat, they had a somewhat misshapen look to them. There was something exciting about her tight clothes, though. It was, in a queer way, more erotic than seeing a naked woman. Her skin and soft flesh, there just below the surface, close enough to touch. What would Nell do if May touched her? Would she be afraid? Or did she long and long for it too? May was almost sure that she did. There was something in the hungry way she looked at May, something in the way her glance had lingered over the ladies in the ball gowns stuck to the wall.

May swallowed. She came over and sat beside her.

'It's all right,' she said. Her mouth was dry, and she thought for a moment that she wouldn't be able to speak. 'There's nothing to be afraid of.'

Nell's wary expression did not change.

'You should see where we lives,' she said. 'Whole family has two rooms the size of this. Eight of us. And you have a whole room to yourself! What wouldn't I do with me own room!'

The temptation was too much for May.

'What would you do, with your own room?' she said.

Nell thought. Then she grinned.

'I'd have a whole bed to meself,' she said. 'And I'd come home from work, and I'd just *lie* in it. And I'd stretch out me arms and me legs as wide as they'd go. And then I'd ring the bell for that slavey of yours, and I'd say, 'Bring me two slices of seed-cake in bed, and look sharp about it!''

May had never rung for Mrs Barber and asked her to bring her seed-cake in bed in her life. Even Mama never exactly *ordered* anything.

'Mrs Barber, dear,' she'd say. 'You couldn't be an angel and do the dining room over tonight instead of tomorrow, could you? Only Miss Hazelwood said she might call round, and it's still rather gluey from the banners May and I were making, and I would help, only I've got these circulars to take round, and May's already late for her rehearsal, aren't you, darling? I'm *awfully* sorry to put you out.'

Mrs Barber had practically raised May; she was more likely to give May orders than the other way around. But she didn't bother explaining that to Nell. Instead, she leant ever-so-slightly closer, her eyes never leaving Nell's.

'Is that all you'd do?' she said, softly.

Nell tensed. Her face was so close that May could feel the breath from her parted lips against her cheek. She could see the mark of an old scar under her eye, and the tide-line of dirt behind her ear, where she'd washed her face after leaving the factory. She could see the lines and tiny craters in her skin, and a freckle on her nose. Nell's breath was shallow. Her cheeks were flushed. But she didn't move or speak. She simply sat there, her mouth slightly open, her dark eyes never leaving May's blue ones, watching her with a curious intensity of expectation, waiting.

May leant forward so that her lips were touching Nell's. Nell drew in her breath as though she'd been given an electric shock. She was trembling. May touched her dark hair and drew it off her cheek. Nell's lips opened, and then they were kissing, properly kissing, and May felt as though the electricity had been transferred to her body, and she was crackling with it, all over, flooding her arms and hands with electrical charge.

They came apart and looked at each other. Nell said, fiercely, 'Where'd you learn to do that?' She sounded angry, as though she thought May had been holding kissing-girls tea parties every Saturday and not sending her an invite.

'Margaret Howard in the stationery cupboard,' said May. The mood had gone, and she wasn't sure if she was relieved or sorry. 'Girls are always having pashes on each other at my school. Mama says it's all our unresolved sexual frustration. Didn't they at yours?'

'No,' said Nell. She looked a bit bewildered. 'We had boys.'

May smiled, her open, wide-mouthed smile. She was so full of happiness, she felt as though it was overflowing. She wanted to kiss Nell again. She wanted to find out everything about her; her family, her home, her work, to gobble it all up and make it her own. She wanted to touch Nell, to see what she wore under her grubby blue jersey; not a corset or a bodice, surely? A shirt? A vest?

'Quakers say all life is sacramental,' she said, instead. She reached out and touched Nell's lips. Nell flinched. 'Even this,' she said, very gently. 'Even this.'

Mother, May I?

After she'd gone, May wandered downstairs. Her mother was sitting by the fireplace, reading a copy of the *Daily Herald*. She looked up as May came in.

'I like your friend,' she said.

'So do I,' said May. She came and leant against the side of her mother's chair. Her mother put her arm round her.

'My little girl, growing up,' she said, which May supposed was her way of telling her that she had a very good idea of what had been going on upstairs, and she didn't exactly disapprove. 'You will be careful, won't you?'

'I'm always careful,' said May, which was a joke. May was many things, but cautious was not one of them. Her mother laughed.

'Don't hurt her,' she said, which seemed like an odd thing to say; surely Mama ought to be more worried about May getting hurt? 'She doesn't look like a child who's had much experience of the world,' she said, which was even odder; Nell had left school, after all, and had a job, and been on Suffragette marches where one attacked policemen with sticks. It seemed to May that she had far more experience of the world than May did herself. 'To a child like that . . . you're a lot to lose.'

'Nell isn't a child,' May said. 'She's fifteen.' Her mother smiled, and kissed her.

'It's nice to see you so happy,' she said. 'Just . . . you have a lot of power over her, you know. Think about how you use it. She doesn't look like a girl who's had much out of life, that's all.'

Belonging

Teddy had not mentioned the action at Buckingham Palace again. Perhaps he hoped it would quietly be forgotten, and over the last couple of weeks Evelyn had found herself wondering if perhaps it would be. Then she told herself firmly that that would be funking it. Other women went to prison for their beliefs. They starved themselves. If they could do that, Evelyn could march down a street.

And if Teddy felt so strongly about it, he could damn well come with her.

When she put this to him, he agreed, grumbling.

'Though I feel we've already taken our share of edible missiles for the cause,' he said, as he met her at the omnibus stop. 'Are you getting the wind up yet? Because if you are, we could always go for a picnic instead. Or to the pictures. Or there's a chap I know who's having a luncheon party—'

'I'm not getting windy,' said Evelyn, firmly.

'Pity,' he said. 'Look here, old thing, the king isn't going to care about your bally missive. Why don't we go to the zoological gardens instead? We could have a ride on an elephant. I haven't had a ride on an elephant since I was six years old.'

'I thought you were supposed to be a feminist?' said Evelyn.

'I am,' said Teddy. 'I'm the sort of feminist who doesn't want the woman he loves to get clonked over the head by a policeman. We're a small but vocal minority.'

'Ass,' said Evelyn.

The aim of the action was to present a deputation to the king. Ministers and Members of Parliament being so unsympathetic to the cause, the Suffragettes had decided to bypass them, and go right to the top. They would march from Grosvenor Square to the Wellington Arch on Constitution Hill, break through the police cordon, and hand their petition to the king himself as he rode past. The action had been publicised across Britain, and women from all sorts of suffrage societies were expected to attend.

The Hampstead Suffragettes gathered at the omnibus stop by the church, and rode into town together, banners under their arms and rosettes pinned to their chests. They joined the crowds at the back of the rally and waited as the suffrage societies assembled. Neither Evelyn nor Teddy had seen a big rally before. Evelyn had never even seen a picture of one. She was astonished by the scale of the thing. There must have been hundreds – maybe even thousands – of women. Men too. Every suffrage society in London seemed to be there.

Those women who had been to prison marched together in a guard of honour. Evelyn thought how strange the world was. At home, a woman who'd been to prison was a dangerous, unwomanly creature. But for these women at least, she was a heroine. Evelyn was aware of the two ideologies sitting alongside each other in her head; the nice young girl from Hampstead who wanted to be respected, and the rebel woman who wanted to bring down the pillars of the world. Could one be two such different people at the same time? she thought, and then, Was anybody ever not? Was there anybody who was only ever one sort of person, all the time? And if there were, would such a person be admirable, or dangerous? When at last they set off, these thoughts were still chasing each other around her head.

She had expected trouble from Teddy, but Teddy, as though in illustration of this principle, was at his most affable and charming, marching alongside nice Miss Plom, a socialist schoolmistress.

'I do think it's *unfair*,' she was saying, 'the way some people have everything and others have nothing. If people could just be persuaded to *share*, the world would be such a *nicer* place, don't you agree?'

'Oh, rather!' he said enthusiastically. 'All those ghastly aristocrats, bathing in champagne. Shocking fellows. Guillotine the lot of them, I say!'

Evelyn came up to him and put her arm through his.

'What are you playing at?' she whispered. He waggled his eyebrows at her.

'Well,' he said. 'I *don't* think we ought to be here, but you clearly do, so here I am. And since we *are* here, you can't grudge a fellow a bit of fun, can you? Don't look now, but there's a terribly keen-looking female trying to catch your attention.'

A girl in the group behind the Hampstead women was

waving at her. Evelyn was just beginning to wonder why it was she looked vaguely familiar when the girl came running up.

'Hullo!' she said. Evelyn looked at her blankly. 'Don't you remember me?' she said. 'I sold you a copy of *Votes for Women* and then some scab chucked a chestnut at you – remember? And now here you are!'

'Oh!' said Evelyn. 'Oh – yes . . .'

'May,' said the girl. Evelyn introduced herself, and Teddy, who shook May's hand enthusiastically. The fresh air, the people, and the singing seemed to have put him in high spirits.

'Ripping day for a spot of criminal violence, isn't it?' he said.

'Oh, we don't want any *violence* . . .' May began, and Teddy laughed, kissed her hand, and said he would expect nothing less.

Evelyn, watching her, wondered if there was more than one May? Did she have a secret life of her own? Evelyn couldn't quite picture it.

'Isn't it wonderful?' May said. 'Don't you just feel . . . so *alive*? Oh, don't you feel sorry for girls who don't have any purpose in life?'

Evelyn didn't quite know how to answer that. For as long as she could remember, her life had been a series of battles and frustrations. Was that something to be thankful for?

'The girls at school,' said May. 'They just want to get married and have babies. Who wants babies when you could be fighting a holy war?'

On the banner behind her, Joan of Arc was lifting her torch with all the fervour of a young woman who knows she's going to be a martyr. Nobody could look less like a martyr in a holy war than May, with her long hair with a blue ribbon in it, and her bony, rather rabbit-y face. But she evidently meant what she said. Evelyn began to wish that she believed in anything as fervently as May did. She looked around her, at the assembled hundreds of womankind. A boy in the street called, 'Oughtn't you be home minding the baby?'

'Oughtn't someone be home minding you?' Miss Plom called back, and the Suffragettes cheered. May caught Evelyn's eye, and grinned.

'Isn't it nice to *belong* to something?' she said.

Belonging. Evelyn wasn't sure she had ever *belonged* to anything. Family, she supposed, and England in an abstract sort of sense. And Teddy of course. If one could belong to people. Did she belong to the Suffragettes? Did she want to? Perhaps she did. Perhaps it would be nice to feel as ardent as May or as joyful as Miss Plom. Evelyn couldn't remember ever feeling as enthusiastic about anything as May seemed to about suffrage. To her, this was a battle for the right to . . . to . . . to *exist*, not a crusade. There was nothing *nice* about it. It was fight or suffocate slowly to death in respectable Hampstead.

'Oh yes,' she said to May. 'Glorious.' And she hurried forward to catch up with Teddy. He had given up on Miss Plom and moved on to teasing Miss Colyer, who was telling him very earnestly all about vegetarianism.

'I know it *sounds* a little eccentric,' she was saying. 'But, really, I feel *remarkably* healthy. Why, I haven't had a *single* bilious attack since I gave up meat, and my dyspepsia is *quite* gone. And Miss Fitzpatrick says the same, don't you, Miss Fitzpatrick?'

'Indeed I do,' said Miss Fitzpatrick. 'I used to catch a chill every winter, regular as clockwork. And now! Not at all!'

'Heavens!' said Teddy. 'But just think of the poor doctors. Why, if everyone went vegetarian, you'd put them out of business entirely. And then where would the poor dears be?'

Evelyn came up and put her arm round his waist.

'You ought to be ashamed of yourself,' she whispered in his ear, and he gave her a look of quite devastating innocence.

Miss Colyer lifted her chin and began to sing, '*Rise up, women, for the fight is hard and long.*'

Miss Fitzpatrick beamed, and joined her voice to Miss Colyer's.

'*Rise up in thousands, singing loud a battle song.*
Right is might, and in strength we shall be strong,
And the cause goes marching o-o-on.'

Evelyn had never heard the song before, but she knew the chorus of course, and joined in. Beside her, Teddy threw discretion to the wind and lifted his voice to the others'.

'*Glory, glory, hallelujah! Glory, glory, hallelujah!*
Glory, glory, hallelujah! The cause goes marching on.'

'Hurrah!' said Teddy, and kissed the top of her head.

Sadie

May was marching with her mother and the Quaker suffrage society, the Friends' League for Women's Suffrage. Nell, of course, was marching with the East London Federation of Suffragettes. The various suffrage societies had assembled in their various meeting-places, then come together and waited, in increasing numbers, for the march to start. There were home-made banners and costumes, and people of all ages and social persuasions. Everyone was there, from the Actresses' Franchise League to a battalion of Lancashire mill-girls in wooden clogs. There was an elderly woman in a bath-chair, with a sign reading: MOTHER, GRANDMOTHER, TAX-PAYER, SUFFRAGETTE. There was a little girl in a straw hat decorated with Suffragette ribbons.

May – impatient at waiting – had come down the phalanx until she found the ELFS, and Nell.

'Nell! Nell!'

Both girls were excited, and a little nervous of what was about to happen – in May this came out in a giddiness and a tendency to gabble; in Nell in more awkwardness than usual, and a nervous tendency to clench her fists and move restlessly from one foot to the other.

May grabbed Nell's arm.

'Hello! You came! I mean, of course you came – but – well – it's so good to see you!' She glanced at an elderly suffragist who was watching them curiously, and dragged Nell out of earshot. 'Come and meet my friend Sadie!' she hissed, in what she probably thought was a whisper. 'She's – well, she's – you know. *Like us*.'

Sadie was leaning against a shop window, smoking a cigarette. Nell had half expected her difference to be obvious, the way she supposed her own must be. And in a way it was; everything about this girl said *rebellion*, from the bobbed hair with the black bandeau and no hat, to the cigarette in the long jade holder, to the neat little ankle-boots clearly visible below her hemline, and the red lipstick. But despite the short hair, Sadie was definitely *feminine*. Nell felt a queer shiver go through her at the sight of her. Despite everything May had said, she had never quite believed in this other world of *people like us*. Was she about to be admitted to it?

Sadie drew in a long, slow breath of tobacco and blew it out slowly, watching Nell appraisingly.

'Well,' she said to May.

'This is Nell,' said May, excitedly. Beside Sadie she looked even younger than usual. Sadie shot Nell a look that Nell couldn't quite interpret, somewhere between pleased and amused and conspiratorial. 'She's one of the East End Suffragettes.' She beamed at Sadie, all teeth and happiness.

'Aren't you the cat who's got the cream?' said Sadie, amused.

She nodded at Nell, then, seeing another woman waving to her across the crowd, gave an insouciant wave in the woman's direction, pushed herself off the wall, said, 'See you,' to May, and was gone.

'You see?' May said, excitedly. 'You don't have to hide everywhere – I told you. What did you think – isn't she wonderful?'

Swank, was what Nell thought. But good-looking swank. She scratched her arm.

'Yeh,' she said shortly. She didn't trust herself to say more, but the blood was thumping in the veins. *People like me*, it seemed to be saying. *People like me. People like me.*

A Militant

By the time they reached the Wellington Arch, the gates had been closed, and the police were massed around it, on horseback and on foot. Large crowds had gathered to watch the affray. Evelyn's stomach clenched. For the first time, she realised that Teddy might have a point. This wasn't the part of *Joan of Arc* where she gave noble speeches and everyone cheered. It was the part where the cavalry charged.

By the time Evelyn and Teddy reached the gates, the battle – and it *did* look like a battle, despite the interested spectators and the petticoats – was already in full force. As far as Evelyn could tell, the mass of women were pushing against the police cordon, while the police attempted to drive them back. The line of policemen stretched far across on either side of the Arch. Evelyn glanced at Teddy.

'Heavens,' he said. 'I had no idea the royal family were so uptight. All this fuss just so as not to read a lady's letter!'

'Rude, I call it,' said Evelyn. She felt a little shaky. The noise of the battle – she couldn't think of it as anything other than a battle – was immense. The women around the cordon were yelling and roaring. She reached out and took Teddy's hand. He gave it a squeeze.

'Funking it, are you?' he said.

'No,' she said firmly.

'I am,' he said. 'Oh well. Into the Valley of Death and all that, eh?'

'Sometimes,' said Evelyn grimly, 'I wonder why I don't just leave you at home.'

Afterwards, they sat in the Maison Lyons at Marble Arch, and drank cup after cup of tea and ate shortbread fingers. The tea-room was full of women shoppers, and families, and parcels, and bulging shopping bags, and waitresses squeezing between the tables with plates of sandwiches, and a three-piece band playing an enthusiastic Gilbert and Sullivan medley, and the whole thing left Evelyn rather breathless.

'What just happened?' she said.

'I think,' said Teddy, 'that *that* was what they call police brutality.'

'It was frightfully brutal, whatever it was,' said Evelyn.

She wasn't sure how many women had been arrested, but it was dozens. She had watched as they'd been forcibly dragged to the police vans, kicking and yelling and thumping the policemen. She'd seen one woman grabbed by her breasts and pulled to the ground. Another had been beaten with a nightstick.

'To be fair to the policemen,' said Teddy. 'Those women of yours were dashed ferocious. I jolly well wouldn't want to meet one of them in a dark alleyway, I can tell you that.'

'One of *us*, you mean,' said Evelyn.

But she agreed with him. 'Unwomanly', the Suffragettes were called, which Evelyn had always thought something of a joke. Plump, socialist Miss Plom, unwomanly! Or little Miss Colyer, all in violet!

But after today, she wasn't so sure. She had seen one woman use what looked like a horse-whip against a policeman. Another had attacked the police sergeant with a walking-stick. You could hardly blame them for retaliating, could you?

It was the Suffragette beaten with a nightstick who had quailed her. She'd watched as the woman had crumpled, and Teddy had put his hand on her shoulder.

'Enough?' he'd said, rather white in the face, and she'd nodded.

Evelyn believed, in theory, that a woman who hit a policeman was no worse than a man who hit a policeman. And sometimes, after all, policemen *did* need to be hit. Several of today's policemen, she felt, had certainly deserved everything they'd got.

But it was one thing to hold these principles in theory, and quite another to see them enacted. Evelyn had never set much store on behaving like a lady. But to see women behaving like those women had behaved today . . . it made her feel cold.

She looked up from her shortbread, and saw that Teddy was watching her with an odd expression on his face.

'Evelyn – don't go on any more marches like that, will you?' he said.

'I don't see what business it is of yours if I do or I don't,' said Evelyn.

'I'm serious,' he said. 'Sell papers if you want, wear sandwich boards – I don't suppose you'll get much more than rotten fruit thrown at you. But – stay away from that sort of thing, won't you?'

'We'll see,' said Evelyn. She had been more shaken by the action than she cared to admit. This did not, however, mean she intended to let Teddy tell her what to do.

'Evelyn, you could have been killed,' he said, and she said, impatiently, 'Oh, don't be such a prig. Isn't there anything you'd risk your life for?'

'I'm blowed if I can imagine what,' said Teddy. 'Not a cause anyway. There's people I might die for.'

'Oh, people,' said Evelyn. She thought gloomily that this was probably the difference between Teddy and herself. She knew one *ought* to risk one's life to save someone like Hetty from a house on fire, but when it came down to it, she could never quite picture herself doing so. The Emancipation of Women was a much simpler thing to imagine dying for. But Teddy, who was so careful and sensible – Teddy would leap into the flames for Hetty without so much as blinking.

It was a rather depressing realisation, and to distract herself from it, she broke off a large piece of shortbread and said, 'You'd jolly well better not get any ideas about rescuing me from any burning buildings. I'll do my own rescuing, thank you very much.'

'Ah, modern woman,' said Teddy. He reached over, took the last piece of her shortbread, and popped it in his mouth. 'So romantic!'

Release

Nell was yelling at the top of her voice. It had started out as: 'Votes for women! Votes for women! Votes for women!'

But as the noise had increased – the whistles blowing, the women screaming – it had become something less coherent, a violent, muddled, joyous, furious howl of rage.

Oh, how she *loved* this. There they were, all those people who spent their lives crushing her and her family: policemen, lawmakers, toffs, *men*. She swung the nightstick and roared. Perhaps they'd arrest her. She wouldn't care – not her! Nell had never been arrested, but she'd always secretly rather wanted to be.

Only then she supposed she'd lose her job, and she couldn't do that. So she didn't *actually* hit any policemen and she didn't *actually* break any windows. But she joined the mass of petticoats pushing against the police cordon, and she joined her voice to the roar of women and she put all her rage into it; rage at the jam factory where they paid her half as much as the men, rage at all those washdays she'd had to stay off school, rage at the boys and girls of Coney Lane. She roared with rage at the whole great world of men.

And she bloody loved it.

Consequences

Two newspapers ran a story about the Suffragette rally, the *Daily Sketch* and the *Daily Graphic*.

In Evelyn's house, the only paper that was read was *The Times*. Evelyn, therefore, did not discover how the rally had been reported until Monday evening.

She had a piano lesson on Monday afternoon after school, so it was past five o'clock when she came through the front door. She was barely into the hallway when Kezia – who had obviously been lying in wait for her – shot out of the drawing room.

'I say,' she said. 'You are for it! Father's so angry he's practically throwing off sparks. Someone at the office showed him a copy of a newspaper story with a picture of you and Teddy in it. There's going to be the most awful row.'

'Is there?' said Evelyn. She took off her school coat and hat with the closest thing to an air of unconcern as she could manage. 'I really don't think it's any of Father's business if I choose to spend my Sunday afternoon visiting Buckingham Palace.'

'My hat!' said Kezia admiringly. 'Just you try telling that to Father, that's all.'

'I shall,' said Evelyn. As she did so, the door to her father's study opened, and he appeared, looking unusually grave.

'Could I talk to you for a moment, Evelyn, please?'

Father's study was off-limits to the children, except in times of high drama. The day Teddy and Evelyn had run away to join the circus. The day Evelyn had won the senior school scholarship. The awful day when their tiny, month-old baby brother had died of scarlet fever. It didn't matter how many times Evelyn told herself she was practically a grown-up now. Being called to Father's study still gave her an awful, sinking, headmistress's-office feeling somewhere in the pit of her stomach.

Her father was sitting behind his desk, with a copy of the *Daily Graphic* on the table in front of him. He handed it to Evelyn.

'Would you like to explain this to me, Evelyn, please?' he said.

Evelyn took the newspaper. There, under the headline SUFFRAGETTE RIOT AT BUCKINGHAM PALACE, was a photograph of the women marching. At the front of the photograph was Teddy, his face shaded under his boater, but clearly himself. Clearer still was Evelyn, a few paces behind him, her face turned towards the crowd with a vague, rather distant expression.

Criminy! she thought. She really couldn't have asked for a more dramatic unveiling. She laid the paper down on the table and said, still aiming somewhere near unconcern, 'Well. Since you and Mother decided I couldn't be educated, I've become awfully interested in the rights of women. It suddenly seemed so – well – so *relevant*, so Teddy and I went to a suffrage meeting at the Albert Hall. It was jolly interesting, actually, so then I joined the local Suffragettes in Hampstead. And then at the weekend we walked to Buckingham Palace; there's nothing criminal about that, you know. If anything, it was the policemen who were breaking the law, and—'

'Enough!' Her father was staring at her. 'Evelyn, this isn't some sort of a joke. I don't think you realise at all the people you're associating with. You don't know – how could you? – the things these women do. Really dangerous, mindless acts of violence. You could end up in prison. You could very easily end up killed. There aren't many things that are worth dying for, Evelyn. Is this one of them?'

Evelyn had a sudden, undaughterly urge to laugh.

'But, Father,' she said, as patiently as she could, 'of course I know all that. I was marching with women who've been in prison yesterday. They aren't at all what you think they are. I think you'd like them if you met them.'

'Like them!' He blinked. 'My dear!' He put on his glasses and then took them off again. 'I can quite see that you might think going to prison was glamorous –' (He's thinking of Joan of Arc, Evelyn thought, remembering the days when she and Kit and Teddy had played at St Jeanne in the garden, and Evelyn had been tied to the pole of the washing-line with a skipping rope and martyred.) – 'But really, dear, a prison cell is anything but romantic.'

What in heaven's name do you know about prison? Evelyn

thought. Up until that moment, she had had no intention of volunteering for prison duty, but suddenly it seemed remarkably appealing.

'I do know,' she said. 'But when something's important, isn't it worth suffering for? Like in war. This is a sort of war, you know.' She saw her father's blank expression and said, gently, 'A war for freedom.'

'Freedom!' He started to laugh. 'Darling!' he said. 'You're hardly a white slave, are you? What freedoms could you possibly want?'

She looked at him helplessly. *How can I make you understand?* she thought.

'Everything,' she said. 'Father, everything. I want to go to university. I want to earn my own living, doing something *real* and *useful*, like Kit will. I want to vote for someone who stands for the things that *I* want, not what my husband wants. I want to have the same rights as a man for – oh, for all sorts of things. The right to see my own children if I get divorced. The right—' She stopped. Her father was looking at her in bafflement.

'But, Evelyn,' he said. 'I hope you'll never have to earn your own living. I hope you'll have a family, and children of your own. Would you really rather live like Miss Perring, at the edge of someone else's family?'

'I'd like,' said Evelyn fiercely, 'to live in a world where women can do everything men can.' Her father was shaking his head. And suddenly she felt the fury rising inside of her. 'It's not funny!' she said. 'Don't you dare act like it's funny, or I shall scream!'

Her father's lips tightened.

'Very well,' he said. 'Supposing you did have a vote and there was an election tomorrow – who were you intending to vote for?'

'I –' Evelyn hesitated. The shaming truth was, she hadn't the faintest idea. She had only the vaguest notion of what the various political parties stood for. She knew her father voted Tory, and always had done, but she still wasn't sure exactly what the difference between the Tories and the Liberals was. The Suffragettes wanted you to vote Labour, because they were in favour of women's suffrage. But Labour were hardly going to win an election, so she couldn't see how this was supposed to help. Also, it felt rather disloyal to Teddy's father to vote for his workers when he had such trouble with strikes and so forth. But she was damned if she was going to vote for her father's party, and she was damned if she was going to vote for the Liberals and that cad Mr Asquith, who was responsible for force-feeding, and the Cat and Mouse Act, and all sorts of other beastlinesses.

Deciding, as ever, to go with the answer most likely to annoy her father, she said with dignity, 'I would vote for the All-for-Ireland League. I think it's about time those poor old Irish got Home Rule.'

'The All-for-Ireland League!' He laughed. 'My dear Evelyn! They hardly put up candidates in Hampstead!' He shook his head. 'I know elections are the current fad amongst you girls,' he said. 'But women can't be expected to understand politics, and it's not fair to ask you to try.'

Evelyn flushed. She hated to be made to look a fool.

'Well, and how am I supposed to know any better?' she said. 'I'm not even allowed to read the newspaper! *If* I had a vote, I'd damned well read up on the candidates, *which*, if I may say so, is more than most men do!'

She knew *damned* would upset him, and it duly did. His expression hardened.

'Well,' he said, 'that's as may be. But I am *not* going to stand by while you throw your life away. These women are not heroines, Evelyn. They are violent, barbaric criminals.' He stood up. 'You are not to see any of these people again,' he said. 'Nor are you to see Teddy, until he can learn a little responsibility. You are to come *straight* home from school – and if I can't trust you to do that, I shall have to ask Miss Perring to accompany you. And once you're home from school, you are not to leave the house, unless accompanied by your mother, or Miss Perring, or me. *Do I make myself clear*?'

Evelyn flushed.

'Perfectly,' she said. 'And you have the *nerve* to ask what freedoms you think I don't have!'

And she turned on her heel and marched out of the study, slamming the door behind her, to the admiration of Hetty and Kezia, who were watching from the stairs.

Evelyn always liked to have the last word.

A Meeting Place

The Religious Society of Friends, commonly known as Quakers, met for worship on Sunday morning. The Meeting Room was large, square and filled with long wooden benches, arranged in concentric squares around the table in the centre with the Bible and *Christian Faith and Practice*. At the far end of the room was the elders' gallery, where May's mother sat with the other elders. May could see her now, her hands folded in her lap, her expression quiet. The room was perhaps half full of Quakers, all similarly silent.

May let her gaze wander around the Meeting. Her school-friends found the Quakers baffling whenever she'd tried to explain them.

So you just sit, *in* silence?

Yes.

But why?

You're supposed to listen. To God, or . . . the Holy Spirit, I suppose. Quakers don't think religion is about what you read in the Bible or what people tell you to believe – although it's about that too, of course. They think it's about what you can say, yourself. That's why we don't have priests, or ministers. We're all just as equal as each other.

It was one of the things she loved best about them. All of the jobs in a Meeting – from keeping the accounts to visiting the sick and managing the burial ground – were divided up between the members of the Meeting, men and women. Equality, to May, wasn't just a political goal, but a religious truth. In what other religion could a woman like her mother sit there on the elders' bench, her pale hair – already beginning to turn grey at the temples – threatening to tumble down out of its hairgrips? In what other religion could May herself stand up and speak, if the spirit moved her?

And all of these people would listen.

May knew that she was supposed to be listening too. But she wasn't. She was thinking instead, of a single word, repeated.

Nell, she thought. Nell, Nell.

May had met Nell three times since that evening in her bedroom. Once, they'd gone to Victoria Park and walked round and round the little pathways while Nell talked about the Suffragettes and May talked about the Sapphists. The second time, they'd been to a Picture Palace and seen a Charlie Chaplin picture, and held hands in the dark. And then there'd been the action at Wellington Arch. May had not been involved in the violence – the pacifist Quakers kept as far away from it as they could – but she had seen it, a little of it. She didn't know if Nell had been a part of it. She supposed it wasn't very likely. There had been a lot of women on the march, after all, and most of them hadn't been fighting policemen. But still.

She closed her eyes, and pictured Nell as she had seen her at the Bow Baths Hall, ready to take arms against anyone who opposed her. She knew perhaps she ought to be worried about Nell, but she wasn't. She found herself almost hoping she *had* been in the violence, which was rather an awful thing to think when you were supposed to be a pacifist. But that mental picture of Nell, Saturday night in hand, taking on the British constabulary, was so glorious. It frightened her a little, how exciting she found it.

Nell, she thought. *Nell.*

That was a girl you could fall in love with.

Short, and Containing Much Wailing and Gnashing of Teeth

It was, of course, not only Evelyn who was in disgrace. In the row that followed the newspaper picture, several other things had come out, including Teddy's presence at the Albert Hall meeting and the copies of *Votes for Women* which were still being delivered to Evelyn at Teddy's address. Teddy too had been summoned into Father's office and treated to another long lecture; Evelyn didn't know exactly what had been said, but he had come out looking rather subdued. He hated not to be thought well of. Not only was Evelyn forbidden to see him, he was banned from the Collis house until further notice. Evelyn was more ashamed about this than she liked to admit; although he had never exactly said so, she knew how important their family was to Teddy.

'I do feel a heel,' he told Evelyn. They were on their way upstairs; Teddy had been granted ten minutes in the nursery to say goodbye to Hetty and Kezia. 'Uncle John's quite right – it was a bit thick of me to go behind their backs like this. They've been frightfully decent to me, you know, over the years.'

'They'll get over it,' said Evelyn callously. 'And it's none of their damn business if I choose to be a Suffragette anyway. I tell you who won't get over it though – young Henrietta. I hope you're prepared for an awful scene.'

This turned out to be quite true. Hetty was so upset by Teddy's banishment that they ended up spending their last ten minutes together comforting her. When it came to it, Evelyn had no time to do anything except clasp Teddy's hand and whisper, 'I'll write – don't fuss, Teddy – and tell your mother I'm still coming to her meeting, no matter what Father says.'

Teddy looked rather as though he wanted to protest, but it was too late.

Evelyn's father was in the doorway, and he had to go.

A Lady Visitor

'When shall I see you again?' May had asked, after the Picture Palace. And then, 'I'd love to see where you live – may I?'

Nell had flushed. Then, remembering Keir Hardie in Parliament, she said, 'If you like.'

May turned up at half past six, just as Nell's mother was serving tea. Nell, bringing her up the stairs, said awkwardly, 'It ain't much, like.'

'I don't mind,' said May. 'I say, though, did you see the fighting at Wellington Arch? I thought you might have been in it.'

Nell snorted.

'Not me!' she said, which was true as far as it went. She hadn't actually *hit* anyone. 'Wish I had been, though. That would've been something!' They reached the landing. From behind the closed door, May could hear the hubbub of children's voices. Nell hesitated. 'Well,' she said. Then: 'It's a bit full.'

It certainly was. Both of the Swancotts' rooms were filled

with furniture. Every flat surface was covered in ornaments, or crockery; even the ceiling was criss-crossed with washing-lines hung with children's clothes and babies' napkins. The room was crowded with children clamouring for their tea. Nell introduced them one by one.

'That's me brother Bill. He's a butcher's boy, and he thinks he's all that – but he ain't. This is Bernie. He's ten. He's a sweetheart, ain't you, Bernie? And Dot – she's six. She's a terror. This is me little brother Johnnie. He's three. And the baby's Siddy. Are you going to wave to the nice lady, Siddy?'

May waved to the baby, and was shown around the two rooms. The bedroom had a large brass bedstead, in which Nell and Dot and Johnnie slept top and tail with their mother and father. There was a orange-crate cot by the bed for the baby. Bill and Bernie slept on the sofa in the kitchen. The kitchen had no range, but only a cheap gas stove. May knew from her mother's Fabian friends how expensive the gas stoves were, and how more often than not dinners made on them would be left half cooked rather than waste another penny on gas.

She was invited to share the family tea, but refused politely, saying she'd already eaten. She knew there wouldn't be much food going spare. Tea was bread and dripping and hot, sweet tea for everyone except Bill, who also got a slab of fried ham. The children mostly ate standing up, a hunk of bread in one hand and a mug of tea in the other, and then ran out to play in the street, Dot lugging Siddy under one arm. Bill tipped his cap to May and disappeared 'off out', but the others didn't look round. One of Bernie's friends had acquired a roller-skate, rescued from the rubbish bin by a sister who was a nursemaid, and all the boys were desperate for a go. May and Nell went to fetch the water from the pump downstairs, then went down and sat on the step, leaving Nell's mother to the washing-up. Johnnie, imprisoned in his high chair, kicked and yelled as the others went outside.

'Oh, give over, Johnnie, do,' said his mother. 'I'll take you out when me work's done, if you're good. He's that fretful,' she said to May. 'I don't know what to do with him most days.'

The street, like all the side streets in Poplar, was full of boys, some chasing the boy on the roller-skate, the rest engaged in a game of cricket. The girls, as far as May could tell, didn't play. They sat in little gaggles on the steps, minding the babies, who, being live and wriggling, were far more interesting than any of May's dolls had ever been. May thought they seemed to be having a jolly old time of it.

It wasn't all jolliness, though. Bernie, excited by his turn on the roller-skate, had been overcome by a fit of coughing and had had to relinquish it. His narrow face was pinched and white, and she had been astonished to learn that he was ten years old – he wasn't much bigger than his little sister Dot. She wondered at the five-year gap between Nell and Bernie. Had there been other children there, who had died? Was that the sort of thing one could ask? She thought of the tea, and the hunks of bread and dripping. It wasn't much, particularly for Nell, who was in full-time work, and the mother, who had an air of permanent exhaustion.

Nell was watching her a little anxiously.

'I know it ain't much,' she said. 'I mean – with all them kids in, like. Mum does her best, but it ain't easy . . .'

'I liked it,' said May. She smiled at Nell, trying to show her how much she *had* liked it, how she wasn't going to swank about her own home or talk down to Nell about hers. 'It's – well, it's friendly. I liked your mother. And I liked your brothers and sisters too.'

Nell grunted. The two of them were silent, sitting on the step. May said, 'How come there aren't any children between you and Bernie?'

To her surprise, Nell grinned.

'That's cos me dad was in South Africa. He were a soldier, in the Boer War.'

'Oh.' May was rather taken aback. 'Your poor father.'

'What's so poor about it?' Nell demanded. She was proud of her dad. Not everyone had a dad who'd been to South Africa.

'Well –' May didn't quite know how to answer this. Quakers were pacifists. All the Quakers she knew took it for granted that wars were dreadful, violent things, which no sane person would ever want to be involved in. 'Wars are simply frightful, aren't they? Quakers are against war,' she explained. 'We wouldn't fight even if there was conscription, like there is in France and Germany.'

Nell blinked.

'That's barmy,' she said, frankly. 'What's wrong with wars? If people fight you, you have to fight back.'

'No, you don't.' May leant forward eagerly. 'Soldiers only fight wars because their officers tell them to. Your father didn't have anything against the Boers personally, did he? He just killed them because he was told to. Well, that's not right. All the soldiers should have said they wouldn't, and then they'd have had to use diplomacy instead. That's what the Quakers would have done. Quakers say there's a bit of God in everyone. So if you kill people, you're killing God.'

'You're cracked,' said Nell. She leant back against the door and dug her pipe out of her pocket. 'I don't believe in God,' she said.

May sighed.

'That's all right,' she said. 'He's there whether you believe in him or not.'

A Life Full of Purpose

Evelyn had said that she was going to go to Teddy's mother's drawing-room meeting, and she meant it. She and her mother had both, in fact, been formally invited, but her parents – fortunately for Evelyn – had a dinner engagement, and her mother had turned down the invitation and promptly forgotten all about it. Even more fortunately, it was Miss Perring's evening out – she was going to a concert at the Crystal Palace.

'I am asking you to stay here with your sisters,' Evelyn's mother said to Evelyn before she left. 'I believe I can trust you not to run off and visit that boy as soon as my back is turned. Am I right?'

'I wouldn't know about that,' Evelyn said. Evelyn considered it below her dignity to lie. 'But I can't think where you got the idea I'm such a flirt from. Teddy and I never did anything we need be ashamed of.'

Her mother raised her eyebrows.

'I never believed you had,' she said. But she had kept the dinner engagement. And Evelyn had to do nothing more than wait until Miss Perring had left, put on her hat and coat, and walk out of the door.

She could not help feeling guilty about this. She justified it to herself all the way to Teddy's house. *It's not as though there's anything* wrong *about the Suffragettes. And I* did *tell Teddy's mother I was going to be there – and Teddy – and Mother's always going on about how important it is to keep your promises. And what right have they got to tell me what to do anyway? I'm nearly eighteen. I'm not a child. And what's more important, after all, obeying your mother, or fighting for your freedom?*

She arrived at Mrs Moran's house in a bad mood. Mrs Moran had arranged all the chairs in the house – there were a surprising number of them, once they'd been scavenged from the kitchen and the dining room and the bedrooms – into rows in the drawing room. The speaker was a young woman called Mrs Leighton, a friend of Miss Wilkinson's. She was standing at the front of the drawing room, hands neatly clasped in front of her, waiting for the assembled women – and it was mostly women – to quieten down and let her speak. Teddy was standing at the back, leaning against the wall as though to distance himself from the attendant women. Evelyn felt an unexpected flutter of excitement at the sight of him. This wasn't entirely comfortable; she looked quickly away, slipped into the back row and concentrated on studying Mrs Leighton. She looked calm and quiet and not at all nervous – hardly surprising, Evelyn thought, when one considered that she regularly spoke on street corners, and in packed meeting rooms full of angry anti-suffragists, and at busy, open-air rallies.

Compared to those things, Mrs Moran's drawing room must seem like very small fry indeed.

As Mrs Leighton stood waiting, the women gradually stopped speaking and were silent. Those who were still talking were nudged by their companions until they too became quiet. Mrs Leighton waited, holding the silence. Then she began to speak.

'All my life,' she said, 'I waited for something that would give me purpose. Something I could do that would mean something. I thought I might find it in my husband, but I didn't – although we loved each other, loving him wasn't enough to fill a life. I thought I might find it in my house, but I had a small house and an excellent housekeeper, and an active mind which was not to be filled with housework. I was sure that I would find it in my child, but I found that, though I love my little boy, I do not have the sort of mind that can be satisfied by bending itself to the whims of an infant.'

She paused. The room was silent. This was not at all what they had expected to hear. But there was a focus to the women's attention which had been lacking from previous drawing-room meetings Evelyn had attended.

'Florence Nightingale,' Mrs Leighton went on, 'once wrote –' she opened a piece of paper and read aloud – '"O weary days! O evenings that seem never to end! For how many long years I have watched that drawing-room clock and thought it would never reach the ten!"' She smiled, without any hint of self-consciousness. 'I felt when I read that, that Miss Nightingale had spoken for me, and for thousands of women like me. That – and I say this without particular pride, for truly I am a most ordinary women – that I was a creature full of potential, which had been tossed onto stony ground like the corn in the parable. My father, my brother, my husband – they all lived lives full of purpose and interest. They had work to do and they did it.

'I know that making a home and a family are fine things to do with one's life; I am very proud of my home and my son. But I also knew that they were not enough to satisfy me. And when I spoke to my friends, I found that most agreed with me. They had entered life hoping for more, and had been disappointed.

'It was this which led me to the Suffragettes. Our critics say that we go to prison for the fun of it – to which the only answer is, what sort of life have they made us lead, that we are driven to suffer such hardship for amusement? I did not go to prison for fun. The three weeks I spent in Holloway were the most wretched of my life. But it is true that I am a Suffragette not just because I believe – passionately – that modern society wastes and destroys the talents of half of its population. I am a Suffragette because for the first time in my life, I feel as though I have a purpose, a goal. I feel as though I am useful. I am powerful. I am doing the job I was put on this earth to do.

'In two weeks' time, I am going to take part in an action which will very probably result in my going to prison again. It is a simple action – any one of you ladies here could take part, and would be welcome. I am not a courageous woman; I am afraid of going to prison. I am afraid of the hunger strike. But I am more afraid of the life I would be forced to live if I had never found the Suffragettes.'

She paused. The silence was electric. Evelyn could feel the focus of all the ladies in the room fixed on this slight young woman standing before them. She half expected Mrs Moran to stand up and volunteer to take part in the action, but she didn't, of course. And then Mrs Leighton began to talk about statistics and reforms from countries where women had already been emancipated, and the moment passed.

After the talk had finished, there was time for questions, which were less combative than Evelyn had predicted. And then the women broke into applause, and the maid was summoned to bring in the tea, and the business part of the evening was over.

Mrs Moran's friends were talking amongst themselves. Some looked scandalised. A few even looked thoughtful. Evelyn went up to Mrs Leighton, who was arranging her pamphlets and copies of *Votes for Women* on the coffee table.

'About that action,' she said. 'The one you spoke about. About it—'

Behind her, she could hear Teddy stirring uneasily. She ignored him.

'Yes?' said Mrs Leighton.

'I'm in,' said Evelyn Collis. 'If you want me. I'm in.'

An Ordinary Member of the Public

Mrs Leighton's action was a simple one. Three Members of Parliament were speaking at an open meeting at a public hall in Camden. Several of the Suffragettes had purchased tickets and would enter as ordinary audience members. Such actions were common enough that policemen were likely to be guarding the entrance; however, Mrs Leighton did not foresee any problems.

'It's astonishing,' she said, 'how easy it is to disguise oneself as an ordinary member of the public when one *is* an ordinary member of the public, you know. If we all looked like the harridans in newspaper cartoons, we'd have a far harder job of it.'

Partway through the meeting, these women would stand up and demand whether or not the Members of Parliament supported women's suffrage. They would continue to press the question until they were evicted.

Meanwhile, their supporters – including Evelyn – would be gathering on the pavement outside. When the dignitaries left the building, the Suffragettes would do all they could to bypass the policemen, reach the MPs and continue their demands. They were to do so, Evelyn was instructed, until they were arrested.

This all sounded straightforward enough. But it quickly got worse. Once convicted, all of the women would be expected to begin hunger and thirst strike immediately. Evelyn would have to refuse to eat or drink until she was too weak to stay safely in prison. Then she would be released for a week on licence to recover, after which she would be rearrested, and would have to start the whole thing again. She would keep on doing this until she had served her entire prison term.

'It's a lot to ask,' Mrs Leighton said, holding her teacup and slice of Madeira cake, while Evelyn tried desperately to look as though they were discussing the weather. 'Take some time to think about it perhaps, and let me know.'

'I don't need time to think about it,' said Evelyn.

Other ladies were moving forward to talk to Mrs Leighton. Evelyn squared her shoulders, moved aside, and went to look for Teddy.

He was waiting on a chair in the hallway, pretending to read the newspaper. Evelyn, remembering her father's jibes about her ignorance, glanced at the front page, but it didn't look very interesting. HEIR TO AUSTRIAN THRONE MURDERED IN SARAJEVO the headline said. She wondered vaguely why any English person was supposed to care what happened to Austria.

Teddy clearly didn't. He shot up as she came through the door, grabbed her by the wrist and pulled her into the morning room. She said, 'Ow!' And then, 'Teddy, get *off* me, can't you? That *hurt*.'

His face was tight and furious.

'You've volunteered,' he said. 'Haven't you?' And then, when she didn't answer, '*Haven't you*?'

'So what if I have,' she said, a little sulkily. He dropped her wrist.

'Evelyn!'

'Evelyn *what*?' She faced him. 'What are you going to do about it? Forbid me from going? You *couldn't* be such a scab as to tell my father.'

'Oh, couldn't I, though? What sort of a fellow doesn't tell a chap when his daughter – his *schoolgirl* daughter – is about to get herself flung into gaol? It's hardly cricket, is it?'

She said, despairingly, 'You *beast*. Is that how you think of me – as a – a *schoolgirl*?'

'Well –' He had the grace to look awkward. 'I mean, not exactly, but—'

'And I suppose you think it's your job to protect me and revere me and keep me in my proper sphere and all that bosh?'

'It's my job to tell you when you're being a bloody fool!' he said, pushed at last to his limit. 'You think this is all some sort of game – holy martyrs and whatnot – but you know what happens to martyrs, don't you? They get roasted at Tyburn. Haven't you seen enough of this mess already to know what it's going to be like – the policemen, the cell, the – the feeding-tube?'

'They don't use the feeding-tube any more, *actually*,' she said. He looked for a moment as though he were going to strike her. She was suddenly very tired.

'All right,' she said. 'Fine. I won't go.'

'Evelyn—'

'I *said*, I won't go. There, is your blasted honour satisfied now? Get out of my way.'

'Of course you're going to go,' he said. He wasn't arguing. He was stating a fact. She'd hoped he might have had the sense to leave it.

'I don't believe what I do or don't do is any business of yours,' she said. 'In *fact*, I believe my parents have expressly forbidden you to have any contact with me whatsoever. Perhaps I should tell my father what use you had for *that* little edict. Or wouldn't that be cricket?'

'Evelyn, for God's sake! This is *serious*!'

She rather wished she *had* accepted his bally marriage proposal. She would have liked an engagement ring to throw at his feet.

'Have you only just realised that?' she said. 'How quaint the human male is.'

And before he could think up a response, she'd gone.

Names

'Why *do* you wear boy's clothes?' said May.

The two of them were up in May's bedroom. Nell was restless, wandering around the room, touching May's postcards, picking up her ornaments and putting them down again. She felt the force of May's attention on this most private part of herself, and panicked.

'I dunno,' she said briefly. 'Cos I looks such a guy in petticoats.'

May sensed the lie, sensed the wall, and retreated. Then, cautiously, she said, 'Mama has a friend who dresses like you. I mean, she wears her hair short, you know, and all her friends call her Cyril. But her name is Mary really. Mama told me.'

Nell's mouth was working silently, but she did not look up from the china shepherdess. At last, she said, 'Don't nobody mind?'

'Well –' May tried to be honest. 'Someone wrote a beastly lot of bosh about her once in a newspaper article. And boys in the street call things – and men too, sometimes. But none of Mama's friends care. And Miss Jones doesn't either – at least –' May was still trying to be honest. She was naturally honest anyway, but she was also – dimly – aware of how important it was never to lie to this girl, of how important all her words might be to the rest of her life. 'At least, she's never told me she minds. But then she wouldn't, would she? She's a grown-up, and I'm just a kid. But she's always rather grand about people who say things. *Blithering wretches*, she calls them. What do you call people who say things to you?'

'I don't,' said Nell. 'I just punch them.'

This was not entirely true, but it sounded impressive. Honesty mattered far less to Nell than it did to May. She was more interested in the woman with the man's name.

'Do lots of ladies do that?' she said. 'Use men's names, like?'

'I don't know,' said May, still trying to be honest. 'I only know Miss Jones who does. And Mama's got a book all about – about – about people like us, you know. It's called *The Intermediate Sex*, and it's ever so famous. Mr Carpenter who wrote it says there's men and there's women and then there's people in between like you and me, who are a bit of both, and it's just nature and nothing to be ashamed of. It's jolly interesting.' This review was somewhat disingenuous; May's tastes ran more to storybooks than to anthropology, and she had abandoned Carpenter as too dull for words, somewhere towards the end of the first chapter. But no need to tell Nell that. 'Did *you* ever call yourself a boy's name?' she said.

Nell flushed. May thought she wasn't going to answer. She wondered if she shouldn't have asked. It *was* a horribly personal question. But then Nell, in a low voice, said, 'When I were little, I used to pretend I were called Arthur.'

'Arthur?'

'After the Duke of Wellington.'

'Arthur,' May said wonderingly. Then, 'I could call you Arthur, if you liked.'

'No!' Nell's head jerked up. 'No,' she said. 'I ain't a kid.'

'I could call you something else,' said May, cunning May, May who knew the power of a private name. 'What would you call yourself if you could?'

Nell blush deepened. 'I dunno!' she said.

May tilted her head on one side, studying her.

'You might be a Jack,' she said. 'Except your brother's a John, so I suppose you couldn't be. Maybe you should be something short from Ellen. Eli. Or Lenny. Or Len. Or—'

'I ain't a Len!' Nell protested. She was watching May with a sort of wonder. 'What's it like in your head?' she said.

'It's full of you,' said May, honestly.

'Danger' Duty

The day fixed for Evelyn's protest was Monday the thirteenth of July. Evelyn should have been at school, of course, but this was all to the good – her absence wouldn't be noticed until much later. If the protest had been on a Saturday, things would have been much more complicated.

Breakfast was a noisy, friendly affair. Kezia and Hetty argued amicably enough over the jam spoon and the butter dish. Hetty was chewing on her toast, smearing jam halfway across her cheeks, and relating the plot of *Stalky and Co*. in a rambling fashion to anyone who would listen, which was most of Miss Perring, about half of her parents, and a quarter of Evelyn. Evelyn's mother was trying to talk to Evelyn's father about the missionary tea she was taking the younger girls to that Saturday.

'Of course, it doesn't *matter* if you don't come, John, but they do always ask after you, and Mrs Fisher in particular would be *so* pleased—'

'It's a ripping tea, Father,' Kezia interrupted. 'Mrs Robinson brings the best meringues you *ever* tasted, and—'

'Father,' said Hetty, giving up on *Stalky*. 'Father, who do you think was the bigger giant, Goliath or Polyphemus? Miss Perring says Goliath, but *I* don't see how. Goliath was a man, wasn't he? But Polyphemus was a cyclops, so—'

This evening, thought Evelyn, all this happiness will be ruined. She felt obscurely that she ought to warn them somehow, say goodbye perhaps, or apologise. But she said nothing at all.

Miss Perring took Hetty to her junior school. Kezia and Evelyn went to wait for the motor omnibus from the stop on the road to the Heath. Evelyn waited until they were at the 'bus stop, then grabbed Kezia's arm.

'I'm not going to school today,' she said. 'I'm going to see the Suffragettes.' (Well, that was true, as far as it went.) 'You'll have to tell them at the school office that I came over faint on the omnibus or something and had to go home. It's political rebellion,' she wheedled, as Kezia hesitated. 'It's frightfully important, and you'll be jolly grateful for it when you're emancipated. And I'm going to go anyway no matter what you do, so you might help and save a row.'

'I thought *you* said all that schoolboy chivalry was rot,' Kezia grumbled.

'Sixpence?' said Evelyn, and Kezia beamed and held out her hand.

There was a crowd of perhaps twenty women gathered around the door of the Civic Hall, wearing suffrage sashes and rosettes, and waving variations on the usual VOTES FOR WOMEN placards. They were singing, noisily and cheerfully, and not at all like people who were planning on getting arrested. Several women were busy thrusting handbills at passers-by, most of whom hurried past, heads down. Four policemen were standing on the corner, watching, obviously uneasy. They had made no move against the Suffragettes yet, but their presence made Evelyn wary. These were the policemen they would have to charge when the meeting was over. These were the policemen they would have to persuade to arrest them.

'Sometimes the constables get too rough,' said Mrs Leighton. 'They should arrest you when you start to show resistance, but they don't always. If it's getting dangerous, stop fighting and cause some property damage instead. Once you start breaking windows, they have to do something about it. I'd always rather not smash up some poor grocer's shop, but sometimes they leave you little choice about it.'

'All right,' said Evelyn. She took the stone that Mrs Leighton offered her and put it in her pocket-book. Someone had pasted a handbill with some argument for *Votes for Women* around it. She wanted to say something jokey, something about bricks, it being a brick, or her, or Mrs Leighton, or the handbill, but she couldn't find the right words to frame it, and then, thinking about it, she realised that probably it wouldn't have been that funny, so she turned away and busied herself selecting a placard from the pile: NO TAXATION WITHOUT REPRESENTATION, this one said.

Not that Evelyn paid tax.

But it rhymed.

Sort of.

There were twelve women who were planning on being

arrested, and the rest, Evelyn supposed, who were there to support them. The others would not actually break the law, but would content themselves with shouting slogans, giving out handbills and singing.

Placard in hand, Evelyn squared her shoulders and went to join the women. Most were strangers, but there *was* Miss Wilkinson from the West Hampstead Franchise Society, and a dark-haired young woman called Miss Miraz, who Evelyn had been introduced to on the march to Wellington Arch and been rather overawed by, because she was an actual student of chemistry at Imperial College, and seemed to Evelyn to be everything a New Woman ought to be. She smiled at Evelyn encouragingly, but Evelyn was too shy to do more than mutter a 'Hullo' and turn away.

The Suffragettes were singing now, to the tune of *Auld Lang Syne*:

> *'I saw a man in tattered garb,*
> *Forth from the grog-shop come.*
> *He squandered all his cash for drink,*
> *And starved his wife at home.*
> *I asked him 'Should not woman vote?'*
> *He answered with a sneer.*
> *'I've taught my wife to know her place,*
> *Keep woman in her sphere.'*

Evelyn didn't sing. She didn't feel like it, and anyway, she didn't know the words. She moved away from the other women and began walking up and down, her placard high in the air, trying to make herself believe she was doing something very important, and so wouldn't have to talk to anyone.

She wasn't funking it. She *wasn't. Anyone* might get the wind up about a thing like this. It didn't mean anything.

And nobody could be such a worm as to back down now.

They waited outside the building for what seemed to Evelyn like for ever, but must only have been about an hour and a half. She was grateful for the other women, and for the banner and the chants. Belonging. A group of women, all together. That was what she'd wanted, wasn't it? Did she feel like she belonged, now? She couldn't say. A little, perhaps. But mostly what she felt was fear: a low, dull, wholly selfish terror.

At last, they could hear the sound of voices from within the building, as the audience began to move out. The policemen tensed – or was it Evelyn's imagination? The women certainly did. It seemed unlikely that the dignitaries would leave by the main entrance where the Suffragettes were protesting so prominently, so women had been sent to stand unobtrusively at the stage door, and tradesman's entrance.

'What if they don't come out?' Evelyn asked.

A Suffragette sniffed. 'Well!' she said. 'We'll stay here all night, is all. Those policemen will get bored of it before we do.'

She lifted up her voice and began to sing, the song Teddy had sung at the rally, '*Rise up, women, for the fight is hard and long . . .*'

This time Evelyn joined in.

The doors to the hall opened, and the crowds began

streaming out. Some glanced at the Suffragettes, but most walked past without looking, rather hurriedly, as though afraid they would be propositioned. Evelyn raised her voice, to avoid having to think about the fluttering sensation in her chest. She wondered what had happened to the Suffragettes inside the hall. Had they been arrested? Ejected? Held in some back room in the Civic Hall?

'*Glory, glory, hallelujah! Glory—*'

'Here we go!'

It was one of the women who'd been sent to watch the other entrances. She'd been running, face flushed and hat askew.

'They're coming out by the tradesman's entrance! Hurry!'

The women began to run. Evelyn ran with them, cursing her skirts that tangled against her legs as she went. Behind her, she could hear the policemen blowing on their whistles. She didn't dare look back. It was happening. It was really happening now.

'Do you support votes for women?' Mrs Leighton was yelling, ahead of her. 'Do you support a woman's right to vote?'

There were more policemen. Where had they come from? There was a policeman behind her, holding a nightstick. The memory of the action at Buckingham Palace flashed into her mind, and she stumbled. The policeman grabbed her arm. She struggled, twisting herself, trying to remember the term of ju-jitsu they'd done at school. The policeman pulled her arm upwards and she yelped in pain. Behind her, somewhere, Miss Miraz cried, 'Oh, I say! Steady on!'

Her voice brought Evelyn courage. She kicked the policeman

squarely in the shins and he swore. She remembered suddenly what one was supposed to do about holds, twisted out of the policeman's grip, and bolted towards the other women, and the two honourable Members of Parliament, who were, after all, who she was supposedly there for in the first place. But then there were arms around her, and her hands were being yanked behind her back, and there was cold metal around her wrists. It was over. All that worry, and the whole thing had lasted perhaps four minutes in total. And, she realised, as they dragged her towards the Black Maria, she hadn't even managed to shout 'Votes for Women!'

As they clapped the handcuffs shut, she remembered with a sudden start of horror that she'd forgotten to tell her parents what she was going to do. 'Going to see the Suffragettes', she'd told Kezia, but that now seemed woefully inadequate; they'd be bound to worry when she didn't show up to dinner. She should have left them a note – or posted them a letter – or *something*. They would think she'd been kidnapped or – or run down by a motor omnibus – or *anything*.

No. Teddy would know what had happened. Surely they would ask Teddy when she didn't come home. And surely, surely he'd remember what today was.

'Come on, now,' said the policeman, not unkindly, and she stepped up into the van, looking over her shoulder for a last glimpse of freedom.

And there he was.

He was standing outside the Woolworths on the other side of the road, rubbing his hands down the side of his grey flannel trousers. He wore an odd, closed expression, something that wasn't quite shame, or fury, or dread, but a mixture of the three. She couldn't tell if he was angry with her or with himself, and suddenly it seemed immensely important that she should know.

'Teddy!' she called. 'Teddy!'

But they shut the doors behind her.

Roly-poly Pudding

Nell was, by nature, very honourable. The Swancotts were a respectable family. If Nell had been the boy she some times thought she ought to have been, she would have treated May right. There would have been nothing that could have brought her dishonour. A kiss in the park, yes, perhaps, but nothing else.

With a girl and a girl, though . . . Nell didn't know what the rules were. *Were* there rules? It wasn't as though they could wait until they were married, after all. So did that mean they should do . . . nothing? Ever?

Her thoughts kept returning to something May had said to her once, that their love was somehow holy, untouchable. Was that true? What she felt about May, what she *thought* about May . . . her cheeks burned. It wasn't holy. But, at the same time, perhaps it was. May was a perfect thing, a true thing.

Nell sometimes thought she was the one, true, honest thing in her whole life.

• • •

She went round to May's house for supper again, despite her misgivings; the desire to be alone with May was stronger than the awkwardness of the nice house with the piano and the parlour and the slavey. She sat politely and ate vegetable curry and jam roly-poly pudding and said, 'Yes, Mrs Thornton,' to May's mother, ever so nice. But all the time she was looking at May and thinking, Oh, to be alone with you! Oh, to have a door to shut against the world!

After supper, Mrs Barber disappeared into the kitchen with the washing-up, and Mrs Thornton disappeared into the parlour to deliver a piano lesson to a little red-faced boy in a sailor suit. And May smiled at Nell and said, 'Come upstairs, won't you, and look at the new book Mama gave me.'

But when they were upstairs, and the door was shut, she took Nell's hand and said, 'What's the matter? No, don't tell me. Come here and kiss it better.'

May's mouth tasted of Mrs Barber's roly-poly pudding. She kissed Nell, and Nell responded with a force which took May aback. There were weeks and weeks of longing in that kiss, years perhaps, years of frustration at keeping so much of herself hidden from the world. Months of claustrophobia and anxiety came out, all of a sudden, there where their lips met, and May, after her first jolt of surprise, was dizzy with it. She kissed Nell back, leaning closer over her body, tongue against tongue, heart against heart. Her heart was pounding. The blood was rushing in her veins.

Nell's hands fumbled at the buckle of the belt of May's gymslip, her hands slipping in their urgency. She yanked at the belt, and it came undone; May laughed and pulled the gymslip over her head, revealing the blouse and the petticoats, with the black lisle stockings, and presumably the suspenders below. Nell gasped and paused for a minute, laying her hand against May's chest.

'What?' said May, but Nell shook her head, and reached for the buttons, pressing her mouth against May's as she did so. May was finding it hard to breathe. Is this what love was supposed to feel like? Nell's cheeks were flushed. Her fingers were working at the buttons on the blouse, her mouth still kissing May's. May realised belatedly that she should perhaps be doing something similar, and she unbuttoned Nell's jacket, and then the rough shirt underneath. She could see the neat pattern of Nell's mother's stitches in the shirt fabric. Presumably it had once belonged to Nell's brother. The intimacy of it was dizzying. The buttons were made of bone, smooth and round and creamy-white under May's fingers. *I love you to the bone. I love you to the core.*

Below the blouse, May wore a liberty bodice, and below the liberty bodice and the petticoats, she wore long, all-in-one combinations.

Nell grunted. 'Ain't there any of you at all under all that?' she said, and May felt a bubble of laughter rising up inside her.

'Stow it, you goose,' she said, and stopped her mouth with a kiss. Nobody had told her that doing this would make her feel so full of joy. Her knowledge of sex, beyond the basic facts, was limited to Shakespeare, and several rather grown-up novels belonging to her mother, in which sex was a matter of great worry and difficulty. Nobody had told her it would make her want to laugh and laugh with delight.

'What you laughing for?' said Nell.

'I don't know,' said May. 'Because I'm happy?'

Nell's hand had found May's breast. Her other hand was fumbling underneath her petticoats. She stopped now, and looked at May.

'Are you sure?' she said. 'Are you . . .? Because I can stop if you ain't.'

May reached out a hand and stroked the side of Nell's cheek. She could see the confusion mingling with the pleasure on her face. How happy I am, she thought. How lucky we are each to have found the other.

'Yes,' she said. 'I'm sure.'

Afterwards, they lay together in May's bed, breathless, May curled in the circle of Nell's arm, the rough, heady scent of cloth and sweat around her. She rested her head on Nell's shoulder, finding, as so many lovers had found before her, how perfectly the two of them fit.

It felt strange and exciting to be so close. The intimacy of it. She could feel Nell's heart beating through her shirt. The smell of carbolic soap in her hair. She could reach out and touch the skin on her hands and face. There was something beautiful about the hardness of the callouses on her fingers. And how thrilling to rest like this, Nell's arms around hers, as though they had a perfect right to be together, as though nothing could ever separate them. *I love you*, May whispered in her head, saving the words, not wanting to say them yet, wanting to enjoy their possession like a secret, like Rumpelstiltskin's name in the fairy tale, the power by which the miller's daughter won her child. *I love you. I love you. I love you.*

A Room in White Porcelain

Getting arrested, Evelyn decided, was quite simply the most sordid thing that had ever happened to her.

She had been taken, along with the other Suffragettes, to a local police station, where she had been searched, and her money and her school scarf taken away from her – to prevent her hanging herself, it was explained. Evelyn felt the urge to giggle; it seemed so queer to be in a police station in her school uniform, and queerer yet for such an innocent object as her school scarf to be considered a possible self-murder weapon. When the policemen filled out the charge sheet she told them she was eighteen, which was not strictly true, but was what she had told Mrs Leighton, and she didn't want to be revealed as a liar in court.

The cell she was taken to was small and bare. It was horribly, disgustingly filthy, so filthy that Evelyn felt the hairs on her arms rising in revulsion at it. There was a persistent low-level stench of urine, and vomit, and something worse. There were black beetles scurrying in the corners of the room; one ran across Evelyn's arm and made her shriek.

The cell was tiled with white porcelain bricks, and contained a plank bed, a W.C., a hot-water pipe, a horsehair pillow and two blankets. There were flies buzzing over the W.C. There was a gaslight behind a thick glass guard which was kept burning all night, and a tiny window set too high in the wall to see through. The window, Evelyn was pleased to see, really was barred. There was a spyhole in the door, and a sort of letterbox arrangement through which her food was posted. The food was the same for luncheon and dinner: bread and nasty, rather slimy margarine, served with an even nastier cup of tea. Evelyn ate and drank it anyway. She'd be hungry enough once the hunger strike began.

At first the Suffragettes knocked on the walls and called to each other – cheering things like: '*Bon courage*!'

And: 'No surrender!'

But there is a limit to how much you can shout through a prison wall, and after a while, the drunk in the cell next to Evelyn yelled at them to, 'Stow it, you daft cows!'

They carried on for a bit, just to show him they didn't care what he thought, but his presence was something of a quash on their spirits, especially when he began ranting and swearing at them. Then he was loudly and violently sick on the other side of Evelyn's wall, which made Evelyn want to throw up herself, it was so disgusting. Captured rebels in adventure novels never had to share their captivity with people like that.

Mostly, however, the lock-up was simply boring. Evelyn was so bored, she was reduced to reading her schoolbooks – a Euclid, a Virgil, and a copy of *The Tempest* edited for schoolgirls. Evelyn liked Virgil usually, but he was poor company in a white porcelain room which smelt of vomit and urine. If Aeneas had ever ended up somewhere quite so beastly, some goddess would be bound to come along and rescue him. *The Tempest* was simply idiotic. There was only one woman in the whole thing, and she was a frightful drip. How could people possibly take Shakespeare seriously when he wrote rot like that? And Euclid was not to be endured. Nobody could expect a girl to care about angles and lines in a prison cell. She wondered what her parents were thinking. Would they come to her hearing? Would they ever speak to her again? They were bound to punish her when they found out. Perhaps they'd lock her in her bedroom for ever. Perhaps they'd pack her off to the country to live with her grandparents. This whole thing had been a stupid idea. She wished Teddy were here. He'd say 'I told you so', but she wouldn't care.

It would be worth it just to see him again.

The next day, she was woken early, issued with yet more bread and greyish margarine, which she was too nervous to eat, and allowed to wash in a basin of cold water. She, the drunk (now sober, and looking very sorry for himself), and the other Suffragettes were bundled out into the yard. Evelyn thought she had never been more grateful to see other human beings in her life. She hadn't realised quite how awful being completely and utterly on your own was. It was like you weren't fully human somehow. She had never thought she liked other people, much. But she could have kissed the other Suffragettes.

'All right?' Mrs Leighton said, glancing at her, and she nodded gratefully. All right. So far.

She, the drunk, and the Suffragettes were loaded into two Black Marias. Inside, the vans were divided into little stalls, just large enough to sit down in. Other prisoners had scrawled things on the walls: *Bob Elliott, begging, one week. Jimmy Barnett, drunk and incapable, three shillings.* Evelyn looked for Suffragettes' names, but could find none. Her heart was beginning to hammer inside her, and her arms were tingling with nerves. A little voice was singing in her head: *court, prison, hunger strike. Court, prison, hunger strike.*

She felt sick.

At the magistrates' court, they were again unloaded into the yard, and abandoned. This yard was already busy; as the morning went on it slowly filled with a mixture of policemen, petty criminals, a few men who were presumably lawyers, and the twelve Suffragettes. And there they waited.

And waited.

It was a warm July day, so Evelyn wasn't cold, and the Suffragettes were all together. The other women linked arms and sang suffrage songs. Evelyn joined in at first, but soon stopped. She didn't feel like singing. She was dirty and uncomfortable, her dress itched, her hair was hot and grimy, and she didn't feel at all triumphant; she just wanted this to be over. Once again she was aware of the ambivalence she always felt around the Suffragettes – the uneasiness of her alliance, and the wariness she always felt about her place in their union. She liked the belonging, but it made her restless. It made her want to argue, to escape.

The prisoners were called in one by one as their cases were heard. It didn't seem to take very long. There was a balcony over the yard along which they were led out afterwards. They held up fingers to their friends below to show how long they'd been given. One week. Two weeks. Three. Four. Evelyn supposed that she ought to be nervous, but she wasn't, much. The time for nerves had passed. Mostly she was restless, and bored.

Miss Wilkinson was talking to a thin, nervous-looking woman who had been arrested for begging.

'But I never done it,' she was saying to Miss Wilkinson. 'A lady asked me to help her with her bags, out of her cab, see? And when I done it, she give me thruppence. And then, when she were gone, the policemen come and said I were begging. But I never were. I told them to find the lady, and she'd tell them, but she were gone by then, and I don't suppose they ever found her neither.'

'But they won't put you in prison, will they?' said Evelyn. 'Just for taking thruppence from a lady?'

'Won't they, miss?' said the woman gloomily. 'One month, my sister got, for begging – and she weren't begging neither, she were selling lavender – her young man being out of work, and the children hungry. If your children were crying for food, miss, you'd go begging, I don't wonder. I can't go to prison for a month, miss – I got five children at home. Whatever'll they do without me?'

The Suffragettes nodded sympathetically, and agreed that it was a shame.

'When women have the vote, we'll pass laws that'll make sure your children are looked after,' Miss Miraz told her. Evelyn wondered if it was true. The Suffragettes promised so much. Would any of it really ever happen?

At last, the twelve women were called into the magistrates' court and told to wait. The courtroom was full of people. It was dizzying, like the school hall on play night. Evelyn stared into the crowd, trying to find familiar faces. There must be Suffragettes there, surely? Had any of the Hampstead Suffragettes come? Had – heaven forfend – her *parents*? They wouldn't, surely? How would they know where to come?

Mrs Leighton nudged her and pointed upwards. There was half a bench of women in suffrage colours, all waving. At the end of the row – and Evelyn felt her heart give an enormous bound – was Teddy. He wasn't waving. He was leaning forward, his hands gripping the back of the bench in front of him, staring and staring and staring at her. His face was set, and very pale, and his eyes burned.

Evelyn – it was the strangest thing – felt as though something inside her had burst open. Seeing him there was like coming home. Like feeling safe for the first time in what felt like her whole life.

She couldn't stop looking at him. The courtroom and the other women felt very far away. Her heart was pounding tremendously inside her. *Of course*, she thought. *Of course, it was you I wanted.* She had never felt anything so clearly. She wanted to shout it out to him, to pull away from the other Suffragettes and run up the courtroom aisle and tell him right now: *Of course it was you I wanted.*

'Evelyn,' said Mrs Leighton, and she dragged her attention back to the judge.

The hearing was astonishingly brief. One of the policemen gave evidence that the Suffragettes had attacked him, and that he'd been forced to arrest them for his own protection.

'The liar!' Miss Miraz whispered indignantly. 'He can't say that, can he? Can't we stop him? We can call our own witnesses, can't we?' She looked into the crowd. 'Miss Gregory's there, look – I'm sure she'd come up and say that never happened.'

'No fear!' said Mrs Leighton. 'Not unless you want her held up for contempt of court. Just stay quiet – they never listen to what we say, anyway.'

'But that's outrageous!' said Miss Miraz. She'd gone pink.

After the policeman had given evidence, the magistrate asked if the Suffragettes had anything to say. Mrs Leighton and the other women shook their heads, but Miss Miraz stepped up.

'Excuse me, your worship,' she said. 'But that policeman isn't telling the truth. We didn't attack him, or hurt him – we just tried to push past him to get to the hall. If you don't believe us, you can ask him to show you the injuries we're supposed to have given him. Why! I bet he hasn't a single bruise!'

The policeman bristled.

'Calling me a liar, are you?' he said. 'You just listen to me—'

'All right, all right,' said the magistrate. 'That's enough. Two weeks, second class, the lot of you. And an extra week for you, Miraz, for contempt of court.'

'I – what?' said Miss Miraz. 'That's—'

'And if you're not careful, it'll be two,' said the magistrate. 'Next case!'

The women were led away. And now, all at once, Evelyn was really afraid. Prison. Real prison. And not with the other women – from whom it suddenly felt desperately important not to be separated – a cell on her own. To hunger strike. The panic fluttered at her stomach. She glanced up at Teddy. He was standing, looking very white, his hands still gripping the back of the bench. It seemed desperately important to speak to him, to tell him – but a policeman's hand was on her shoulder, pushing her forward.

She turned her head back to look at Teddy as they went out of the court, twisting it round to keep his face in sight for as long as possible. She tried to store up every particle of it in her memory – the line of his jaw, the slight tremble in his mouth, the light curls that tumbled over his ears, and the blue eyes full of anxiety. *It might be the last time I ever see you*, she thought, and then she told herself firmly not to be a bloody idiot. *Two weeks*, she thought. *That's nothing. That other woman's getting a month for helping a lady with her parcels.* But it wasn't the two weeks that were worrying her.

It was the hunger strike. Hunger and thirst strike.

Starting now.

Alone

The first time Nell had ever fallen in love with a girl, she'd been eleven years old.

The girl in question had been Mabel Tonge, who sat two desks along from Nell at school. At eleven, Nell had been old enough to know that girls didn't fall in love with other girls. For the longest time, she'd tried to convince herself that what she felt for Mabel Tonge wasn't love. She *liked* her, that was all. It wasn't often Nell liked other girls, so that, surely, must be what the funny, nervous, butterfly-y feeling she felt around Mabel was about. Other girls, mostly, didn't much like Nell either; she wasn't quite a girl and she wasn't quite a boy, and that made them wary and a little contemptuous. Nell minded and she didn't mind. But when it came to Mabel, she minded a lot.

Mabel Tonge was a blackboard monitor, the best speller and the best skipper in the class. Nell thought she was perfection itself. She would watch her in class, whispering secrets to her deskmate Mary Henson, and thought she'd die of envy. What wouldn't she give to have that dark head whispering secrets to her!

But even at eleven, Nell knew it wasn't exactly friendship she wanted with Mabel. What she did want, she wasn't sure. Something grander and nobler, like Sir Walter Raleigh laying down his cloak for Queen Elizabeth across a 'plashy place'. Or like Sir Lancelot dazzling the Lady of Shalott on his war horse with the burnish'd hooves. Nell wanted to protect Mabel from muddy puddles and black magic. She wanted . . . she didn't know what she wanted. She didn't dare to look at it face on.

But she was ashamed of it, even so. It *wasn't* normal. It wasn't how other girls felt. The other girls giggled about boys, but Nell thought that even if she lived to be a hundred she wouldn't understand why. The boys Nell knew were noisy, chaotic, blood-and-guts types, all scabby knees and fisticuffs. They lived more interesting lives than the girls did, but Nell couldn't imagine wanting to marry one of them.

Girls, though . . . girls were beautiful. Everyone agreed on that. She didn't see why anyone would rather marry a boy over a girl.

Nell rarely thought of Mabel Tonge these days; she'd gone to work in a steam laundry in Poplar, and was walking out with an Irish boy from the docks. But the older she got, the harder it was to ignore the fact that something about her make-up was intrinsically inverted. That there were rules about how girls were supposed to behave, and she seemed built to break them all.

There was very little space for introspection in Coney Lane. There was very little space for *breathing*, Nell sometimes thought. She was used to it, them all living on top of one another, they all were. Mostly the younger children were out playing in the street, or at school. She and Bill went out too, when they weren't working. You had to.

They hung around in gangs, like adolescents everywhere, the girls watching the boys and the boys watching the girls watching them. There was still cricket, sometimes, the boys showing off and the girls in little huddles shooting them admiring glances. Nell hated it.

'Mating rituals!' said Bernie scornfully. He was clever, was Bernie. But he was right too. It was a mating ritual, only Nell was all wrong, like Albert Kumar's monkey, who thought Albert's father's fox terrier was its mother, and tried to chase sticks and roll over like she did. Albert Kumar's father was a Lascar who'd come to Poplar on a ship from India. He'd bought the little monkey from another Lascar and given him to Albert, but it was the fox terrier who'd adopted him.

Nell often thought of the little dog, barking and barking in panic as her strange son leapt about the room, from the table to the fireplace to the top of the dresser and back again. When the boys fooled for the girls in Victoria Park, she felt just like that monkey, a creature from a far-off country, dropped down amongst the soot and smoke of the East End docks, longing for the jungle.

Could you be homesick for a place you didn't even know existed?

Sometimes, as she washed herself in the Public Bathhouse, she'd sneak sideways glances at the other girls as they undressed, then down at her own body, short and squat and awkward. Other girls felt like a different *species* to Nell. She'd decided as a child that she wasn't one of them, and as an adult that feeling had only grown. *What* are *you? s*trangers said to Nell in the street, or sometimes *What* is *it?* which was worse. Nell never knew what to say.

How could she? She didn't know the answer to their question herself.

She just knew that whatever it was, it was a desperately lonely thing to be.

Until May came along.

No Surrender

The cell was small and bare. As Evelyn was a Suffragette prisoner, and expected to hunger strike, she was assigned a hospital cell. The main difference between this and last night's cell, as far as she could see, was that instead of the bare boards she'd slept on last night, she had an iron bedstead. And somewhere close by, she could hear a baby crying.

It had been a very long day. After the trial, the Suffragettes had sat in a small room for what felt like hours, waiting to be processed. A few years ago they would have been given prison clothes, but to Evelyn's relief, that did not happen now. She was allowed to keep her own clothes. She was expected to wash, however. She'd been longing and longing for a bath all day, but when she was presented with it, the bath was cold and the water greyish. Looking at it, Evelyn wanted to weep.

'Couldn't you at least change the water?' she said to the guard, her desperation conquering her previous resolution to keep quiet and stay out of trouble.

'All prisoners must wash before being admitted to prison,'

said the guard, in a rather bored tone, as though she hadn't asked the question. And Evelyn, recognising defeat, began to undress.

She was not permitted to wash herself, and had to submit to the ministrations of the guard.

Instead of last night's porcelain, the walls of her cell were whitewashed and much graffitied. I DID IT FOR MY CHILDREN, read one message, rather pathetically. MAY GOD HAVE MERCY ON OUR SOULS said another. NO SURRENDER a third. Others were crude, or obscene.

DETECTIVE SMITH KNOWS HOW TO GEE.

TELL HIM HE'S A C—— FROM ME.

Evelyn hadn't the first notion what it was that Detective Smith knew how to do. The obscenity was a new word too, although she understood the violence of it. It was an ugly, dirty thing to share a cell with. She'd hoped that Holloway might be better organised than the police station, but this cell was just as filthy as the other. There was a low-level, grey, grimy beastliness about everything. She felt, very much, a stranger in an unwholesome place. I should never have come here, she thought, very clearly. I should never have come.

She banged her fist on the wall of the cell.

'Hello!' she called. 'Hello! Are there any Suffragettes here?' No answer. She did the same on the other side.

'Hello! Hello!'

Nothing.

She was alone.

There was something desperate about being alone. The Hampstead house was always full of people: Mother, Father, Christopher in the vacs, Kezia, Hetty, Miss Perring, and before

Miss Perring, the nursemaid, Ann. Cook and Iris, the between-maid. Friends of Mother's coming to call, or their own school-friends coming for tea. And all of the everyday people, knocking on the front door or the back – gypsies selling heather, the vicar wanting subscriptions for the church roof, the clock-winder, the coal man, the butcher's boy, the baker's boy, the newspaper boy. Teddy. School was full of people. The streets of Hampstead were full of people. Evelyn, in all her seventeen years, had never been really alone before in her life, and it terrified her.

'No surrender,' she said, out loud. 'No surrender, no surrender, no surrender. Oh, criminy. Oh, Teddy, I do wish you were here.'

After a while, two warders came into the cell, carrying a chair and a table with a tablecloth. They left, and soon returned with plates of food, of quite a different quality to the bread and margarine she'd been given in the police station. Tea. Steak. Fruit. Jellies. Brand's Essence. A large earthenware jug of water. This food, Evelyn soon realised, was to be left permanently in the cell, to act as a constant temptation. She discovered that she was not, in fact, very tempted. She felt much too tired and nervy to eat. And too thirsty. She had been given nothing to drink since that morning. The water was very tempting indeed, so she took the jug, and the teapot, and the milk jug, and she tipped them out onto the floor. Then she felt better.

Perhaps tomorrow, she thought, when she was hungrier, the food would bother her more. But in all her time in gaol, she discovered that it could not touch her.

A woman on hunger and thirst strike does not care about food. Almost from the first, she craves only water.

By the next morning, Evelyn's throat was dry and parched and her head was throbbing. At first it was an annoyance, but it soon became all she could think about. It didn't help that she had no other distractions (although what could distract you from dying of thirst?) She was denied both exercise (and therefore companionship) and books from the library as punishment for the hunger strike. She took to walking from one side of the cell to the other, backwards and forwards, talking to the walls as though they were a friend; Teddy perhaps, or one of her friends from school, or Mrs Leighton.

'Well then,' she'd say, 'this is a pretty mess I've found myself in, isn't it? I must look a guy. I wonder what Mother is telling her friends. I wonder if I was in the papers. Do you think I might have been?'

Neither Teddy nor her schoolfriends were very impressed. And as the day went on, and the jug of water was replaced, none of them could see why she didn't give in and take a sip, just one sip, just a little sip, no one need ever know!

'Mrs Pankhurst wouldn't take even a little sip,' Evelyn told them sternly.

'Oh, hang Mrs Pankhurst!' the imaginary Teddy cried. 'You'll make yourself ill if you carry on like this!'

'That's rather the whole point,' Evelyn told him. She liked telling him, it made her feel very grand and noble. But she did wish her own imaginary friends might be more helpful. In the end, she took to tipping the water out onto the floor of the cell as soon as it arrived, so as not to be tempted. But it was hard.

Mrs Leighton was a better companion.

'Just think of what you're doing this for,' she said. 'Just think of the other women in the other cells doing this same thing. You don't want to be the only one who gives up, do you?'

'No,' said Evelyn. She gritted her teeth, and kept walking.

But soon she began to wonder how long she could bear this. Her tongue was coated in a foul-tasting gunk, and felt huge and hot and swollen. Her saliva – how disgusting! – was thick and yellow. A bitter-tasting phlegm rose constantly in the mouth. She longed to be sick, but although she tried again and again, she could not manage it. What little urine she could pass was dark and painful. And as night fell, she discovered that she could not even sleep. Her thirst and her headache overpowered everything else. She sat on the bed, hunched forward with the blanket wrapped around her shoulders and shivered. The police cell had been warm, but here she was constantly cold. The wardress gave her a hot-water bottle, but it burned her skin, and left the rest of her body as cold as before.

Soon, it hurt too much to walk. Added to the throb of her headache was a constant pain in the small of her back, and other sudden, stabbing pains in the abdomen and stomach.

'Heavens,' she said, still trying desperately to pretend she was cheerful. She bent double, listening to the flutter of her heartbeat. It was as though there was another Evelyn, a detached, observant Evelyn, who could watch this torture without being immersed in it. She leant forward, clutching her stomach. Some Suffragettes had lasted as long as six or seven days on thirst strike before they were released. Evelyn wondered how on earth they had managed. She listened to the baby still crying somewhere close by in the prison hospital, and wondered how long she could endure.

Changeling Child

It had taken May much longer to realise she was different.

None of May's friends knew many boys. May didn't, certainly. There were people's brothers, but mostly, of course, they were away at school. She knew a couple of boys through the Quakers, but not well; they were older and rather distant. There had been boys at children's parties at Christmas, and boys at the dancing class she'd attended for a term, but you couldn't call that *knowing*, exactly. There were three boy cousins in Scotland, and really, that was it.

Despite this, all the girls at May's school were in love. Barbara was in love with young Nelson and with a red-headed boy who worked at the stationer's on the corner. Winifred was in love with Edmund – they'd been doing *King Lear* in English that year – and also Miss Cage, the games mistress. It was quite common to be in love with mistresses. There simply weren't many other options.

The mistresses themselves rather frowned on love. People who stared out of the window at boys, or dressed 'flash' in order to attract them, were the subject of stern lectures on the perils of being 'forward'. May, without really thinking about why, knew that sort of girl was not quite nice; not in the Fourth Form at least. Nobody had ever said anything about falling in love with a girl, though. Falling in love with a girl was a different order of things entirely, something pure and beautiful, almost holy.

It had taken May until she was fourteen to realise that she only ever fell in love with women, or girls. This had come to a head last year, with a passionate, week-long relationship with Margaret Howard, involving lots of secret kissing and intense discussions about the nature of love. Then, just as suddenly as it had begun, Margaret Howard had decided May was too 'immature' and 'peculiar' and that had been that.

The suddenness of Margaret's about-face had bewildered May, and forced her to confront the fact that what she thought of as love was quite different to what other girls thought. She'd taken this problem – as she took most problems – to Mama, who'd listened with unusual seriousness and said, 'There's much more of this about than there used to be, you know – I expect it's one of those perils of modernity we hear so much about. I've got a frightfully interesting book about it somewhere.'

And she'd lent May Edward Carpenter's *The Intermediate Sex*.

'Do be careful though, darling,' she'd added. 'You know *I* don't mind what you do. But I rather think Miss Cooper might think it fearfully Freudian, or immoral, or inverted, or something awful like that.'

May had promised. And although she hadn't managed to

get very far with Carpenter, what she *had* read had charmed her. A whole separate species of people, who weren't quite men and weren't quite women! It was like discovering you were a changeling, or a princess raised by swineherds. And then May's mother – very casually indeed – had pointed out women amongst the suffragists who were part of this secret tribe, and that was even better.

Nell had always hated being different.

But May revelled in it.

Home

Evelyn lay on her side on the narrow bed. She curled up into a ball and pulled the blanket over her shoulders, but she was still cold. The cell shouldn't be this cold in July, should it? She couldn't stop shivering. It was like panicking, this shivering. She curled herself tighter together and put her hands under her armpits. When she tried to sit up, her head ached and she was dizzy, so then she didn't try it any more. But she was so thirsty. How long did it take someone to die of thirst? How long had she been in prison? It made her head ache to try and calculate it, but it must be days now. Three days? Four, five? Could it be as long as a week? It couldn't be, could it?

The ache at the small of her back was worse. It hurt more when she tried to move. She felt like an old woman. Could hunger striking give you rheumatics? Why had no one ever told her it felt like this?

She pushed herself up. There was a ringing in her ears and then the room was swinging around her in giddy, drunken sweeps. She tried to stand, and found herself on the floor.

She tried to sit and found that she couldn't, so she stayed where she was. Everything was ghastly. Everything hurt.

How much longer could this last?

'You're going home,' said the wardress. 'Home. You're going home.'

She opened her eyes, slowly. The wardress was leaning over her bed, peering into her face as though curious to see if she might have died, or slipped into unconsciousness. Evelyn was horribly afraid she was thinking about slapping her. She was a big, broad woman, with big white hands, and when she saw that Evelyn was awake, she pulled back and said, not unkindly, 'Here, won't you drink something?'

And she gave Evelyn a mug of water. Evelyn took it in both hands. They felt clumsy and painful and stiff, as though they had forgotten how to be hands. She gripped the mug as tightly as she could. If she dropped it, she thought she would cry. She felt very close to tears. Her ears were ringing so loudly she thought she might faint. She couldn't faint, with cold water in her hands.

The water tasted like nothing earthly. It had its own flavour, subtle but beautiful. It was cool and delicious and strangely heady, like wine. She drank slowly, savouring every mouthful. She felt that nothing she would ever drink again would ever taste as beautiful as this.

The woman waited while Evelyn drank, and then gave her a folded piece of paper. Her brain didn't seem able to take in what it was; the words were blurring and jumping before her eyes. It took several readings before she managed to grasp its meaning. It was a release on licence for seven days. She had been in Holloway without food or water for six nights. In seven days' time, she would have to come back in to finish the remaining eight days of her sentence. She had a hysterical urge to laugh. She had managed to persuade them to release her; for what? In seven days' time, the whole obscene charade would begin again. She thought of Mrs Pankhurst, serving a three-year sentence in six-day chunks, and felt a new respect for her. How could she possibly find the courage to do this again and again and again?

Two wardresses took her into a taxi-cab and gave her address to the driver. Evelyn leant back against the seat and closed her eyes. The cab was cold, and her spring coat was light; she was shivering. Why weren't the wardresses cold? Was it because of the hunger strike? Or was she getting ill? She thought she might be getting ill. She thought she had never felt so tired in all of her life.

The taxi turned into Evelyn's road, and stopped before her house. It felt very strange to see home still standing there, looking just as it had when she'd left. Had it really only been seven days since she'd seen it?

One of the wardresses sat in the taxi with Evelyn, while the other went up to the door and rang the bell. After what felt like an age, the maid, Iris, answered. She spoke to the wardress, then peered out of the door at Evelyn sitting there in the back of the cab in her spring coat, shivering like it was midwinter. She disappeared into the house. Whatever was she doing? Then Evelyn's mother appeared in the doorway and ran down the garden path and opened the door to the cab.

'Oh, Evelyn!' she said, and Evelyn was astonished to see that she was crying. Her brisk, sensible mother, crying in the street!

They were in the hallway, and Hetty was at the bottom of the stairs, staring, and her mother was shouting for help. There were the stairs, which were so hard to climb that they made her sob in pain, and her mother and Miss Perring had to half carry her up them. There was a bed in a warm room, with a fire in the grate, and light so bright that it hurt her eyes coming through the window. The Collis children only had fires in their bedrooms when they were ill. So perhaps I really am ill, thought Evelyn.

There was a doctor with an old-fashioned black Victorian doctor's bag, who talked in corners with Mother. *What are you saying?* Evelyn cried, but the words wouldn't come out properly. *I'm quite all right*, she wanted to say. *I'm not ill at all. I'm just tired.* But nobody seemed to hear.

Mother was trying to make her drink a cup of milk. It felt absurdly, luxuriously rich, like drinking cream. She could only manage half a cup before she began to cough, and then she was crying, because she felt so sick and tired. Her hands looked impossible, like old women's hands, or the hands of corpses. They had been very pale and slender when she'd come out of prison – frighteningly so – but now that she'd begun to drink again, they'd gone scarlet. They hurt so much that she cried aloud when Mother tried to give her the cup of milk, and Mother had to hold it for her. Her whole body hurt.

The doctor was taking her temperature. *I don't have a*

temperature, Evelyn wanted to say. *I'm just tired because of the thirst strike.* But he carried on taking it anyway. Evelyn's head still hurt too much to argue. *And I've got to go back there!* she remembered suddenly.

'Don't make me go back!' she cried aloud. 'Don't make me!' And she struggled to sit up, and the room blurred, and hands were pushing her down again, but she cried aloud, 'I can't go back there! I can't!'

It was later, and everything was dark, and there was a pain in her stomach that hadn't been there before, and she was shivering very hard, so she must have a fever, and when she tried to lift her head, the room began swimming around her, and nothing felt right.

Teddy, she thought, and then, Oh, God, Teddy was right. I've done something dreadful to myself and now I'm going to die. She felt the panic rising inside her. She couldn't die! Not yet. She hadn't meant to make herself as ill as all this. Surely there was some way to take it back?

'I'm sorry!' she cried, but she wasn't sure if the words came out. 'Teddy, I'm so sorry! Teddy, I want you! Teddy!'

But she was sinking again. The world was fading out of focus. She fought to stay awake, to make them understand, to stop this thing, whatever it was, from overwhelming her, but she couldn't hold her mind together, she was falling, falling, falling, and everything went to black.

August 1914

In this dread hour when the fate of Europe depends on decisions which women have no power to shape, we, realising our responsibility as mothers of the race, cannot stand passively by. Powerless though we be politically, we call upon the governments of our several countries to avert the threatened and unparalleled disaster. Women see all they most reverence and treasure, the home, the family, the race, subjected to certain damage which they are powerless to avert or assuage. Whatever its result, the conflict will leave mankind the poorer, will set back civilisation, check the amelioration in the condition of the masses on which the welfare of nations depends. We, women of twenty-six countries in the International Woman Suffrage Alliance, appeal to you to leave untried no method of conciliation or arbitration which may avert deluging half the civilised world in blood.

Appeal for mediation sent by the offices of the International Woman Suffrage Alliance in London to the Foreign Secretary and Embassies of all countries likely to be involved in a war, July 29th 1914

Mafeking

The Women's Peace Movement meeting finished at ten o'clock on the evening of the 3rd of August. Eleven o'clock in Germany. At midnight, German time, unless something miraculous happened, Britain would be at war.

For years, Europe had been a sort of domino-run of alliances, treaties, grudges and unfought battles. The assassination in Sarajevo had been the fallen domino which had sent the others toppling in every direction with a speed that – to May, whose knowledge of international affairs was limited – was astonishing.

The day before, Germany had invaded Luxembourg. They had sent an ultimatum to Belgium – with whom Britain was allied – demanding safe passage. If Belgium did not agree to let them pass, they would invade.

All day, the newspapers had been full of outrage at the thought that Britain might not uphold its 'moral obligation' to support 'plucky little Belgium'. May's mother, generally, was very much in favour of keeping your word – and of supporting the underdog, which plucky little Belgium definitely was – but there was something rather terrifying about that domino-run. The newspapers talked as though any war would be brief and glorious, but most of May's mother's friends were less optimistic. At best, people would be killed. At worst . . . it didn't bear thinking about.

The British government, however, did not share their concern. They, in turn, issued an ultimatum to Germany. Withdraw from Belgium by midnight, or Britain and Germany would be at war.

The Women's Peace Movement, naturally enough, had been loud in their condemnation of this decision. Representatives from all sorts of groups were there – suffragists, of course, but also the National Federation of Women Workers, the Women's Labour League and the Women's Co-operative Guild. Only Emmeline Pankhurst's WSPU was absent. The meeting had drawn up a resolution condemning the conflict and demanding that Britain attempt a peaceful reconciliation. A deputation of women were sent to take this to Downing Street. May and her mother stood in the street, listening to the news boys calling the evening papers, full of the day's speeches in Parliament. It was a hot, heavy evening. Motor cars rattled past. The street was full of suffragists. No one wanted to go home, but nobody quite knew what else to do. On a night like this, the thought of their oven of a house was more than they could bear.

May's mother had been talking to some of her friends. She came over to May.

'Some of the NUWSS ladies are going to Whitehall to wait

for eleven,' she said. 'There's quite a crowd there, apparently. Would you like to go too? It'll be a moment in history, I suppose. Like the Relief of Mafeking – do you remember?'

'Mama, you know I don't,' said May. 'I was a baby! But do let's go. I couldn't bear just to sit at home and do nothing.'

'I always hoped you'd remember,' said her mother. 'But, there! I don't suppose you'll ever forget tonight.'

May supposed she wouldn't, whatever happened. She wondered where Nell was, if she was waiting for eleven somewhere too. Did Nell want a war, or didn't she? How strange that she even had to wonder! May had never thought about why she was anti-war, any more than she'd thought about why she was anti-pestilence or anti-famine. They were just obviously bad things, weren't they? But nobody else seemed to agree. Everyone at school was desperate for a war. Would Nell be too? Her father had been a soldier, after all. And the East End Suffragettes were the breaking-windows, socking-policemen sort. But Nell couldn't really actually *want* this.

Could she?

There was a small crowd of people in Parliament Square, watching the clock. It was half past ten already. In half an hour it would be midnight in Germany.

The crowd was mostly quiet. There were no shouts, no cheering, no banner-waving. Mostly people just stood in little groups, whispering to each other. They were the strangest collection of people too. On one side of May were three young men in top hats and tails, who looked like they'd come straight from a supper party, or an evening at the theatre. They were smoking cigarettes and saying very little, but their eyes kept looking back to the clock. On her other side was a gaggle of railway workers, still in uniform. Behind them was a cluster of girls a few years older than May, all in calico summer frocks in bright colours.

'All right?' said May's mother. May nodded.

The hands of Big Ben crept closer to eleven. The tension in the air grew palpable. The people around them quieted. Would something happen? A last-minute change of plan, an eleventh-hour telegraph from Berlin? Surely something must?

And then the minute hand moved to twelve. The great *bongs* of Big Ben began to toll. And suddenly the tension broke, and everyone was shouting.

'War is declared! War is *declared*!'

People were hooting. They were cheering, and embracing each other. One of the young gentlemen threw his top hat into the air and cried, 'Whew!' and laughed.

'We're going to war! We're going to war!' the railway workers were shouting. They kept slapping each other on the back and shaking their heads. Another young gentleman, this one in a grey flannel suit and a boater, hurried over and shook hands with all the suffragists.

'Do beg your pardon,' he said, rather confusedly. 'Terribly exciting, eh? A war! Jolly good show, what?'

And he shook May's hand for a second time, took off his spectacles, wiped them on his handkerchief, then went off to shake hands with the railway workers, repeating, 'A war! A real war!' to himself.

Suddenly, everyone was talking. These people who a few

moments ago had been so quiet and solemn seemed all at once to have a great deal to say, and most of what they seemed to have to say was, 'War is declared!'

More people were coming out onto the streets. The press around them was growing. May's mother – perhaps remembering the riot in Bow – grabbed her hand and said, 'Come on! Out of the crowd!' and began to push onto the road. But it was slow-going. The stunned look on people's faces was being replaced by a sort of giddy hysteria. A group of men outside a pub were singing *Rule, Britannia!*, very loudly and tunelessly. The young gentleman in the boater and all his friends joined in. Someone somewhere released the cork from a bottle of champagne and sent it spraying over the heads of the crowd to ironical cheers. A girl in a white dress caught up the end of her sash and waved it over her head shouting, 'Death to the Hun!'

A car full of young men and women came careening down the street at high speed. The young woman in the driving-seat was honking the horn furiously. The young men in the back seat were whooping. May's mother glanced at them nervously, and pulled May closer.

To May, the enthusiasm was baffling. These were the men who would be soldiers. Didn't they understand what that meant? It felt strange to have come straight from a meeting so concerned with the viscera of war – civilian casualties, economic destruction, loss of nationhood – into a noisy playground celebration. Any one of these young men might be killed. Didn't any of them care?

At the other side of the square was a small anti-war demonstration.

'This war does not concern us!' a man shouted as May and her mother walked past. The demonstrators looked rather out of place amongst the general party atmosphere. But even so, May watched them a little guiltily. It felt so wrong just to be walking around, watching. Like the young woman driving the car, she wanted to do *something*.

'Should we join in?' she asked her mother, but her mother shook her head.

'Not today,' she said. 'Let's get home. We'll have work enough tomorrow.'

A Telegram

The telegraph boy came when Nell's family was at breakfast. Meals were a complicated business for a family of eight. Nell's father, Bill and Nell all had to be at work by eight, which meant breakfast by a quarter past seven; bread and margarine for Nell and her mother, bread and dripping for the men, who had a long day of physical work ahead of them. Both Johnnie and the baby had woken too, and wanted feeding. Bernie and Dot were still in bed, but awake. Bernie slept on the sofa in the kitchen, and Dot was woken when the rest of the family left the big double bed.

The telegraph boy was Tommy Parkin, who had once sat across the schoolroom from Nell and blown spit-balls into her hair. He looked almost unrecognisable in his smart blue uniform, shiny regulation boots, and blue hat. He knocked sharply on the kitchen door – which was open – and announced, 'Telegram for Mr Swancott!'

Everyone – even Johnnie – looked at Nell's father in astonishment. Her father, however, didn't look that surprised.

He seemed, Nell thought, as though he'd been expecting something like this. His face, as he looked at Tommy Parkin, wore an expression almost of dread. He got up laboriously, took the little brown envelope from Tommy, and opened it.

'No reply,' he said to Tommy, who left.

'Well?' said Nell's mother, as soon as he had gone. 'What is it? Is it bad news?'

Nell's father handed her the telegram. Bill and Nell and Bernie scrambled up and over to read it.

It was very short.

'*Mobilise*,' said Nell's mother. She stared at him in alarm. 'What does it mean? Eric? *Eric*?'

'It means we're at war,' said Nell's father, which Nell already knew, because the newspaper boys had been shouting about it all morning, and Mrs O'Farrell had already been up to talk it over with her mother and father. 'They're calling up the reserves. It's back to the army, old girl.' But he wouldn't look at her as he said it.

'Calling up the reserves!' Nell's mother cried. 'But you can't! Tell them you can't, Eric. You've got six kids to feed!'

'I ain't got no choice, Lil,' said Nell's father. His face was rigid. 'They'll give me a couple of days to get meself together, but that's it. If I don't go, it's desertion.'

'They shoot deserters, don't they, Dad?' said Bernie. Nell's father didn't answer. He went into the bedroom, and pulled the family suitcase out from under the brass bedstead. Dot scrambled over to the side of the bed, crying, 'Dad! Dad! Dad, what's happening?'

Nell's mother shrieked, 'Eric! How'm I going to pay the

rent if you go off to war? Is the army going to pay it for us? Well, is they? Answer me! *Eric*!'

'Is you going to Belgium, Dad?' said Bernie.

Nell's father rummaged in his pocket and handed her mother something which chinked. Nell's mother stared at it. It was a thruppeny bit, and three farthings.

'That's all I've got, love,' he said. 'You'll have to make do until I can send some back.'

Nell's mother stared at him, terrified. You could not feed and house seven people on what she earned, even with the extra Nell and Bill brought in. It simply could not be done.

Nell's father bent his head and kissed her forehead.

'You'll manage somehow, pet,' he said, awkwardly. 'You always do.'

And he opened his suitcase.

11

Evelyn missed the declaration of war. She missed her last weeks at school. She missed her eighteenth birthday, and the long-planned 'coming-out', the German advance on Paris and rebuttal at the Marne, and all of the excitement, the shouting in the street, the enlistments, the soldiers and the hastily planned weddings. For many weeks, she missed everything.

As she slowly got well, she began to learn what had happened to her. She had had appendicitis; a common side-effect of hunger strike, apparently. A doctor had come to the house and operated on her, 'Right here, on the nursery table, in your bedroom!' said Kezia, to whom this was the most exciting part of the whole business. But something had gone wrong, and the wound had become infected, and Evelyn had gone from having one serious illness straight into having another.

Naturally this had meant she'd been unable to return to prison, as her licence required. By the time she was well enough, the government had announced a general wartime amnesty for suffrage prisoners. Evelyn was ashamed of how relieved she felt. More than anything, she'd dreaded going back to prison.

She had never been really, seriously ill before, and she didn't like it. At first, she had been too ill to care about anything, and her days had been a confused, shivery, miserable blur of fever, and aches, and always feeling tired.

In those semi-delirious days, it was not Teddy or the little girls who she wanted, but, astonishingly, her mother and Miss Perring. Miss Perring, whom Evelyn had always rather scorned, turned out to be exactly the sort of person one needed when one was sick. She seemed to know almost by telepathy when Evelyn wanted water, or company, or an extra blanket, or when Hetty and Kezia were getting too much for her. Evelyn marvelled at how little attention she had given to this woman; with whom, after all, she had spent more time than her own parents.

'How did you get so good at looking after people who are ill?' she asked, one day, and Miss Perring replied, 'Caring for my own mother when she was dying.'

And Evelyn realised with a pang that she'd never – in all the years she'd known Miss Perring – once wondered about her own family.

Her mother, too, was a surprise. Evelyn had supposed that her mother would be very angry about prison, and the hunger strike, and the Suffragettes, but the subject was never mentioned at all. Instead, her mother would bring her mending into Evelyn's bedroom, and read aloud from the old nursery favourites: *The Pickwick Papers*, and *Puck of Pook's Hill* and *Alice in Wonderland*.

It was very strange to go to prison a schoolgirl, and to wake up an adult, in a world at war. Even in the few months that she'd been ill, the world had become a very different place indeed.

Hetty and Kezia were eager to tell her all about it: who was getting married in a great hurry, who had already joined up, who had rushed out and bought half the grocer's shop on the first day of the war.

'There are soldiers drilling every day on the Heath,' Hetty told her excitedly. 'There's soldiers everywhere you go, everyone's joined the army, practically. Kit's desperate to go too, only Father says he's too young and he's to finish his education. But Kit went back to Oxford and he says nearly all the boys have joined up already; there's just cowards and the medically unfit left, Kit says, and the foreigners. And his college is full of soldiers now, and they're ever so sniffy about the students. Half the colleges have soldiers billeted there, or they've been turned into army hospitals, Kit says. He stuck it out for three days, then he came home and said either Father had to let him enlist, or he was just going to sit around until Oxford sent him down for not showing up to lectures. But Father says he's too young – *I* don't think nineteen is too young, do you? I think it's rather an awful thing to have a brother at home in a time of national emergency. But you know what Father's like.'

Kezia and Hetty were both very excited about the war. They'd been on a rally supporting the soldiers, and Hetty's guide troop had already started making bandages for the wounded, which seemed a little premature to Evelyn.

'Captain says it's especially important to look smart and always wear our uniforms properly,' Hetty announced. 'She says it's every Englishman or woman's duty to maintain discipline and morale and that way we can show the troops how much we support them. Isn't it marvellous?'

'Did you tell Captain you'd got a sister who assaulted policemen?' said Evelyn, amused.

'Gladys did,' said Hetty. 'Captain said that sort of thing was all very well in peacetime, but in war we must put our differences behind us and work together to defeat the Hun. I told her you would. You will, won't you?'

'I suppose so,' said Evelyn. She felt rather bewildered. Mrs Pankhurst had been very vocal about how the needs of the country should come before the needs of the Suffragettes. Evelyn knew she was right. The whole point of the suffrage campaign had been to make life as difficult as possible for the government. But in wartime, wasting government time and money would put British soldiers at risk. It was the sort of thing traitors and resistance fighters did; it would, in a very real sense, be doing the enemy's work for them. Of course the Suffragettes couldn't do that. And yet . . .

She was filled, once again, with the impotent rage that had dogged her for most of her childhood. That this one thing that was so important to so many women had once again been trumped by the preoccupations of bloody men. *Is it worth dying for?* Teddy and her father had said to her, the implication being that it wasn't. And now this other *thing*, this vague thing, that seemed to be mostly about treaties and alliances and other people's battles, this thing *was* supposed to be worth it.

And the worst of it was, she didn't exactly *disagree*. It wasn't that she thought they ought to break their promises and abandon their national duties. It was just . . . rather insulting to realise that the rights of British women sat quite so far below the rights of Belgians in the British psyche.

She had seen very little of Teddy at first. Evelyn was not sure if this was because he was still forbidden to enter the house, or because she was too ill to be allowed visitors outside of family. For a long time, she had been too ill to notice who was there and who wasn't. But when the world began to settle down, and her head to clear, she had asked after him.

'Where is he?' A terrible thought struck her. 'He hasn't joined the army, has he?' He wouldn't, surely, without seeing her, or at least writing? Would he?

'No, no, of course not,' her mother said reassuringly.

'And you aren't still angry with him, are you?'

'No,' said her mother, rather surprisingly. 'Goodness, no!' And, seeing Evelyn's questioning expression, 'How could I be angry with him? Not now . . .'

She meant not now they were at war.

'Can I see him?' she said. 'I *do* so want to.'

'All right,' said her mother, rather anxiously – this was in the days before Evelyn was allowed even to sit up in bed, and everyone was very worried about upsetting her. And Teddy had been brought upstairs to visit.

'Hullo, old man,' he said. There was something fearful hovering behind his eyes, which hadn't been there before.

'Hullo,' she said, and held out her hand.

'Goodness,' he said, and his voice wavered. 'Don't you ever

do that to me again. I think I aged ten years that week you were in prison. And then you come out and throw this at me!'

'I'm sorry,' she said, and he took her hand and squeezed it.

'It's all right,' he said. 'After due consideration, I have decided to forgive you.'

She gave a hiccupy gurgle of a laugh. Then . . .

'Teddy,' she said. 'Teddy. You came to the action.'

'Well, of course.' He sounded surprised.

'But I was so ghastly to you.'

'Well, yes. You were rather hideous. But you didn't think I'd let you face that on your own, did you?'

She felt her eyes fill with tears.

'And you didn't tell Father I was doing it.'

'No. It didn't seem quite the thing, somehow.' He winced. 'There was rather a scene about that, I'm afraid.'

'Poor darling.' Of course, he'd had to tell them what had happened to her. It occurred to her for the first time what an awful job that must have been.

She rubbed her eyes. Goodness! To do all that . . .

It did make one look at him in a different light.

That was the sort of partner one wanted. A man who would tell you to your face when he thought you were acting like a bloody fool, and then stand beside you when you went ahead and did it anyway. There wasn't one man in a thousand who would do a thing like that.

Want

The next thing that happened was Nell's jam factory closed down.

'But why?' said Nell, when the foreman told them.

'Governor's enlisted, hasn't he?' said the foreman. 'So've half the men on the shop floor. Who's going to run the place? *And*,' he said, with an air of importance, 'there's no money in jam, anyway. Half the market's gone, ain't it? We can hardly sell jam to the Huns any more, can we?'

'But there must be money in jam!' said Mrs Dunbar, who lived two streets over from Nell, and had four children to feed. 'Everyone eats jam!'

The foreman shrugged.

'Set up your own factory, then,' he said. And that, it seemed, was that.

'Don't fuss,' Nell told her mother. 'I'll get work. You'll see.' But it wasn't so simple. Half the East End factories were closing. And those that weren't were swamped with applications.

Domestic jobs were being lost as well, as every male member of the middle classes who could was joining up. The gentry apparently considered it a point of honour to 'do without' male servants, and more and more women were seen driving their own cars and 'making do' without chauffeurs or handymen.

'Patriotic duty!' said Nell's mother, furiously, when Mrs Prickett's son was told that his services would no longer be required, as Mrs Thomas believed it was her patriotic duty to release young men of an age to serve in the army. 'Where's your duty to them's that need to pay the rent?'

A week later, Nell's mother also lost her job. This was a blow, but hardly a surprise. The socialist organisation existed in a state of permanent near-crisis. They were perpetually disorganised and underfunded, and the war was the straw that broke the already-bowed camel's back. The foreman told Nell's mother that Britain was in a national emergency, and nobody bought skirts in a state of national emergency. He advised her to try and get work making soldier's uniforms – 'There's a national shortage' – but there were no uniform factories anywhere near Poplar. Nell's mother asked the Suffragettes if they thought it was worth moving for the work, and was told it was unlikely; the uniform factories, like those in Poplar, were inundated with women. Nell's mother wept, and Siddy cried, and Bill swore, and Dot said, practically, 'What's we going to do?'

'I don't know,' said Nell's mother. She wiped her eyes furiously on the edge of her shawl. 'We'll think of something. Don't worry.'

But it was impossible not to. Nell's mother's wage had meant more than just money. Since their father had gone, Bernie and Dot had been getting free dinners at school. Now, however, because their mother was an able-bodied woman who did not work, the Poor Law stated that they could not be given charity.

'How am I supposed to work?' Nell's mother raged at the school ma'am. 'Do you have work? If you have it, I'll do it. There *ain't anything*.'

'I'm sorry, Mrs Swancott,' said the school ma'am. She did look sorry. 'I wish I could help you. But the law's the law.'

'If those children end up in the workhouse,' said Nell's mother. 'It'll be on your conscience. You and your bleeding Poor Law!'

'We won't end up in the workhouse, will we, Nell?' said Bernie that evening, as they sat on the step of the house watching the children playing in the street. Bernie's little face was whiter than ever, and his eyes were huge. He wouldn't survive the workhouse.

'Course we won't,' said Nell. 'Don't be daft. We'll be all right once Dad's money comes.'

'I could work maybe,' said Bernie. 'Mum were working when she were my age. I don't care about school. I could be a delivery boy, like Bill.'

Nell ruffled his hair.

'You!' she said. 'Not likely! Who'd ever think you were fourteen? And if you ain't fourteen, you ought to be in school. That's law, that is.'

'Most folks don't care about that,' said Bernie, which was probably true. But still . . .

'Go to school, Bern,' said Nell. 'We'll be all right.'

The only wage now coming into the household was what Bill could earn as a delivery boy, and that barely covered food and coal. Almost as soon as war was declared, prices had begun to rise. Dealers sent men to all the small shops, to buy up their stock and drive prices up still further. Anything imported from the continent disappeared. So, of course, did anything made in places like Nell's jam factory which had closed. Those who could afford to panic-bought coal and bread and soap and tinned food, which of course just made things worse. That autumn Nell's days became a desperate trudge from office to office to household to household to factory to factory, looking for work. There was none. Everyone Nell knew was in a similar position. Everyone was hungry. Everyone was cold. Everyone's babies were crying, their children grizzling, the frailer members of the family were beginning to fall sick. Everyone was desperate, and as the weeks dragged on, the desperation rose.

The biggest worry was of course the rent. One of the houses in the street across from Nell bore a calico banner which read:

PLEASE, LANDLORD, DON'T BE OFFENDED,
DON'T COME FOR THE RENT TIL THE
WAR IS ENDED.

It had been impossible for some weeks since for Nell's mother to pay her rent to Mrs O'Farrell, which in turn meant Mrs O'Farrell couldn't pay their landlord.

'I don't want to give you notice,' Mrs O'Farrell said. She really didn't. The few shillings Nell's mother could scrape together each week were better than nothing, and who knew how long it would take to find new tenants? 'But . . .'

Letters from Nell's father came from an army camp. All soldiers were supposed to receive a month's pay on mobilisation, but this had not happened. He didn't know why. He didn't know when it would come. Once they were paid, he would be allowed to send half his wages home, but nobody had been paid anything yet. There were forms you were supposed to fill in to make sure that your wife got her share of your wages, but these forms had not materialised. Everything was chaotic and disorganised. They didn't have proper equipment yet. They didn't even have proper barracks. They were sleeping on straw mattresses on the floor of a church hall. He missed them. He loved them. He didn't know when he would be sent to France.

Meanwhile, Nell's mother was raising money the only way she had left. Day after day, she loaded their possessions into the perambulator in which, until recently, she had taken her shirts to the factory. Day after day she joined the queue of women outside the pawnbrokers, pawning everything except the barest essentials. Their Sunday clothes. The china dogs which sat on the overmantel. The wardrobe. The table. The bedstead.

'Soon there'll be nothing left but us,' said Bernie mournfully. 'And then what?'

And then the workhouse. Like most of the working poor, Nell's mother lived in terror of the workhouse. They took your children from you in the workhouse. The work was perishing hard, and the food pitiful. You didn't die of starvation, but you probably died of something else instead. Plenty of people did.

And you never saw your children again.

Nell went down to the Women's Hall and knocked on the door. The Suffragettes were sympathetic, but helpless. Women like Nell and her mother came there every day, all with the same story. They took down her details, and her mother's details, and promised to let them know when there was work.

But there never was.

One of the young ladies who worked for the Suffragettes explained to Nell that her mother could apply for a separation allowance. Nell's mother queued all day at the Bromley Public Hall, along with hundreds of other soldiers' wives and dependants. But the money simply didn't arrive. It seemed to be a symptom of the general disorganisation into which the entire country had been thrown. Who cared about the East End women when soldiers like Nell's father didn't have boots?

In desperation, Nell's mother went to the Poor Law Guardians, then to the Relieving Officer, then back to the Suffragettes at the Women's Hall, and then round the same sad pilgrimage of Labour Exchange, pawn shop and anyone who might have work.

'When they writes up the history of this war,' said Nell's mother. 'I hope they tells about the wives and children starving to death!'

'They won't,' said Nell, gloomy socialist. 'It'll be all "Our Boys", and everyone enlisting and people doing without chauffeurs to help the war effort.'

'Well, they ought to be ashamed of themselves,' said Nell's mother, as furious with the gentry of the future as she was with those of the present.

'*Vive la bleeding révolution*,' said Nell.

The Principle of the Thing

May had always been odd. Somehow, before, it had never mattered. People at school had ribbed her, affectionately, about the suffrage badge on her coat collar, and her vegetarianism (which at school meant eating the vegetables and leaving the chop, or, sometimes, picking the vegetables out of the stew and leaving the rest). But May knew her own friends liked her, even if they thought her a bit queer, and who cared what the other girls thought anyway? Not her!

But now, things were different. Every girl in May's school, every teacher, even the caretaker and the charwomen, everyone was a patriot. The school newspaper ran patriotic stories about ways a 'Keen Girl Could Do Her Bit'. Handicraft classes were taken over by knitting for soldiers. In English, they all had to write patriotic essays about why Britain had to enter the war.

'It's awful,' May said to her mother. 'It's like . . . like it's a *game* or something. Don't they realise people are going to be *killed*?'

But even this aspect of the war seemed romantic to the other girls. May's friend Barbara had a brother who was actually a soldier, and Barbara told May solemnly that her brother had said he would be proud to die for his country – that dying on a battlefield would be a much better way to go than dying an old man in bed, and that he almost hoped he *would* die, and make them all proud. This way of looking at things was baffling to May, but apparently it wasn't to the girls in her form who had all nodded, and agreed that were they men, they would all feel exactly the same way.

May refused to take part in any of the patriotism. She refused to knit for the soldiers, working doggedly on the embroidered handkerchiefs she was making for Mrs Barber's birthday present instead. She wrote a patriotic essay on the idiocy of refusing to even consider a negotiated peace until thousands of men had been killed – a *ironic* idiocy, she wrote furiously, since the final peace would have to be negotiated *anyway*, so why not just do it *first*? She told Barbara she thought her brother was a twit, and she bet he would change his mind when he actually found himself on a battlefield surrounded by *corpses*.

This stance, unsurprisingly, did not win her any friends. People started to whisper things in the halls. An older girl, who May did not even know, tripped her up in the corridor, and laughed when all her books went flying. Arriving in her form room one morning, she found the word TRAITOR! scratched into her desk. From the giggles and whispers amongst the other girls, even May's particular friends, it was obvious that they all knew all about it. The form mistress sighed when May had complained, and said, 'Well, May, you do rather ask for it, don't you?'

The girls at school had been fired up with lust to attack someone – anyone – and since Brightview School for Girls regrettably did not contain any actual Huns, they turned on May. Girls she had never spoken to before hissed 'Traitor!' and 'Coward!' at her as she passed.

'What would you do if a Hun was attacking your mother?' they demanded, at break time. 'What would you do if the Huns invaded and killed us all? That's what would happen if everyone was a pacifist.'

'No, it wouldn't,' said May. 'If *everyone* was a pacifist, the Germans would be pacifists too, and they wouldn't do anything of the sort.'

'Huns aren't pacifists,' said Barbara scornfully. May said heatedly that her mother knew several *very nice* German suffragists who were, and Barbara knew nothing about it. But that turned out to be a mistake too. The girls added 'Hun-lover' to their list of cat-calls, and taunted May with lewd suggestions about what she wanted the Huns to do to her. This was as baffling as it was hurtful. Arguments May could cope with, even arguments where every girl in her form room was against her. Not for nothing had she stood in the street while passers-by threw rotten vegetables at her mother. But the violence and the cruelty of this hate campaign was outside of her experience. You couldn't argue with it. You couldn't fight it. All you could do was put down your head and endure.

It wasn't just at school that May was lonely. The outbreak of war seemed to mean an awful lot of committee work, and May's mother had flung herself into the fray. The National Union of Women's Suffrage Societies was full of pacifists; they had, after all, been saying for years that once women had the vote, there would be no more wars. This feeling was not, however, universal. Most suffragists came from middle-class homes, where the supremacy of King, Country and the British Empire went without saying. Furthermore, both Millicent Fawcett – leader of the NUWSS – and Emmeline Pankhurst – leader of the more militant Women's Social and Political Union – knew that a suffrage movement which came out against the war would rapidly lose all public sympathy.

Mrs Pankhurst had early on declared the WSPU's support for the war, but the NUWSS were less easily swayed. At meeting after meeting, they wavered between grudging support and out-and-out opposition. It was hoped that Millicent Fawcett would officially condemn the war, but she showed no signs of wanting to. And it all meant a beastly lot of extra work for May's mother.

On top of this, there was the Women's Peace Movement, as well as the Quakers, who, in true contrarian Quaker style, were in the process of reviving something called the Friends' War Victims' Relief Committee. Nobody was sure exactly what relief war victims actually needed, but they were determined to find out and provide it. May's mother spent all day rushing from committee meeting to public meeting to lecture hall to picket.

She did, however, manage to find a morning to go down to the school and complain. This had not been a success either. The form mistress had listened politely, and explained that Brightview School for Girls was proud of its patriotic history, and that May should consider supporting her fellow countrymen like her classmates. Men in France were desperately under-equipped, and if May thought making handkerchiefs was more important than keeping a fighting man's feet warm – well! What could the form mistress do? May's mother said furiously that she would take May out of that disgusting school at once, and send her to one of the Quaker schools, Sibford, or Sidcot, but May begged her not to. Sibford and Sidcot were both boarding schools, and May knew how stretched their household finances already were. Besides, she didn't want to go to boarding school. She didn't even want to stop going to Brightview, exactly. It felt like a failure. It felt like giving up. And if May gave up, what sort of person would she be then? It would be just the same as knitting their beastly socks, and she was dashed if she was going to do it.

She was beginning to understand – a little bit – what life must be like for Nell. Nell might be awkward, and prickly, and shy, but not only did she wear what she wanted to wear, she marched down the street wearing it, clutching a banner and singing at the top of her voice. May loved it, but she had never understood it. She thought she did now, a little. If you gave in and became the person other people wanted you to be . . . well, you just couldn't. It wasn't possible, if you were the sort of person May was, or Nell was. May couldn't just go into school and announce that she liked the war now. And Nell couldn't just turn up one day with her hair in ringlets. It wasn't just that she didn't want to, she literally didn't know how she'd even begin. And once you realised that, there wasn't anything left to be but the person you were, as loudly and stubbornly as you could.

But even Nell was no comfort, now things were so difficult for her at home. May had tried to help, but Nell was prickly and proud about 'charity'.

'You ain't a Poor Law Guardian,' she said. 'You're me girl. You can't give me money. Besides, how would I explain it to me mum?'

She would, however, accept meals, and Mrs Barber, who was surprisingly fond of Nell, would make her up parcels of treacle tart and pie and bread and cheese for her to take back on the long walk home to her family.

'You could come and live here with us,' May whispered, as they sat side-by-side on her narrow bed, Nell's thin hand in hers.

Nell snorted. 'Don't be daft,' she said. 'Me, live here! No fear. I just got to get a job, that's all.'

When Nell's problems were so obviously so much more important, it felt absurd to talk about the girls at school. She felt, as she often did around Nell, like a child. Not that Nell asked. She was too locked-up in her own difficulties. May was vaguely resentful of this; Nell should have *known* that things were bad. She shouldn't have *had* to tell her. Of course she knew it wasn't important, compared to what was happening to Nell. But she should have cared *anyway*.

She didn't say any of this, of course. But she thought it. Things didn't stop being awful, just because someone else's problems were awfuller, any more than you stopped being happy just because someone else was happier. You could still be perfectly miserable about people at school, even if your girl *had* lost her job. People dying in fields in France didn't make

Nell's mother any happier, did they? Other people's problems made you feel *worse*. Or they did if you were any sort of person at all.

It would have helped if Nell had at least *pretended* to understand May's principles. But May suspected that Nell found her and Mama's pacifism rather amusing. She supposed she couldn't really expect her to agree with them; after all, her father was a soldier. But she could have *tried* to understand, at least.

She felt ashamed even thinking this. But she couldn't help it. Sometimes it seemed to May as though she lived in another country to the girls at school. But Nell? Nell's life was so different that she might as well live on the other side of the world.

Up

Christopher Collis had – finally – been allowed to join up. He was offered a commission in a London regiment and went off wild with excitement to training. The German advance on Paris had been halted, but the Battle of the Aisne was showing no signs of being won by either side, and Christopher said joyfully that the war now wouldn't be over until next year at least. Evelyn's father was resigned and her mother quietly anxious. The girls were full of pride. Hetty immediately began knitting him a wobbly scarf in regimental colours, while Kezia took to telling everyone about 'my brother in the army'.

Both of Teddy's older brothers had also enlisted. Stephen was in an army camp near Reading, but Herbert, who'd been in the OTC all through Marlborough and Cambridge and was a reservist, had actually been sent to France. Evelyn didn't know anyone else who was really in France. Hetty and Kezia flung themselves on Teddy every time he appeared, demanding to know what it was like 'out there', but Teddy was rather vague. Herbert sent dutiful letters to his mother, mostly demanding cigarettes and sweets, but they were short on details, giving a general impression of disorganisation, endemic low-level chaos, and boredom.

'Has he killed anybody yet?' said Kezia, and Teddy laughed and said he had no idea, but if Herbert had, he doubted very much that he'd write home and tell Mother and Father about it.

She'd seen rather a lot of Teddy over the last couple of months. A lot of his art-student friends had joined up, and she got the impression he was rather lonely. She'd been finally allowed to move downstairs, and he would come and sit on the end of the couch and draw her funny pictures of what was happening in the world outside. A significant proportion of the art students, apparently, considered themselves too internationalist and intellectual to want to fight. Teddy said he could see their point, if he squinted at it from a distance, but this didn't stop him drawing rather sneery caricatures of them all, with long hair and painter's smocks, tittering about the Germans while Christopher and Stephen and Herbert went off to defend them. She could see he resented being assumed to be one of their number, which worried her. So far he'd shown no inclination to join up himself, but she knew he wouldn't wait for ever.

They were no longer allowed to be together unchaperoned, and had to endure either Evelyn's mother or Miss Perring sitting in the easy chair with darning or knitting or letters, pretending this was where they'd intended to spend the afternoon anyway. This made conversation rather difficult. Evelyn had all sorts of things she wanted to say to him, private things, intimate things, and instead was stuck talking about soldiers, or art students, or books. It was maddening. She felt as though something huge and mysterious and vital had happened to her – to him – to both of them – and it was forced to stay trammelled inside her. Every time he left she swore that next time she would tell him, Miss Perring or no. She would wait with increasing impatience until he got there – all the time he wasn't there she felt as though she was half alive, waiting . . . and then when he did arrive her courage would fail her again. How could you possibly tell someone you loved them with your mother sitting next to you, darning Father's socks?

At the end of October, he came round to visit again. Evelyn was on the couch in the drawing room, wrapped up under a blanket in front of the fire, picking rather dully at a half-finished cushion-cover left over from last term's needlework class. She perked up as she heard his voice, and her mother got up and went to greet him. There was a long pause, in which she could hear the murmur of their voices in the hall. Then he came into the room, alone, and shut the door behind him. Her heart began to beat rather quickly.

'Hullo,' he said, uncertainly, twisting his hat between his hands.

'Hullo,' she said. 'You'll muck up the brim if you keep doing that, you know.'

'What? Oh!' Teddy let go of the hat and looked around for somewhere to put it. He set it down on top of the couch, then changed his mind and put it on the coffee table instead. Then he sat in the easy chair.

'Look here,' he said. 'I – that is – the time has come – I mean . . .'

It wasn't about her at all. It was about the war. Her disappointment made her harsher than she'd intended.

'You want to join the army,' she said.

'Yes,' he said. 'I rather think I ought to. I didn't at first – I can't quite see me in a tin hat somehow, can you? But – well – when it comes down to it, I find I don't quite like the thought of letting all the other chaps do the dirty work for me.'

'You mean all the other fellows have joined up and you feel a heel,' she said.

Teddy grimaced. 'I don't say that isn't a part of it,' he said. 'But it's more . . . there's a job that needs doing, and they've asked for volunteers, and – well – when it comes down to it, none of my excuses really hold. I did think *you* might have understood that.'

'I suppose so,' said Evelyn. *What about me?* she wanted to say, which was ridiculous, and childish, but she couldn't help herself. She was only now realising that if he joined the army he would go away and she wouldn't see him again for months and months – perhaps ever. 'You must do as you think best,' she said instead, which was nearly as bad. The worst of it was, she didn't exactly *disagree* with him. Of course he couldn't be the only sensible chap still left behind in classes while everyone else was in France. Of course, if anyone had to go, it ought to be young, unmarried men like Teddy. But while those things were very easy to think in the abstract, even surprisingly easy to think in reference to Christopher, with his thick brown Collis hair all cut short and his brand-new second-lieutenant's uniform, Evelyn's patriotism faltered when she thought of laughing, curly-haired Teddy getting blown to pieces somewhere. Teddy's workmanlike assessment of the problem irritated her too. Kit, she knew, longed to be a hero. Evelyn had secretly always rather fancied herself as the next Emily Wilding Davison. But Teddy sounded like a boy scout volunteering to do the washing-up.

What happened to 'No cause is worth dying for'? she wanted to say. Are the rotten Belgians really so much more important than . . . than my emancipation was? She knew this was a beastly selfish way of looking at things, and the knowledge made her furious.

'Well then,' said Teddy. 'The other thing is – that is –' She glared at him, and he stopped. 'Look here,' he said. 'Do you want to marry me or not? Because I jolly well want to marry you, and if you don't – well – I do think you might tell a fellow, that's all, so he knows where he stands.'

'I suppose you think I'll say yes just because you're going to go and get your head shot off,' said Evelyn coldly.

Teddy flushed. 'There's no need to be such a cat about it,' he said. 'If you don't want to, you don't, that's all.'

'I didn't say I didn't want to,' said Evelyn. She felt suddenly ashamed. She had been waiting for this moment for months, and now when it had come, she'd gone and ruined it. 'Oh, Teddy, I am being a brute. Of course I'll marry you.'

'Really? Will you really, though?'

'Honestly, truly. I've been – ever since that day when you came into court, I've been – I mean, I've been wanting to tell you. I – well.' She stopped in confusion. 'I'd love to marry you,' she said. 'I can't think of anything I'd like more.'

Teddy didn't seem to know where to look. He picked up his hat, put it down again, picked it up, looked at it for a moment and then rammed it on his head. The corners of his mouth were twitching upwards in a most undignified fashion.

'Oh,' he said. And then he really did grin. 'Jolly good.'

The Ghost of Christmas Future

Later, when the congratulations, and the embraces, and the exclamations over Teddy going away were over, when everyone's health had been drunk, and Teddy had gone home to tell his parents the good news, and Hetty and Kezia had been packed off to bed, Evelyn sat alone on her couch in the drawing room. She felt curiously wide awake. She sat with her half-embroidered cushion-cover on her lap, but she didn't pick it up. She stared instead into the drawing-room fire and thought, I am engaged to Teddy! I am engaged to be married! But it didn't feel real. It belonged to a make-believe world, a when-the-war-is-over world. Where would they live? What would she do all day? Would she have a job? Would they have *children*? Perhaps Teddy will die, she thought, but that didn't feel real either.

She heard a noise, and turned to see her father come into the room. He shut the door quietly behind him and sat down beside her.

'Well,' he said. 'So I have a daughter who is engaged to be married.'

'Yes,' said Evelyn.

'And a son who is determined to get himself killed just as soon as ever he can.' He exhaled. He looked tired, Evelyn noticed. His civil service job, which had always sounded rather dull, now seemed to involve enormously long hours and late nights. Evelyn realised guiltily that she still didn't know exactly what he did for a living. The old nursery explanation: 'doing figures for the government' suddenly sounded incredibly childish. And of course he was old, older than other people's fathers. She felt a stab of guilt. She had never, not even for a moment, considered that it was her job to look after her parents, but for the first time she began to appreciate how hard Kit joining the army must be for them. Another sort of daughter, she realised, might have been sympathetic and comforting. She could hardly have been less comforting if she'd run away to join the circus.

'Kit's just trying to do his bit,' she said, awkwardly. Her father gave her a wry smile.

'Oh yes,' he said. 'In the most bloody and dramatic way he possibly can. I know.'

Evelyn didn't know what to say to that, so she changed the subject.

'Chin up,' she said. 'At least I'm behaving myself now. I'm going to be a good little housewife for the rest of my life. You ought to be delighted.'

Evelyn's father did not greet this pronouncement with the enthusiasm which might have been expected.

'My Evelyn,' he said. 'Engaged at eighteen. I never pictured you marrying young. I rather thought you'd want to go off and raise some hell first.'

This surprised Evelyn.

'I thought you wanted me to be married,' she said. Her father smiled.

'Oh well,' he said. 'I never imagined you'd pay the slightest bit of attention to what *we* wanted. You never have before.'

Suddenly, Evelyn felt hope rising inside her.

'Father,' she said. 'Teddy and I aren't going to get married for ever so long – not until the war's over, anyway, and probably not until Teddy finishes college after that. Couldn't – oh, couldn't I go to Oxford while I'm waiting? Teddy wouldn't object. I think he'd like it. And I expect I could pay you back when we're married. Or perhaps I could teach, or something – I can't imagine I'd be much earthly good at it, but someone might pay me something. Please, Father. Just think of the money Kit's saving you by being in the army instead of at university. Don't you want me to do something with my life?'

Evelyn's father blew out his breath. He leant forward, his face half in shadow, half warm in the light of the flames. Evelyn waited, holding her breath. She felt as though the whole course of her life were being weighed, and just by breathing right, or sitting in a certain way, or saying the wrong thing, she might tip the balance in the other direction.

'Doesn't it frighten you?' her father said, suddenly.

'Doesn't what frighten me?'

'A whole generation of young men. This war with Europe looming over them like the Ghost of Christmas Future. Aren't you afraid?'

'No,' said Evelyn honestly. 'I mean – a bit for Teddy and Christopher. But mostly I think it's thrilling. Don't you?'

'Me?' said her father. 'I think it's terrifying.' He put the palms of his hands together in a gesture rather like a child saying its prayers. He rested his forehead on the tips of his fingers and closed his eyes. Evelyn wondered if he *were* praying. Then he raised his head. 'Go to Oxford if you want to, daughter,' he said. 'I won't stand in your way. There are too many lives going to be broken in this war, without us breaking another.'

A Storm in a Hobnailed Boot

It was a rainy Saturday, the worst sort of day. All of the Swancotts hated rain. The children, cooped up with nothing to do and nowhere to go, fought and made trouble and got under everyone's feet. Nell's mother was in a foul temper because the floor needed mopping and the windows washing, and the blacks leaded, and how could she do any of that with all the children here? Dot and Bernie, catching her bad temper, quarrelled noisily in the corner over nothing at all, and Dot pinched Bernie on the arm and Bernie pulled her hair, and Dot screeched and knocked the cotton-reel Johnnie was playing with off the little table on his high chair, and Johnnie began to cry and woke Siddy, who started to howl.

'Bleeding hell!' cried their mother. 'Can't I get a moment's peace in here? Shut your gobs, the lot of you, before I shut them for you!' And she handed Siddy to Dot, lifted Johnnie out of the high chair, and shooed the younger children into the bedroom.

'And don't come out till you can behave yourselves!' she yelled.

That left Nell and Bill, Nell cutting the mould out of a bucket of potatoes her mother had bought cheap at the market, and Bill toiling over a pair of Bernie's boots. The sole had come away at the toe, and flapped about when you shook the boot. Obviously Bernie couldn't wear them out in the rain, so equally obviously someone had to mend them.

Boots were Nell's father's job. He had a tin box full of scraps of leather, and a shoemaker's needle, and hobnails, and a little tin of dubbin for waterproofing the leather. As the man of the family, this job now fell to Bill, but Bill, it seemed, didn't have the first idea how to mend a pair of boots. He was sitting by the range staring glumly at them. At last, he pulled out the leather needle and, rather doubtfully, began to unwind the thread.

Nell, also in a foul mood, had been waiting for this. Why should she be stuck chopping potatoes when Bill, who didn't have a clue what he was doing, was allowed to do her father's work?

'You don't want to *sew* it,' she said scornfully. 'The hobnails've come out – see there. You got to nail it back on. Fancy you not knowing that!'

Bill flushed. He was sixteen and three-quarters, which wasn't at all an easy thing to be in November 1914. Several of his older friends had already joined up, and had come back from the Recruiting Office to swank about it to the girls and the younger boys. They had made it very clear to Bill that men joined the army, and little boys stayed at home with their mothers and sisters. Bill's father, indirectly, had rather exacerbated this view of things. Bill adored his soldier father, and from early childhood had loved to hear his stories of army life, and the Boers, and the 'natives' in Africa. Bill's father knew this perfectly well, and used the army as a way to manage his sons.

'Look sharp, private!' he'd say. 'Wash that face and polish those boots, or I'll have you drummed out of the regiment.'

For years Bill had dreamed of joining the army like his dad, and it was a bitter thing to have this long-prophesied war with Germany finally come and to have missed out on it by so short a hair. By the time he was old enough to join up, it would all be over. Right now, Bill was feeling much less of a man than he should be, and his sister Nell lording it over boots was the last straw.

Bill had suffered quite a lot for Nell's sake over the years. A little sister who was better than you at cricket and football! A little sister who guyed herself up like a boy, and spat, and fought, and smoked a pipe, and swore! Bill considered it his brotherly duty to defend her, and mostly he did just that, but he couldn't help but resent it sometimes. It wasn't as though she was ever grateful! Why couldn't she just behave like other girls did? Didn't she know the things people said about her? Even now, when things were so tight, she still insisted on going around in all that get-up. Who did she think was ever going to give her a job, dressed like that? And then for her to say a thing like that? It was too much.

'How dare you?' he spluttered. 'How bloody *dare* you? What do you know about it, anyhow?'

'More than you does!' Nell sneered. She had been longing for a fight all morning. 'Why don't you come and chop the potatoes, and let me show you how it's done?'

'You – you – you!' Bill swore.

His mother said, 'William Swancott!' but he ignored her.

'You think you're so clever!' he raged. 'Don't you know everyone's laughing at you? Who's ever going to marry a girl like you? Who's ever going to give you a job? If you were a *proper* man, you'd care more about feeding those children than swanning about looking a guy! If you can't behave like a woman, at least behave like a man, and put on something sensible and get a bleeding job!'

His words stung. He was, Nell knew, quite right. But – but – 'You think I don't know that?' she cried. 'How *can* I dress like a girl? How? Tell me how! *What am I supposed to wear*?'

She was right. There was nothing. Her only dress, the one she'd been forced into on Sundays and packed off to Sunday School with the other children ('Only time your dad and me gets any peace, Sundays! Off you trot!') had been pawned way back in August. So had her mother's spare dress. And in any case, Nell was shorter than her mother and broader in the chest – she couldn't have fitted into her clothes. In better times, her mother might have managed something – Dot had had a costume for the Suffragettes' annual May Day pageant made out of an old bedsheet, and several times she and Nell had run up entire items of clothing overnight when last-minute disasters had happened to trousers or shirts or skirts. But right now there was no money for cloth, or thread.

'You should've thought of that before, shouldn't you?' Bill raged. 'You ain't a kid any more, are you? And you ain't a man neither, so stop bloody pretending you is! This war is gonna be won by *men*, not girls in they's brothers' clothes! How many Huns is you gonna kill? None!'

He was almost crying. So, to her horror, was Nell. She knew the other kids talked about her, knew she would never be a boy, not really. But her own family! Bill! She had never, never thought he felt like this.

'Yeh, cause you's killing so many, ain't you?' she roared. 'Why ain't you joined up then, if you feel like that about it?' She gave him a look of pure scorn. 'Think I'd still be here if I was you?' she said. 'Not bloody likely!'

He launched himself on her. She fought back, with all of her Suffragette training, mixed up with years of bare-knuckle fighting in the streets of Poplar. Fighting like a girl who knew ju-jitsu, and how best to attack a policeman! And fighting like an East End boy as well. Bill was taller than her, and stronger, and furious with rage, but she was winning. The other children were in the doorway, Dot shrieking, Bernie crying, 'Oh, stop it! Stop it!'

'Enough! Enough, I said! Stop it right now!'

She felt a bony hand at her elbow, a bony shoulder shoved between them. Her mother was forcibly pulling Bill off by the scruff of his neck, the way she used to when they were smaller than Bernie and Dot were now.

'Outside!' She gave Bill a cuff on the cheek. 'I don't care if it *is* raining. Go up to the park, go to Jim's house, whatever. Don't come back till you've got your head on straight. D'you hear me?'

Bill swore, and wiped his hand across his cheek, which was

bleeding, Nell realised guiltily, though not much. But he went. Nell's mother turned on the children in the doorway.

'Mum, Mum, Nell's crying—' Dot said.

'And you!' their mother bellowed. 'Back in that room and play nicely, or you'll be out on your ear, and all.'

They disappeared. Nell's mother rummaged in her pocket for a handkerchief, and handed it to Nell, who took it, furious with herself. Crying, over bloody Bill! Her mother tutted to herself, sat down at the table, and began to peel the potatoes at twice the speed Nell had managed.

At last, Nell managed to calm herself. She came and sat beside her mother, handed back the handkerchief and muttered, 'I'm sorry.'

'S'all right.' Her mother pocketed it. 'Lord knows, I've wanted to weep enough times since this bleeding war started.' She began to chop the potatoes into quarters with neat flashes of the knife. Then suddenly, decisively, she said, 'You know Bill didn't mean that, didn't you?'

Nell shrugged. Bill *had* meant it and he *hadn't* meant it, she knew. It was complicated. Just like he was right and he was wrong, all at the same time.

Her mother sat back and regarded her with exasperation.

'My God, girl,' she said. 'Do you know how proud I am of you? The whole world wants to knock us down and you just keep on fighting, don't you? God didn't make the world the way you wanted it, and you're damn well going to rip it up and rebuild it right, ain't you?'

Nell blinked. Her mother had never said she was proud of her. Ever. Mum didn't say things like that. She yelled, and commanded, and kissed you, and worried you, but she didn't say she was proud.

'I know I ain't a proper daughter—' she began, awkwardly.

Her mother hooted.

'Proper daughter!' she said. 'What am I, Queen of Bloody England! You're me daughter, and that's enough for me. Now go find your brother and make it up, d'you hear me?'

She pushed Nell out of the door and Nell went, reluctantly. It was still raining heavily. She looked up and down Coney Lane, but there was no sight of Bill. He'd probably gone round to one of his mate's houses. That's what she would have done in his place.

She hunched her shoulders against the rain, wishing she had a coat, and hurried towards the high street. There, in the shelter of a shop front, she dug out her tobacco pouch. It was almost empty, but there were enough scrapings left to fill the pipe half full. She lit the pipe and drew in the smoke, then released it in a long, slow exhale.

She didn't know what to feel. Mum, Bill, everything. It was too much to keep in her head. Mostly what she felt was despair. She would *never* belong. *Never*. Meeting May had made her hope that perhaps there was a space in the world for people like her. Maybe there was if you were someone like May. But for someone from a family like hers? Never. If even *Bill* thought those things about her . . . And the worst of it was, he was right. How could she possibly carry on dressing like this if it meant the workhouse for Bernie and Dot and Johnnie and Sid?

But how could she possibly do anything else? The thought of dressing herself up like her mother in petticoats and bodices filled her with a physical revulsion so strong she thought she might vomit. It would be like . . . like getting married to George or Albert or Robbie or one of the other boys on the lane and pretending to love them. It would be like joining the Anti-Suffrage League and protesting against Miss Pankhurst. It would be like dressing up as a German and shooting at her father. It was impossible. The whole thing was impossible. There was nowhere to go and nothing to be. She had thought May was a refuge, but May was just a window, showing her a world she could never enter.

She leant back against the wall and closed her eyes. I wish I was dead, she thought, very clearly. She was cold, she was hungry, and she was more exhausted than she had ever been in her entire life. The thought of going home, getting up the next day, doing it all again, was more than she could bear.

Bill had not gone round to a mate's house. He was too angry. The quarrel was too private. And – though he would never have admitted it – he was too worried that Nell might be right.

He clenched his hands into fists in his pockets and offered a silent, furious curse to the world that had made him sixteen at a time when the only men who mattered were those aged eighteen to thirty-eight. Everything important was happening overseas, and here *he* was, a *boy*, while in France the men who mattered were *men*.

He went stumbling down the high street, kicking his boots

in the puddles and sending up little angry sprays of water. Already there were dividing lines drawn in the sand: Those Who Were There and Those Who Weren't.

Of course, most of the boys he knew Weren't There yet. They were in training camps. They came back to Coney Lane on leave in stiff new uniforms and shiny new boots and swanked about impressing the girls. But they would be.

And he wouldn't.

She was still standing there, the pipe in her hand, when Bill came back down the road. He had been walking round the streets of Poplar in a fury, thinking of all the things he should have said to his sister, and how he should have said them. Yet at the same time, he couldn't help but wonder if his mother was right. Nell wasn't a bad sort, not really. A bit peculiar, but who wasn't? And a fellow really ought to stick by his sister, oughtn't he? Of course, everything he'd said was perfectly true, but still . . . perhaps he *oughtn't* to have said it.

He pushed angrily past a woman with a perambulator, and saw her, her head tipped back against the wall of the tobacconist's, her eyes closed. Her dark hair was slicked wet by the rain, and her shirt clung to her chest. She looked – Bill thought – utterly defeated. He was shocked and ashamed. A man shouldn't make a girl look like that, even if she *was* a rum sort of girl. Women were emotional creatures, everyone knew that. That was why you had to treat them gently, and not punch them in the face the way you would a boy. Nell might *look* a boy, but she was a girl really, and if she wanted to forget it, it didn't mean he should.

He went over to her and leant against the wall beside her, bumping his shoulder against hers. She started and flinched away, then saw who he was. He saw the shutters go down in her eyes; she was wary, he saw, preparing herself for another attack.

'Look here,' he said, awkwardly. 'I shouldn't have said them things I said. It weren't right. I'm – I'm sorry, all right?'

She looked at him wearily, with that same dead gaze.

'It dun't matter,' she said. 'Don't worry about it.' She closed her eyes.

He said, a little panicked, 'It does, though. I am sorry, honest I am. You believe me, don't you?'

She stared at him for so long that he thought she wasn't going to answer. He began to grow afraid. He hadn't *meant* it. Or – if he had, he hadn't meant to hurt her quite as hard as all that.

'Nell . . .' he said. 'Nell, old girl. We're mates, you and me, ain't we?'

At last, she seemed to see him. She gave a 'Ha!' and took a puff on her disgusting cheap tobacco. 'All right,' she said. 'If you want. What does it bloody matter, anyway?'

But he noted that she didn't apologise.

Kneading

Mrs Barber was in a bad mood. She was making the bread for the next day, pounding it against the tabletop as she kneaded it. May sat in the kitchen and watched her. Her mother was giving an anti-war lecture in Southampton. She'd been doing a lot of this lately. May much preferred it to the committee meetings, because at least she could come along and give out handbills. But tonight was a school night, and May's mother wouldn't be home until gone midnight, so May was once again left with Mrs Barber.

'Your mother,' said Mrs Barber, 'had better watch out. She's going to be getting herself in trouble, one of these days.'

'Mama?' said May, surprised. 'Why? Has someone said something?'

'Has someone said something!' Mrs Barber slammed the dough against the table. 'That John Catlin ought to know better, he ought. As if your mother would conspire with Germans!' John Catlin was the postman, and an old enemy of Mrs Barber's. 'Still,' she went on, 'I've a good mind to tell her, she shouldn't be sending off for foreign German papers. People do talk.'

'Do you mean *Jus Suffragii?*' said May. 'Darling Mrs Barber, that's not German. It's Latin. It's the paper of the International Woman Suffrage Alliance.'

'Huh,' said Mrs Barber. 'Well, he is a fool, then. As if Germans would be writing in a Latin newspaper!'

Jus Suffragii was published in English and French, but May did not bother to correct her.

'Actually,' she said. 'There was a letter from German suffragists in this one, sending greetings to everyone else. We sent them a greeting before Christmas too. Women don't want to fight wars, you know, Mrs Barber, especially not suffragists. We're all for equality and justice, not one set of people being better than everyone else.'

'Tell that to Mrs Pankhurst,' said Mrs Barber darkly. Mrs Pankhurst had been very vocal recently on how everyone ought to give up fighting for votes and start fighting for Britain instead.

'Mama says,' said May, 'that some women in the IWSA want to organise a peace conference just for women, with representatives from all the countries in the alliance. It's going to be in the Netherlands, she says. Won't that be marvellous?'

'A peace conference!' said Mrs Barber. 'What good will that do? Women can't stop this war, dearie. Only the men could do that, and they won't. Like little boys, they are. If Mr Asquith and the Kaiser were in my nursery, I'd bang their heads together until they were ready to kiss and make up.'

May giggled.

'I bet the Kaiser wouldn't,' she said. 'I bet he was a *horrible* little boy. But, Mrs Barber, that isn't true, you know. Mr Asquith and the Kaiser aren't the ones fighting this war – it's ordinary people like us. If everyone just refused to fight, they'd *have* to make it up. There was the most glorious article about it – Mama showed me. It said that governments oughtn't to be allowed to decide anything like foreign policy without everyone in the country being allowed to vote on it – *everyone*, do you see? Women too. Women won't ever vote to go to war, you know, Mrs Barber, it's only men who think like that. If we could just get the vote, there wouldn't ever be any more wars, *ever*.'

The old arguments came out easily enough. But even to May, they rang a little hollow. Women had been depressingly eager to send their sons and husbands off to France. Millicent Fawcett had outraged May's mother by declaring that it was treason to even talk of peace – a declaration which was rather baffling given the nature of most of her organisation's official statements. It was one thing for old Mrs Pankhurst to change her mind, but for Mrs Fawcett to do the same!

May's mother had resigned her membership in a fury, along, it must be said, with a rush of other women. But even so. May loved the idea of the modern, twentieth-century woman, who would throw off the stale old traditions of Victorian England. It was deeply depressing to discover that Modern Woman was just as nationalistic and war-hungry as Victorian Woman had been.

Mrs Barber knew this as well as May, but she did not say so. Mrs Barber loved May and her mother – almost as much as she would have loved a child of her own. But she considered them both incurable innocents, and saw no reason to disabuse them of their quaint notions about basic human goodness. Quakers believed there was that of God in everyone. Mrs Barber thought there might be exceptions.

'Well!' she said to May. 'That's a lovely idea, dearie, but Mr Asquith won't let your mother go to the Netherlands and talk to Germans, you know. Why! He'd arrest her as a spy, like as not, and send her to prison.'

'Mama wouldn't care,' said May. 'And neither would I. Just let Mr Asquith try, that's all!'

Consolation

It was a miserable day in December. Nell couldn't bear to go home. She turned instead towards May's house. At least it was *warm* in May's house. (Although it wasn't, actually; the living-room fire was a sputtery, resentful, hiccupy little thing, and May never had a fire in her room unless she was ill. May's room was actually colder than home. But May was always happy to lend you jerseys. And of course they had other ways of keeping themselves warm, when it was just the two of them.)

And at least it was quiet. At least you could hear yourself *think*.

At least there was food.

There was less food than there used to be, though. Nobody had much food these days, even the nobs. Nell was never sure *quite* how much money May's family had, and of course one couldn't ask. There was the slavey, Mrs Barber, and the nice house, and the fancy school, and Mrs Thornton was a gentlewoman, of course. But all of May's clothes were worn and darned and let-down, and her mama had to work, and there were the pitiful fires, and Mrs Barber's grumbles about the price of bread, and the food all vegetables. Vegetables were what you ate when money was so tight you couldn't even afford a Sunday roast. Even as hungry as Nell's family were now, they still ate bread and beef dripping for tea.

So it was a mystery. Different rules evidently applied if you were gentry. Nobody actually said anything about food, but Nell was given the general impression that, while of course they were very sorry for her trouble, and of course she was always very welcome, perhaps it wouldn't be politic to come round *all* the time. Not with prices what they were at the moment, and May's mama so busy with her anti-war work, and no time to teach piano.

Not that she should *stop* coming. But just . . . well. She knew.

Nell did. She was painfully proud, and would have died rather than have Mrs Barber think she was trying to scab off May's generosity. As a result, she turned down so many invitations that May began to wonder if she'd done something to offend her. It didn't help that autumn was now here, and you couldn't just sit in the park like you could in summer. And May had school, of course, and prep in the evenings. And, and, and . . .

But Nell couldn't stop seeing her. May, to Nell, was like opium. Like brandy on a cold day. Like an electric shock. She made everything *blaze*. What did all the petty mess of manners matter when there was May there, waiting?

So she still came.

She just saved May for days when everything was most desperate.

Today was a desperate day. This morning, she'd been offered a job as a milkman's mate. She kept this job for a total of five minutes until a boy, coming too late, cried in bitter jealousy: 'You can't give it to her, mister! She's a girl!'

'Don't be daft!' said the milkman, roughly, and then, in sudden doubt, 'You ain't, is you?'

Nell hesitated, but before she could answer, the boy cried, 'Yeh, she is! She's Bill Swancott's sister! Look at her: she's got titties and all!'

'You shut your face!' cried Nell in fury, but it was too late. The damage was done.

'What you doing dressed like that anyway?' the milkman said. 'It's disgusting, that's what it is. Like them women what goes round setting fire to things. Mad, they are. Someone ought to lock them up before they hurts someone. What's your mother think she's playing at, letting you go about dressed like that? I ain't being funny, love, but no one's going to give you a job looking like that.'

The guilt and the misery twisted up inside of her all day, until she could bear it no longer and went round to May's, uninvited and unannounced.

Mrs Barber answered the door.

'Hello,' she said. 'Didn't your mother ever tell you it's polite to give notice before descending on a family for supper? What if we were otherwise engaged?'

Nell had never done any such thing before in her life, and this welcome rather crushed her.

'I'm sorry,' she said. 'I does usually, honest I does, ma'am. I don't need nothing to eat, I ain't hungry. And I can go away if May's busy. I don't mean any trouble, ma'am, honour bright I don't.'

'All right,' said Mrs Barber, her face softened, almost imperceptibly. 'As it *happens*, Mrs Thornton's been held up at a committee meeting, so we've supper going spare. And in *this* house, I hope we wouldn't make a guest go hungry. But just you remember for next time, you hear me?'

'Yes, ma'am,' said Nell. 'Thank you, ma'am.' And she scurried inside.

May – hearing her voice – was coming down the stairs.

'Hello,' she said. 'Don't mind *La Barber*. She's in an awful wax because Mama's been out every night this week, and Mrs Barber thinks she'll give herself TB or something. Did you ever hear anything so absurd? I say, though, what's up?'

Nell explained. 'It ain't nothing, not really . . .' But the further into the story she got, the more upset she found herself becoming. As she got towards the end, she was horrified to hear her voice begin to wobble and tears start in her eyes. She was going to cry! She never cried! Boys didn't, and if boys didn't, neither would Nell. Living in such close quarters, it was essential to learn how to keep your feelings locked away, and Nell was an expert. Yet here she was, almost crying on May's landing, over something as stupid as this!

May said, 'Nell! Nell, it's all right. Come on. What a beastly man. You don't want to listen to people like him. You never do usually, do you?'

Nell sniffed and rubbed her nose with her sleeve. This was awful! It wasn't at all how you were supposed to behave, especially around your girl. Men might drink, when things got bad, but they never, ever cried. Nell didn't think she'd ever seen her father cry. Not when the baby died. Not when Bernie had diphtheria. Never.

'Naw,' she said, turning her head away. She felt she couldn't bear sympathy, on top of everything else. She could face any cruelty, but kindness always destroyed her.

'Hush. Hush. Nell. Darling Nell.' May's hands were on her face, and she was kissing her, her eyes, her cheeks, her mouth, her nose. Nell was shaking. 'Nell. Nell, my love. It doesn't matter what they think. I love you. That's what matters. Darling Nell, please don't cry.'

Nell pulled herself away.

'You what?'

'I love you. Didn't you know?'

Nell blinked at her. She rubbed her eyes, trying to buy herself time, to take in what she'd said. May loved her! Her! Nell! A blazing star of a girl like May, and she loved her! It wasn't possible. It bewildered her.

'Aren't you pleased? I won't say it again if you don't want me to.'

Pleased! Pleased was too small a word for what Nell felt. It was as though her whole world had been turned topside-up. She couldn't contain it.

'You love me?'

'Yes.'

'Are you a loony?'

'I don't think so.' Now May was laughing. 'Why? Don't you love me?'

But Nell couldn't sort that one out either. It all seemed so simple for May; you had two people, and they loved each other, and that was that. But May to Nell was more than love. She was joy, and torment, and magic, and terror, and lust, and hope, and despair, and secrets, and truth, and sin. May was a lodestone in a bewildering world. She was everything. How could you take all that and call it love?

But if it wasn't love, what was it?

'Go on now,' she said weakly. May took her hands in hers.

'It's all right,' she said gently. 'I'm not going anywhere. I belong to you, and you belong to me. You know that, don't you? Come back when you've worked it all out. I love you. I promise. I'll be right here, waiting.'

March
1915

I thought of the armies marching now along the great main thoroughfares of Europe, everywhere bringing destruction to peaceful homes . . . the cries of fatherless children, the groans of injured men; a gigantic arrest of human progress . . . beneath all a great hunger, till famine prove the victor . . .

The night long, as I grieved there in my solitude, the men called up to war yelled on, in quenchless mirth.

The Home Front, Sylvia Pankhurst

Tea Parties, Euclid and Knitting

For Evelyn, the first six months of the war passed in something of a daze. She felt strangely dislocated – from the rest of the world, but also from herself. All of the things that had previously ordered her days had disappeared: school, Teddy, her schoolfriends, even the Suffragettes. In the usual course of things, she would have 'come out'. There would have been parties and dances; Evelyn's friend Joyce had been to a dance organised for the entertainment of soldiers, and another to raise money for Belgian refugees. But for a long time, she had been too ill for parties.

Fortunately for Evelyn, as she began to grow stronger, she found that the work for her Oxford Scholarship examinations took up most of her time. To pass these, she would have to know a great deal more than what was taught in a small second-rate private girls' school. She had weekly lessons in Latin and Greek with Miss Dempsey, as well as further sessions at a boy's crammer in Hampstead, wrestling with Euclid and the baffling intricacies of geometry. The work was hard, but it was exactly the sort which suited Evelyn, and it was a relief to be worrying about conjunctions and irregular verbs instead of what might very shortly be happening to Teddy and Christopher. Any time spent not working was swept up by her mother, who insisted that she take part in the busy life of middle-class Hampstead, a seemingly endless round of tea parties, and dinner parties, and bridge parties, and church bazaars, and war work, which mostly seemed to mean knitting. Evelyn and her mother both attended first-aid classes run by the Red Cross, accompanied by an enthusiastic Kezia, whose one hope seemed to be that the war would last until she was old enough to go out to France as a stretcher-bearer.

Teddy and Christopher had both managed to get commissions in London regiments. Neither of them had yet gone out to France; Teddy's regiment was in an army camp near Brighton, while Christopher's was somewhere in Kent. Christopher minded being in England ferociously, but Teddy seemed happy enough where he was. He sent Evelyn letters full of vivid pencil sketches of soldiers, and Brighton children playing in the streets, and still lifes of souvenir shops and army barracks, and revolvers.

'Probably best to burn these as soon as you get them,' he wrote cheerfully. 'Simply frightful things could happen if they get into the wrong hands.' Evelyn didn't burn them, of course, but stuck her favourite pictures up around the mirror on her dressing-table and glared at them whenever she was feeling black-doggish. She was rather surprised by how much she missed him. How ridiculous to feel like this, like a girl in a penny romance! She told herself firmly that she was a modern woman, and had more important things than boys to worry about. But it didn't seem to make much difference. She still missed him like anything.

The Oxford examinations were held at Easter, in a hall full of earnest-looking schoolboys, most of whom had no intention of taking up their places if the war still happened to be going on in October.

'But, of course, it'll probably all be over by then,' one boy told Evelyn gloomily. 'Just my rotten luck my birthday's not till August.'

Evelyn could only hope he was right.

Every Man Will Do His Duty

There were fewer boys in Coney Lane now. It seemed to Bill like everyone had joined up, everyone who was eighteen anyway, though when he said this to Mum she said, 'Don't be so daft! What about Clarence? And Robbie? And Dolly Ivey's Leonard – he's still around, ain't he?'

'Len Ivey is a scab and a wart,' said Bill. 'If he joined the army, he'd probably desert. You don't think I'm like him, Mum, do you?'

'Don't you talk like that about your elders, young man . . .' Mum began, and the subject had been dropped.

Bill longed for conscription, then he would *have* to join up, no matter what Mum said about it. If the war was still going on when he was eighteen. Which it mightn't be.

He was beginning dimly to understand that this war was more than an adventure, or a chance to serve your country. That for the young men of his generation, this would be the defining experience, a bloody Freemasonry to which you would either belong, or would spend your whole life knowing that when this moment had come, you'd been found wanting.

In 1915, Bill was seventeen. You couldn't join the army until you were eighteen, and you couldn't serve overseas until you were nineteen. Unless the war somehow managed to drag on for another year and a half, he would never be part of it.

But the recruiting officers didn't ask for identification. If you said you were nineteen, they took your word for it. Why – Tommy Parkin had joined up last month, and he was younger than Bill was. Everyone on Coney Lane knew he was only sixteen, but no one had said anything. He was in a training camp right now, while Bill was still here, pedalling round the East End on his uncle's bicycle. Though he would never have admitted it to her, Nell's words still rankled. Would she really have joined up, if they'd let girls in the army?

He didn't know. But sometimes he thought she might have done. She wasn't afraid of anything, Nell. There were times when he wondered if what she had said was true. She *would* have been more than a man than he ever would.

The situation at home had eased a little. Their father had finally been allowed to send some of his wages home, which helped. And before that, Miss Pankhurst and the East End Suffragettes had opened a cost-price restaurant in the Women's Hall. You paid for your meals, so the Suffragettes said it wasn't quite charity, but they gave Nell's mother a whole sheet of meal tickets for free and told her to come back for more if she didn't find work.

The restaurant made stews of the sort May's mother liked. Beans and lentils and split peas and root vegetables with the skin left on. Nell thought it sloppy stuff, but it amused her to be eating the same sort of vegetably things May did. Several of the East End women thought it was an outrage, though.

'Who do they think we are? Animals?' Mrs David said furiously. 'You wouldn't eat this muck, would you, miss?'

'I certainly would!' said the woman the Suffragettes had hired to cook the food. Nell recognised the fervour in her voice, and grinned to herself. 'Don't you know, half the good of a vegetable is the skin? Why! In the Irish Potato Famine . . .'

But Nell didn't wait to hear about the Irish Potato Famine. She took her bean stew and her bread, and went to find the rest of her family. Her mother gave her a tired smile.

'Why couldn't the government have done something like this?' she said. 'Instead of leaving it to the women?'

'Too busy making guns,' said Nell briefly. She didn't often agree with May's mother, but on this, she had to admit, she had a point.

To Bill, though, it was degrading, taking charity from women. And it *was* charity, whatever the women said about it. A man was supposed to support his family. Not that anyone expected a seventeen-year-old to support a family of seven, of course. But *still*. Bill had been down the docks, asking if they'd take him on in his father's place, but they hadn't even considered it, not seriously. So many men were out of work now, naturally they wouldn't give a man's job to a boy like him. So he was stuck working for his uncle. As a grocer's *boy*.

Bill's father had rather liked the East End Suffragettes; he thought they had pluck. But Bill knew they were against the war, or Sylvia Pankhurst was, anyway. You only had to read those papers they had lying around the Women's Hall. It drove him to distraction to think he was taking food from traitors and anti-British creatures like that.

There were recruitment posters up all over Poplar and Bow. Men pointing at you and shouting at you and shaming you. Bill had seen women giving out white feathers to men who weren't in uniform; they did it on the high street, right in public in front of everyone. If you were given one, it meant you were a coward. Bill was bicycling down Poplar high street when he saw them, so they hadn't actually given one to him. But they *might* have done.

There was a poster on the wall outside Uncle Jack's grocery:

HOW TO JOIN THE ARMY.

The nearest Recruiting Depot is listed below.
Present yourself personally before the Recruiting Officer,
who will give you all particulars of Terms of Service,
Pay and Allowances. You can be medically examined
and attested at this depot without loss of time.

Every time he walked past it, it felt like an accusation. He'd always said he was going to join the army like his dad, as soon as ever he turned eighteen. What sort of heel would wait until *after* a war was over to join up? And what sort of a time would he have, serving under men who'd actually been there?

Each time he walked past the poster, his resolve grew. It

took such an age to train people, anyway. Even if he joined up tomorrow, he'd probably never actually make it out to France. But it wouldn't matter. It would be something, to say he'd been in the army. Nobody would be able to sneer at him then.

It was a wet day in March when he came home late from work. The kitchen was the usual suppertime chaos: Dot and Bernie fighting over the right way to lay the table, Siddy crying because he wasn't allowed to play with the bread knife, Nell complaining to anyone who would listen about the crowds outside the factories waiting for day-work, and why didn't the government set them planting vegetables, or something, if we were all so blimming short of food?

Bill took off his cap, threw it onto the table and said, 'You can have my job if you wants it. I quit.'

'You what?' Nell stared at him. 'Why?'

Bill didn't look at her.

'Cos I joined up, that's why.'

She stared at him. He kept her gaze, a challenge in his eyes. *Who's the man now?*

'You never!' Their mother looked up from the dinner pot and the moment was gone. 'William Swancott, you go straight back to that recruiting officer *right now* and tell him you're seventeen. I mean it! War may be going badly, but we ain't desperate enough to start sending kids to the Front Line, and we ain't about to start with you.'

'No,' said Bill. He took off his jacket and hung it on the coat hook on the back of the door. He turned to face his mother. '*And* I told them I were nineteen, so I expect they'll send me to France. You ain't stopping me, Mum. It's my war too. And I'll send home money and all, once I'm settled.'

Nell, over by the fireside, could see her mother trying to decide whether it was worth marching down to the Recruiting Office herself, and deciding against it.

'And anyway,' Bill went on. 'I've done it now. I can't leave, it'd be desertion. Imagine what Dad would say if I deserted!'

Their mother started to argue, but Nell could see that it would be no good. Bill had won.

She watched him, torn between envy and dread, guilt and pride and fear.

How much of this was her fault?

The Sniper and the Hun

Nell lay on May's bed and stared at the soot stains on the ceiling. May was talking about conscription, which she and her mother were sure was going to happen soon, and what a disaster it would be if it did. Nell found she couldn't summon much energy to care. If there weren't enough soldiers, you'd have to get some from somewhere, wouldn't you? The Germans had conscription, didn't they? So if we wanted to beat them, we'd probably have to have it too. This was so self-evidently obvious to Nell, she was baffled that it seemed such an evil to May. But arguing with May was never a good idea. It wasn't as though you stood any chance of getting her to listen to you.

The longer the war went on, the harder Nell was finding it to sympathise with May's pacifism. Right now, her father was in the middle of his first battle, in a godawful-sounding place in Belgium called Ypres, which nobody knew how to pronounce. Nell had always imagined battles lasted a day or two; you lined up your men, they lined up theirs, you both charged, and when the smoke had cleared, you counted up the casualties and declared one side or the other the winner. But these battles just seemed to go on and on and on, and the whole time Ypres did, you couldn't forget that Dad was in it. You flinched every time there was a knock on the door, in case it was a telegram. You couldn't bear to read the casualty lists in the newspapers, but *not* reading them was worse. Imagine if something happened to Dad, and someone like Mrs O'Farrell found it out first! It didn't bear thinking about.

'Mama thinks they might make an exception for people with a conviction against fighting. But I don't expect they will. It's not like anyone in this idiotic country even *believes* in pacifism. Even you don't, not really.'

Nell had hoped her uncle might give her Bill's job, but this hadn't happened.

'You're having a laugh, ain't you?' he'd said, when she'd asked. 'Get your mum to teach you sewing, love, you're too old to mess about like this.'

He'd given the job to her cousin Lionel, who was not-quite fourteen and awful. He stole, and pinched, and needed everything explained to him three times over before he understood it. Nell wasn't sure whether to laugh or weep.

'Hmm?' She realised May expected her to respond. 'I believe in pacifism! I want peace just as much as you. I just . . . well, war's *here*, ain't it? I don't see what good not fighting's going to do, except make the Germans win.'

'But it's not about what *good* it does,' said May, sitting upright on her knees. Nell recognised the zeal in her little face, and groaned inwardly. Quakers were called Quakers because early Friends were supposed to quake with the power of the

Holy Spirit. May, Nell thought grimly, would have fit right in. 'If you've got a religious conviction against fighting – which we do, because it says in the Bible *Thou shalt not kill*, and you can't argue with that, can you? – then it doesn't matter what happens after you kill someone. The point is, killing is wrong, full stop, so whatever happens after it is wrong, no matter how good you think it's going to be.'

'That's cracked,' said Nell, goaded at last. 'Like – what if some Hun were going to blow up a school, and you could stop him by shooting him, but you didn't, cos you was a Quaker, and then he blew up the school. All them kids would be dead, and it would be your fault. You'd have killed them just as much as the Hun did.'

'I would not!' said May, delighted. 'That's such rot. You might as well say their parents killed them by sending them to school. Real life doesn't work like that. And you can't *know* he's is going to blow up the school. Maybe he'd change his mind. And you can't *know* what's going to happen if you kill him either. Maybe all his friends will come and blow up the Kensington Olympia in revenge. By that argument,' said May, with relish, 'you could do *anything* if you thought the ends justified the means. You could kill Mama and give all her money to the poor. Or the king – he's got heaps of cash. I bet you'd save loads of lives if you killed the king and sold the Crown Jewels and gave the money to poor kids. But you don't. Cos it's wrong. So.'

This was why Nell hated arguing with May. She was wrong. Nell was sure she was wrong. But she just twisted up all your arguments and left you in a tangled mess, trying to follow the threads.

'But this ain't a real Hun,' she said, deciding to ignore May's unexpected plot to bring down the monarchy. 'He's a pretend one. Say you *knew* you could save them kids. There's a Hun with an actual gun, actually shooting people right now. And you's a sniper and you can stop him. You would, wouldn't you?'

'No, I jolly well would not,' said May. 'And don't say Hun, that's an awful word. Germans don't go around shooting kids any more than we do; it's just propaganda, Mama says. But I still wouldn't. I'd try and stop him without hurting him. I'd go and tell the police—'

'Who'd shoot him. How's it different if they does it and not you?'

'Because they're the police! You can be against the army and for the police! The police try *not* to kill people if they can avoid it. The army kill as many as they possibly can! If we were sending an army of policemen to arrest the Germans, I wouldn't have a problem!'

'I would!' said Nell. 'They'd get blown to bits.'

'Well, that would be unfortunate,' said May, with dignity.

Nell began to giggle. After a pause, May joined in.

'Goodness,' said Nell. 'You is a card, you know that, don't you?'

'But you love me anyway?' said May. She had been asking this a lot lately, teasingly, like it was a joke, like it didn't mean anything. She did it so as to get Nell used to the idea. To try and fool her into thinking it didn't matter whether they loved each other or not. But it did matter. Of course it did. And the longer Nell brushed it aside, the worse it was, she knew.

May had never said she loved her again. But those words, once said, couldn't be unsaid.

And after all, *didn't* Nell love her? So why was she so afraid to say so?

Keeping her tone very carefully light, she kissed the top of May's head, so as not to have to look into her eyes.

'Course I does,' she said. 'You're me girl, ain't you? Even if you is a loon.'

Bloody Men

The telegram came on Saturday while the family were eating dinner.

'Telegram for Miss Evelyn,' said Iris, and Evelyn started. No one ever cabled her, except relations on her eighteenth birthday, as a sort of treat. It must be from Teddy.

It was. It read: SHOVING OFF MONDAY MOTHER AND FATHER MOTORING DOWN TOMORROW CAN YOU? BEST LOVE T

'Shoving off?' said Hetty, who was reading over her shoulder. (Wasn't anyone *ever* going to teach these kids manners?) 'Does that mean going to France? He's going to France!'

'Oh, darling,' said her mother. She held out a hand to Evelyn, who ignored it.

'Mr and Mrs Moran are going down to Brighton to say goodbye,' she said. 'Teddy wants me to come too – I may, mayn't I?'

'Tomorrow?' Her mother expression changed. 'Oh dear, I don't think so.'

'Why ever not?'

'Well –' Her mother's face twisted. 'An army camp, darling, really?'

'Teddy's parents are going to be there,' said Evelyn. 'I'm hardly going to wander about on my own and wait to be ravished!'

This was exactly the wrong thing to say. Her father said, 'Evelyn!'

And Hetty said, 'What does ravished mean? Daddy?'

And Kezia, with maddening superiority, 'It's *frightfully* rude, Het, you wouldn't like it a bit.'

'Please don't be tiresome, Evelyn,' her mother said. You would think she was a child, the way they treated her! 'And anyway –' as though this closed the discussion – 'you know Aunt Mary is coming tomorrow, so you couldn't possibly. Could you pass the mustard, Kezia?'

Kezia passed the mustard with a rather mulish expression. Evelyn sat, astonished. Had that just happened? Had her mother really just told her she couldn't go? She wasn't a schoolgirl any more. She was eighteen. She was engaged to be married. If something awful happened to Teddy, this could be the last time she ever saw him. She experienced once again the bewildering sense that here she was, dealing with life-shatteringly adult experiences, while living with people who insisted on treating her like a sulky child.

'You can't forbid it,' she said. 'You simply *can't*.'

'And yet it seems I have,' her mother said stiffly. She had been far too relaxed with Evelyn, and look what had happened as a result. She liked Teddy's parents very much, but she had still not forgiven Teddy's mother for that awful Suffragette meeting where Evelyn had apparently got into this whole mess in the first place. And as for letting them chaperone her daughter – well!

Evelyn's mother had already had to suffer a daughter in a prison cell, and had accepted that she would probably have to suffer a daughter at a university. She was not about to suffer a daughter who was an unmarried mother, particularly since Teddy could hardly be made to marry her if he were blown to bits.

She had no intention of explaining this at the dinner table, however, and since Evelyn had only the vaguest notion of how babies were conceived, this part of her mother's reasoning passed her by entirely. She was horrified.

'But he could *die*,' she said. 'This might be the last chance I have to see him, *ever*. Imagine if it were Kit or Father! Imagine how you'd feel! Imagine how you'll feel if he gets *killed*!'

'I expect I'll be able to live with myself,' said her mother, who knew full well that were anything to happen to Teddy, she would probably remember today for the rest of her life.

'I hope Kit gets shot to pieces, and then you'll know how I feel!' Evelyn said furiously, and was sent to her room in disgrace.

The next morning, when she came downstairs all prepared to sulk and rage, there was a letter waiting on the breakfast table for her. It informed her that she had been awarded a place to study Classics at Somerville College, starting in October. She was so blindsided by this that she could only stare.

The breakfast table was as noisy as usual. Hetty and Kezia were squabbling about lipstick.

'Scarlet lipstick,' Kezia was saying, 'and long red nails, like talons. That's what I'm going to have. And those eyebrows that look like they've been painted on. And—'

'Lipstick is vulgar,' said Hetty, and Kezia said, snubbingly, 'People of twelve don't know the first thing about it.'

'I do!' Hetty cried, indignant. 'I do know! Captain said—'

Evelyn dropped the letter onto the table.

'You might be interested to know,' she said. 'That they've offered me a place. At Oxford.'

There was a pause while the family absorbed this information. Then her father said, 'My dear! Congratulations.'

And Kezia said, 'Great Scott!' and made everybody laugh. Evelyn scowled. She still wanted to be angry, and it didn't suit her at all to be happy and congratulated. Mostly what she felt was frustration, that what should have been a grand and important moment had been spoilt by the awfulness of Teddy going to the Front.

Later, upstairs in her room, she wrote him a long and furious letter about it. *Everything I ever do gets overshadowed by Bloody Men,* she wrote, and then tore the whole thing up. It was impossible to be angry or self-absorbed in letters to someone who was busy packing their bags to go to war. Your letter might so easily be the last thing they ever read.

Nobody, she thought, in a sudden rage, understood what it was like to be told something was the most important thing in all the world, to follow it, to *believe* in it, and then to have it pulled away from underneath you.

It didn't help that she wasn't at all sure whether her most important thing had been the right to an education, or votes for women, or if, in fact, it had always been Teddy all along.

Cranquettes

For much of the early part of 1915, May's mother had a new scheme; helping to organise the Women's Peace Congress.

The Women's Peace Congress was going to be held in the Hague. Representations were going to be sent from all of the warring countries, and many of the neutral ones too. It wasn't just going to be suffragists either, although it was mostly the suffragists who were doing the organising. All sorts of women's organisations had been invited. Women lawyers. Women factory workers. And so on.

'Mama says,' said May to Mrs Barber, as she helped her clean the family silver, 'that the fighting countries couldn't ask the neutral countries to negotiate peace without looking weak. But women can. We don't care about looking weak the way men do. Just think! What if we managed to stop the war – women like us?'

'I'll believe that when it happens, dearie,' said Mrs Barber doubtfully. Mrs Barber, May thought, had a very prosaic mind.

To May, the conference was everything wonderful. It was hope, and vindication, and pride, and proof; proof that women could do everything men could do. Stop the war! Why not? Women, talking, peace-making, doing all the things women always did, in homes across the world. Wasn't that a better way to end a conflict than standing in a trench getting shot at?

This was real peace work, and the thought of it made May blaze with the joy of it. This wasn't the sort of peace work where you stood aside and let the German soldier blow up the children. This was stopping the gunner, stopping *all* the gunners, stopping everything.

Nobody else was talking to people on the other side of the war, as far as May could see. Nobody except the women. Imagine if they *did* make peace!

Wouldn't *that* be one in the eye for Barbara?

For most of the first half of 1915, she lived for the conference. She begged her mother to be allowed to address envelopes, fold letters, do whatever needed doing to help. One hundred and eighty women were going to the conference as British representatives, including Nell's heroine, Sylvia Pankhurst. May's mother was going too. It was more complicated than it would have been this time last year, due to the introduction of something called a passport. You had to apply for one before you could leave the country; supposedly to stop you travelling to Germany and fraternising with the enemy.

'But you *are* going to be fraternising with the enemy,' said Mrs Barber.

'I certainly hope so!' said May's mother. 'Don't worry, though,' she added, unpinning her hat and letting it drop onto the sideboard. 'What harm can us women do anyway?'

At first, it seemed as though the British government were going to take this line. But then, a week before the conference, it was announced that all of the women were to be refused permits – the Home Office having decided that it would be 'inconvenient' to hold a political conference so close to the war. One of the organisers managed to secure a meeting with the Home Secretary, who agreed to issue passports to twenty-four of the women, not including May's mother. But there was little time to celebrate. Almost immediately afterwards, it was announced that an Admiralty Order had closed the North Sea to all shipping until further notice.

'Well!' said May's mother. 'You can't say the government isn't taking us seriously now!'

'You'd think they *wanted* to be at war,' said May. But she had to admit that such a public condemnation was rather thrilling.

The newspapers, however, disagreed. The *Daily Express* ran an article describing the women as 'cranquettes' and 'sorrowful spinsters'. Other newspapers were similarly scathing.

May's mother was serene. 'Better to be mocked than ignored,' she said. 'Mockery means they're worried.'

In the end, it was decided that – as it had been promised that passports *would* be issued to the women – the best thing to do was to send all the delegates to Tilbury, since it was understood that one last boat would still be allowed to leave for Holland. A special train was put on from London, and May and Mrs Barber went to see it off. It was rather exciting to spot all the famous Suffragettes – Mrs Barber was particularly impressed with Lady Ottoline Morrell, the celebrated pacifist.

But both of them were left feeling rather depressed when the train had pulled away without them.

'Next time your mama starts looking for a new project, can we campaign for equal rights to seaside excursions?' said Mrs Barber.

It seemed, however, that even equality for women was too much to ask for. First the British representatives were told that there would not be enough time to process their passports before the boat sailed. Then they were told not to worry as another boat would be sailing. At last, the passports appeared. But as the Home Secretary handed them over, he informed the women that another Admiralty Order had been issued, and the new boat had now also been cancelled.

Furious, May's mother and the other British 'peacettes' waited in Tilbury. They waited a week. They waited another. They waited while women in the Netherlands laid out the terms on which peace would have to be made, and argued about how women activists might help that peace come to fruition. And in Bow, May waited for news from her mother. She made Mama promise that she would cable just as soon as ever there was good news, even just tiny good news, even if just one delegate was allowed to go, on a sailing boat even, anything.

Just tell me, Mama, promise, she wrote, and her mother promised.

But no cable arrived.

And then the conference was over, and no boat had come.

A dugout in the dark
THE FRONT
Somewhere in France

Darling Evelyn,

I am writing this UNDER FIRE. Other soldiers might faint, or tremble, or wave machine-guns about. NOT ME. I am sitting at this rickety little table, as close to the lamp as I can get, and calmly writing you a love letter. 'Of what great stuff is that Edward Moran made of!' you no doubt exclaim. I don't suppose you had the slightest idea what a dashing young fellow you were engaged to. Well, to be frank, neither did I. Maybe all that yelling they did at basic training has done me some good.

Heavens! That was rather a close one. They make a tremendous noise coming down, and all the earth shakes, and things sort of leap up into the air; you have to keep a tight hold on the ink jar and the lanterns, or you risk starting a fire. It's rather thrilling, actually. To be at the centre of the action at last, after so long hanging around at the edges. Reminds me of the time I was finally allowed up to bat at prep school after two terms as Third Reserve. I was so nervous, I whacked the ball straight up in the air, it landed right in the wicket-keeper's hands, and that was the end of my brilliant cricket career.

Thanks for the chocolate and the slippers – they have been much admired! Here is a picture of me protecting the Line in the nicest slippers this side of Paris.

They're calling for me – I'd better go.

Best love,
Teddy

The Lusitania

The beginning of May, and the war had suddenly come much closer to home for Nell.

Since the start of 1915, the newspapers had been full of the new submarine warfare. Not content with firing on naval shipping, U-boats had begun attacking merchant ships carrying food and other supplies to Britain. Everyone in Poplar agreed that this was just the sort of thing you would expect from Germans. May pointed out that we were doing exactly the same thing in the Adriatic, and how exactly was a naval campaign designed to starve German civilians any better?

May had a very irritating habit of popping up in Nell's head when Nell least wanted her.

Nell heard about the sinking of the *Lusitania* at work. She'd picked up a week's worth of day-work in a bottle factory, and was busy, like the other girls, putting on her hat ready for the journey home. The late editions of the newspapers were being called in the street. The forewoman came into the hallway holding the paper.

'Have you heard the news?' she said.

They crowded around her. LUSITANIA TORPEDOED BY GERMAN PIRATE, the headline read. A passenger ship. Not even a British passenger ship; a neutral American liner. Shot at without warning by an enemy submarine.

'There's a thousand people dead, they think!' the forewoman said.

A thousand people. The girls couldn't comprehend it. It was like the *Titanic* all over again, but this time it was people who'd done this thing. The war. Nell could hear May's voice in her head: *Now can't you see what an awful thing war is?*

But the other factory girls took a different view of things.

'It's a disgrace, that's what it is!' said Betty, who worked next to Nell. 'How could anyone torpedo a passenger ship? With women and children aboard!'

'That's just what them Boche is like,' said another girl, with a ferocity which surprised Nell. 'They don't care about people – they just want to win the war. They's all the same. We have to show them we won't stand for it, that's all!'

May's voice in the back of Nell's head was asking how exactly vowing to fight a war until 'the last man standing' – as the British government had done – showed a concern for human life. Nell thought May was probably wrong about this – torpedoing women and children was a different thing to killing soldiers who were, after all, trying to kill you – but she was still taken aback by the other girl's words.

'Not *all* Germans is like that,' she said cautiously, thinking of May.

But the girl wouldn't listen. 'They ain't like us,' she said firmly. 'They ain't been brought up civilised like what we has.'

The view in Coney Lane when Nell went home was somewhat more sanguine. Nell's mother, rather predictably said, 'Ain't it a shame?' and 'Them poor little kiddies.' But, perhaps influenced by Miss Pankhurst and those bits of the *Woman's Dreadnought* Nell had brought home, she said very little about the Germans.

Mrs O'Farrell, bringing up the post, muttered rather darkly that, 'Someone ought to teach them what's what,' but no one paid her much attention – it was lunchtime, and the kitchen was in its usually Sunday-lunchtime chaos, with six people in the dining room at once, all trying to eat, all taking up more space than there really was to fill.

After lunch, Nell, feeling restless, wandered out into the street. The children were playing soldiers again, marching up and down, with broom handles for rifles tucked under their arms. Nell wanted to tell them that it wasn't a game, that their brothers and fathers really were dying in a real war.

But probably they knew that already.

The older boys gathered on the street corner were talking about the *Lusitania*. Nell hopped onto the wall beside them. It was much the same sort of things the factory girls had been saying, but here there was another undertone. That same line Mrs O'Farrell had said: 'Someone ought to teach them a lesson.'

And this time the boys were nodding in agreement.

'Take Mrs Danks,' George Cormack was saying. 'I never trusted her. What's she doing in this country, anyway? Why doesn't she go back home where she belongs?'

Mrs Danks was the German wife of Mr Danks, the

tobacconist on the corner. Nell said, fairly, 'Well, she's married to Mr Danks. And she got kids here, ain't she? And anyway, they doesn't let people go to Germany any more, you know they doesn't.'

'I bet they'd let Huns go back to Germany if they wanted to,' said George. 'Why! I'd be ashamed to live in enemy land, if I were her. I reckon she's a spy.'

The other boys made noises of assent.

Nell hooted. 'A spy! What's she got to spy on in Poplar?'

'There's all sorts,' said Robbie Farr, stoutly. 'There's . . . there's heaps of soldiers in Poplar now, and . . . and there's morale . . . Huns is always wanting to know about morale on the Home Front, ain't they? And anyway –' and this was indignant – 'even if she ain't a spy, that ain't the point. They ain't like us, Germans. George is right. We ought to show them they ain't wanted here no more.'

There was more murmuring from the boys, but this time there was a sort of purpose to it. George got up and picked up a stone from the road. He tossed it reflectively from hand to hand.

As though it was a signal, Robbie got up and picked up another stone, a bigger one. The other boys stood too, a little warily. Nell could see one or two of them glancing at each other uncertainly – *Are we really going to do this? Were* they really going to do this? They weren't, were they? But there was something of the same feeling as one got before a Suffragette action, the same tense, communal waiting, the same sense of people nerving themselves up. Nell had waved banners while women had thrown stones through windows, and flung themselves on policemen in the hope of being arrested. She recognised the tension, and then the glorious exhilaration of release. It was like fighting when you were a kid. It was like finally telling someone what you really thought of them. It was the joy of doing something violent, and brutal, and forbidden. It was wonderful, but it was dangerous. It could get you killed, and if it didn't, it could get someone else killed.

The boys didn't know that, though. They stood, looking warily at each other, and at George, who was still tossing his stone from hand to hand. After a moment, he moved away, almost idly, as though his mind were on something else altogether, towards the high street. The other boys followed.

Nell, rather unwillingly, hopped off the wall and joined them.

'What's you doing?' she said, although she knew the answer, of course she did. 'George? This ain't funny.'

'Who's laughing?' said Robbie. George didn't answer.

They moved, with the same dreamy, unspoken air, onto the high street. Most of the shops were closed of course, it being a Sunday, although the pub on the corner was still open for luncheon, and there was a clump of older men outside with beer tankards, watching the passing traffic and laughing. A newspaper boy passed by, still calling out about the *Lusitania*. A motor omnibus went past, with a lady conductor on the back step, rammed full of people coming back from work. Most of the London 'buses had gone to France, Nell knew. Right now they were full of soldiers, travelling to the Front. The thought made her rather sad. Even the 'buses had gone to war.

The boys had picked up more stones and rocks along the

way. There was a tumbledown wall by the church which provided them with several pockets full. Nell had had stones thrown at her before. They hurt if they hit you, but mostly they were easier to avoid than the wet rubbish, which stuck in your hair and stained your clothes. But she knew other Suffragettes who had not been so lucky. Miss Urwin had had her arm badly broken where a stone had hit it. And she had never seen eight boys all going against one person before. It worried her.

'You ain't going to throw them stones at Mrs Danks, is you?' she said, uneasily.

'They killed all them kids on the *Lusitania*,' said Robbie. 'They didn't care, did they? This is war. It ain't a picnic.'

'But you ain't at war with *Mrs Danks*,' said Nell. She heard, suddenly, May's voice in her head, talking about the Germans who had been sent to internment camps. *They think they're the enemy.* And she'd replied, *They is the enemy.* Which they were, of course. But not *Mrs Danks*.

The Danks' tobacconist's was next to another pub. It was closed, of course, but there was a light on in the flat above the shop.

'They're in,' said Nell.

'Good,' said George. Then he drew back his arm and flung the stone through the window.

The window shattered with a glorious *SMASH!* People passing in the street stopped to look, but no one intervened. The younger boys cheered. One – a year or so older than Bernie – threw another stone through another pane. Another *SMASH*. Tremendous. Nell shivered. Oh, she'd *missed* this.

'Filthy Boche!' shouted George, and the other boys joined in.

'Hun-lover!'

'Sausage-eater!'

'Baby-killer!'

'Stop it!' cried Nell.

The door to the flat opened, and Mr Danks came out. He was a large, red-faced man, and he was holding a poker in what he obviously hoped was a threatening manner.

'What the bleeding hell do you think you're doing?' Mr Danks said.

The boys quietened. For the first time, they began to look uneasy. They glanced at each other, looking for a leader. Robbie said, boldly, 'Tell your wife to go back home.'

'She is home,' said Mr Danks. He stepped forward and the boys retreated. Perhaps that was all that was needed. Perhaps nothing was going to happen after all. Behind Mr Danks in the dark hallway, Nell could see the pale faces of several children, including a boy a little older than Johnnie, with thick yellow hair. Did their father know they were there?

But now the men from the pub had seen what was happening. One, a large man with a reddish beard and a tattoo in the shape of an anchor, came over to them. He reached into the tobacconist's window and, with a quiet, but rather menacing deliberateness, pulled out a pack of cigars.

'The spoils of war, eh, boys?' he said. He opened the packet, pulled out a cigar and stuck it in his mouth. Then, with the same deliberate calm, he struck a match and lit it.

'Oh, you can't!' Nell cried. 'Stop it, can't you? What's Mrs Danks ever do to you?'

Another child's face had appeared at the upstairs window. The man shook his fist at it. He picked up a stone and aimed it at the window where the child was. The face ducked down. The man flung the stone and the window imploded. Nell said, 'You *brute*!'

The man turned on her.

'You what?' he said, but before Nell could answer, she was interrupted by a furious voice.

'You! Here, you! George Cormack! Does your mother know what you're doing?'

It was Mrs Cohen, one of the Suffragettes. She grabbed George by the arm, and shook him. 'Throwing bricks through a poor citizen's window! Ought to be ashamed of yourself, you ought! And you!' She turned on Nell.

Nell said hastily, 'I weren't! I were trying to stop them!'

'And a piss-poor job you was making of it, wasn't you?' said Mrs Cohen. She glared at the man with the cigar in his mouth. 'And you can piss off back home, and all!'

The man looked at her levelly, his eyes lingering on the old VOTES FOR WOMEN badge on her coat collar. He took the cigar out of his mouth and ground it, very deliberately on the pavement.

'Women like you,' he said slowly, 'makes me sick to think of yer. Get yourself back home to yer poor kids where you belongs.'

Then he pulled back his arm and punched Mrs Cohen in the mouth.

The boys gasped. Mr Danks thrust his children back through the door and shut it on them.

'Oh, you *swine*,' he said, almost joyfully, and leapt down the step, poker raised. The man from the pub's friends surged forward.

Mrs Cohen yelled, 'You cowards! Why ain't you in France, if you cares so much about beating up Germans?'

Nell leapt into the fray. For the first time in almost a year, she felt alive. This is what it was about! Fists, and knuckles, and all that ju-jitsu the Suffragettes had taught her, all those months ago in Victoria Park. May might sneer at violence, but that was only because she didn't know how glorious it could be.

A righteous fury, condensed into the end of a fist.

At last!

By the time the policemen arrived, she had bruises all down one side of her stomach, a bleeding hand, and the traditional Suffragette bird's-nest hair. Mrs Cohen fared worse – three cracked ribs and a foot that she couldn't walk on for a week. But Nell didn't care. Mrs Cohen had called her 'A hero' and even George and the other boys had been grudgingly admiring. No one else on Coney Lane knew ju-jitsu. Only May had been a bit sniffy – 'You *punched* him?' she'd said, when Nell told her about it – but Nell didn't even care. As far as she was concerned, it was worth it.

The Danks closed up their shop and moved out of Poplar. Nell never did find out what happened to them.

And for the first time, the war felt like something real.

October
1915

Why We Oppose Votes For Men

.1.

Because man's place is in the army.

.2.

Because no really manly man wants to settle any question otherwise than by fighting about it.

.3.

Because if men should adopt peaceable methods women will no longer look up to them.

.4.

Because men will lose their charm if they step out of their natural sphere and interest themselves in other matters than feats of arms, uniforms and drums.

.5.

Because men are too emotional to vote. Their conduct at baseball games and political conventions shows this, while their innate tendency to appeal to force renders them particularly unfit for the task of government.

Alice Duer Miller, 1915

A sunny window-seat, overlooking a quad
Oriel College
Oxford
October 1915

Dearest Teddy,

Thank you for your letter, which arrived last week. Your French farmer family sounds wonderful! I love the story about your corporal and the goose – it jolly well serves him right! And I can just picture you making pictures for the little French children. Say 'salut!' from me and tell them to keep my best boy safe until he comes home.

I am now a student! Miss Collis, studying Classics at Somerville College. Except right now we're all living in Oriel, because Somerville is a soldiers' hospital. I feel v. queer and grown up and rather as though I were playing a part. I suspect the other girls all feel just the same, but of course no one admits to anything, and we all go about smoking cigarettes and talking a little more loudly than necessary about Great Works of Literature.

Have been here a week and a half and so far all is well. The girls on my corridor are jolly good sorts. We all said we were sure we would not be up to the work – we shall see! The reading lists are fairly ghastly, I own, but since I fought so hard to get here, I suppose I must just put my head down and get on with it.

Mother brought the little girls to help see me settled in. We took them for a punt and ices on the Isis. They thought Oxford very grand, and were particularly taken with the RAF aeroplanes, which all take off from Port Meadow. Hetty says she would like to be a student and read all day, Kezia not very taken with the gown and hat, said they made me look a guy (they do, a little, but am v. proud to be wearing them, so do not care). Hetty sends you a kiss and her best love, and wants to know if you have met any Germans yet. Kezia asks me to tell you not to get killed. I told her you had no intention of doing any such thing, but she said to tell you anyway, and so I do. I hope this letter will make you smile and remember;

Your own,
Evelyn

Another Telegram

They'd been at war for over a year. Nell's father had been promoted to sergeant, out there in Belgium somewhere. His letters sounded cheerful enough, but then, Dad always did. Dad wasn't one to grumble. You heard such awful stories about the trenches, but Nell knew, no matter how dreadful things got, Dad would never dream of saying anything that might worry Mum. His letters were full of the excellent rations, the good lads in his platoon, and kisses to the babies. And that was it.

Once again, the East End Suffragettes had come through for the Swancotts. Miss Pankhurst had opened a toy factory. Most toys in Britain had come from Germany, and were now in short supply. She got several of her art-school friends to design stuffed animals and wooden toys, and the East End women made them up. There was a nursery for the babies and children too small to go to school, which also provided food and milk for children who had been nearly starving to death.

'They pays properly too, Mum!' said Nell, but her mother didn't need persuading. She loved Miss Pankhurst, and she adored the nursery. There were more toys there than Johnnie and Siddy had seen in their entire lives, including a real-life rocking horse like something from the story books Nell remembered from Board School. To hear Nell's mother talk, the nursery might be the most wonderful thing that had ever happened to her.

Nell's mother was one of the women chosen to stitch up the toys. It was simple enough sewing, and the wages were, of course, good. The Suffragettes were rather lax about work rates and keeping to time; Nell's mother was used to piece-work, and it made a welcome change to be paid by the hour.

None of the East End ladies had ever run a business before, so there were a few hiccups at first, but generally speaking, the toys were well received. There were baby dolls in all the different colours one found in the East End – black, white and brown – and all sorts of animals beyond the usual nursery bears. Even Selfridges put in an order.

'Just think!' said Nell's mother. 'Dukes and duchesses shop in Selfridges. Perhaps one of them will buy one of our toys for their children!'

'We should put grenades in them,' said Nell, only half joking.

Although many of the women had done sewing work before, few had any woodworking experience. Miss Pankhurst had found a German gentleman called Mr Neiderhofer to explain how the German toys were made. Nell grinned a little to herself when she heard about him. It was just like Miss Pankhurst to hire a German. A few of the women muttered to themselves when they heard about his appointment, although of course no one would say anything directly to Miss Pankhurst. And actually, most of them found themselves liking gentle, dignified Mr Neiderhofer. Nell did, when she came in to see where her mother worked. Perhaps, she thought, May's mother might have been more right about the Germans than she cared to admit.

The money Nell's mother earned – with the half pay their father sent them – was enough to keep the family solvent. Nell had still not been able to find full-time work, but she picked up bits of day-work and odd-jobs – an afternoon minding a baby here, some work in her uncle's shop there. It was frustrating, when people were so obviously needed to replace the men who'd gone to the Front, that everyone was still so reluctant to employ women. For the first few months of the war at least, it had seemed that girls were allowed to knit socks or be nurses or nursing assistants, and not much else.

Bill's ambitions were similarly frustrated. He was still stuck at a training camp, waiting to go out. Nobody seemed to have realised he was only seventeen. He wrote them short, dull, dutiful letters on the backs of the letters Mum sent. *The weather is good. We are not going to France yet. Love to all.* Nell was grateful that she didn't have to worry about him yet. Which made the news, when it came, all the more appalling.

Nell had picked up another piece of day-work; minding a neighbour's children while she visited a wounded husband in a London hospital. The telegram was waiting on the table when she came home, she knew as soon as she walked into the door what it said.

Dad. Her lovely dad had been killed.

But it wasn't Dad. It was Bill.

Bill. Bill who was underage, Bill who needn't have joined up at all. He hadn't even made it to France; he'd been killed in an accident on a training exercise. You couldn't even pretend he'd died for his country, although she supposed he had, technically. Bill. Bill who had cared so much about being a man, and who had only gone because she had said those awful things to him.

And now he was dead.

Nell felt numb with it. Her mother had obviously been crying, and so had Bernie and Johnnie; Dot was standing by the table, twisting her hands around her skirts, looking very pale.

She couldn't take it in, it didn't feel real. All she could think of was practical things; someone would have to tell her father (her mother could barely write and her words were dreadfully chicken-scratchings-y, normally she dictated her letters to Bernie or Nell). Someone would have to put the dinner on. Bill's wages wouldn't be coming in now, and someone would have to make up that shortfall.

Bill was dead.

And it was her fault.

'Oh, Mum,' she said. And then, 'I'll put the kettle on,' because she couldn't think of anything else to say.

And Bernie said, 'Mum, when I'm grown up, *I'll* be a soldier like Bill and won't I make them sweat for what they done to him?'

And her mother said, 'No, you bleeding well will not!'

And Bernie started to argue, and Nell had a sudden, horrible urge to laugh, because if she'd sat down and imagined the scene: Family Receive Tragic News of Son's Death, she wouldn't have imagined anything remotely like this. But then her mother began to weep again, and curse, *curse* the Kaiser and the government and the Germans and Bill himself, and the tears were pouring down her face so that she quite frightened Nell.

And Nell was the oldest now. The man of the family.

Because Bill was dead.

'Mum, please,' she said. And, to Dot, 'Here, run and get some brandy from Uncle Jack, can't you? Mum's had a shock.' And Dot, looking somewhat like a rabbit Nell had disturbed once hop-picking in Kent, disappeared out of the door and down the stairs.

And then Uncle Jack was there, and Mrs O'Farrell, and Mrs O'Farrell's eldest two girls, and Jeannie from down the road, and Auntie Maudie was making the tea, and Jeannie was cutting the bread and butter for dinner, and someone else was handing Mum a cigarette, and Nell was a child again.

But she didn't forget.

This is my fault, she thought, watching them all crowded into the tiny room.

And, I've got to make it right.

Though how she might do that, she couldn't imagine.

Later, when she crept out of the house and round to May's to tell her the news, Nell half expected her to be awful about Bill. Not deliberately awful, but just . . . what Nell secretly thought of as straight-through-a-brick-wall awful. Which was Nell-shorthand for, May was exactly the sort of person who would knock a hole through someone else's brick wall, if she thought it was the right thing to do, and then when the wall owner tried to stop her, she wouldn't even apologise. She'd just start trying to convince him she'd been in the right all along.

Which was what the Suffragettes were like too, of course – some of them literally did blow holes in walls.

But it was exhausting, sometimes, when it was your girl doing it, and your brother was dead.

Nell had expected May to say it served Bill right for enlisting, or to tell her this *proved* how awful the war was (as though she'd somehow failed to notice that wars killed people). But actually May did none of these things. She was properly shocked, and sympathetic, and interested, and she wrote Nell's mother a letter saying how sorry she was, which Nell hadn't expected, and she told Mrs Barber (her Mama was out at a committee meeting), and Mrs Barber said it was a shame, and her poor mother, and gave Nell some apple dumplings to take back home to the children.

Nell should have been relieved, but she found the whole thing deeply uncomfortable. She had wanted to be *angry* at May, and instead she found herself having to be grateful.

She *hated* being grateful, and she *particularly* hated being grateful to May, who would always have so much more to give than Nell would ever have to return.

A Sort of Hopelessness

It was a hard autumn, and a hard winter.

All summer, *Jus Suffragii* was full of articles about what a success the Peace Congress had been, but May couldn't help but be depressed. Perhaps Mrs Barber and the girls at school were right. If people really wanted to blow each other up this much, was it mad for the suffragist women to think that *they* could stop them?

The members of the newly formed International Committee of Women for Permanent Peace – 'What names you women do come up with!' said Mrs Barber – were optimistic. They agreed that the next thing to do was to persuade the leaders of neutral countries like America to organise peace talks between the warring countries. Representatives from the conference set off to meet with as many government officials as they could. This was rather exciting, even from a distance – May's mother knew several of the women who were involved in these meetings, and would often greet May cheerfully with announcements like, 'Good news, darling! Woodrow Wilson's agreed to see us!' May often wondered what the girls at school would say if they knew pacifists were industriously travelling all across Europe, meeting with secretaries of state, prime ministers and even the President of the United States. May's mother seemed very optimistic about their chances too – apparently someone in Sweden had said Sweden would actually organise a peace conference if the Suffragettes could prove the warring countries really would accept peace talks, and since all of the warring countries had apparently said they would, this was a very good sign.

'Imagine!' she said. 'If women like us *did* end the war!'

'They really would have to give us a vote then,' said May.

But she found it hard to scrape up much optimism for the International Committee of Women for Permanent Peace and their supposed talks. Surely nothing would actually come to anything?

For Nell, it was a time of bitter, bone-deep unhappiness. After Bill died, a sort of hopelessness had descended on all the Swancotts. Things had been hard before, of course. But you had been fighting for . . . well, for something. And you knew things would come right in the end, somehow, eventually. You just had to put your head down and push through it.

Now . . . well, somehow the heart had gone out of everybody. Mum pretended that everything was still all right, everything was *fine*.

'And get those dirty boots off my nice clean floor! And stop fighting, for *heaven's* sake, couldn't anyone get a *moment's* peace in here, with all these kids blimming *screaming* all the time? Can't you all just get *out* and let me *be*!'

It was like that all the time, or it felt like it. It was exhausting. The little ones felt it too. Dot was so . . . so *angry*, always. You asked her to do something and she'd *argue* with you. 'Why? Why should I look after the baby? Why can't you? Why do *I* have to stay home from school to do the washing? Can't Nell do it? She doesn't have a job. Well, can't Bernie, then?' Nell had been that little girl herself, when she was Dot's age (she suspected this was where Dot got it from). She'd never appreciated how irritating she must have been.

Bernie just went very quiet. Quiet wasn't a quality that got you very far when there were eight of you – six now – living in two rooms. But Bernie had always been like that. (Nell was quiet too, but when she wanted something, she *fought* for it. Bernie just worried over it, like a dog with a bone.) He was Nell's favourite brother, all elbows and knees and round blue eyes. She worried about him. She'd always worried about him.

'All right, Bern?' she said, and he looked at her over his bread and margarine and said, 'Nell, is someone going to shoot Dad too?'

'Dad!' she said. 'No fear! Them Boers didn't get him in South Africa, did they? And he's ever so much older and clev-erer now than he were then. I expect them Germans is more worried about him getting *them*.'

She smiled at him, but the blue eyes didn't look persuaded.

And then, at the beginning of December, Dad *was* hit. Not dangerously, thank God; a piece of shrapnel had embedded itself in his leg. But it would mean several months in England, in hospital and convalescing. And as long as he was at home, he wouldn't be earning.

He'd asked to be taken to a London hospital, but in the usual bureaucratic chaos had somehow ended up in Liverpool. Nell's mother had managed to scrape together the money for the fare to visit him, but there hadn't been enough for the children to come too. Nell's mother said he seemed cheerful enough, only rather worried about the family. He'd sent Bernie and Johnnie cap-badges taken from German prisoners of war, a little wooden peg-doll for Dot, and kisses for all the rest.

Now the family had lost Bill's money *and* Dad's money within two months. It was just like last year all over again. Every time they got themselves together, Nell thought fiercely, something else always bloody went wrong. Less money meant more belt-tightening. Less food – no meat, and more bread for everyone. More borrowing from Nell's uncle, who'd only just been paid back the money he had lent them after the last crisis. It was exhausting. How much effort it took just to keep afloat. And for what? Two miserable little rooms, dark and damp and freezing cold in winter. What was the point of it all? What was the point of any of it?

Even May failed to cheer Nell. In fact, May was beginning to irritate her, with her big, clumsy smile and her earnest insistence on the necessity of her mama's latest loony social improvement scheme. It just seemed so . . . unimportant. Who *cared* about Germans in internment camps? Who cared about blimming pacifists who didn't want to fight? What difference did they think it would possibly make?

A bullet an inch to the left, and Bill would have been alive. A piece of shrapnel an inch to the right, and Dad would have been dead. Those were the things that mattered. Those were the things that made a difference.

Everything else was noise and blether.

Amiens
France

Arrived in Amiens this evening, for rest-break. Too tired to write. I send you instead the week's drawings. Enclosed are a picture of:

Corporal Aspey drinking tea.
Private Mattingley and his new machine-gun.
Two French children picking through a ruin.
French prostitutes out in the sun. Don't they look swell?
Captain Lassiter's horse. The horse, believe it or not, is called Blackie. A fine name for a war horse, I don't think!

I don't imagine you can possibly know how much I miss you, and how much I wish I were home in the old nursery with you and the little girls, drawing your faces instead of all these blasted soldiers.

Your own,
Very weary,

Teddy

A tea shop on The Broad,
Oxford,
December 1915

Teddy,

I think I'm in love.
Not with another man, don't worry, but with Oxford. Teddy, I don't know if I can explain to you what it's like. For the first time in my life, people are taking me seriously. They listen to me when I say things, they pull me up when I say something idiotic (which I do, a lot), like I ought to have known better than that. They expect so much! It's exhilarating. I'm not used to anyone expecting very much of me at all. Not like this, anyway.

I tell you what else is exhilarating. The people – the other girls, I mean. It's so strange to meet other girls who get excited by the same things I do. Did you feel like that when you started art school? There's a girl called Miss Billingsley who's in one of my tutorials and has rooms on my corridor. We spent about an hour yesterday evening sitting on her bed talking about how much we loved dear old Homer. Imagine doing something like that in Hampstead!

I love my work too. It's hard – of course it's

hard – there's never enough time to read everything you're supposed to read, particularly if you want to join societies and so forth, which I do – I'm in the debating society, and the bridge club, and the tennis club, and Miss Billingsley wants me to join the dramatic society next term, but I don't think I will, because I'll never get anything done if I do. But I love . . . just learning things. Working all day and knowing more at the end of it than I did at the beginning. The tutors are so clever too, and they know so much more than the mistresses at school did. I feel like my brain is being rewritten, all my nerves unravelling and reknotting themselves – it's disorientating, of course, but it's perfectly thrilling too. I feel like I'm unfolding, and I'm just wild to see what I'm going to unfold into.

Teddy, I might not be the same person I was when you left me. I'm growing up. I'm turning into someone else. It's marvellous, but it's rather frightening too. I do hope you'll still want this new Evelyn. I can't bear the thought of having to be a grown-up without you.

Best love,

Evelyn

Ice

The two little rooms in Coney Lane were almost unendurably cold. Coal was more expensive than Nell had ever known it, and food had to come first. Winters were always cold of course, but somehow this one felt more desperate than it ever had before. Perhaps because everyone was so hungry.

Mornings were the worst. Not nights so much; they all slept snuggled up together in bed, so that was all right. But waking up with the ice tracing delicate, fern-leaf patterns on the inside of the window panes, the contents of the chamber pot frozen under the bed, stumbling up and out of bed to fumble with your bare hands for your boots, to light the fire for breakfast . . . it was unbearable. Nell's hands were raw and red with the cold, every day, all the time. She had chilblains on both her hands and her feet; red, swollen blisters that made her wince and cry out with pain when she walked or tried to use her hands. Washday was agony; plunging her wounded hands into the icy rinse-water, standing in the yard in the pale frost, turning the mangle-handle. Waking up the next morning to see the clean clothes hanging from the ceiling, all covered in a thin layer of frost. Having to brush off the frost before you put the linen on.

It wasn't to be endured.

But you had to, all the same.

All the family had chilblains. You just did, every year. Everyone did, even swells like May did. Even the babies did. No matter how many layers Mum dressed Siddy in, he was never warm. But this year it felt worse, somehow. Nell felt fragile and brittle, as though she'd lost all her reserves of strength, as though whatever it was that made her go on had broken. The littlest thing made her want to snap, and hit something.

All the children had colds, all the time. Siddy had an awful cough, that made Nell's heart clench every time she heard it. A baby like Siddy shouldn't cough like that. And it was only a matter of time before one of them – Bernie probably – fell ill.

Bernie had always been sickly. His life was punctuated with semi-regular crises – diphtheria, rheumatic fever, a bad attack of influenza which had nearly killed him when he was four. Bernie had always had a somewhat other-worldly quality, perhaps as a result of all his illnesses. He was openly and unashamedly their mother's favourite.

'You gives your kids the love they needs,' she'd said once, and Nell thought this was probably true. Her mother had given her minimal interference in her life – something she had always been grateful for – and a defensive arm when she'd needed it. What she gave Bernie was long, sleepless nights sitting up with him when he was ill, work she could do from home when he was kept away from school, and a protective streak a mile wide.

The morning when Bernie woke up, his skin burning hot to the touch and weeping, they called in the doctor. You had to, no matter what it cost. The doctor told them what they already suspected: it was pneumonia. A child could die of pneumonia. Nell's mother went up to the infirmary looking for a bed, but was told all the beds were being used by soldiers, and civilian illnesses had to take second place.

'Keep him warm, and give him plenty of fluids,' the doctor said. He didn't have time for more; both his partners had gone to the Front, and much of the infirmary's work had been added to his case load.

Keep him warm was easy to say, but nearly impossible to deliver in a world where the price of coal had nearly doubled since the war began. May's mother lent them spare blankets and jerseys, she wanted to give them money, but Nell refused and May's mother didn't press it. Nell was grateful for the blankets, but nothing could alleviate the desperate coldness of their room except coal. And coal cost money.

Nell needed a job. She knew she did, but it was hard to find one when she also had to sit with Bernie while her mother was at work. Bernie was not a difficult patient, but he was a demanding one. He would cry, and Nell wouldn't know how to comfort him. His temperature gave him hallucinations – once he thought his father had come home from the war with one side of his face burnt away, like a man they'd seen in the garden at the infirmary – and he'd screamed and screamed and screamed. Another time he thought the Germans had invaded and were marching up the high street. This was exactly the sort of work Nell hated most – sitting alone with Bernie in a darkened room. She had always hated to be still.

Once Dot came home from school and was free to sit with Bernie, Nell went job-hunting again. There was more work now than there had been at the beginning of the war and, at last, more interesting jobs were becoming available to women. There were women staff at the Underground stations, and there were rumours that women might soon be allowed to drive the omnibuses – imagine, a woman omnibus driver! Wouldn't that be something? There were jobs more immediately connected with the war effort too. Nell knew a girl who'd got a job inspecting and cleaning guns brought home from the Front.

'You for the war or against it?' said her mother affectionately, when Nell told her about this. But Nell couldn't answer. She was for defending England against the Germans, and against the way the war seemed to trample on women like her mother, and children like Bernie. And herself. Perhaps, when it came down to it, she was just against being the one who was left out of things. Again. She agreed with Miss Pankhurst that the war seemed to benefit the bosses and no one else. And yet . . . she watched the soldiers marching up the East India Dock Road and dreamed secret dreams of being a new Polly Oliver, who cut her hair close, and stained her face brown, and went for a soldier to fair London Town.

Except she was in London Town already, and it wasn't particularly fair. And neither was France, by all accounts.

Spring was coming. There would be another offensive; there always was, in spring, and by then Dad would be back out there and no doubt would be in it. The longer he was over there and Nell was stuck here, the less happy she was about it.

It was in this mood that she came across an advertisement at the Labour Exchange. Positions available at a new shell factory which was opening on the edge of London. It would mean leaving home and finding digs near the factory, but the money was all right. Twelve shillings a week. Even once she'd paid her room and board and someone to sit with Bernie, there'd be money left over to send to Mum and the kids. The more she thought about it, the more exciting the idea was. A life of her own, away from Mum's watchful eye. A room in a boarding house, perhaps with other girls who worked at the factory. Her own bed! Good money to spend on tobacco, and newspapers, and whatever else she wanted. And to be connected to the battlefields that were swallowing up the boys and men of Poplar. Perhaps she might make a shell that Dad would one day fire at someone, or one of the boys from the street – Moshe Ayers perhaps, or Jimmy Mitchell. Perhaps her hands would save somebody's life – or destroy it.

Even that was strangely exciting. The violence of the Suffragettes had always excited Nell, the joy of letting out all that pent-up energy and frustration by kicking a policeman, or smashing a window, or making yourself a Saturday night and taking it to a meeting stuffed into the pocket of your jacket. The bombs I make could kill people, she thought, as she copied down the address of the factory. Not could. Would.

The only thing was, how in heaven's name was she going to explain it to May?

Respect

May's mother was out at a campaigning meeting. Nell came round for dinner.

Nell had been coming round for dinner a lot more recently. She'd been a bit reluctant about this at first – 'It's charity, ain't it?' – but May had been firm.

'It's helping your mother. Just think of all the food you would have eaten at home – she can feed it to everyone else. And, besides, it's campaigning work. You can keep the plight of the East End women burning bright in the minds of prominent suffrage campaigners like Mama. Just think of all the good you'll be doing.'

May and Nell ate dinner alone in the dining room. It was a sort of vegetable stew, followed by apple pie. Mrs Barber still talked wistfully about a nice chop, but she had owned that vegetarianism did at least make cooking easier, now meat was so shocking expensive.

Nell was quiet throughout dinner. She still looked out of place at May's table, although she and Mrs Barber seemed to understand each other. Mrs Barber – unlike most people when first presented with Nell – had accepted her without question, a result, presumably, of all the 'funny folk' May's mother was in the habit of bringing home after Fabian and suffrage meetings. That meant a lot to Nell. But she had admitted to May that she found the whole concept of servants odd.

'Ain't it queer, having someone live in your house who ain't family?' she'd asked May.

May said, 'Mrs Barber sort of is family. I mean, she looked after me quite as much when I was little as Mama did.'

'She ain't family if you pays her to do it,' said Nell, firmly.

May was sure Nell was wrong – she loved Mrs Barber just as much as she loved her mother – but she could see how peculiar the whole thing must look from the outside.

After dinner, the two girls went up to May's bedroom. Outside, it was dark. May drew the curtains, and dimmed the gas. She had always liked the intimacy of the semi-darkness, particularly with Nell there. She held out her hand.

'All's well?' she said.

Nell nodded.

'Yeh,' she said, but she didn't look all right. 'I just . . .' she hesitated, then she said, all in a rush, 'There's something I got to tell you.'

'All right,' said May.

Nell looked away, into the shadows at the corner of the room. She couldn't seem to meet May's eyes.

'I got a job,' she said.

'A job?'

'Yeh.'

May was aware of something hovering just out of sight. A big bad wolf waiting to eat her up.

'What job?' she said, warily.

'In a factory,' said Nell. She hesitated, then added, with obvious reluctance. 'Making bombs, like.'

May had known it was coming – what else could it be, what other kind of job would make Nell so wary? But it was still a blow.

It was Barbara from school all over again. It was exhausting, being hated, especially exhausting being hated every single day, especially, *especially* exhausting being hated every day by people who used to be your friends. Nell was a refuge. There was too little safe ground for May right now. There were too few places where she didn't have to justify herself. This news was a betrayal, and it hurt more than she knew it ought.

'You aren't going to take it, are you?' she said.

'I have to,' said Nell. 'It's Bernie . . .' and then, hopelessly, 'You know how it is.'

'I do not!'

'No,' said Nell, wearily. 'You don't, does you?'

'I'm sorry about Bernie,' said May. 'I really am. But – it's not asking much, is it? Not taking a job. People do all sorts of things for their principles, much worse things. They go to prison! They go on hunger strike!'

They go to war, Nell thought, but she didn't say it. They go to war, and they die, like Bill died, like my father might, and if you don't give them the weapons they need to fight with, they can't just turn around and come home, no matter what the Quakers say. They just die.

And we've had enough death in our family already. Bill died. And it was my fault. Those things I said . . . And I never apologised neither. (This had been bothering her more and more as the weeks had gone on. Bill had apologised for the things he'd said, and it had never even occurred to her to do the same.) If Bernie dies and it's my fault too . . . I can't bear it.

And you shouldn't need me to tell you this, she thought, with a spark of fury. *Nobody* should need to be told this. What sort of a person thinks principles are more important than a little boy?

'It ain't me,' she said. 'It's Bernie! I told you! You can't ask someone *else* to die for what you believe in!'

'Why not?' said May, swift as her mother. 'The government is, aren't they?'

It was the final straw.

'Can't you just . . .' she said. 'Can't you just bleeding *stop*? For one minute? You sound clever, but it ain't the same thing at all, and you know it! Them soldiers – they *volunteered*. My dad volunteered. Bill volunteered. And they didn't do it cos they've been duped by the government, neither! They done it cos it's their *duty*, cos they're *brave*, cos they want to – to defend their country! To protect their families! To stop the Kaiser coming over here and turning England into bleeding Germany!'

'Your dad didn't volunteer for anything!' May said shrilly. 'And Bill didn't join up because he was brave! He joined up because he was sick of staying at home and being treated like a kid! You *said*—'

Nell felt like she'd been slapped. People *didn't* say things like that. You just *didn't*. Somebody's brother died, you didn't tell them he wasn't brave. You didn't use them as a point in an argument. You had a bit of Goddamn *respect*.

What sort of a person was May that she didn't *know* that?

Nell couldn't believe it. She *couldn't*. She was so angry that if May had been her wife, she might have hit her.

'Don't you say a *word* against my father!' she said. 'Nor Bill! My dad volunteered to fight the Boers, and it's the same thing! He's been out there for years, keeping you and your *stupid* mama safe, when he might have been killed any minute, and all you can do is sneer at him! And how *dare* you say something like that about Bill? How bloody dare you? For Christ's sake, have a bit of respect!'

May had gone white.

'Get out,' she said.

'Now, look here—'

'I mean it. Get out right now and never come back.'

'Too right, I will!' Nell stood up, a year's worth of fury coursing through her veins. 'You haven't got a bloody clue, have you?' she said. She spat on the floor. 'I should have left months ago!' And she was gone.

For Ever

It took her a long time to walk off her fury. At first she was too angry to think. Her mind was buzzing with all the things she should have said to May, all the things she should have said to her idiot mother, a grown woman who thought helping *German prisoners* was more important than helping children on her own bleeding doorstep! For Christ's sake! But slowly, as she walked, her anger began to fade.

At first she was walking blindly, through the familiar streets of the East End. Then she realised that her feet were taking her towards Coney Lane, and she veered away. She couldn't bear to go home. She couldn't face the closeness of those rooms, no peace, no hiding place, nowhere that one could just be *quiet* and *alone*. And her mother would be sure to ask after May, and she didn't think she could cope.

I can't, she thought. I can't.

She turned instead the way she had come, towards Victoria Park. It suited her mood to be walking. She couldn't go home. She couldn't go to May's. There was nowhere she could go.

Now that her anger was gone, all she felt was exhaustion and a terrible weight of despair.

She had known this would happen. She felt, walking through the evening twilight, that she had always known it would happen. How could it not? What, after all, did she have that would keep someone like May bound to her? She had read none of the books May had. She could never follow any of her wild leaps of logic (although sometimes she wondered secretly if that was her fault or May's). May cared about helping Germans and pacifists. Nell cared about making life better for ordinary women like her mum, and helping soldiers like her dad, who would *die* without weapons. They both wanted peace and they both wanted the vote. But they came at it from such different angles, was it any wonder they never seemed to understand each other? What sort of life could they ever have made for themselves? Where would they have lived? What would they have *done*?

Nell was fairly sure that May had not thought very much about what sort of future – if any – the two of them might have had together. Nell herself had never mentioned it, it seemed too fantastical and faraway. But she had thought about it, sometimes.

In that dream, they shared a room, perhaps two, nothing fancy. But those rooms were their own. Their own space. Nell was obsessed with the idea of her own space, a room that belonged to no one but her. The fact that she allowed May to share this dream was a greater honour than May would ever realise.

They had worked, the two of them. At what, Nell wasn't

clear, although in her more fanciful moments they had managed to work for the causes they believed in, the way Miss Pankhurst did. This, of course, was all *after the war . . .*

After the war . . . They would be campaigners, socialists, feminists. All of the things that the most wonderful women Nell knew were. They would move in May's world, a world, if May was to be believed (and Nell still wasn't sure that she was), where their . . . abnormality . . . would be accepted and forgiven.

Nell did not, quite, believe in this vision. But she loved it. She loved it the way the exile longs for home. She felt as though she'd been caged in all her life, and May had set her free. And now . . .

Now all of that had gone.

She felt a sob rise up inside her, and she clenched her jaw against it. She couldn't cry. She *wouldn't*. But she felt very tired. She felt as though she had been fighting her whole life for something she could never have, something it was not possible to have, because it did not exist. The Suffragettes might one day get the vote, but she . . . how could she have what she wanted, when she didn't know herself what that was? To live in a world where she was accepted and loved for who and what she was. Was it possible? May had allowed her to imagine that perhaps it was. But how could it be? She and May still lived in the world, didn't they? You couldn't ask the whole world to remake itself just to please you.

She had reached the bridge over Limehouse Cut, the long, narrow canal which ran through Bow. She stopped walking. She thought that she had never felt so tired and hopeless in all of her life. The whole world was going to Hell, and her own small part of it was crumbling. And how dark it was! She had never been to Victoria Park in the dark – what would it look like? And then she realised that of course, the park would be closed. The gates would be locked. It felt like the final straw. She wanted to sink down in the road and never get up. She wanted to sleep for ever.

She looked down at the dark water of the canal. A woman had been found floating there last year. A suicide. Nell couldn't swim, and the water looked icy. She didn't think it would take very long to drown.

Looking down, she felt a wave of relief at the thought. She could simply give up. And, after all, why not?

It wasn't that she wanted to die. It was simply that she was so tired of living. And for what, exactly? What exactly was she fighting for? The war had taken even that away, Nell's glorious battle for freedom. What did women's freedom matter now? What did anything matter?

She put her hands on the wall of the bridge, and watched them resting there, the skin pinched and white. She lifted her knee up onto the parapet.

'All right, lad?'

The question made her start. A man – perhaps one of the bargees from the canal – was peering up at her, looking concerned. She slithered down, awkward and embarrassed.

'Yeh – yeh. I'm just—'

He didn't look convinced.

'Whatever it is, it'll look better in the morning, I swear.'

Oh, Lord! Her face was hot with shame. Her only thought

was to get away as quickly as possible, before he started asking questions and expecting her to explain. And what if he called the police? Suicide was a crime, wasn't it? Self murder? They could put her in prison. And then whatever would Mum say?

'Yeh,' she said. 'Only I weren't – I were just – I got to get home.'

And she stumbled away, and down the road. Back towards Coney Lane, and tomorrow.

•

Choice

May told herself that she didn't mind about Nell at all. *At all.* What had she and Nell had in common, really, besides a sort of quirk in their make-up? Hardly anything. Nell had left school at fourteen and worked in a factory! And she didn't believe in *any* of the things May believed in. She didn't even believe in God! Her father was a soldier!

May was now more isolated than ever at school. The girls had begun to tire of attacking her, which was something. Perhaps they were a little sorry for how they'd treated her, or perhaps they'd simply got bored. Either way, nobody made any attempt to make it up, and May was too proud to try. She ignored them, and they ignored her. It had been a relief at first, but now it was almost worse than their campaign of attrition. It was as though she'd disappeared. It was a strange, rather disorientating feeling. And it was lonely.

May missed Nell most when she was loneliest – Nell might not have agreed with, or even understood, what May was doing, but she would have understood what was happening to her now. Her mother understood, but her mother was so busy nowadays. The rare evenings she was home were taken up with the piano lessons she still had to squeeze around her busy schedule. May was mostly left with Mrs Barber, who was brisk but sympathetic.

'They're a pack of silly cats, that's what they are,' she said, reassuringly. 'You come here and help me make some toffee, and don't you worry about them no more.'

Toffee-making was something they'd done together when May was a little girl. She was too old to be comforted by toffee, but it comforted her nonetheless. She could not help but think of Nell, though. Nell would have loved making toffee, and her brothers and sisters would have loved eating it.

'Whatever happened to that nice little friend of yours in the breeches?' Mrs Barber said. 'Don't you think you ought to make it up, whatever it was you quarrelled over?'

'Nell,' said May grandly, 'is dead to me. Please do not mention her name again.'

But she didn't mean it, exactly. The longer she went without seeing Nell, the more she missed her. She'd thought perhaps Nell would come round and apologise for what she'd said, but she hadn't. And nothing, nothing would induce May to apologise to her. Apologising would mean giving in, and she *couldn't* do that. If she gave in, everything would crumble, and she'd have nothing left. She'd be just as bad as those suffragists who'd given up all their campaigning when the war began.

Not all of the suffragists had given up campaigning, but so many had. Now it all seemed to be arguments about war work, and peace work, and should female munitions workers be paid the same as the male munitions workers, and nobody seemed interested in the vote any more. May cared about all of this, of course. And she was depressed that so much of Mama's campaigning work seemed to exclude her. May had been on several anti-war marches, and to several local public meetings. But most of Mama's work seemed to be committees, and public meetings in provincial towns. Nobody, she thought, with a blind sense of fury, understood what it was like to give your life to something you'd thought was the most important thing in all the world, and then to have it suddenly pulled away from underneath you.

It didn't help that she wasn't at all sure whether the most important thing in all the world had been the suffragists, or Mama, or Nell.

She went to Quaker Meeting, and the problem buzzed around her head, worrying away in the quiet. Even here she couldn't be at peace. In other churches you just had to listen to the pastor, but here you had to listen to God, which was much worse. What God said was between you and Him. And He might not say the same thing to everyone. That was why some of the young Quaker men had enlisted, and some hadn't, and the Meeting had respected that. It was the young man's decision. Whether he went or stayed was between him and God.

This morning, May was wondering if maybe Nell's decision was between her and God as well.

Except that the Quakers had thought about it, at least. Had prayed about it. Had Nell thought about it at all?

A woman in front of May stood up to speak about the

German submarine attacks in the English Channel. She asked the Quakers to pray for the merchant seamen, swept into a war not of their choosing. Another stood and asked the Quakers to pray for the German conscripts on the submarines, also part of a war not of their choosing. An old man stood up and ministered about choice – what did it mean? How true was it to say those men *didn't have a choice*? Doesn't everyone always have a choice? Those seamen could desert, or object, or resign, after all. Or were there some things that you simply didn't have a choice about? Some decisions that you couldn't make any other way, without ceasing to be yourself?

It was horribly pertinent. Ministry in Meeting was like that sometimes. That old man might have been speaking to her. *I ain't got no choice*. That's what Nell had said. May didn't think it was true. She didn't think a Suffragette like Sylvia Pankhurst would have taken that job, no matter how ill her little brother was. Would May have done it, if it were Mama who were sick? Would Mama have, if it were May?

There were Quakers who wouldn't, she knew. The American Quaker John Woolman had left his wife and daughter to come to England and ask English Quakers not to support the slave trade. He'd died in England and never seen them again. May had always rather admired him. Now, she wondered. What *would* she have thought, if Mama had let May die rather than sign up to make shells?

She didn't know. But the grief of Nell's betrayal – it felt like a betrayal, like a punch to the stomach – was staggering. She felt, obscurely, as though this were a battle between people like Mama and herself, and people like Barbara and the girls at school. And although she'd always known that Nell didn't feel as strongly about this as she did, she'd trusted that Nell would understand the impulse behind it, even if she didn't share it. That she would respect the choices May and her mother had made.

It wasn't the factory! she told an invisible Nell, silently, in her head. *I could have forgiven the factory! It was the way you didn't seem to* understand *why it was important! You didn't seem to* care*!*

May had always cared, all her life. She didn't understand why it was so important to Nell to dress the way she did – although she loved it – but she understood that it *was* important, and she thought she would die to defend her right to do so. She had assumed that Nell felt the same way about Mama and herself.

But you didn't, she said silently. She was supposed to be listening to God, but the only person she wanted to talk to was Nell. *You didn't care at all.*

There was a part of her which knew she was being unfair, but she couldn't seem to stop herself.

June
1916

Dover Beach

The sea is calm tonight.
The tide is full, the moon lies fair
Upon the straits; on the French coast the light
Gleams and is gone; the cliffs of England stand,
Glimmering and vast, out in the tranquil bay.
Come to the window, sweet is the night-air!
Only, from the long line of spray
Where the sea meets the moon-blanched land,
Listen! you hear the grating roar
Of pebbles which the waves draw back, and fling,
At their return, up the high strand,
Begin, and cease, and then again begin,
With tremulous cadence slow, and bring
The eternal note of sadness in.

Sophocles long ago
Heard it on the Ægean, and it brought
Into his mind the turbid ebb and flow
Of human misery; we
Find also in the sound a thought,
Hearing it by this distant northern sea.

The Sea of Faith
Was once, too, at the full, and round earth's shore
Lay like the folds of a bright girdle furled.
But now I only hear

Its melancholy, long, withdrawing roar,
Retreating, to the breath
Of the night-wind, down the vast edges drear
And naked shingles of the world.

Ah, love, let us be true
To one another! for the world, which seems
To lie before us like a land of dreams,
So various, so beautiful, so new,
Hath really neither joy, nor love, nor light,
Nor certitude, nor peace, nor help for pain;
And we are here as on a darkling plain
Swept with confused alarms of struggle and flight,
Where ignorant armies clash by night.

Matthew Arnold

Offensive Behaviour

It was odd, Evelyn often thought. In wartime, any number of disasters could happen, and here in England it would be days before you found out, weeks even, sometimes.

Here you all would be, going about your business, and your world would already have ended without you even knowing it.

Evelyn was home from Oxford and back in her parents' house for the long summer vac. Each time she'd come back, the house had felt different. This time, Miss Perring had left: she'd gone to work as a clerk in the Ministry of Munitions.

'You should have seen her,' Kezia told Evelyn gleefully. 'She came downstairs and told Mother she felt she owed it to her country to support the war effort, now Hetty and I were old enough to look after ourselves. Can you imagine? Good old Perring! Hetty and I were sure she was going to go and tend war-wounded or something, but she's picked about the dullest job she possibly could, of course. Mother was rather dashed, but Hetty and I are glad she's gone. It's ever so much nicer being in charge of ourselves.'

Iris had left last year to work in a munitions factory, meaning that most of the household work now fell on Cook and Mother and the younger girls and, in the holidays, Evelyn herself. Hetty was thirteen now, and Kezia fourteen, and Miss Perring was right that in theory they didn't need much looking after. But, said Mother, it was astonishing how much time one seemed to spend chivvying them to get to school on time, or dressed for dinner, or to finish their prep.

Then too, there was even less food than there had been at Easter. This vac, Mother's conversation seemed to be full of shortages, and queues, and the price of butter. By the time she had been home two days, Evelyn was ready to scream. But then almost immediately, she had something else to worry about, something so huge it made all Mother's anxiety about food seem small and meaningless.

You always knew when there was going to be a big offensive. The men weren't supposed to tell you about it, but they all did. They sent you letters that said things like, 'we're moving closer to the Front' or 'we've all been issued with new equipment'. Sometimes they sent you goodbyes, or told you they loved you. Sometimes they even sent coded messages – Kit had agreed, very solemnly, that if he ever mentioned *Treasure Island*, it would mean that an offensive was about to begin – something that had terrified Evelyn's mother and father the year before, when, forgetting this, he'd sent them a letter cheerfully telling them he'd been billeted with a real-life Captain Flint. And it wasn't just you who got letters like this. Everyone did. Everyone with a son, or a brother, or a sweetheart 'over there'.

As June faded, it seemed to Evelyn that everyone was

talking about the big offensive that was going to happen. Mrs Waiting, whose daughter was a VAD in a hospital in Reading, said over the bridge table that the hospital had been told to expect a hundred and fifty casualties in the next week. She delivered this news as though it was an exciting piece of gossip. Evelyn felt sick. Her eyes rose, involuntarily, to meet her mother's, and saw what she was sure was her own expression reflected in hers.

Before an offensive, the artillery battery against the enemy grew worse. For days, they could feel the pounding of the guns from France, making the earth quiver beneath their feet. When they were at their worst, the walls of the London house vibrated with the violence of them. They seeped into Evelyn's dreams. The constant presence of fear was like a weight, pressing down on your chest. Or like a finger pulling on your nerves, tighter and tighter, like a child twisting a piece of elastic until either it cut off your circulation entirely, or it snapped. But the guns got on everyone's nerves. Kezia spilled marmalade all down the front of her school blouse, and Mother shouted at her for being careless, and Kezia, astonishingly, burst into tears right there at the breakfast table.

'If the guns are like this here, what are they like at the Front?' said Evelyn.

'Unbearable,' said Father. He closed his newspaper, laid it very deliberately on the breakfast table, and walked out of the room.

On the first of July, the guns stopped. Hetty ran into Evelyn's room to tell her, as though it might be something she wouldn't have noticed.

'What does it *mean*?' she said.

'Juggins,' said Kezia, following close behind. 'It means the battle's begun.'

A letter from Christopher arrived that morning. It was scrawled in pencil on a dirty scrap of paper and read simply:

Frantically busy – no time even to read Treasure Island. *Soon I shall find out how brave I really am. I hope and pray I shall make you proud. Kisses to the girls, and best love to you all,*

Kit

Which was queer, as Kit had never been religious, and, so far as Evelyn knew, had never prayed for anything in his life.

That evening, the newspapers were singing.

GREAT BRITISH OFFENSIVE

ATTACK ON A TWENTY-MILE FRONT

GERMAN TRENCHES OCCUPIED

BRITISH GAIN IN TERRIFIC DRIVE

The days when the newspaper belonged to Evelyn's father and to Evelyn's father alone were long gone. Now even Cook

– who had two brothers on the Western Front – could take you through every last intricacy of the Verdun campaign. The family spread the paper open on the drawing-room table and crowded around.

'OUR CASUALTIES NOT HEAVY,' said Hetty, pointing to one headline. 'Look!'

Evelyn's mother gave her a scornful look.

'Nobody,' she said, 'attacks on a twenty-mile front without heavy casualties. Aren't you old enough to know better than to believe newspaper headlines?'

Hetty looked hurt.

'Well,' she said, defensively, 'the battle's over now, anyway.'

'No, it isn't,' said her mother. 'It's barely begun.'

Teddy, who'd never been one for long or descriptive letters, sent not a letter at all but a picture, which did not arrive until almost a week after the battle had started. The picture showed himself, in uniform, leaning against the wall of a trench. All around him were men, also in uniform, clutching rifles. Evelyn recognised Kit and Stephen and Herbert amongst the soldiers, although she knew for a fact that Herbert was not involved in the offensive at all, but was in a London hospital with enteric fever. The other men were staring out over No Man's Land, waiting for the order to attack, but Teddy was looking in the opposite direction, down at an open letter in his hands. Floating above the letter, like a djinn in an illustration from *The Arabian Nights*, was an incredibly detailed pencil drawing of Evelyn's face. Evelyn was astonished that he could produce so accurate a picture of herself, apparently from memory and the two rather formal photographs she'd given him. She remembered suddenly that day in the courtroom, the day they'd sent her to Holloway and she'd tried so hard to fix his face in her memory. Now, she found herself struggling to remember what he looked like, conjuring only a vague mental picture of curly, laughing Teddy-ness. But his drawing of her was perfect, right down to the tilt of her head and the strands of hair tumbling out of their grips.

Teddy often sent drawings of himself. Usually these were caricatures, laughing at Evelyn, blowing her kisses, reacting with horror to senior officers shouting in his ear, or army food, or a rat poking a comical head out of a tea-mug. The Teddy in this picture was not comical. His uniform was dirty and threadbare. His boots were covered in mud. The hand that did not hold the letter held a rifle. And his expression as he gazed at the pencil-Evelyn was old, and wistful, and sad.

Underneath it he had written, *Is it worth dying for, Evelyn?* It was signed with his name and the date. *Edward Moran, June 1916.*

The picture had been sent a week ago. Evelyn stared at the pencil-soldier. She felt sick. She had no idea whether the man who had drawn it was even still alive.

Factory Girl

Two years, they'd been fighting. Would the war *never* end? To Nell it felt as though it had been fought for ever, and would continue to be fought for ever, and every day the news seemed worse. The Fall of Kut, the death of Kitchener, the awful, bloody, dragging battlefields of Verdun. Nobody ever exactly said the British were losing, but everyone thought it, and below every conversation about the war was the thought, *How much longer can this go on?*

Nell wondered if ever again people would care so much about things that were happening so far away in other countries. Good news could lift your spirits for the whole day, but bad news sent them plummeting. And there was *so much* bad news. It ground you down, it really did. It made you wonder what had happened to the world? What had happened to *people*, that they'd make a world as desperate as this? And what sort of world would be left when it was over?

Nell was living in a boarding house set up for girls who worked in the shell factory. They were almost all older than she was, but not by much – the eldest was nearly thirty, but most were around eighteen or nineteen.

She was not entirely sure how she'd found herself there. The weeks after the break-up with May had left her in a daze. She'd wake up with a start and realise that she'd got up, got dressed, eaten breakfast and was halfway through the morning and could remember none of it. She supposed she – or, more likely, her mum – must have found the boarding house somehow (she remembered vaguely a conversation about an advertisement in a newspaper), but there were whole days and weeks that seemed to have muddled past without her even noticing. And then one day, a whole month had passed, and for the first time she found herself able to look around and see where she had landed.

The boarding house was a large Victorian terrace in a grimy street that must once have been a fashionable place to live. The girls slept in dormitory-like beds, eight to a room, with a small curtain you could pull around the bed for privacy. Some of the girls complained about this, but to Nell, who had never had a bed of her own since she'd grown too big to sleep in an orange crate, it was an astonishing luxury.

Breakfast and dinner were provided by the woman who ran the house. The food was fairly basic – 'There's a war on!' – and Nell was sure they were being overcharged, but it beat bread and margarine. There was a small kitchen where the girls could make tea and cocoa, and Nell would buy bread and potted meat and make up sandwiches to take into work the next day. She felt absurdly grown up and important. At first she had missed the noisy, cosy muddle of family. It had felt very strange, that first night, sleeping in a room where she knew nobody. She'd been surprised, however, at how quickly she'd settled into her new life. The days were so long, you didn't have time to feel homesick.

The other girls twitted her less about her clothes than she'd expected. The first day had been awful, walking into the shared dormitory, the other girls' eyes like flames at her back. The whispers, then the inevitable comments.

'Look here, I ain't being funny, but you know this is a girls' dorm, right?'

What on earth were you supposed to say to that?

And then, 'I ain't trying to cause offence, right, but what *are* you? Peggy sez you're a girl, but you ain't, are you?'

What are you? What *was* she? How could she ever explain, when she wasn't sure of the answer herself?

But after the first couple of days, it had settled down. Being so young helped. She was such a child – it wasn't much fun to tease her. Or maybe it was just that everyone else had their own worries; brothers and sweethearts in the war, money troubles, boy troubles. Or perhaps because everyone was a little older, so it didn't matter quite so much that you didn't look exactly the same as everyone else.

Even so, the boarding-house dormitories were *incredibly* female. On Saturday evenings, they filled up with clouds of scent, powder compacts spilling open on the windowsills, stockings hanging on the sides of the bed. Nell had never felt more awkward, more like an imposter than she did sitting there in Bill's old breeches, watching the girls dolling themselves up for a night at the pictures. There seemed to be so many different ways to be a woman. There was Mum's way, all babies and housework and rough affection. There was the munitionette's way: curlers, and lipstick, and meeting men round the corner from the boarding house, so the landlady didn't see. And then there were the Suffragettes. Sitting in the dormitory, watching the girls, Nell realised perhaps for the first time how lucky she was to have encountered women like Miss Pankhurst, for whom being a woman meant *doing* something. Fighting. Working. Even May's mother, with all her committees . . . at least she *did* something. Nell had mixed feelings about May's mother, but she would rather be her than a girl like Gertie who slept opposite her, whose one interest in life seemed to be finding a fella.

For work in the factory, she had to wear a uniform. This was a long, shapeless blue dress, and a blue cap to tuck her hair under. None of the girls were allowed to wear their own clothes into the factory, for fear they'd bring in metal which might spark and set off an explosion. Even the metal hook-and-eyes on corsets were banned, as, of course, were jewellery, hairpins, and Nell's hobnail boots. They had to wear clumsy wooden clogs, like mill-girls. The floor of the factory was carpeted in asbestos to prevent fires; they had to wade through it to get to their workstations.

All of the girls hated the uniform. They complained loudly, 'They doesn't have to guy us up like this, does they?'

Nell hated her own uniform, of course, but privately she thought there was something rather exciting about the similarity of them all. When you first came into the factory, all you saw was the mass of blue dresses. Then, as you got closer, the features resolved into individual faces – an eye, a cheek, a strand of hair escaping from the cap. There was nothing whatsoever erotic about the lumpy uniforms. But there was something exciting about how different each girl looked in the same dress, how somehow, just by the bag they carried, or how they set their cap, or whether they wore powder, or lipstick, or no make-up at all, they changed the whole timbre of their appearance.

The days were long, the work was hard and – despite what the press said about munitionettes in fur coats – poorly paid, although Nell earned more than she had in the jam factory. This was a Suffragette issue too, Nell knew. The Pankhursts had fought hard for equal pay for male and female munitions workers, but had succeeded only in securing equal pay per shell made, something the factory neatly circumvented by paying them by the hour. Still, Nell earned enough to have some left over to give to Mum and Bernie when she went home on Sundays. And she knew that it helped her mother, not having to feed her.

Her job in the factory was filling up 'gains' – which were like cartridges, only bigger. She had a table with a glass dome on top of it, into which she had to put her hands, and fill up the gains tight with a kind of black rock, which was the explosive charge. The principle was easy enough, and she soon got used to it – it wasn't much different from any other sort of factory work, really, for all the recruitment posters boasted about girls who were helping win the war. The only difference was, whatever it was in the black rock dyed your skin bright yellow. It dyed your hair too, if you let it slip out of your cap, and most of the girls had a few ginger locks around their face. You got used to it, when all the others looked the same. Some of the girls would scrub and scrub at their skin in the evening, trying to wash away the dye, or whatever it was, and spend hours covering their faces and hands with powder. Others saw it as a badge of honour – a medal of service, as it were.

Nell had little time for thinking about May, for which she was grateful. There had been six days in Poplar while her accommodation and travel necessities were arranged which didn't bear thinking about. She'd been in an agitation of nerves, shouting at Dot and Johnnie for getting in her things, screaming at her mother for 'fussing', and arguing with everyone about nothing at all. Luckily, they'd put it down to worry about leaving home and starting the new job, but she knew she couldn't behave like that again. She would have to keep better control of herself in future, and so she welcomed the long days, the strangeness of the new environment and the sheer physical exhaustion. Even if May had forgiven her the munitions work, she would have seen very little of her anyway; what days off she had, she spent with her family in Poplar, helping her mother with the washing-up and the younger children. Siddy was two now! Johnnie was five! Bernie was twelve, and had shot up over the last two months. He was still too skinny, though; they all were, but you noticed it most in Bernie. He looked like a weed in the dark. He'd taken a long time to recover from the pneumonia, and Nell knew her mother still worried about him. Probably she always would. And then there was her father, who was finally back with his platoon in Belgium. Nell and her mother didn't know how to feel about that; they needed the money he sent them, but now the fear that something would happen to him had begun again.

Mostly what she felt was a sort of dull weariness. A kind of ache. A sense of something important, that had been there before and now was gone. Nobody, she thought wearily, understood what it was like to have your whole life transformed by something you'd believed to be the most important thing in all the world, and then to have it suddenly pulled away from underneath you.

It didn't help that she wasn't at all sure whether the most important thing in all the world had been the Suffragettes, or her family, or May.

By Your Leave

As the days went by, it became clear even to Hetty that this battle – the Battle of the Somme – was something different to the others. With every day that passed, the newspapers seemed to get more hysterical about it. Her mother's friends were able to talk of nothing else but whose son was 'in' it and whose had escaped. The week after the battle started, Evelyn's father took the whole family to a concert in London. On the way there, they saw the wounded soldiers coming off a hospital train at Charing Cross. Dozens of them, hundreds perhaps. Everything from the walking wounded to men lying comatose on stretchers or wheeled in bath chairs. Men missing limbs. One man whose whole face was covered in bandages. It was horrible, and rather terrifying.

Evelyn's mother said, 'Come on, girls, don't stare.' But she was staring herself. Evelyn couldn't take her eyes away. She was sure that one of the men she saw would be Teddy, like something in some awful story in *The Girl's Own Paper*. But of course, none of them were.

It had been nearly a fortnight, and they had heard nothing

from him. A postcard had arrived from Christopher nine days after the battle began, saying he was well and a letter would follow shortly. Teddy's parents received a letter from Stephen saying that his battalion had not yet been involved in the battle at all, although they expected to move up the line in the next few weeks. But from Teddy, there was nothing at all.

Evelyn couldn't stop thinking about the last time she'd seen him. It had been about a month before he'd gone out to France, and he'd cabled from camp to tell her he'd been given an unexpected three-day leave. She'd been wildly excited and horribly nervous; what would it be like to see him again after so long? What ought they to do? Would he want plays and concerts, or quiet walks on the Heath? It had to be absolutely perfect, she knew, because it might be the last time she ever saw him alive.

She had completely forgotten, of course, that it might also be the last time his parents, grandparents, art-school friends and brother ever saw him alive. And none of them had realised he would come back from camp with a list of last-minute kit it was apparently essential to have before one went out to France. When it came to it, they spent all of one day rushing from shop to shop trying to buy alarming-sounding things like ammunition clips, and morphine, and gun oil. And another confusedly trying to see various family members, and a hurried evening at a music hall. It might be the last music hall he ever sees, Evelyn remembered thinking, and then told herself not to be such a goose.

On the last day, his parents, with unexpected tact, seemed to wake up to how little time the two of them had had together.

They said their goodbyes at the house, and left Evelyn to see him off at the station.

They took the Tube to London Bridge, and waited on the platform. There was a frightful lot of people waiting for the Brighton train, including an awful lot of soldiers, presumably also going back to camp. Some also had sweethearts or family there to see them off, others were alone. If Teddy recognised any of them, he didn't greet them.

Evelyn thought, as she had been thinking all leave, how strange it was to see him in uniform, with his curly hair all shorn off, and a straggly attempt at a moustache. She was struck once again by how unlike himself he looked, as though the man she loved had been trimmed and squeezed into an unfamiliar and rather frightening mould. She wasn't at all sure she liked it.

They stood awkwardly on the platform, not touching. Both, though neither would admit it, were rather dreading the goodbye. If this were to be the last time you ever saw him, then nothing you could say could ever possibly be enough. And yet one simply *couldn't* be such a scab as to weep and cling and make a scene, like that awful mother down the platform was doing. Evelyn knew one was supposed to be brisk and cheerful and encouraging, and all that rot. But since she had never been remotely brisk or cheerful in her life, and since what she really wanted to do was howl, she was left feeling awkward and bad-tempered and resentful.

Teddy, glancing at her, said, 'Buck up, old thing, it isn't as bad as all that. It's only Brighton.'

She tried to smile.

'I know,' she said. 'I'm sorry. I'm being a brute. I just – well.' She stopped, then: 'Look. Do you remember after that action – with the king – when you told me you couldn't imagine a cause worth dying for? Don't you think it's rather – I mean—'

'You mean, wasn't I a sanctimonious twit?' said Teddy. 'It's all right, I do appreciate the irony.'

'I didn't mean that. And you were quite right, anyway. It was an idiotic thing to do.'

'Naturally it was. All of the best things are.'

Evelyn blinked. She wasn't sure what to do with this. Had he changed his mind? Did he think she'd been right after all? She wanted to pursue it, but time was running out. And her own question was more urgent.

'I meant –' she hesitated – 'Teddy, *do* you think it's worth dying for – honestly?'

He looked at her, and she was taken aback by the seriousness of his expression. She had expected self-deprecation, or a joke about how he'd only joined up because all his art-school friends had, and England Expects, and Public Schoolboys Doing Their Bit and all that.

'Do I think Belgium's worth dying for? It probably is, but I don't know that I would; I rather like being alive. It's not that I object to Belgians, but it isn't like I know them, you know. Do I think you – and Hetty – and Kezia – and my mother and father – do I think you're all worth it . . .?'

He stopped. She knew this was the point in the conversation where she was supposed to fling herself on his neck. Instead, she just felt irritated. Why did *Teddy* get all the fun of dying for his country? If either of them were going to sacrifice themselves for a noble cause, she did rather think it ought to be her.

And – *damn him* – it wasn't as though he were *wrong*, either. Teddy, she thought, as she often had before, would be much easier to deal with if he wasn't so often bloody *right*.

'Oh, marvellous!' she said, so loudly that the sweetheart on the other side of her (who was, she noted bitterly, pulling off brisk and cheerful with élan) looked at her in surprise. 'I suppose you want me to be *grateful*? Because now, when you get blown to bits, at least I'll know it's *my* fault. You might—'

'Evelyn Collis,' said Teddy. 'I love you more than I'll ever love anybody, but you're the world's worst goop. Shut up and kiss me, can't you?'

Evelyn opened her mouth and then shut it again.

'All right,' she said.

He leant forward and kissed her, on the mouth. At first it was hot and wet and clumsy, and then, suddenly, it wasn't. He seemed to know exactly what to do. Had he kissed other girls before? She supposed he must have done. Who? When? She closed her eyes, then opened them again and pulled apart, horrified at herself. Kissing a man in public! And enjoying it! What on earth must the other passengers think? She felt awkward and angry, and – worst of all – some treacherous, womanly part of her just wanted to beam and beam and beam.

They looked at each other for a long moment. Teddy was flushed, and his mouth was displaying a most inappropriate tendency to turn itself up at the corners. Her face felt hot. She wanted to hurry away from him as quickly as possible, and, bizarrely, to lean forward and kiss him again.

'I've been wanting to do that for a long time,' he said.

'Oh,' she said, ridiculously. 'Did you like it?'

'You are an ass,' said Teddy. 'Of course I did.' His mouth won out over his manners, and he beamed at her. 'I dare say you'll think me frightfully indiscreet,' he said. 'But could we do it again?'

It was the only time she'd ever kissed him. She couldn't stop wondering if she'd ever do it again.

Adults

In July 1916, May was seventeen.

Seventeen, as far as several of the girls in her form were concerned, was practically an adult. One or two had already left school; one to volunteer in a London hospital, another to help care for a brother who'd been invalided out of the army. But most of the girls were still there.

The war fervour of the early years was gone, though. The war was a fact of life, and a bloody one at that. Adults might – and did – talk about 'glorious sacrifice' and 'brave heroes'; the newspapers were full of letters from mothers celebrating the exploits of their dead children. But strangely – or perhaps not strangely at all – the girls in May's classroom had stopped caring. They all knew boys who were in France, or Italy, or Egypt, or Belgium, or Turkey, or Palestine. Some had brothers or fathers or cousins out there. Barbara even had a sweetheart in Egypt – or she claimed she had a sweetheart, a boy who lived at the end of her road and had joined up on his eighteenth birthday. But the jingoism of the early years had been replaced by boredom, and in some cases cynicism. Now, when the mistresses talked about glory and sacrifice, the girls giggled and yawned and rolled their eyes. It was considered sophisticated to be very above the grown-ups' nationalism. Several of the girls in the Upper Sixth were now avowed pacifists. Even the Lower Sixth had lost interest in the war, except to moan about food shortages, and the dull, pinched diet of thin bread, watery stews, and endless greyish margarine.

Somewhere along the way, without speaking about it or even really acknowledging it, the girls had made it up with May. The death of Barbara's brother in April had helped. No one, of course, had reminded Barbara that in 1914 she'd said that she'd be glad if this happened. When it *had* happened, it had so obviously been something about which no one could possibly be glad. May had not said 'I told you so', either. Maybe she was growing up too; in 1914, she probably would have done. Instead, later that day, as they were going for a gymnastics lessons, she'd caught up with Barbara and said quietly, 'I'm sorry about John.'

Last year, Barbara might have sniffed, or turned her head, or pretended not to hear. But perhaps she too felt this quarrel was too petty to continue, because she simply nodded, and said, 'Thank you.'

No more was said. But after that, May found that none of the girls seemed interested in their campaign of attrition. They might not exactly be *friends*, but they would consent to hand her a sheet of blotting-paper, and to pass the salt. As the weeks went past, May found herself on a hockey team with several girls in her form, who permitted her to walk across from history with them and talked about tactics in quite a friendly manner. She got a part in the school play – not a big one, but a speaking part – and Mary Waterfield, who was in her form and also in several of her scenes, spent all of one French walk telling her in dreadful French how nervous she was about it. And then Winifred and Jean decided to put on a revue of songs and comic skits to raise money for the starving children in Belgium, and invited May to take part, and May persuaded Barbara to recite, and even managed to bite her tongue when Barbara announced she wanted to do that awful, patriotic *Horatius at the Bridge*.

Lars Porsena of Clusium,
By the Nine Gods he swore
That the great house of Tarquin
Should suffer wrong no more.
By the Nine Gods he swore it,
And named a trysting-day,
And bade his messengers ride forth,
East and west and south and north,
To summon his array.

East and west and south and north
The messengers ride fast,
And tower and town and cottage
Have heard the trumpet's blast.
Shame on the false Etruscan
Who lingers in his home,
When Porsena of Clusium
Is on the march for Rome!

May was sure Barbara thought her a *false Etruscan* and had chosen the verse on purpose to say it, but she smiled and said nothing and even offered Barbara a role in her skit about sweethearts waiting for letters. And the other forms came along to watch, and said they liked it, and it seemed as though the girls had come to a tacit agreement that her period of ostracisation was over.

And perhaps Barbara had meant the verses for John, after all.

Things were changing at home too. At the beginning of 1916, the government had finally introduced conscription. Ireland was exempt, which just went to show, May's mother said angrily, what happened when people threatened to riot if you passed a law, and why were pacifists in Britain so willing to let this pass without challenge?

'Because they're pacifists?' said May, amused. 'Mama, you aren't really suggesting the Quakers should start a riot, are you?'

'Oh, I suppose not,' her mother said. She looked tired, May thought, to her surprise. Mothers didn't look tired. Mothers were all-powerful and all-knowing; a mother who was a human being, and rather a worn-and-darned human being at that, was a new concept, and not entirely a pleasant one.

Conscription changed everything. The act included a clause that said those called up could apply for an exemption on the grounds of 'conscience'. But since it gave no indication of what might constitute a genuine conscientious objection, almost all of the young men who applied found themselves either imprisoned for desertion, or shunted off into non-combative alternative roles. Since 'non-combative' could mean anything up to and including digging trenches, naturally most of the men refused.

Outside of Quaker and suffrage circles, most people seemed to have a pretty low opinion of conscientious objectors. May remembered her argument with Nell about it. Wasn't it better to kill one person if it saved the lives of dozens of others? That was the argument they used in the conscientious-objector tribunals too. May could see it made a sort-of sense, if you took God out of it. The problem with believing in God was that you had to do what he told you, even if it seemed cracked. She wished she'd said that to Nell. She wondered what Nell would have said back.

That was still the only time Nell had ever said she loved her. May wondered if she really had. Had she missed May at all, these long months, the way May had missed her?

Anti-conscription meetings were held each week in Finsbury Park by young men awaiting their conscription notices. May went most weeks, her mother when she could. She sold copies of the *Daily Herald* and other anti-conscription literature to the crowds, which seemed to grow larger every week – or was it May's imagination? There were agitators there too; most weeks, the stage would be overturned by supporters of the war. But the men carried on speaking regardless. May wrote an article about it for the school magazine, and the editors published it without complaint; it aroused very little comment from the other girls either. In fact, Winifred said confidentially to May that her brother had told her that someone in his battalion had actually been part of a court-martial of a conscientious objector and he – Winifred's brother – thought it a crying shame.

So there was that.

Postcards From the Dead

Field postcards were a thing soldiers sent. You usually got them after a big offensive, which was all very well if one arrived, but rather shattering if one didn't.

Evelyn's friend Joyce called them *Postcards from hell. Postcards from the dead* was what Miss Kent called them.

'Because if they aren't dead now, they soon will be, won't they?'

Miss Kent was a girl on Evelyn's corridor last year, who had been inclined to be rather hysterical about the war. She came from one of those towns where the whole battalion had gone over the top one day and never came back. Since this battalion had included both of Miss Kent's brothers, her cousin, the boy who did the gardening and the handyman, Miss Kent was understandably cynical when people talked about 'glorious sacrifice' and 'our brave boys'. Most of the girls in college avoided her, as though her bad luck might be contagious. Evelyn had, when she first arrived, considered it a test of basic human decency to talk to her, but as the war dragged on, and waiting for letters became more and more nerve-racking, she'd begun to lose heart. It was also basic human decency to be reassuring to someone when that someone had a fiancé on the Front Line, wasn't it?

Miss Kent was inclined to be cynical about fiancés, on the basis that most girls only got engaged because of the war. This was, of course, technically true in Evelyn's case, but she felt it missed the point somewhat. She and Teddy would have got engaged *eventually*.

'I wouldn't ever have married anyone else,' she'd explained to Miss Kent, and Miss Kent had said, 'Well, at this rate, you won't marry anybody.'

After that, Evelyn decided even basic human decency had its limits, and made friends with Miss Foxwell instead, who was small, timid, looked about fifteen, and told Evelyn in a tremulous voice that she was *sure* she was going to fail *everything*.

It was now over three weeks since the Battle of the Somme had begun. Evelyn, assisted by an anxious Hetty, took to reading the casualty lists in *The Times* every day, but casualty lists were peculiar things. Men might easily be missed from them, or lost in No Man's Land, or appear with their name misspelt, and anyway, if someone you were related to was killed, you did rather expect to be told first.

'Perhaps he's been taken prisoner,' said Hetty. 'Or – or – perhaps he's been tragically wounded, and he's forgotten everything except your own sweet face, only of course that isn't any use without your own sweet name and address, so he's lying there bleeding heroically being *oh so brave* and cheering the nurses with his dear ways. People do forget things when they're wounded. There was a story all about it in *The Girl's Own Paper*. And then one day, he'll see some sight made holy by the memory of your presence, and it'll all come flooding back, and he'll just *know*.'

Or perhaps he's dead, thought Evelyn. But she didn't say it. What would be the point?

At last, when Evelyn had wound herself up into such a state of tension that every knock on the door had turned into a telegraph boy, a field postcard arrived. Hetty, who had charged to the door at the sound of the postman, picked it up from the mat and shrieked, 'He's alive!'

Evelyn felt as though her heart had stopped. She was dizzy with relief and, for a moment, she was sure she was going to faint. She clutched at the breakfast table. She had not realised, until that moment, how sure she'd been that he was dead.

The field postcard, however, was frustrating. It read:

NOTHING is to be written on this side except the date and signature of the sender. Sentences not required will be erased. If anything else is added the postcard will be destroyed.

Underneath this alarming pronouncement were the possible answers, which Teddy had marked through with a pencil.

~~I am quite well.~~

I have been admitted to hospital

{ ~~Sick~~ { ~~and am going on~~ well.
{ wounded { ~~and hope to be discharged soon.~~

I am being sent down to the base.

I have received your { letter dated ...June 26th...............
{ ~~telegram ,,~~ ....
{ ~~parcel ,,~~ ....

Letter follows at first opportunity.

~~I have received no letter from you~~

{ ~~lately~~
{ ~~for a long time~~

Signature only. } Edward Moran

Date ....15/07/16...........

(Postage must be prepaid on any letter or postcard addressed to the sender of this card.)

Evelyn sat on the bottom step and read through the postcard again and again. She still felt rather dizzy, and Hetty and Kezia's noisy interest was not making things any easier.

In the plus column was the obvious fact that Teddy was not only not dead, but was apparently well enough to sign his name – and that definitely was his signature, not a nurse's, though rather shaky. So that was good. Nothing *too* dreadful could have happened to someone well enough to sign his name, she told herself. In the minus column was that ominous ~~*and am going on well*~~. Fiancés, Evelyn thought fiercely, *also* had a responsibility to be reassuring, and of all the things that ~~*and am going on well*~~ might be, reassuring it was definitively *not*.

Hetty seemed to have decided that it was her job to be cheering, which she did with great gusto – the relief of knowing that Teddy was alive, which had wiped Evelyn out, seemed to have invigorated her.

'Not going on well is *good*,' she said. 'Maybe it means something that'll get him sent home. Maybe for ever! He's probably just being stupid and honest and doesn't know you're supposed to be "going on well" even if your legs are falling off – which they won't be,' she added hastily, seeing Evelyn's face. 'You don't get field postcards when people's legs are blown off, you get kindly letters explaining that they're quite all right really and very cheerful considering. Enid in my form's Auntie Mary got one, and Enid said her Auntie Mary said it was the most ridiculous thing she'd ever read. And,' she went on cheerfully, 'he's left the *letter follows* bit uncrossed. So you'll know soon anyway.'

And with that Evelyn had to be satisfied.

Gas

The answer came a few days later, in the form of an official letter to Teddy's parents. Teddy had been shot 'in the abdomen', and had also been the victim of a gas attack. He was in a hospital in France, but was on the list to be sent home to England as soon as possible. This, Evelyn knew, might take days, or even weeks. Teddy's brother Herbert had had to wait nearly a week for a boat-train home.

'And it's always worse after a big offensive.'

Evelyn and her parents, and Teddy's parents, pooled what information they had about gas attacks. It could kill you. If it didn't kill you, it burned the inside of your throat and destroyed whole chunks of your lungs. Like the feeding-tube, thought Evelyn, with a shudder. Whatever she'd expected Teddy to face in France, she'd assumed he'd be safe from *that*.

Herbert, when appealed to for information, had not been very forthcoming.

'Good God!' he said. 'Poor little devil. Well, with any luck, he's out of it now.'

Evelyn tried to picture him, but the problem with war-wounds was that the official words covered so many possibilities. 'Shell-shock' seemed to mean everything from nightmares and headaches to men who were literally unable to speak or move. 'Gunshot wound' could mean everything from death, to permanently invalided, to simply grazed. She, Hetty, her mother and Teddy's parents had all written, but the letter Teddy had promised never arrived, which Evelyn told herself was almost certainly down to postal delays, and *nothing* to worry about. But to her astonishment, she found herself praying. She, Evelyn Collis, who had never believed in Father Christmas, let alone in Jesus!

Dear God, she prayed, and then stopped. She wasn't sure exactly what she wanted. A Teddy perfectly all right and unhurt? A Teddy so ill that he wouldn't have to go back to France, like Herbert seemed to expect? Or just a Teddy who was alive?

Dear God, she prayed at last, with more honesty than she'd ever used to anyone before, even Teddy. *Let him not die. Let him come home safe. Let him still love me, and let me still love him. Let him still be Teddy, please God, and everything else will come out right.*

A Bailiff With a Teacup

May had grown used to the fight for women's suffrage taking a back seat to the fight for peace. So it was something of a surprise when she came home from school on Friday to find a bailiff sitting in the corner of the back room, drinking a cup of tea and eating a biscuit. He was rather a portly bailiff, with a round red face, and a shiny red bald patch on the top of his head.

'Hello,' said May, and the bailiff raised his teacup and said, 'Afternoon, miss.'

May's mother was hovering by the table, her fingers drumming nervously on the pile of unsold *Votes for Women*. She seemed full of a sort of pent-up excitement. Something, May thought, was obviously up.

'What's happening?' she asked, and her mother said, 'It appears I've been declared bankrupt. It's rather exciting, isn't it? I don't believe I've ever had a debt in my life before.'

May could only stare. Bankrupt! It was impossible. Money was tight, but it wasn't *that* tight. Also, Mama was a Quaker. She wouldn't buy something she couldn't pay for. Mama's stockings were so old, the darns had darns on them, and she'd had that same dingy brown handbag for as long as May could remember. If they couldn't afford something, they didn't buy it. They paid their bills.

'I don't understand,' she said, and her mother said, 'It's the tax resistance campaign, darling. No taxation without representation, remember? We don't pay our taxes until the government gives us a vote.'

May did remember. Her mother had been very involved in the campaign, and she and May had stood outside the court-room protesting when Princess Sophia Duleep Singh had been taken to court for non-payment of taxes. The government had impounded a diamond ring and sold it to pay her fines, but a Suffragette friend had bought it back for her, which May secretly thought was stupendously romantic. Princess Sophia was a very glamorous Suffragette; she lived in Hampton Court and had known Queen Victoria.

'Most of the tax resisters gave it up when war was declared,' May's mother was saying, 'but *I* couldn't do that, of course. Anyway, the tax office kept sending me summons, and I just kept ignoring them, and then last week I got a letter telling me I owed them fifty pounds and they were turning me over to the Bankruptcy Court. Imagine!' She gave a gurgly, slightly hysterical giggle and said, 'This is Mr Moss, darling. He's a bailiff. He's coming to live with us for six weeks, though I can't *think* where he's going to sleep.'

Mr Moss said, 'Anywhere will do, ma'am. *I* ain't particular. Kipped in all sorts of holes, I have, and it's nothing to what our boys on the Western Front have to put up with, now *is* it?'

May supposed that it wasn't, but she wasn't really interested in where Mr Moss was going to sleep.

'Why is he coming to live with us?' she demanded. 'I didn't know bailiffs did that! I thought they just came and took all your things away!'

'A common misconception, miss, if I may say so,' said Mr Moss. 'Your mother, now, she has six weeks to find that fifty pounds what is due and payable. Beg, borrow, steal – *we* don't care how, stealing notwithstanding, which we couldn't be said to countenance. *I'm* just here to make sure she doesn't do away with these here goods and chattels, what you might say are collateral, and what His Majesty's Government, *if* the debt is not paid, will be forced – not what I'd prefer, miss, *given* a choice – to seize and distrain in payment of said debt. *You* see how it is, I'm sure.'

'Not really,' said May, who didn't. 'You mean you're going to stay in our back room for six weeks, and if Mama doesn't pay the government fifty pounds at the end of it, you're going to take away all our things?'

'That's exactly what he means,' said her mother.

'Do you *have* fifty pounds?' Fifty pounds was a lot of money. It was more than Mrs Barber earned in a year.

'That's beside the point,' her mother said. 'The government claims to have started this war to fight for democracy. If they care that much about democracy, I do think they might actually practise it.'

May agreed, of course. And she thought she knew why her mother had continued the tax resistance campaign while so many others had abandoned it; it was beastly to have given up the cause just because of this idiotic war. But she felt bewildered by the reality of it.

Three years ago, she knew she would have been wildly enthusiastic about this. Sacrificing everything for the suffrage cause! Privation! Publicity! Principle! And she still was in favour, she supposed. Certainly having decided not to pay tax, she quite saw that her mother couldn't turn round and say, 'Oh, it's too difficult now, sorry.'

But at the same time . . . it wasn't as though the newspapers were even interested in suffrage any more. It wasn't like there were hundreds of them all doing it all over the country. As far as she could tell, it was just Mama and a couple of other pacifists. So what difference would it really make?

She went upstairs and looked around her bedroom; the books, the clothes, the patchwork quilt her grandmother had made for her when she was a little girl. Would they take all her things as well as Mama's? Would they take all Mrs Barber's?

There was a knock on her door and her mother came into the room.

'I am sorry, darling,' she said. 'I should have talked to you about this. I never imagined it would ever get to this stage.'

'I know,' said May. 'It's all right. It's quite exciting, really.' But she didn't want her mother to believe her, and her mother didn't.

'We do have the money. I've been keeping it safe – I intended to pay them when we finally got our freedom, you see. I would rather stick it out, because I *do* think it's important that the cause isn't forgotten, and it would be awful to give in the very moment it got hard. But it's an awful lot to ask, I do know that. Say you want to stop and I'll pay them now. Shall I?'

Should she? A very large part of May wanted to say yes. But . . .

'No . . .' she said. 'Mama, of course not.' She gave her mother a wan smile. 'Imagine that man living in our back room for six weeks. Whatever do you think he'll make of us?'

What Are You Going to Do?

It was another Sunday afternoon. Nell had been home for dinner, but Johnnie and Siddy were chasing each other, yelling, through the two rooms, and she felt she couldn't bear it any longer. She had escaped to the offices of the East London Federation of Suffragettes and was stuffing copies of the *Woman's Dreadnought* into envelopes; dull work, but necessary. Nell preferred envelope stuffing to selling; you got to sit down, and you didn't have to deal with cat-calls and rotten vegetables. Nell got quite enough cat-calls, without going looking for them.

The little office was warm and cosy. There were three women, and Nell, and an old gramophone, playing music-hall songs.

'How old are you now?' said Mrs Cohen, suddenly. Mrs Cohen had taken something of an interest in Nell since the business with Mrs Danks.

'Seventeen,' said Nell. 'Why?'

'And what are you going to do with your life?' Mrs Cohen persisted. 'You can't spend it all in that nasty factory, can you? What are you going to do when the war ends?'

Nell was used to this sort of question, and grimaced. However, she liked Mrs Cohen, so she answered, politely enough, 'I ain't never going to get married, Mrs Cohen, so don't tell me I ought to. I ain't that sort of girl.'

'Bless you!' said Mrs Cohen. 'I didn't mean that. I never thought you were the marrying sort, dear. Some girls are and some girls aren't, and that's all there is to it. No, what I meant is, if you aren't going to marry, what are you going to do? You're a modern girl, you are. You should look around you. Look at what the Suffragettes are doing! Why, there's Mrs Stevens, who used to work with your mother at the toy factory. Look at her! She's only gone off and set up with a toy business of her own down south, and a very good thing too, what with her poor husband coming back from France so poorly, and her having to earn the money for all those children.'

This question took Nell somewhat by surprise. She had never given much thought to her future. One didn't, really. One got a job, and if there wasn't a job, one looked about until there was one. When you grew up, you got married, and had children. If you didn't get married, you lived in a room somewhere, and worked. That was all there was to it.

'Bright girl like you,' Mrs Cohen was saying. 'How much you earning, now?'

'Twelve shillings a week,' said Nell. 'Which is rotten – the men get twice that.'

'Aye,' said Mrs Cohen. 'But they're doing all right, your family, aren't you? Your mother's working. And your father's sending money home, ain't he?'

'Aye,' said Nell. She wondered where this was going.

'Well,' said Mrs Cohen. 'So, there's money for you to train at something else, ain't there? After the war, all the men are going to come home – they're going to want their jobs back, aren't they? You need to start thinking about that. All these jobs for women – they aren't going to last.'

'I s'pose not,' said Nell. She'd been thinking about this too. 'Doing what, though?'

'Well!' said Mrs Cohen. 'That's up to you, ain't it? What do you *want* to do?'

Nell was quiet. She folded the copy of the *Woman's Dreadnought*, put it in the envelope, and licked the flap. Then she dropped it on the pile for Mrs Cohen to add the stamp.

'I'd like to work in an office,' she said at last, rather shyly. 'With me own desk and me own typewriter. And people calling me Miss Swancott and fetching me biscuits. And I'd do shorthand and typing and . . .' Nell was vague about what people did in offices. 'And write letters and things. Like them professional Suffragettes, at WSPU.' She was thinking of the women who worked at the charities May's mother was involved with. Or the people who worked at the Trade Unions. Could you get paid for that, or did you have to do it for love, like May's mother did? 'Or them Trade Unionists,' she said. 'Can you do that as job?'

'I don't see why not,' said Mrs Rasheed, another Suffragette, who was listening to this conversation. 'I think you ought to organise a strike at your munitions factory. Make them pay you what they pay the men!'

'Not bloody likely!' said Nell.

She bent her head over her envelopes to hide her confusion. She was used to people telling her she ought to act more like other girls did. It was rather bewildering to be told instead that she ought to act more like herself.

There's a Long, Long Trail A-winding

Teddy came back to England at the end of August. Evelyn had been sure he'd be sent to a London hospital, so it was rather a blow to discover that he'd somehow ended up in Bristol. She'd had to fight to be allowed to visit him; at first, to her horror, her mother had wanted to come too.

Still, she was fortunate that he'd been wounded in the vac; Somerville would never have allowed it. Teddy's parents had gone down the week before, but Evelyn had been forced – loudly complaining – to attend a family wedding instead. Permission to visit, alone, a week later was something in the nature of a parental olive branch.

Teddy had, at last, sent several letters from the French hospital, but they'd all been rather uninformative, and had read rather like the dutiful missives he'd been forced to write from prep school. *How are you? I am fine. The food is awful. Teddy.*

It was a wet, blustery sort of day. The train was full of soldiers singing.

We're here,
Because we're here,
Because we're here,
Because we're here.
We're here,
Because we're here,
Because we're here,
Because we're here.

They were drunk, Evelyn realised. She and the other occupant of the first-class compartment – a portly lady in a dark purple dress – exchanged surreptitious glances of horror. But she needn't have worried. The soldiers were riotous, but perfectly respectful; one, an Irish lieutenant, even insisted on fetching her mackintosh down from the luggage rack and carrying the portly lady's suitcase off at Bristol.

Teddy's hospital was in an old workhouse. A lot of soldiers seemed to be in places like this; Evelyn's friend Joyce's husband was in a Masonic hall. The workhouse had been abandoned some years previously, and it showed. There was a damp smell, which the hospital disinfectant hadn't quite managed to cover. Many of the windows were boarded up. It reminded Evelyn of a dead thing. Of an animal with an untreated wound, dying slowly.

It reminded her of prison.

Teddy's ward was a large room, with long, high windows. There was a gramophone at one end, blaring out *There's a*

Long, Long Trail A-winding, which seemed an odd choice for a hospital, but the men didn't seem to mind. The room was full of men, and for a terrifying moment, Evelyn couldn't find him. Had he changed so much? What would he say if she couldn't recognise him? Or – oh, God, had something happened to him? She was beginning to panic when she saw him, lying propped up in a bed by the window.

It was over a year since she'd seen him. What sort of person was he now? The trenches were foul. Everyone knew that. It was all rats and mud and people dying in unspeakable agonies and heaven knew what else. Going to France changed people, everyone knew that too. It had changed Christopher. He'd come home at Easter quieter, thinner, and somehow older – a young man instead of a boy pretending. But Christopher had always been distant and rather superior, so Evelyn hadn't minded much, though she knew Mother had. Teddy was different. She couldn't bear it if Teddy wasn't Teddy any more.

She studied him, almost afraid to speak. He was thinner too, and his face was a queer bluish-white. He had a sketchbook open in his lap, a pencil in one hand and a cigarette in the other. Kit smoked now too, but she hadn't known Teddy did. There was a scar she didn't recognise down his cheek, and – more than that – something altered in his expression. *He's grown up*, she realised, and although she tried to laugh at herself, she knew it was true. She came forward, rather nervously, and then he looked up and saw her, and his face came alive all at once, the way an electric lamp does when you turn on the bulb.

'Hullo!' he said, and she knew it would be all right.

'Hullo, Ted,' she said, rather tremulously. There wasn't a

chair, so she sat on the edge of the bed and looked at him, taking in every feature of him, trying to get used to the altered lines of his face.

'It's so good to see you,' she said.

'You too,' he said. 'Do you know, I've been waiting and waiting for you to come? I couldn't sleep all last night – it's a beastly noisy ward this, something's always waking you up – and I kept looking at the clock and thinking, *Twelve hours and Evelyn'll be here*. I suppose that's rather absurd, isn't it? But there you go.'

'It's not absurd at all,' said Evelyn. 'I've been doing just the same – for days, ever since Mother said I could come. How are you? I mean – how are you feeling? Do you know,' she said, trying to speak lightly, 'I don't even know what's wrong with you.'

'Oh,' he said. 'Well. A bit of shrapnel in the lungs and another that just grazed the stomach. It was a dashed close shave, that last one – stomach wounds are pretty bad news.'

'And they said you'd been gassed?' It was the gas that had worried her most; it sounded so awful.

'Not really. I mean, I wasn't sharp enough with the gas mask, that's all. But it wasn't much. I wouldn't be here if it had been.'

'Oh.' She wasn't sure what to say to that. 'Are you in much pain?'

'No . . . it's not so bad.' She suspected he was lying, but she didn't push him. 'It's dull, that's all,' he said, suddenly fretful. 'And it's so *noisy*. A fellow never gets a minute to himself.'

'That does sound rotten,' Evelyn agreed. Privately, she already thought the noise was a bit much, and she'd only just got there. 'Won't they let you come home?'

'Not for an age, worst luck. And then it'll only be for a week or so. They don't let you convalesce at home now – it'll be a convalescent hospital, though I thought I'd see if they'd send me to one in Oxford. That would be rather decent, wouldn't it?'

'Frightfully decent,' she said, though she couldn't imagine how she'd ever manage to see him. You couldn't just go and visit young men unchaperoned, even if you *were* engaged; girls got sent down for less. But it didn't seem the time to say so. 'And will – Herbert thought – when he thought you'd been gassed, I mean – he thought you might be out of it.'

'Well,' he said. 'I might. They think my lungs are going to be mucked up for ever. But the doctor thought I probably wouldn't be. It won't be France, anyway. It might be teaching cadets – my CO said he'd write and recommend me. I'd like that.'

'Yelling at Tommies for not polishing their boots properly?' said Evelyn. '*Really?*'

'I'm quite good at it, actually,' said Teddy mildly. And she felt, with a sudden, sickening swing, the chasm of experience widening between them. She thought about next term, about him convalescing in one of the colleges and her not being allowed to see him, and then once he was well, him going off to God-knows-where to shout at new recruits, and perhaps her not seeing him again for months and months and months. She felt she couldn't bear it. Even with the promise of a week or so's leave at home, she couldn't.

'I think,' she said, 'we ought to get married sooner rather than later.'

He blinked.

'Are you sure?'

She nodded.

His mouth worked in silent conflict. Then he said, 'Look here. I didn't want to worry you, but I suppose you ought to know. I might not ever get properly better. They don't know, but . . . I mean, it's possible. Things still get pretty sticky sometimes, even now. I might not be able to teach cadets, even.'

'You could still draw, though, couldn't you?' said Evelyn.

For answer, he tipped up his sketchbook to show her. A picture of the soldier in the opposite bed, dozing over a penny paper. She took the book from him and flicked through it. A soldier with his leg in plaster. Another in a bath chair. Six sketches of the same soldier reading a novel, smoke curling up from a pipe. The interior of a hospital train, with soldiers sleeping in bunk beds three high. All the pictures seemed to be of soldiers. Once, not that long ago, they'd been of girls.

'Well then,' she said, trying to sound cheerful. 'That's all that really matters, isn't it? And your father would always make sure we were all right, wouldn't he?'

'I expect so,' said Teddy. 'I must say, it would be rather nice.' He tried to sit up, and immediately began to cough. Once he'd started, he didn't seem able to stop. Evelyn looked at him in alarm, wondering if she ought to summon a nurse, but at last he managed to calm himself. He lay back on his pillows, his face horribly blue, and closed his eyes. Then he opened them again and gave her a pale smile.

'Goodness,' he said, and, astonishingly, she saw that his eyes were full of tears. 'We do do dramatic proposals, don't we?'

She took his hand and squeezed it.

'Goose,' she said. But for some reason, she felt rather like weeping herself.

Mr Moss

May and her mother soon got used to Mr Moss sitting in the corner of the back room. He was the very soul of consideration. At first, he insisted on eating his own food; awful-looking meat-paste sandwiches in paper bags, which his wife brought in every morning, and bath buns, and steak and kidney pies with mashed potato from the café around the corner.

But after a few days of this, Mrs Barber told him not to be so ridiculous, and that nobody who lived in this house was going to eat meat-paste sandwiches while *she* worked here. After that, he very scrupulously paid Mama a few shillings a week in return for his meals, which he ate in the kitchen with Mrs Barber.

He spent most of his time sitting in May's father's armchair in the corner of the back room, reading a battered copy of *David Copperfield*. At night he slept in the armchair under his overcoat and a blanket. (He refused May's mother's offer of a pillow.) He smoked a clay pipe full of foul-smelling cheap tobacco of the sort Nell favoured, but out of respect for their furnishings, he always took this out into the back yard. There was very little space in their house for another person; the ground floor consisted of the parlour, where May's mother gave her piano lessons, the back room, where May and Mama sat of an evening, and where they ate their meals, and the kitchen. But Mr Moss, evidently embarrassed by his imposition on such a respectable family, did his best not to impose. When Mama had company he betook himself off to the parlour or the kitchen, though the company invariably found him fascinating and insisted on interrogating him about his life: Did he spend *all* of it living in other people's houses? Weren't people dreadful to him? Whatever did his wife and family think?

At first, May resented him. It was awful having him sit there, no matter how apologetically, imposing himself onto what little time she had with Mama. She was rather ashamed of this; last year she would have viewed it as her duty to befriend and convert him. But being unhappy seemed to do funny things to a person. It made it harder to be kind. It made it harder to forgive. When you spent all your energy being unhappy and angry and buffeted and bruised, you didn't have much left for Mr Moss.

But it *was* rather rum, having him sitting there in the corner while she tried to eat her rice pudding. You *couldn't* just ignore him, or May couldn't, anyway. Instead, she gave him a copy of *Votes for Women,* and *Jus Suffragii,* and *Rebel Women*, and told him since he was here, he ought to find out about the injustice he was propping up: 'Because you *are* a tool of the government, you know, though I don't suppose you intended to be. Probably you thought you were going to be sitting in the bedroom of some rake like Steerforth, and then you got Mama instead. But I *do* think now you might rebel against our oppressors and join the suffrage cause.'

'I dare say you do,' said Mr Moss, very seriously. 'But I dare say *Mrs* Moss would have something to say about it if I lost my job a-protesting for her freedom. Come, miss! Can't you have a word with your mother about this bankruptcy business? I hate to think of you ladies living here without all your nice things.'

'Oh no,' said May. This was the sort of conversation she was used to, the sort she'd once relished. It was rather cheering to have someone to lecture on the importance of principles again.

In return, Mr Moss told her about his wife, Esme, and their two grown-up sons, one of whom was in Belgium and the other in France. May asked if his wife was lonely at home without him, and tried to persuade him to invite her around for dinner, but this he would not do.

'I'm sure I don't want to impose, miss,' he said.

It was nice, when Mama was away, to have someone to talk to. She found it hard to take the threat of him seriously. Surely the government wouldn't really take all their things away.

Would they?

And then one day, they did.

Everything

They took everything.

Two men – not Mr Moss – came and loaded it all into a cart. Everything except their beds and their clothes, and Mrs Barber's personal effects. (May's mother argued for May's personal effects, but unsuccessfully). They took the carpets and they took the curtains, they took the books and the saucepans, the waste-paper baskets and the dinner plates. They took the family photograph album with all May's baby photographs, and the pictures of May's father.

That was the one thing that *did* make May's mother cry.

They took the piano.

'But I need the piano!' said her mother. There was panic in her voice. They'd known this was coming, of course, and they'd both done all that they could to prepare themselves. But Mr Moss had assured her she'd be allowed to keep the piano, just as workmen were allowed to keep their tools.

Without a piano, she couldn't earn a living. They could, May realised, be in serious trouble.

They were already in serious trouble.

• • •

She went upstairs and into her bedroom. They had left her the bed, with a heap of clothes piled on top of it, and the fashion-plates and the picture postcards stuck up on the wall. Nothing else. Without the bookcase, the wardrobe and the chest of drawers, the room looked strange and shabby and surprisingly large. There were dustballs where the furniture had stood, and a large, rectangular patch on the floor where the carpet had been.

She felt almost nothing.

That wasn't true. She didn't feel devastated, or bereft; May had never cared very much about possessions. In fact, she was surprised by how little she minded. You should care more than this when your whole life was carted away, shouldn't you?

Mostly what she felt was bewilderment and a realisation of how impossible it would be to live in the house without all the small, essential objects that kept it in motion; dishcloths and lavatory paper and waste-paper baskets and armchairs, none of them very difficult to obtain in themselves, but to put them all together from nothing! It seemed a monumental task. And not just armchairs, but her *father's* armchair, and the picture of her mother that one of her aunts had painted when she was eighteen and the dear old print of *St Isumbras at the Ford* that her father had put up in the nursery when she was a child. All gone. As it often did, the thought of Nell flared into her mind. She remembered those days after war was declared, when Nell's mother had gone to and from the pawn shop, her perambulator piled high with china dogs and rag rugs and candlesticks and picture frames. Had they ever got any of their things back? She had never asked, and the thought made her hot with shame. There hadn't ever been much in those rooms that wasn't useful. She should have bought some of it back. It wouldn't have been charity. It would have been a romantic gesture; she could have found a way of doing it that Nell wouldn't have minded.

Or could she? She and Nell had always seemed to rub each other up the wrong way. Probably she'd have done it wrong, and instead of being a grand romantic gesture, it would have ended in a row.

She should have tried though. She should have done *something.*

She sat on the bed. A small but insistent voice in her head was asking, *Is it worth it?* If every woman – or even every Suffragette – in the country had stopped paying taxes, it would have meant something. But this? Who would even care? It might be news for a few weeks, if her mother was lucky, and then it would be forgotten.

It won't make any difference, said the voice in her head. *It'll cause a frightful lot of upset, for you and Mama and Mrs Barber, but it won't get us the vote.*

It made her uneasy, that little voice.

It suggested that doing the right thing was a lot more complicated than she'd thought it was, and she wasn't at all sure that she liked it.

The Rest of Your Life

Secretarial course, said the advertisement. *Evening class.* It started at seven thirty, which was a bit of a rush from the factory, and it wasn't cheap, but it wasn't prohibitive either.

Miss Swancott, Secretary. Nell tried out the words in her head. They felt rather grand. Would she have to wear a skirt and blouse? Would they *let* someone who talked the way she did (and looked the way she looked) work in an office? Although secretaries didn't just work in offices, did they? They organised the affairs of gentry, and catalogued things, and . . .

They'd never let you anywhere near the gentry, Nell told herself firmly. She wasn't sure they'd let her on the *course*, even. At least she wouldn't be the only woman there, the way she might have been before the war. Female secretaries weren't so uncommon now. But would she be able for it? Shorthand, and typing, and whatever else secretaries learnt?

If it's awful, I don't have to stay, she thought, but of course she did. You couldn't pay all that money and then quit because you were frightened.

You aren't afraid of a typewriter, are you? she said. And she wasn't. But she *was* afraid. And although she filled out the form, and took out the postal order and addressed the envelope, she didn't post it. She carried it around with her for days, in the bottom of her pocket.

It was still there on Friday, when, as they were coming out of the factory, another girl caught up with her.

'It's Nell, isn't it?'

She was dressed like Nell in the munitionette's uniform and, like Nell, her hands and face were stained canary-yellow. Unlike Nell, however, her nails were carefully trimmed and varnished. And unlike Nell, she was smiling.

'I'm Jane,' she said. 'Jane Percy. Listen, what do you think about football?'

She was older than Nell, but not by much – she looked perhaps eighteen or nineteen.

'I dunno,' Nell said, rather taken aback. 'Cricket's my game. But I like it well enough.'

Jane looked pleased.

'Do you?' she said. 'That's good. I rather thought you might. Look here. They're wanting to start a football team – for the munitionettes, you know. They're trying to set up a league with the other factories – just for fun, you understand. We've got ten girls, so I thought you might like to be an eleventh.'

Nell looked at her suspiciously. Was she being insulted? But Jane's face showed nothing but honest interest.

'Well . . .' she said.

'You needn't stick it if you don't like,' Jane coaxed. 'But

I thought of you at once when I heard about it, and I *did* hope you might have signed up.' She opened her eyes a little wider. 'I rather fancied playing on a team with you.'

Was she *flirting*? Nell looked at her hard. She looked back innocently.

Confused, Nell stammered, 'Oh – well – I mean—'

'Good-o!' Jane beamed at her cherubically. 'I'll let you know when we've got somewhere to practise. I used to be in a girls' football team before the war, and we had *ever* such a jolly time.' She winked at Nell, raised a hand in airy farewell, and headed off back the way she'd come.

Nell watched her go. She was tall and muscular, and walked with the easy grace of someone who works hard for her living, but has never had to go hungry. Her munitionette hat dangled loose from her hand, and her hair hung long, dark and shiny down her back.

Nell, watching her, realised she was grinning.

She put her hands in her pockets and touched the edge of the envelope. The thought of it still made her nervous, but now she thought perhaps she would be able to cope. As if Fate were trying to tell her something, she turned out of the factory gates and saw the pillar box on the corner. Quickly, before she could change her mind, she took the envelope out of her pocket and put it through the slot.

There.

It was done.

Dizzyingly, Deliriously Happy

September, and with it, Teddy, home at last from hospital and installed in Christopher's bedroom for a giddy, glorious two-week-long leave. At the end of it they would be married, and then Teddy would go off to a convalescence hospital on the Isle of Wight, and Evelyn would go to the perfect little doll's-house cottage that had been found for them in a village on the edge of Oxford. She had never cared about decorating before, but she found it was rather fun to go through the cloth in her mother's sewing chest, trying to decide if red or green curtains would be best in the living room. And then when Teddy was well enough, he'd come and join her and start his new job training recruits at Cowley Garrison.

'And we'll all live happily ever after,' said Evelyn.

She was dizzyingly, deliriously happy. This last year at Oxford had been gorgeous, of course, but there had always been that worry about Teddy (and, to a lesser extent, Christopher) gnawing away behind it. And now it was gone. Now Teddy was coming *here*, to her own *house*, for the first time in *years*. And in two weeks' time they would be *married*, and then they would be *living* together, and be together for *always*. She felt quite un-Evelynishly giddy about the whole thing.

It had been decided that Teddy would spend almost all of his leave with the Collises. The war had been disastrous for Teddy's father's factories, which made cheap porcelain figurines of shepherdesses and cherubs and so forth. Nobody wanted shepherdesses in wartime, which was just as well, as Teddy's father had lost half his workers to the forces. He was busy trying to diversify into something more practical, but this meant much of his time was spent in his offices, and he had little to spare even for Teddy. Teddy's mother was out all day too, running a National Kitchen, and everyone agreed it would be dull for Teddy all alone at home.

And so you're coming to us! Evelyn wrote. *Huzzah!*

She felt like a child on Christmas morning, breathless and excitable, and inclined to giggle.

'Why!' her mother said in astonishment. 'You look almost like a real girl for once.'

Another day, Evelyn would have been insulted, and probably furious. Today, she just wanted to laugh. Who cared what her mother said any more? Teddy was coming home!

The wedding was to be held in the church where Evelyn had been christened, the one they'd gone to as children for Christmas Day services and summer fêtes. Evelyn's mother had made her dress, in white organdie, from a pattern from *Vogue*. If she'd expected gratitude, she was disappointed, Evelyn found it hard to care at all about the dresses, the flowers, the music, or the food. Everything was going to be so pinched and scrabbled-together anyway. Why waste your time worrying about it? Evelyn thought she could have been married in a paper bag and it wouldn't have mattered, so long as Teddy was there.

Teddy, they quickly realised, still wasn't very well, even now. He tired very easily, and spent much of that fortnight asleep on the drawing-room couch, while Evelyn tried to interest herself in her neglected Ovid. Besides his parents and Herbert, they saw hardly anyone at all. They spent their days quietly together (when Hetty and Kezia would let them) Evelyn reading aloud, Teddy drawing. (He still drew mostly soldiers, even here in her drawing room. Soldiers marching, soldiers sleeping, soldiers stumbling through the mud. It was a little disconcerting.)

'Draw me, won't you?' she said, and he said, 'Eh? What? All right,' but he left the drawing half finished, and she didn't have the heart to remind him.

When the younger girls weren't there, they would talk about the life they'd have together in Oxford. Teddy wanted four children, she two, so they agreed three would be fair.

'Horace, Augusta and Algernon,' said Teddy, and she said, 'Beast!' and he laughed, delighted.

'I'm terrible at housework,' she said. 'You do know that, don't you?'

'I never expected anything less,' he said. 'Hurrah for slatterns, say I. We'll eat currant buns, and potted shrimp, and Gentleman's Relish in bed, and to hell with the washing-up.'

'That does sound rather heavenly,' she said. 'And we'll never, ever make the bed. Except on Sundays.'

'Naturally on Sundays we'll be perfectly respectable,' Teddy agreed. 'We'll go for constitutionals on Christ Church Meadow, and tip our hats to the dean.'

The wedding was the last Saturday before his leave was over. Evelyn had been disappointed that they wouldn't have a honeymoon, but they'd had so little notice of the leave that even this last Saturday had been a scrabble to organise in time. And actually, now she'd seen how ill he still was, she was rather relieved.

'We'll have a real honeymoon when the war's over,' she told him. 'We'll go to Italy and look at the ruins of the Colosseum.'

'Crikey, you are a romantic,' said Teddy.

Teddy wore his uniform, with his new first lieutenant's pips. Hetty and Kezia were bridesmaids in pale blue muslin. Christopher and Stephen were both still at the Front, but Herbert was there as Teddy's best man.

The reception was held in the church hall. There wasn't much food, but there was a real cake, for which all the guests had donated sugar, or butter, or milk, or eggs. There were telegrams from Teddy's friends on different fronts all over the world; there was even a rather lewd telegram from his unit, which made his mother shake her head and Herbert chuckle. The whole thing was ever so much nicer than Evelyn had expected. She had supposed it would be like her friend Joyce's wedding last year, everyone hanging around in ghastly clothes, making polite conversation with other people's aunts. But it turned out to be quite different when it was all your *own* aunts.

She had never before felt so loved, or so surrounded by people who wished her well. It was an unnerving feeling, and one she wasn't entirely sure she was comfortable with.

She was relieved that they weren't expected to stay for the dancing, since by half past six Teddy was looking exhausted. Her father had booked them a room in a hotel, and Evelyn had a new going-away outfit with a little blue hat to wear, which made her feel frightfully grown up. They sat in the back seat of the cab and waved goodbye, while everyone cheered and waved back and called 'Good luck!' Then the cab turned the corner, and suddenly it was over.

'All right?' she said to him, and he nodded.

'Just tired.' He took her hand and smiled at her. 'You?'

'I'll say.'

He was watching her with an odd expression on his face, a mixture of pride and anxiety.

'I don't think I've ever seen you look so happy,' he said. 'I hope to God we aren't making a terrible mistake.'

'Oh, Teddy!' she said. 'Do stop talking such rot. It'll be all right, I promise it will.'

'I expect you're right,' he said, but he didn't sound sure. She rested her head against his shoulder. He put his arm round her.

'I love you,' she said.

'I know,' he said. 'I just hope it's enough.'

Doors, Open and Shut

It had taken an age, but things for May were, finally, settling down. There had been a month when they'd lived with May's grandparents in Greenwich, while May's mother had cobbled together dishes and dressers and dining-room tables from friends and acquaintances. The Quakers had, as ever, been bricks, and had unearthed all sorts of furniture from box rooms and outhouses and attics. May's grandparents had donated their piano, mostly unused since their children had left home, and although May's mother grumbled that it was ancient and awful, it seemed to suffice for lessons. It was transported to their little house, and May's mother bicycled from Greenwich to Bow each day to give lessons in the bare parlour.

The suffragists, meanwhile, had declared May's mother a heroine. There had been stories about her in *Votes for Women*, the *Manchester Guardian* and the *Daily Herald*. Donations and offers of help had been forthcoming from all sorts of unexpected quarters, and at last they were able to move back home and at least live, if in rather more straightened circumstances than before.

May secretly suspected that her mother rather enjoyed all this drama. It was all right for Mama; *she* didn't have to spend her evenings staring at the spaces where familiar things had once belonged. Sacrificing everything for a cause was rather a grand and exciting thing to do. Having everything sacrificed for you by someone else was just awkward and frustrating and difficult. (That flash of Nell again. *You can't ask someone* else *to die for what you believe in!* It was beginning to dawn on May that she'd probably behaved very badly towards Nell.)

She pushed the thought down; there was nothing she could do about it now, after all. Her mother bought her a subscription to a circulating library as a sort of apology for the loss of the books, and though of course it *didn't* make it up, she discovered E.M. Forster, Edith Wharton, G.K. Chesterton, and a whole lot of H.G. Wells that the school library didn't seem to have heard of. Which helped.

Perhaps due to the publicity surrounding the case, the Treasury seemed determined to make life difficult for them. Their gas was cut off, on the pretext of seizing the money they had paid on account, and it was with some difficulty that they managed to get it restored. Their post was diverted and opened in the hope of intercepting money.

At last, their furniture and other possessions were sold at auction. May and her mother made up a list of the most important things and were able to buy almost all of them back, although May's secret hope that the photograph albums might be sold proved unfounded. But the money raised from the auction, together with money seized from the gas company and the postbag, was enough to pay the debt.

'I hope you aren't planning on repeating this performance next year,' Mrs Barber grumbled. Mrs Barber's as-you-wish-ma'am face had grown rather forced over the last year.

Mama flinched, almost but not quite imperceptibly. May hadn't thought of that. But of course, if you'd decided not to pay your taxes until women had the vote, you had to *keep* not paying your taxes until women had the vote. How long would it be? Years, probably. For the first time, she felt actually angry at her mother, a confusing sort of feeling, since she knew perfectly well that she herself would probably have done exactly the same. But at least it would have been her decision.

She wasn't sure whether what she felt was selfishness, and a lack of commitment to the cause, or whether what her mother had done to their family had crossed a line from which she could never return.

Still, for now, there was breathing space, which May sorely needed. She was seventeen. She would be leaving school in July, and then she would have to decide what to do next. She knew she'd be expected to get some sort of job, and the idea was a welcome one. Her mother's idea of war work – anti-war work – had begun to leave her unsatisfied. No matter how hard you campaigned, no matter how many protests you went on and petitions you signed and speeches you gave, *nothing seemed to change*. And it did get awfully dispiriting after a while.

May thought of the cost-price restaurant, and the toy factory where Nell's mother worked. At least they *had* made a difference. They might have saved Bernie's life.

The older she got, the more May was wondering what sort

of difference *she* wanted to make. A couple of years ago, making a difference meant shouting in the street, telling everyone around you as noisily as you could exactly what was wrong with whatever it was they were wrong about. Now . . . she wasn't so sure. *Deeds not words*, Mrs Pankhurst and her Suffragettes said. May was wondering if there might be something in it. Not ripping up paintings and blowing up houses, obviously. But . . . May was beginning to wonder if it wasn't better to build a house than shout about how awful it was that people didn't have one.

'Doesn't it infuriate you?' her mother said. 'How few jobs there *are* for women? Teacher or companion or secretary . . . wouldn't it be wonderful if after the war we could carry on being 'bus conductors and machinists and stretcher-bearers?'

'Hmm,' said May. She agreed, of course, but . . . 'I wouldn't mind being a teacher,' she said.

March 1917

How Doth the Little Busy Wife

How doth the little busy wife
Improve each shining hour?
She shops and cooks and works all day,
The best within her power.

How carefully she cuts the bread,
How thin she spreads the jam!
That's all she has for breakfast now,
Instead of eggs and ham.

In dealing with the tradesmen, she
Is frightened at the prices,
For meat and fish have both gone up,
And butter too, and rice has.

Each thing seems dearer ev'ry week,
It's really most distressing,
Why can't we live on love and air?
It would be such a blessing!

Wartime Nursery Rhymes,
Nina MacDonald

Points

'May! It *is* you, isn't it?'

It took May a moment to recognise the woman in the coat with the Red Cross armband on the sleeve. Then, 'Sadie!'

She could feel the smile splitting her whole face. She couldn't help herself. Sadie, after all these years! Sadie!

'It's so good to see you!' she said. And she meant it. Sadie felt like a door to another time, a time when all the tumble-down houses were new and standing. Sadie!

In the three years since she'd seen her, Sadie had changed so much as to be almost unrecognisable. The red lipstick and the little earrings and the defiant bare-headdedness had gone. Instead, she was wearing what looked like army boots, and a trench coat so ragged it looked as though it had been used to carpet a barn dance.

'What have you been *doing*?' May said, and Sadie went into a long description; she'd been driving an ambulance; no, not on the Front Line, here in London, picking up men from the stations and taking them to the military hospitals. 'I want to get over there – and I think I will soon, only it's so difficult . . .'

She looked tired, May thought, and much older than she had three years ago, which was hardly surprising, she supposed. Everyone knew how overworked the VADs and the nurses and the ambulance drivers were. How strange to think of Sadie driving an ambulance!

'How . . .' She sought for the right platitude, and couldn't find it. 'Exciting' was callous, but 'awful' seemed inadequate (although of course ferrying bleeding soldiers about *must* be rather awful). She supposed the bromide she was looking for was something like: 'What good work all you girls are doing!' which she couldn't quite bring herself to say.

Sadie saved her by changing the subject and asking what May was doing now. May launched into a long convoluted explanation, which included handing out leaflets, and the marches, and the speaking in parks, and the school play, and the peace conference. Sadie listened vaguely. It occurred to May that perhaps an ambulance driver would think the war a good idea. Plenty of people still did, after all. She didn't know which side of the internationalist/patriotic suffrage split Sadie had come down on. She'd never thought of her as a patriot. But you never knew, did you?

Sadie didn't seem particularly interested in peace-building, though. She waited until there was a break in the flow of words, then said, 'And what happened to Nell?'

May shrugged. 'I haven't the faintest idea,' she said stiffly. Sadie gave her a questioning look.

May sighed. 'She's working in a munitions factory,' she

said. 'Making shells! To blow people up! You'd think she'd know better!'

'Half the world is blowing up the other half,' Sadie said mildly.

'Well, they shouldn't,' said May.

Sadie raised her eyebrows. May had the grace to feel embarrassed.

'I'm sorry,' she said. 'But shells are quite a different thing to ambulances, you *must* see that. Principles are *important*. Don't you think they're important?'

Sadie was quiet for a moment. 'Perhaps. But don't you think people are important too? This time next year, we might all be living in Germany. We might all be dead!'

May was startled. She'd known the war was going badly, but it wasn't going *that* badly, surely?

'Heavens!' she said, trying to speak lightly. 'I don't imagine it's going to come to *that*!'

Sadie didn't answer. Then she said, 'Look here. I admire your strength of feeling. But . . . don't lose your friends over it, will you? People like us . . . we need all the friends we can get. We *have* to stick together if we're going to survive.'

'I know!' said May, although she didn't, not really, not the way Sadie did. 'I know that!'

'Do you?' said Sadie. She scratched the back of her head. 'It's a wretched life this, May. I don't think you realise yet quite how wretched it can be. Hiding everything that's important to you . . . never quite respectable, never quite decent . . . it's such a lonely way to live.'

May looked at her in wonder. She had never thought that

Sadie might be lonely. It occurred to her to wonder what had happened to the glamorous Priscilla. Was she still around, living a romantic anarchist life in Bloomsbury? It seemed unlikely. Was she doing war work like everyone else? Was she *dead*?

'Don't you miss her?' said Sadie, more gently. 'You seemed so happy, the two of you.'

'I'm not the missing people sort,' said May stiffly. But her long fingers were clenched around the strap of her handbag so tightly that her knuckles were white.

Eat Less Bread

Evelyn thought that never in her whole life had she felt so grateful for spring.

Life right now, for Evelyn, was an endless state of struggle, fought blindly, half asleep, in the permanent knowledge that at any one time there were five other things you ought to be doing instead of the thing you actually were.

She and Teddy were living in a cottage in a village on the edge of Oxford. Evelyn had always rather grandly looked forward to the days when, like her mother, she should be in charge of a house, and could ring for tea, or order roast beef and meringues for dinner every day for a week. She had not reckoned with starting her career as a housewife at a time when every vaguely employable woman had been absorbed by the factories or the various armed services, and every household of her acquaintance seemed to be run by a dispiriting series of 'temporaries' of varying levels of incompetence. A housekeeper, or even a maid, turned out to be impossible, and Evelyn was forced to make do with a daily charwoman, whose housework was sloppy and hurried, and cookery skills limited to boiling, and heating up tins. The cottage, which had looked so charming and doll's houseish at first viewing, turned out to be dark, and draughty, and damp. There was of course no electricity, or even gas, forcing them to make do with oil lamps and a temperamental oil stove. And the roof leaked.

These domestic trials were complicated by food shortages, which were only growing worse as the war dragged on. Evelyn and all the other housewives she knew seemed to spend their lives trailing from shop to shop following desperate rumours of butter, or sugar, or meat, or jam. Even when one found such things, they were usually extortionately priced, and Evelyn would be left to stare at the tatters of a budget so optimistically compiled, and wonder whether her household could better survive a lack of bread or a lack of coal. EAT LESS BREAD ordered the advertisements. *Fat chance of anything else!* Evelyn told them savagely, every time she passed.

They had, on top of Teddy's lieutenant's pay, a small allowance from both of their parents, but whether through Evelyn's lack of experience, Teddy's doctor's bills, the wartime prices, or simply the sheer number of unexpected things one seemed to need when setting up a house, they were perpetually short. Teddy was reluctant to ask his father for more; several of his enterprises had folded when the war began, and although no one was exactly explicit about this, it was understood that there was less money to be spared for grown-up sons than there might have been a few years before.

Throughout her childhood and adolescence, it had been Evelyn who had railed against petty injustices and slights, and Teddy who, with laughing good humour, had turned the world right-side up again. Before the war, Evelyn was sure, he would have transformed their leaking cottage and burnt dinner into a grand and comical adventure. But now it was Teddy who struggled, Teddy who needed her to reassure him and raise both their spirits. And Evelyn was very quickly realising that Angel of the Home was not a role to which she would ever be well suited.

Teddy had spent the autumn and winter of 1916 fighting battles on several competing fronts. He had been ill a great deal, first, and terrifyingly, with bronchitis, then, while he was still convalescing, with a bad dose of influenza, *then* a seemingly never-ending series of stomachaches and bilious attacks. These were all the more frustrating because one never knew whether they might be the start of something serious, in which case the doctor must of course be called immediately, regardless of the strain on the budget, or whether they would pass of their own accord. Teddy himself was no help.

'For God's sake, don't fuss,' he'd tell Evelyn irritably, sitting up in bed in jersey and dressing-gown and worsted cap and scarf, to save on coal, his face white and strained, his teeth chattering with the cold. He seemed to feel the cold much more easily since coming back from France, which made the rising coal prices all the more desperate. More than once, when he was very bad, Evelyn had tipped the whole coal-scuttle onto the bedroom fire in a rage, and then been forced to write humiliating letters to her mother, begging for money. This money had always arrived, though Evelyn knew her mother was struggling with domestic crises of her own, and her silent kindness never failed to reduce her to tears. She seemed to be perpetually hovering on the edge of tears, that winter.

Even when Teddy wasn't ill, he had lost the easy cheerfulness which Evelyn supposed it was now her womanly duty to supply. Although he claimed to like his job at Cowley Garrison well enough, he was subject to fits of depression all the more infuriating for bearing no apparent relation to anything tangible. She had assumed that he'd be pleased to be home, but as the war stumbled on, he seemed to resent his comparative inactivity as much as she resented her perpetual busyness.

'At least in France you're *doing* something,' he complained. Evelyn pointed out that most of his letters had been full of how bored he was, but this was evidently the wrong thing to say.

'Oh, what do you understand about anything?' he cried, a question as infuriating as it was unanswerable. He would sit by the oil stove for hours at a time, drawing ghastly pictures of nightmarish landscapes, leaving the washing-up piled in the sink and coloured pencils strewn across the table.

'You might at least *help*,' she said, and then they'd fight, about Somerville, and his lungs, and his pictures, and Cowley Garrison, and whose job the washing-up was anyway. He was utterly ruthless about his art, always had been. Somehow it had never seemed to matter before.

He was sleeping badly. He worried desperately about the men he knew who were still 'out there', and insisted on sending them parcels of cigarettes and sweets that they could ill afford. The arrival of spring, and with it the likelihood of a new offensive, sent him into paroxysms of anxiety. And there was nothing Evelyn could say that would soothe him. After all, there very likely *would* be an offensive. And his friends *would* in all probability be in it.

In April, when the weather had finally turned, the Americans had at long last joined the war, and things had begun to look up, they got the news that Teddy's brother Herbert had been killed in the Battle of Arras.

Teddy had never been close to either of his brothers, both of whom were so much older that they had always been distant, rather glamorous figures in his childhood. Evelyn was therefore taken aback by how badly he took the news. He went so white that she thought he was going to faint, and was violently sick. He followed this with a bad relapse of what she supposed was influenza, which kept him in bed for a week. He seemed to regard this whole episode as a personal failing, despite her efforts to reassure him.

'But we ought to be in London,' he insisted. 'I'm the only one left now. I ought to be looking after Mother and Father, not *ill*, *again*.'

'But you aren't the only one left,' said Evelyn, her frustration rising. Why did *she* have to deal with this? Didn't the universe know how *bad* she was at comforting people? 'Stephen hasn't died yet.'

'You might be a *bit* sympathetic,' he said crossly.

He began to have nightmares. He would wake in tears, and she wouldn't have the first idea how to soothe him.

'They'll pass,' said her mother reassuringly, but they hadn't.

'I love you,' Evelyn whispered, over and over and over, night after night, and he buried his head in her arms and whispered, 'I love you too, old man.'

But love, as Evelyn's grandmother used to say, didn't buy a bonnet for the baby.

On top of all of this, there was Evelyn's degree, which required just as much study and thought and attendance at lectures as it always had. The tutors seemed to Evelyn to have a permanent air of disapproval as she hurried in, the hem of her skirt spattered in mud from the bicycle ride into town, her hastily pinned hair already tumbling down, her satchel filled with books half read and essays barely finished. She seemed to be always behind, that year, and always to be turning down invitations to student affairs she had neither the time, nor the money, nor the energy to attend. Struggling over her books by the light of an oil lamp at the kitchen table, she was beginning to wonder if the degree was even worth continuing with. Only the thought of the alternative, a life filled with housework, and sick-beds, and the toil perhaps of a dreary job in an office somewhere, kept her at it.

Meeting in the Middle

May couldn't stop thinking about it, what Sadie had said to her. And other things too. Nell's desolate expression, that last day in her bedroom. Her mother's warning about treating Nell's feelings with respect. Her feelings about her mother and the bailiffs and the empty rooms, which she still hadn't managed to untangle to her satisfaction. The suspicion that she'd broken something that should perhaps have been handled with great gentleness and care, that things should have worked out differently, and that no matter what else had happened between them, she and Nell should always have been friends.

The May she had been then felt like a different person entirely. A furious, miserable, black and white sort of a person, always simplistic, sometimes cruel. She burned with shame to think of how she had treated Nell; Nell, whose brother had been so ill! Nell, whose family were starving to death! She wanted to find her, and apologise. She wanted to know that Nell had been all right without her.

And she wanted – yes, why not admit it? – she thrilled at

the thought of seeing her again, even after all this time. Nell was the only person she'd ever been properly in love with. (Sadie didn't count, and nor did Miss Cage, the games mistress she'd been puppyishly in love with in the First Form). Nell was still the only person who'd ever made her physically thrill with longing.

She'd spent over a year travelling away from this girl, and now?

All it took was half a conversation with Sadie, and Nell was all she could think about.

She had a day out from the factory on Sundays, May knew. She'd seen her once, coming off the motor omnibus one Saturday evening with her bag. May had ducked behind a pillar box and watched. It had made her feel strange and trembly, just to see her again. She was too far away to pick out any details, but Nell was unmistakable. She hadn't *looked* broken-hearted, or despairing, or bowed down with grief. But perhaps she was. May was surprised at how deeply it had affected her, that brief glance. She'd thought of nothing else for weeks afterwards. She should have said something to her then, but she'd funked it.

Standing here now, at the end of the street, she felt like she was going to funk it again. What did she think was going to happen? She hadn't seen Nell in such a long time. Probably she had another girl now. That boarding house, that factory, full of girls . . . May had spent six years in a girls' school. She knew what happened.

She perched on the wall with a copy of *The Three*

Musketeers on her lap and waited. Every time another omnibus came up to the stop, she tensed. She watched as factory girls, and shop girls, and dock workers, and mothers with children piled off the 'buses, and she clenched her long hands tightly together. She was nervous. More nervous than she'd been when campaigning in Trafalgar Square. More nervous than she'd been of the white-feather women, or the soldiers at Charing Cross, or the men who came to break up the anti-conscription meetings. Public ridicule was one thing.

Nell was something else entirely.

And then, suddenly, so suddenly it took May off balance, there she was.

She wasn't in breeches this time, but her munitionette's outfit. A long, shapeless dress, rather like a nurse's uniform, with a wide, white collar, and a cap to tuck the hair underneath. Her skin was a jaundiced yellowish colour – canaries, they called the munitionettes – and the strands of hair that the cap didn't hide were gingerish. She was taller than May remembered, and in the uniform, with her dark hair tucked away under her cap, she looked almost unrecognisable.

It threw May, seeing her. It made everything she'd been thinking seem suddenly absurd. What exactly was she doing here? What exactly did she expect to happen?

She couldn't answer. She didn't have time even to *think* of an answer. Nell had looked up and seen her. She stared at May, her expression blank with shock. You could hardly ever tell what Nell was thinking by looking; she kept so much of herself hidden, always. Even now, the shock was all May could be sure of.

She couldn't tell, for instance, if Nell was pleased to see her or not.

'Hullo,' she said, and Nell scowled.

'It's all right,' she said. 'I know I looks a guy. You needn't say it.'

'You look like a nurse on the Western Front,' said May. 'In an illustration from one of those stories – you know, "our angels".'

Nell snorted.

'Angel! Me! Not likely! Blimming hard work, that's what it is. But then, what did you ever know about that?'

'That's not fair,' said May.

Nell flushed. 'Ain't it?' she said. There was an awkward pause. Two boys ran past, chasing a cricket ball and yelling.

'How's Bernie?' said May.

'He's grand,' said Nell stiffly. 'Thanks for asking.'

'I'm glad.'

'Are you?'

Now it was May's turn to flush.

'Of course I'm glad!' she said. 'What sort of beast do you think I am?'

Nell had the grace to look chastised.

'I'm sorry,' she said. 'I ain't— Look, what are you doing here? Come to have a go? Cos I ain't interested, all right?'

'No,' said May. 'I just—' This was all going wrong. Perhaps there was just too much stacked against it. Perhaps there always had been. Looking at Nell's furious face, she wondered what she'd ever seen in her. What had they ever had in common, after all?

'I'm sorry,' she said. 'That's all. That's all I came to say. But if you aren't interested – well!'

Nell's face was a curious mixture of fury and indignation. May almost thought she was going to hit her.

'Damn you!' she said. 'Damn you, damn you! After all this time, couldn't you just leave me alone?'

Charcoal

'Teddy! Teddy, dearest, wake up.'

He came awake all of a sudden, with a cry.

'But I have to!' he said.

Sometimes, when he had bad dreams, he woke and fell quickly back into sleep without seeming to realise that he'd been awake or dreaming. Not tonight, though. Evelyn could hear the panic in his voice. She fumbled for the matches and lit the lamp. He cried, 'No, don't! They'll see us!'

His eyes were open, but, still caught in the dream, he didn't see her. Evelyn took his hand in hers.

'Hush,' she said. Sometimes, after a nightmare, he needed help to reorientate himself to the real world. 'That's our lamp with the green shade, look – the one we got for one-and-six in the market, remember? And that's the eiderdown your mother found for us – you've kicked it right off, no wonder you're so cold. There – that's better, isn't it? And there's the awful washstand Uncle Robert gave us as a wedding present. One day I'm going to smash it into pieces and blame it on you. And there's the fireplace, there, and the fire screen with all the shepherdesses, and the funny cottage beams, and the dear old nursery coal-scuttle from home. See? Do you know where you are?'

He nodded, yes. His hand was like ice. He said, 'I'm going to be sick.'

Eight months of marriage had taught her more about illness than she'd thought she'd ever need to know. She bolted for the basin on the washstand and then went over to the fire. While he retched, she shovelled coal onto the embers with the furious abandon of a millionaire's mistress. A bedroom fire, in spring! But it had been a rotten cold April. They'd even had snow, last week.

He was trembling when she came back to bed. She took the basin and set it down on the floor. He said, 'I'm so sorry,' and began to cry.

She climbed back into bed beside him and took him in her arms. He buried his head into her shoulder, still weeping. His pyjamas were sodden with sweat, and his body against hers was rigid and cold. He was much too thin. She whispered, 'Hush. Hush, my darling. I love you.'

At last, he quietened. She said, 'If you tell the dream, it'll be easier.'

He shook his head against her shoulder.

'I can't. It's too awful.'

She said, softly into his ear, 'It's like in fairy tales. If you name the monster, it can't hurt the miller's daughter any more.'

He gave a laugh that was half a sob. They lay quietly together in each other's arms, listening to the putter of the flames, watching the long shadows thrown by the lamplight against the slope of the ceiling.

At last, without moving his head, he said, 'I'm crawling back to the trench. It's night, and the air is thick with smoke from the guns, so I can't see further than my nose, and I have to feel my way forward. I'm following the noise of the artillery, and all the time I'm hoping I haven't got turned around in the dark, and am heading toward the German trenches. But after a while, I know I'm going the right way, because I start to crawl over the bodies of the dead men from my platoon. The earth is vile and sticky with blood, and – worse. I can smell it. And I can hear some poor devil moaning, close by. But I can't stand up, and I can't see, so I can't help him. I just have to keep crawling.'

He began to tremble again as he spoke. She stroked his hair.

'Did that really happen,' she whispered. 'Or is it just a dream?'

'No,' he said. 'It really happened.'

She tightened her arms around him.

'Nothing like that will ever happen to you again,' she said, but she wasn't sure he believed her.

She could feel the tension gradually leaving him. His narrow body growing warmer. She made no move to turn out the lamp, knowing it comforted him, knowing he wouldn't sleep yet, but she let her eyes close. She was beginning to drift back into sleep when he sat up and started rummaging in the drawer of the nightstand.

'What are you doing?' she said, sleepily. 'It's the middle of the night.' He didn't answer. She rolled over, and saw that he was sitting up in bed, his sketchbook and a box of charcoal pencils open on the bed beside him. He was drawing rapidly.

'Teddy, I've got class in the morning,' she said.

He flung down his pencil.

'Look here,' he said. 'I have to get it down before I forget. I can go downstairs if you want, but I can't stop.'

She sighed, recognising the old ruthlessness.

'Don't be a goose,' she said. 'It's beastly cold down there. Just – don't be too long, all right?'

He grunted, but did not reply. The figures were already forming on the creamy paper. It was the picture from the dream. The wounded man crawling. Bodies in the mud.

'How do you know what to draw,' she asked, 'if you couldn't see?'

'I'm naming the monster,' he said impatiently. 'Do you actually need anything? Or could you please just let me work?'

She lay for a while, watching the charcoal soldiers as they appeared beneath his fingers. But it was late, and she had an early tutorial. She turned over onto her side, and closed her eyes.

Stones at the Window

Thud.

Thud. Thud.

May rolled over and closed her eyes.

Thud.

Whatever it was wasn't going away. Something hard, landing against her bedroom window. A bird?

Thud.

She climbed out of bed, went over to the window, and drew back the curtains. Nothing. She looked down. Standing in the street below the window was a dark figure. It held up a hand to May, who opened the window and leant out.

'It's me! Can I come in?'

It was Nell.

May drew back and peered at the clock on her nightstand. Three in the morning. It was very cold. She pulled on her slippers and dressing-gown and hurried downstairs. Nell! What was she doing here in the middle of the night?

She was standing on the doorstep, hugging herself a little awkwardly, as though she wasn't quite sure of her welcome.

'Hello,' she said.

'Hello,' said May. 'What are you doing here? Come in! It's freezing!'

'I weren't sure you'd want me,' said Nell. But she followed May inside. May pulled her coat off the hook and on over her dressing-gown. Nell didn't have a coat. She must be frightfully cold. May took her mother's black coat off the hook in the hall and handed it to her. There was something rather intimate about seeing Nell in her mother's coat – the lining was much darned, and it was strange to think that Nell knew that, when most of her mother's friends didn't. But of course Nell, who didn't even own a coat of her own, wouldn't care about darning. It had always looked shabby and shapeless on May's mother, but it seemed rather exotic on Nell. Nell always looked queer and awkward and most unlike herself in women's clothing, but the coat worked somehow, like the lipstick on the male impersonators at the music hall. *Erotic*, thought May, and shivered. Erotic was the last word she'd ever have thought to use about her mother's old coat.

They went into the back room, and May lit the gas. Nell sat on the edge of her seat, arms wrapped round her chest. May could see her looking around the room, taking in all the changes – the new table and chairs, the spaces where the books had been. She looked nervous. May remembered when she used to come around 'for supper' and sit awkwardly at the dinner table, while her mother tried to talk to her about politics. There was something of that younger Nell still there in this one. But most of that girl was gone. She looked like a woman, a manly woman, but a woman nonetheless. That was erotic too. This woman-Nell was a little frightening, almost a stranger, but then you'd see a flash of the girl May had loved, transformed into something powerful and adult. She shivered again. Nobody had ever stirred such feelings in her as Nell did. She wondered if anyone else ever would.

'You came to see me,' she said.

Nell nodded.

'Yeh,' she said. 'Well. I've got to help me mum with all the baking tomorrow. I'd not get to see you otherwise.'

There was a pause. May waited. Nell scratched on the arm of the chair with her fingernail.

'About what I said . . .' she said.

May waited.

'I dunno why I said it. I just . . . it were all such a mess. You, and . . . War and . . . Bernie, and Suffragettes . . . I dunno.' She looked up. 'But it weren't right, what I said. It weren't fair. So, I'm sorry. That's why I come.'

'I'm sorry too,' said May. 'I was a frightful prig, wasn't I? I knew I was at the time too, only . . . well, it seemed so important.'

'It were important,' said Nell. There was an odd intensity in her eyes. 'That's what I loved about you,' she said. 'How important it were. Remember how they used to laugh at us? And say it weren't worth it, going to prison and that, for a cause? Bet they ain't saying anything like that to the boys at the Front, is they?'

'No,' said May quietly. 'Now Mama and I say it to them.'

Her heart was pumping, the blood throbbing in her ears. To think that Nell had this effect on her still, after all this time! She reached out and touched her hand, lying there on the chair-arm. She half expected Nell to flinch away, but she didn't. Very slowly, very deliberately, May moved her index finger along the side of Nell's finger and up her arm. Nell did not move, but her breath quickened. May's throat tightened. She continued to move her finger, very slowly, up the arm, across her neck and still further up until it touched her mouth. Only then did she lift her eyes to look into Nell's. In the gaslight, they were dark, and the canary-yellow cheeks were flushed. She stared at May and, very deliberately, leant forward and kissed her.

Later, they sat together on the sofa. May couldn't tell if she was comfortable, or awkward, or happy, or anxious, or safe, or a confusing muddle of all these things and more.

'What's it like?' said May. 'The munitions factory?'

'It's all right,' said Nell. 'I gets me own bed.' She grinned a little shyly at May. 'We're all in rows, like a barracks. And the food's disgusting. But the other girls is nice.' Her grin widened. 'There's a football team.'

'Never!'

'There is. Girls' football. Munitionette's league.' She looked delighted at May's incredulity. 'I'm a centre forward.'

'I bet you are,' said May. 'You always were forward.' But she felt rather wistful. In two years, Nell had left home, got a job, set up a new life of her own. And what had May done? Played a nymph in the school play, distributed some handbills, failed to get to the Netherlands and failed to end the war.

'Go on,' said Nell, teasing. (She said it like a Dickens

character. *'G'arn!'*) 'What have you been doing – learning French like a good girl? Or have you left school now?'

It was as though she'd read May's thoughts. But May didn't mind. She wouldn't, actually, have wanted to sleep in a narrow bed in a dormitory full of factory girls. She would have hated to work in a munitions factory. She could, if it came to that, have left school herself if she'd wanted to.

'No, I'm still there,' she said mildly. 'I'm leaving at the end of term.'

'And then sit around waiting for a nice young man to marry?'

She was teasing, but May answered her directly.

'I shall never marry,' she said. 'I'm going to be a school-teacher. I'm going to work in a Board School, just for a few years at first. It's all arranged. And then I'm going to start a school of my own. It's going to be co-educational; just a small one to start with, but it'll get bigger. My father was a head-master, you know. I thought I could be the same. And the girls can learn science, and Latin, and the boys can do needlework, and I shall teach them all that they can grow up to be whatever they want to be. It's going to be simply marvellous.'

'All right for some,' said Nell. 'You can't be whatever you want to be if you comes from where I come from. You get a job in a factory, and count yourself lucky.'

'You don't *have* to,' said May, though she knew it was easy for her to say.

'Well,' said Nell. 'Actually, I . . .' And then she stopped.

'What?'

But Nell shook her head. 'Don't matter,' she said. She was

building up her walls again, May saw. Nell was always such a *hidden* sort of person. She tried not to let herself mind.

They were quiet, sitting together on the sofa, their hands not quite touching. May said, 'Do you want . . .? I mean, are we, could we . . .?'

'Seriously?' Nell raised her eyebrows. May flushed. She supposed it was a ridiculous thing to ask.

'It's not that I ain't flattered,' Nell said. 'But . . . well . . . I got a girl already.'

'Oh.' And then, 'Oh! Is she nice?'

'Yeh.' And Nell grinned all over her face. 'She's a centre half,' she said. Her grin widened. 'She's going to bleeding kill me when I tell her I kissed you.'

May had thought she'd got over losing Nell. It had been so long since she'd seen her, and she'd changed so much. But just now, right at this moment, it was as though she were fifteen again. Evidently there was still an inconveniently large part of her that minded.

Nell caught her expression, and, surprisingly, seemed almost amused by it.

'I never knew you cared so much,' she said.

'Didn't you?' said May. 'What a fool you were.'

A Vote

The nineteenth of June, 1917, was a Tuesday. Evelyn, who had struggled to the end of her Second Year Mods the week before, had spent all morning fagging around town looking for oil and soap, and what felt like all afternoon trying to make sense of Thucydides while standing in a queue for fish – fish, of all things! She had done very badly in the Mods, although not, she thought, badly enough to fail entirely, and was already beginning to panic at the thought of next year. And then it had begun to rain, and cycling up Headington Hill, a coal lorry had gone through a puddle and sprayed her with muddy water, and she was so tired, she wanted to weep.

When she got home, Teddy was sitting by the oil stove in the kitchen, reading the newspaper. He smiled as she came in.

'Look!' he said. 'Did you see?' And he handed her the paper. The Representation of the People Act had been passed by the House of Commons. Universal male suffrage – or as near enough as made no difference – and votes for women over thirty who met a property requirement, or were graduates of certain universities like Oxford and Cambridge, and therefore got an extra vote. (Everyone who'd gone to these universities got an extra vote. Not just women. It was very odd.) Evelyn knew all about it, of course. College had been full of it all last week.

'Oh,' she said, glancing at the headline and throwing it back to Teddy. 'You've got a vote.' She didn't mean it to sound bitter, but it did. Under the previous law, Teddy would not have been eligible to vote in an election; their tiny cottage would have failed the property requirement. Now he had a vote, or would once the bill went through the House of Lords, probably sometime in 1918. And she wouldn't. Not until she was thirty and she and Teddy were no longer living in quite such desperate circumstances, or until she graduated, if she ever did.

Teddy looked hurt.

'You might be a bit pleased,' he said. 'I bought you this.' And he gave her a little posy of flowers. Pansies, in white and violet, and a handful of green leaves. Suffrage colours.

Evelyn took the posy and, to her horror, felt the tears rising behind her eyes. She turned away so that Teddy shouldn't see them, muttering an angry *thank you*. Teddy, however, was still aggrieved.

'There's no need to get in a wax,' he said. 'I thought you'd be happy, that's all. I've been waiting for you to come home so we could be happy together.'

'For pity's sake!' she cried. 'Just chuck it, can't you!'

And the tears were leaking out of her eyes, and running down her cheeks. He stared at her in astonishment.

'Why, you're blubbing!' he said, which only made Evelyn

cry harder. All those long, weary months of unhappiness, of trying to crib for Mods in half-an-hours squeezed from looking after the house, all the constant worry about money, the snide remarks from the charwoman about plates left unwashed and the mess they never managed to get on top of, the darns in her gloves and the holes in her stockings painted over with boot-polish, all the luncheon parties and tennis parties and boating parties she never managed to attend. All this unhappiness seemed to come to a head. She sat on the chair, rested her head on the kitchen table, and sobbed.

'I say,' Teddy said, watching her anxiously. 'Steady on, old man. Look, you'd better have my handkerchief, it's bigger than yours. Goodness, you are having a good howl, aren't you? Whatever's the matter?'

And Evelyn tried to explain, between sobs, that once upon a time she'd thought that being an equal citizen was the most important thing in the world, but now having the vote didn't seem to mean anything at all, and life was just hard, all the time, and how miserable the endless worrying about food, and coal, and rent, and study was.

'And it just goes beastly on and on,' she wept. 'And I never have enough money, no matter how carefully I plan. And I know it's not your fault about your lungs, Teddy darling, I really do, but I *hate* looking after people. And I'm rotten at it, I know I am. I just wish – I wish—' But what she wished, even she didn't know. To be seventeen again? God, no. To not have married Teddy? But she didn't wish that either, exactly. Teddy belonged to her now. She couldn't imagine a world which didn't have him in it. Last year, when a world without

Teddy in it had been a terrifyingly likely possibility, was still too close and awful.

'I wish this ghastly war had never happened,' she said, instead, and began sobbing all over again, which was absurd, because what did she have to complain about, really, compared to so many other people? But Teddy didn't seem to mind. He patted her arm.

'But,' he said, 'my darling idiot. This won't last for ever. Even the war won't last for ever.'

Evelyn sniffled.

'No,' she said, 'but everyone says we'll keep on going until we're down to the last man standing. It's hardly cheering, is it?'

She was thinking of Kit in France, and Teddy's brother Stephen, who was in Palestine.

'Buck up,' said Teddy. He put on a mock-indignant face. 'It might not come to that. We might win, you know.'

It wasn't funny, but Evelyn gave a hiccupy laugh.

'And,' said Teddy, 'next year you'll be able to work. That'll help.'

'Work!' said Evelyn. 'Doing what? Civil service work? I couldn't live in London, and leave you here on your own. What'd you do when you got ill? I can't even teach, now I'm married. I might work in an office, I suppose, if I learnt to type.'

'I can't see you as a secretary,' said Teddy. He was looking at her fondly. 'But you'll think of something. I always knew if either of us was going to do something important, it was going to be you.'

'Don't say that!' Evelyn was distressed. 'What about your drawings?'

'Oh . . .' Teddy shrugged. 'They're all right. But they won't last. Not like the sort of thing you might do, if you wanted to.'

'Like what?' said Evelyn. His certainty astonished and bewildered her.

'How should I know?' He smiled at her. 'Organising something, probably. Look how well you organise me.'

'Organising! Organising what?'

'Search me! Something, though. A business? An army?' His smile widened. 'A revolution?'

'Juggins,' said Evelyn, but his optimism was cheering. 'You need money for businesses. And revolutions, I expect.'

'That's true enough. You'd have to talk to Father about that. He's got heaps of friends who are rolling in it. I bet they'd love to invest money in a plucky Suffragette enterprise. It would be a hell of a thing to puff about at the club.'

'Don't be a goop,' said Evelyn. 'People who are rolling in it don't invest money in business ideas just so they can puff about them in clubs. If they do, they tend to stop rolling pretty sharpish.'

'Oh well,' said Teddy. 'It had better be a good business idea then, hadn't it? Really, though, Father's a brick when it comes to things like this. I'd much rather ask him for a business investment than for money to pay my rotten doctor's bills.'

He reached over and took her hand. She gave him a shaky smile. She rather liked the thought of herself as a businesswoman. She could run a respectable employment agency, perhaps. Or a training college. Or something that gave spinster aunts more interesting jobs than being companions. It must be possible.

'I know I'm a brute to you . . .' Teddy was saying, and she realised with a start that she ought to be listening.

'Oh, Teddy. Darling. You couldn't be a brute if you tried. I'm the one who ought to be apologising. None of this is your fault at all.'

'It's my fault we got married,' he said mournfully. 'I knew it was a bad idea at the time, only I was so beastly selfish. You could be living in a nice icy room in Oriel . . .'

'Getting sent down for sneaking out after curfew to meet dashing young lieutenants in alleyways . . .'

'I'm serious!' said Teddy.

'So am I,' said Evelyn. She felt suddenly enormously fond of him. She leant across and kissed him, on the mouth. He looked pleased.

'What was that for?' he said.

'Because I love you, you chump,' said Evelyn. 'And because you're quite right, of course. You usually are.'

'Oh.' He said. 'Jolly good.' And he kissed her back.

February 1918

Representation of the People Act 1918 before the House of Lords

'What do we want? What is the goal?' said Ann Veronica.

'Freedom! Citizenship! And the way to that – the way to everything – is the Vote.'

Ann Veronica said something about a general change of ideas.

'How can you change people's ideas if you have no power?' said Kitty Brett . . .

'It seems to me that many of a woman's difficulties are economic.'

'That will follow,' said Kitty Brett. 'That will follow.' She interrupted as Ann Veronica was about to speak again, with a bright contagious hopefulness. 'Everything will follow,' she said.

Ann Veronica, H.G. Wells

Chips

May's mother had gone down to Parliament with some of her friends to wait for the news. She had wanted May to come too: 'It's history, darling!'

But May said she couldn't possibly miss work.

'I've got a job, Mama. I can't just chuck it in whenever I feel like it.'

And it wasn't history anyway, not yet. The Lords might vote against it, after all. Although everyone seemed to think that it *would* pass.

May was working as an assistant schoolmistress at a little Board School in Bow. She taught in the most junior class; solemn little scraps of five and six in starched white pinafores and flannelette petticoats, and boys in little grey caps. The work was simple enough, teaching them their ABCs and arithmetic, and how to sit quietly and listen when spoken to. It amused her to think of Nell in a class like this, a fierce, anxious little thing in her brother's breeches.

She was finding things out. She was finding out that she was good at teaching. She was finding out how much she liked it. You could sign endless petitions against conscription, and conscription still happened. But if a child came to you not knowing how to write her name, and left you knowing it . . . Well! That *was* something. You could point to it and say, *I did that*.

She finished work mid-afternoon on the day of the vote, and stayed behind in the little classroom, tidying up ready for tomorrow, catching up on the day's marking. Her mother was going on to a party arranged by one of her Fabian friends; May knew just the sort of gathering it would be, lots of cigarette-smoke, and earnest women with severe haircuts and sensible shoes, discussing politics and the various factions of the suffrage movement, and complaining loudly about everything that was wrong with the bill.

She finished her marking, locked up the classroom and went to catch the omnibus home. A newspaper boy went past, calling the evening edition. May caught sight of the headline and grinned to herself. Good-o.

The omnibus conductress was a young woman a few years older than herself.

'Did you hear about the bill, in the Lords?' said May, and the girl grinned at her.

'Too bloody right I did,' she said. 'About time, is all!'

The omnibus was rammed, as usual. May stood clutching the ceiling strap, looking out of the windows at the people going by. None of the women looked as though being enfranchised meant very much to them.

She was gazing absently at the passers-by, wondering what Mrs Barber had managed to scrape together for dinner, when suddenly she stiffened.

'I'm sorry!' she gasped, fumbling for her bag. 'I'm sorry! I need to get out! I need to get out at the next stop!'

There were some grumbles from the other passengers, but they parted to let her through and off. May scrambled out and, gathering together her skirts, ran back along the pavement to the figure she'd seen from the window; a young woman in a man's suit, her broad back, her easy, male saunter.

'Nell!'

Nell turned. She looked different, May thought, and for a moment she couldn't work out why. Then she realised and she began to grin. She wasn't wearing Bill's old clothes any more. Bill had been long and lanky while Nell was short and squat, so his clothes had never sat right on her frame. But someone – her mother? – had made these clothes for Nell, long trousers and a man's jacket and shirt. *Proper swank!* May thought, and began to grin, and Nell, catching her happiness, grinned back.

'Nell!' said May again. 'What are *you* doing here?'

'Got a job,' said Nell, and her grin widened. 'In Mission to Seamen, at the docks, like.' And it widened again. 'Miss Swancott, secretary. That's me!'

She beamed at May, and May, delighted, beamed back.

'Oh, jolly well done,' she said. And then, 'Do you want some chips?'

They sat on the wall outside the fish and chip shop in Bow. They ate chips out of the newspaper and drank lemonade out of the bottle. The headmaster at May's school would have died of shock, May thought, if he'd known.

'Votes for women,' said Nell. 'Well. Some women. You, probably.'

'And you,' said May. 'Why not?' She smiled at Nell, a proud smile that had nothing in it besides pride. '*I'm* just going to be a school ma'am,' she said. 'You could end up anything.'

Nell snorted, but she seemed pleased. She took another mouthful of lemonade and gave May a sly, sideways glance. 'Did you read what them newspapers was saying about the vote?' she said. 'That it were a – a *thank you* prize for all the war work women did? Being nurses and that.'

'Huh!' said May. 'Mama says politics is all about finding excuses for doing things you were going to do anyway. Everyone knows they would have had to give us the vote eventually. She says the war just gave them something pretty to say so it didn't look like they'd lost. But doesn't it make you *furious*? All those years and years of work we did, and who gets the credit? Mrs Pankhurst and all her lot! Shaming men, calling them cowards – she's a coward, herself! She was just as much for peace as the rest of us were for years and years and years! And then as soon as the war started – what did she do? Started handing out white feathers in the street and telling everyone to join up! And now they're saying the vote's thanks to women like *her*!'

'And me and all,' said Nell. 'I'm a war-worker. What did *you* do in the Great War, Daddy?'

'Tried to stop the bloody thing,' said May. She took the lemonade bottle from Nell and tipped it into her mouth. 'It'll be us they'll remember, anyway,' she said. 'In a hundred years. They won't teach schoolchildren about the munitionettes and the women who threw stones. It'll be the peacemakers who'll be celebrated.'

'Peacemakers!' said Nell, scornfully. 'Ha! It's people like that Emily Wilding Davison and them soldiers what sacrifice themselves to save their wounded comrades what get remembered. Except they won't remember Miss Wilding Davison either, I bet. Women fighting men ain't heroes, is they? Fighting for freedom *for* the government, *that's* heroic. Fighting for freedom *against* it – not bloody likely!' She spat on the pavement to show exactly what she thought of those future historians. 'They won't teach about us at all,' she said. 'History ain't folk like us. It's kings and queens and Mr Lloyd George and swells like that.'

'That's what you think,' said May, with the queer inner certainty that had always been hers, right from a little girl. 'History's about everyone. We made history, Nell. You and I.'

THE END

Historical Note

Most of the suffrage scenes in this book, including the march on Buckingham Palace, the Women's Peace Congress, the cost-price restaurant, the toy factory and Sylvia Pankhurst's escape from the Bow Baths Hall, are based on real events. I have, however, moved them around, and altered a few timescales to suit the story (I don't think there were any Albert Hall meetings in 1914, for example).

In Britain, women gained a limited right to vote in 1918, and voting rights on the same terms as men in 1928. Over the last century, more and more countries have given women the vote; the most recent was Saudi Arabia in 2015. Today, the only country in the world where women do not have suffrage is the Vatican City. A new Pope is elected by cardinals, all of whom are men.

Rights for gay and lesbian people have taken much longer to be realised. Male homosexuality was decriminalised in England and Wales in 1967. Gay marriage became legal in England, Wales and Scotland in 2014.

They say that stealing from one author is plagiarism, but stealing from several is inspiration. I was inspired by many books while researching *Things a Bright Girl Can Do*, but a few deserve special mention. Evelyn's experience of the build-up to the Battle of the Somme is taken from Vera Brittain's *Testament of Youth*. The depiction of a hunger strike is based on Sylvia Pankhurst's harrowing account in *The Suffragette Movement*. The effects of the war on the East End are taken from Pankhurst's *The Home Front*, while much of May's story comes from Anne Wiltshire's *Most Dangerous Women: Feminist Peace Campaigners of the Great War*. The descriptions of drawing-room meetings, walking the streets in sandwich boards and selling *Votes for Women* come from Evelyn Sharp's *Rebel Women*, and the account of life as a tax resister from her *Unfinished Adventure*. The description of a lock-up and a Black Maria come – amongst other places – from George Orwell's *Clink*. And Nell's storyline draws much from Stephen's in Radclyffe Hall's *The Well of Loneliness*.

The title is a homage to *301 Things a Bright Girl Can Do*, a real 1914 book which teaches bright girls, amongst other things, how to build stage carpentry, make a photocopier, and cremate themselves alive as a Christmas entertainment. I hope its authors would have approved of the things my bright girls do.

Acknowledgements

This book began with my editor, Charlie Sheppard, who suggested I might like to write a novel about the Suffragettes. You were quite right. Thank you for your patience, your enthusiasm, and your old-fashioned insistence on getting the book as good as it possibly could be. Thanks also to my agent, Jodie Hodges, for enabling me to have a career as bonkers as this. I feel grateful for it every day.

Thanks to Beamish, the Living Museum of the North; May's house is based on one of your terraces. To Helen Pankhurst for reading the novel in manuscript form, and for all your kind comments. To John Harris for lending me your copy of *301 Things a Bright Girl Can Do*. And to all the authors, friends and Twitter followers who listened to several years of my moaning and enthusing about the Suffragettes. Your enthusiasm for this book has been incredibly heartening.

To all the people who looked after my baby son while I sat in a room typing: Jane Nicholls, Celia Harris, John Harris, Pita Harris, Rebecca Waiting. Thank you. And to Tom, for doing the same things I thank you for every time, on far less sleep.

AMNESTY INTERNATIONAL UK endorses *Things a Bright Girl Can Do* because it asserts the importance of women's rights to education and political representation. Although modern women now have the right to vote nearly everywhere, they are still severely underrepresented socially and politically around the world. Girls still have less access to education globally than do boys. Meanwhile, being lesbian, gay, bisexual, transsexual or intersex (LGBTI) is a crime in many countries. There is a huge amount of evidence to show that girls, women and LGBTI people are discriminated against and subjected to violent assaults and other hate crimes all over the world.

Amnesty International is a global movement of millions of ordinary people standing up for humanity and human rights. We try to protect people wherever the human rights values of equality, justice, fairness, freedom and truth are denied.

Human rights are universal and belong to all of us from birth. They help us to live lives that are fair and truthful, free from abuse, fear and want, and respectful of other people's rights. But they are often abused and we need to be alert and to stand up for them, for ourselves and for other people. We can all help to make the world a better place.

You can take action for people at risk at **www.amnesty.org.uk/actions**

Find out how to start an Amnesty youth group in your school or community at **www.amnesty.org.uk/youth**

And if you are a teacher or librarian, please try our free educational resources at **www.amnesty.org.uk/education**

Amnesty International UK, The Human Rights Action Centre, 17-15 New Inn Yard, London EC2A 3EA
Tel: 020 7033 1500
Email: sct@amnesty.org.uk
www.amnesty.org.uk